PRAISE FOR MIKE NICOL

'Mike Nicol is the rapidly rising star of South African crime fiction. His novels have everything I love about the genre in just the right amount: shady characters, twists, turns, murder, mayhem, humour, wonderful dialogue, white-knuckle pace and lots of authentic Cape Town colour.'

DEON MEYER

'Watch out Elmore Leonard, here comes Mike Nicol'

SOUTHERN MAIL

'A heady mix, and Nicol stirs it with vigour, inventiveness wit … The laconic, street-smart style is so convincingly laid-back that it may blind readers to the artistry of the writing, which is taut and economical'

INDEPENDENT

'In the top rung … Nicol's clipped dialogue and sparse, high-impact prose recalls that of revered American recluse Cormac McCarthy'

THE CITIZEN

killer
country

First published in Great Britain in 2010 by Old Street Publishing Ltd
40 Bowling Green Lane, London EC1R 0NE
www.oldstreetpublishing.co.uk

ISBN 978-1-906964-19-1

A CIP catalogue record for this title is available from the British Library.

Typeset by Martin Worthington

Printed and bound in Great Britain.

killer
country

mike
nicol

CONTENTS

THE HITS

Friday

1

Pollsmoor Prison, 6 a.m. The chief warder frowned. No birdsong. No cacophony. There was kak in the land. You didn't need to be a bloody prophet to know this. The hell of it was he'd just eaten a decent breakfast – thick bacon slices, two eggs, fried tomato, fried banana, toast fried in the grease. The one advantage of the first shift, a breakfast like that. If the old cookie was on duty. The old cookie a lifer with one eye who escaped being dangled over the long drop when hanging was scrapped. All because of the new constitution. The old cookie who should've been dropped for all the grief he'd caused. Other hand, the old cookie did a helluva breakfast.

'You hear that?' the chief warder said to the rookie with him. A young guy, six months out of training. 'There's been shit.'

The young warder looked at him, not even a light in his pupils. Dead brown eyes. Didn't seem to know what he was talking about.

'You feel it?'

The young warder shook his head.

Before he opened the solid metal door with the peep hatch the chief warder knew there was major trouble ahead. He took a look into the corridor. Empty as it should be. The old cookie must've known. Bastard wouldn't say a bloody thing, even though he knew. Wouldn't warn you.

He unlocked the door, let the young warder pull it open. In front of them two grilles, the corridor beyond.

'You hear that?'

'No.'

'The silence. When you hear nothing then there's kak.'

Trouble was in which cell. Five cells on this corridor, could be any one of them. Or all five. Only way was to check first through the peep holes. Still gave him the sweats, these sort of situations. Could be they were planning a mass breakout, come screaming at them waving knives, guns, screwdrivers. No matter what you did the hardware got in. Two weeks back this nine mil with a full load in the cartridge pitched up. Deep in the prison in maximum. How'd it get there? Bloody magic.

'Lock the grilles,' he told the young warder.

What he should do was get backup. But bugger that, have the youngster reckon he was chicken-shit scared? No ways. He heard the locks bang home. Drew his revolver. These savages came at him he'd take down five of them first.

'What're you going to do?' said the youngster.

He glanced at the boy. How old was he, eighteen, nineteen? From some village most likely. Not a township special, this one. Too polite. Welcome to the pisshole, my china. He watched the youngster fumbling to unholster his weapon. 'Stay behind me, okay. If I shoot, you shoot.'

'Why they so quiet?'

'That's what we gotta find out.'

The chief warder went up to the spy hole on the first door, lifted the flap to check the glass wasn't smashed. Last thing you wanted was to put your eye to the hole, some bokdrol sheep turd rams a spoke through your eye. It'd happened one time, they nailed the warder's brain as well. Poor bastard. He was singing with the heavenlies before he hit the floor.

The chief warder peered in at the first cell, the men not even standing up, lying on their beds like it was summer holidays. He banged his gun butt on the metal door. Yelled in Afrikaans, 'Stand up. Stand up.' Watched them get to their feet, twenty-eight of them in a pot meant for ten. Ugly, tattooed, scrawny gangbangers. Could slide a nail between your ribs while they asked you for a smoke.

The peephole fisheyed the room. Far as he could tell from the heaps of bedrolls on the floor no one was baiting him, wanting to lure him in so they could stick twenty-eight bits of sharpened metal into his skin.

'Stay like that,' he shouted, moved on to the next door. Went through the same procedure with the peephole: thirty arseholes in this one, grinning at him. 'Want to check them out?' He moved aside for the young warder. 'Take a long look. You check anything funny, tell me.'

'Like what?'

'You see it, you'll know it.'

His armpits were damp. The taste of bacon at the back of his mouth. Dry. Harsh. This sort of situation brought Cookie's breakfast back very quickly.

The young warder said, 'I don't see anything.'

'Good then,' he said. 'Number three.' He rapped his gun on the metal door. 'Yous just stay like that, hear me?'

Not a response out of them. Everyone shut-up, waiting.

The chief warder scoped cell three, then the remaining two. In them the men all standing up, facing the door. Some bored, some smirking, some giving him the snake-tongue when they saw his eye darken the hole. He walked slowly back to cell three, wondering how to handle this. Call backup? Or go in there?

'What's it?' said the young warder.

'Check it out,' he said. Pointed at the peephole. 'Go on, man, look for yourself.'

The young warder did. Stood back, gabbling in his own language. Grey as ash.

The chief warder gripped the youngster's shoulder. 'Been a rough night in there, hey.' He put his eye to the hole. The convicts standing in two lines. Thirteen one side, twelve the other. On the floor between them a blanket. Under the blanket a body. A dark stain on the blanket at chest level.

He said to the young warder, 'I'm going to unlock the door, okay? I'm going to go in there, okay? You stay here at the door. You watch them. They do anything funny, any one of them, you shoot, okay?'

The young warder nodded.

'Say yes.'

The young warder swallowed. 'Yes, sir.'

'Okay, boykie. Here we go.'

The chief warder unlocked the door, pulled it open. The convicts leered at him. He told them to turn around, face the wall, stand with their hands above their heads. They obeyed. Taking their time, waggling their arses, giving him lots of attitude, but they obeyed. Like he reckoned they would. This wasn't about a breakout. This was about a job. Or gang initiation.

He sucked up some saliva to cover the bacon dryness in his mouth. 'Any one of yous move, you're dead, okay?'

He walked to the blanket covering the body. Lifted a corner. For a moment couldn't work out what he was staring at. Then he got it. The bloody stump of the neck. The chest opened like a box, the heart ripped out. He wondered if the guy had still been alive at that point. Wondered how many of them had eaten it. The head he found in the toilet bowl. Carefully placed in there so the face gazed up at him, blue eyes wide open.

2

Sheemina February tapped a highlighter on the statements scored with yellow. Bank statements spread across her dining-room table. Looked up at the horizon: nothing out there to break the line of sea meets sky. A blue emptiness. She smiled. Caught the reflection of her smile in the window. Kept it muted. Thinking, well, well, well. Here were possibilities.

What made her smile, what she liked about Obed Chocho's bank statements were the large deposits. Multiples of a hundred thousand at a time. Random entries. Mostly electronic. Two cash amounts which spoke of an inside man. Knowing Obed Chocho he'd have an inside man. Or woman. Probably woman. Women were his style.

No doubt though, Obed Chocho was a very rich man. Spent it too. Lived large. But then she knew that. Just had to look at the cars, the bling on the lovely Lindiwe Chocho to know this.

Only obstruction to Obed Chocho's current lifestyle was prison. The reason he'd hired her. 'I hear you're a hotshot lawyer,' he'd said. 'Mighty fine. Show me. Look after my interests.' Why she'd made herself available. Why she'd got an inside man at the bank – men were her style – to get her Obed Chocho's bank statements. Only way to know what she was dealing with. To the cent.

Sheemina February was dealing with the sort of money that pleased her. More especially she was dealing with the sort of deals that pleased her.

She picked up her cellphone went onto the balcony to make some calls. The balcony in shadow, cool. In March the sun halfway through the morning before it reached the front of the apartments. She ran a hand lightly over the dampness on the chrome railing, something soothing about the moisture on her skin. Her left, scarred and tortured. Stared at the mutilation of her fingers, the discolouration, the glisten of water in the palm of her hand. Her rigid hand. No matter how much she willed her fingers they would never close. Nor straighten. Twitch slightly. But not close. They remained claw-like.

She brought up a number on the phone screen. Keyed dial. Listened to the ringing. Before her the quiet back of the ocean was spotted with white gulls. Earlier she'd watched their feeding frenzy on a shoal of small fish. A madness of killing. Nothing to tell of that now from this placid scene.

'Spitz,' she said when her call was answered. 'Are you available?'

'Who is this talking,' came the reply in a weird German accent. Made Sheemina February smile. She looked down at the rocks: low tide, kelp and debris drying on the mussel beds. All very serene.

'Doesn't matter,' she said. 'What's in it is your usual fee plus a percentage. At the request of a man called Obed Chocho. Ring any bells?'

Spitz said yes.

'Good. He has heard about you. He knows your work, that's why the percentage.'

'How many contracts will there be?'

'Two.'

He came back with, 'That is in order.'

Brought the amused smile to her lips again. 'So you're available.'

Instead of yes he said, 'Ja, ja.'

'Do you want the details?'

'It is better not at this time.'

'We'd prefer that too,' she said.

Sheemina February told Spitz to be outside the Meadowlands police station at four o'clock. 'You're in Johannesburg aren't you?' she said. 'Melrose Arch, if my information is correct? You'll have to take a taxi to Soweto. I'm sorry for the inconvenience.'

'That is alright,' he said.

'Pack an overnight bag. You'll be meeting a man called Manga.

Black like you. He'll arrange the transport and the gun.'

'It must be the right calibre.'

'I know about that,' she said.

Next she phoned Manga and set it up with him. Said, 'No funny stuff, okay, Manga. Just get him to Colesberg, to the farm. Let him do the job. Stay out of the way.'

'What d'you think I am?' Manga said. 'I can do this job. I've done that. You don't need to get him.'

'Of course,' said Sheemina February, not suppressing her laughter.

Manga said, 'Don't laugh at me.'

'You're a funny man,' said Sheemina February. Paused. 'Alright, there's a thing you can do for me, Manga. While you're in Colesberg.' She told him what it was, gave him an address. 'You interested?'

'No problem,' said Manga.

She disconnected, slipped the phone into the pocket of her kimono, gave no further thought to what she had arranged. After all it was her client's brief. She turned to face into the apartment, caught her reflection in the glass. There were models that would've killed for her looks, her figure. She smiled. Gazed through herself at her lair. Her white lair. White couches, white flokatis, white walls. She leant against the balcony's railing to admire the room's pristine comfort. Here she was alone. Here no one else had ever been. Here she laid her plans.

She needed to shower, dress, pack a bag. Tonight she would give up the quiet of her lair for her town house. Replace the sea with the rawness of the city: the sirens, the harbour lights, the dark looming mountain, its arms around the scurrying streets as if one day it would crush the human insects nestled there. Tomorrow she would breakfast with the lovely Lindiwe Chocho, get some idea of the lady's sleeping patterns. Now it was started it could not be stopped. Only thing, one other piece had to be pulled into the unravelling: a man called Mace Bishop. The man who'd smashed her hand. Who'd sent her to the punishment camps of Angola. Who'd consigned her to the rapists. The man she sent rosebuds to. The man whose photograph she kept in a plastic sleeve in her handbag.

Mace Bishop in a black Speedo, standing on the edge of a swimming pool about to plunge in. A photograph she'd taken from the other end of the pool. In the days after he'd killed the man she'd hired to kill him. Mace Bishop. She got the photograph. Slipped it from the sleeve, rubbed her rigid fingers over the surface, leaving a smear on the gloss.

Imagined shaving him. With a cutthroat razor from her collection. The collection displayed on the wall. Blades that had shaved famous men. Blades she'd paid a fortune for. Imagined Mace lying back in a Badedas bath. Coming to him, kneeling to lather his face, working the gel into a foam, spreading the foam across his bristles, under his chin, across his upper lip. Her latte hand against his white skin. Stropping the razor, bone-handled, Sheffield steel. Angling the blade down the left cheek along the jaw to the chin. Flicking off the foam. Doing the same with the right side of his face. No rasp, no hair pull, a clean shave. Carefully shaving off the moustache stubble. Then gently tilt back his head, work from the Adam's apple into the soft crop of the underjaw. Mace Bishop lying there with his eyes closed, soft featured. Reaching a hand up to fondle her breasts.

The surprise on his face when she slit his throat.

With the hem of her kimono, Sheemina February cleaned the surface of the photograph. Returned it to its plastic sleeve. Put that into her handbag. There would be time for such fantasies.

An hour later she left the apartment – an elegant woman wearing a grey linen suit, sunglasses stuck in her hair, holding a briefcase in her right hand, her left hand sheathed in a black leather glove.

3

Spitz, outside the Meadowlands police station, put down his holdall and lit a cigarette. Stared at a police van, the cops dragging three bloodied men from the back cage. The men too drunk and messed up to complain. Some at the nearby taxi rank mocked the cops but the taunts went unheeded.

Spitz blew smoke from the corner of his mouth, tipped off the small head of ash. He glanced about for somewhere out of the sun. The pavement was barren, a wide sweep cleared round the police station. No vegetation beyond weeds threaded into the security fence at his back. Sweat started in his armpits. Little chance there would be a thunderstorm to cool down the afternoon.

He could do with a long Stella. Preferably at JB's, Melrose Arch. Some Kal Cahoone sweetly in his ears. A waitress moving about the tables, reassuring her customers that the world was a good place.

Spitz looked at his watch. The man was five minutes late. What he didn't like was people who weren't punctual.

His experience, you weren't punctual it meant you were caught, being tortured, about to be dead. He ground the cigarette butt into the dirt. Also, a man wasn't punctual it meant no attention to detail. This sort of operation, attention to detail was important.

Spitz knew the man he waited for had been on the highway heist. A heist that people talked about. Even given it a name: the Atholl Off-Ramp Heist. That show'd needed attention to detail. Five cars, twenty men. And two more cars to block the highway, split-second timing. Open the cash van, grab the boxes, ten of them, two per car. Nine million in total. Also, the body count impressed Spitz. Three dead guards, one dead comrade. Though he'd heard two coms weren't going to be operative again. Ever.

Which was one of the reasons he hadn't gone into cash heists: the stats were against you. More money, maybe, but you got killed or shot up or arrested.

Spitz didn't know any rich cash-in-transit heisters. Not soldiers. Knew of plenty of big players pulling cashflow from bank heists and carjackings and round-sourcing government contracts and crony deals and land development scams. They got richer and richer diversifying assets. One or two almost richer in twelve years than the Oppenheimers in a century.

Spitz fired up another cigarette, took a pull. Most of them bastards. Bastards like Obed Chocho. Except the deal with Chocho had this percentage. This was a new arrangement. An incentive. One that appealed to Spitz. 'He has heard about you,' the woman had said. 'He knows your work, that's why the percentage.' He checked his watch. The man was ten minutes late.

A voice behind him said in English, 'Yo, captain, am I waiting for you?'

Spitz turned, not liking being surprised, saw this Zulu boy grinning at him.

Manga marked Spitz right off, standing there outside the police station in his pressed chinos and brogues. Neat, dapper. New bag beside him. Saw Spitz look at the passengers getting out of the taxi, check his watch, grind out the cigarette. Not even noticing him. Manga dressed in floppy township. No difference between him and any cousin. Spitz not giving him a second glance. The great Spitz-the-Trigger.

What Manga had wanted to know at the outset was why Spitz? When he got the call from the woman and was told the job and was told Spitz would be his partner he'd protested. 'No, uh uh. Who needs that man, Spitz?'

'You do,' he was told. Because this was not some bang-bang arrangement where he could put the AK on auto and spray a clip far and wide. This was precision work. In out, one shot per.

'I can do that,' said Manga. 'I've done that.'

The woman on the line had laughed at him.

Once, he'd done it. Once only. An assassination that'd taken three hits of brown sugar and not a little brandy in advance. Eight bullets in the execution. The place looked more like a massacre site than a hit, more blood on the walls and ceiling than a slaughter house. Splatter marks in the bedroom, down the passage way, in the lounge and in the kitchen. Only because it was open plan, Manga tried to explain. No, he'd been told, because you messed up in the bedroom. The man's lying in bed with his wife, you're standing over them and it still takes five bullets for the man alone. Three for the woman. And the woman ends up dead outside. That's why you need Spitz. Spitz uses only one bullet per head. No shit on the walls. No smashed furniture, no broken vases. Nobody even attempting to escape. Better to stick to transit heists, she'd told Manga.

Manga reckoned that too. Do the job, get the money, have a blast in some shebeen. Until the deal on this job was laid out: the fee plus a percentage. For being the driver. That's all. Get him there, get the job done. We trust you Manga.

Meaning, Manga believed, they didn't trust Spitz. Hadn't contracted with Spitz before. Knew the reputation, but weren't sure about the man. At the end of it maybe Mr Spitz wasn't going to be on the payroll. Such were Manga's personal conclusions according to gut feel and a working knowledge of Obed Chocho's people.

Personally, he had no social problem with Spitz-the-Trigger. Personally he could hang with anybody, no big deal. Shoot a few beers, tell a few war stories and they were brothers. Personally, though, he'd rather have done the job with someone he knew. Personally Spitz-the-Trigger wasn't high up the list of people he wanted to know.

A man with a shoe fetish! Hey, wena, what's to talk about with a shoe man?

Manga looked down at his Adidas trainers. Stood in the police yard behind the security fence right behind Spitz, Spitz standing there in his polished brown brogues, their shine dulled with red dust. Sharp shoes. But what'd he want to wear smart shoes for in Soweto. They get scuffed in a taxi, ruined on the streets. Okay for a Sandton shopping mall but where they were going brogues weren't the shoe. Where they were going the shoe was light and tight, urban-style.

Manga noted the broad shoulders, the shirt creased in the small of the back from sitting in a taxi. The neat short dreads hairstyle. The way Spitz held himself he might break if he moved. This was the man they said had done some of the hits for high-up people. Manga rolled his tongue round his teeth. He latched the fingers of his left hand into the fence, said, 'Yo, captain, am I waiting for you?'

Spitz turned. He wasn't grinning like Manga. He held up his arm and tapped his watch. 'I am waiting for you. Ten minutes.'

'I've been here,' said Manga. He let go of the fence, jerked his thumb at the door of the police station. 'The man we've gotta see's inside.'

The sergeant they had to see took them to a compound at the back of the police station. About fifty cars in it, a few of them totalled. To the side two rows of good models, mostly new G-string Beemers, some Audis, Subarus, a few sporty Golfs, the sort of cars with fast nought to one hundred specs. Could have been on the forecourt of any northern suburbs dealership.

'I saved you time,' said the sergeant. 'I picked out a car already.' He pointed to a navy BM at the back of the row nearest the compound gate. Three series, the latest model. 'That one. It's fast, it's clean. I drove it. You want to drive it? Fifty-five on the clock. Full service record.'

'Any blood in it?' Spitz put down his holdall, took a packet of menthols from his top pocket.

'Valeted,' said the sergeant, not looking at Spitz. 'Anyhow, a no-shit hijack. No blood in it ever. Guaranteed.'

'Number plates are the original?' said Manga.

Spitz lit a cigarette without offering the pack.

'Sure.' The sergeant grinned, exposing a missing molar, top right. 'With the paperwork backlog it is a week before the car is in our system. Your holiday is a week, né? Until then the car is not missing. Never came in here. But in a week the car is hot stuff.'

Spitz exhaled, the smoke hanging dense in the air before them.

Manga said, 'Let me listen to it.'

'The key is inside.' The sergeant opened the door for Manga to slide in. Said to Spitz, 'This one is okay for you?'

Spitz shrugged. 'I am going for the ride.'

Whatever the sergeant replied, he couldn't hear beneath the whine and roar of the BM. When Manga dropped the engine to idle the sergeant said, 'This car is perfect.' He slapped the roof with his palm. 'Sharp, sharp guaranteed.'

Manga switched off the ignition and eased his legs out. 'How about that Subaru, captain? BM or a Subaru I would choose a Subaru.'

'No problem,' said the sergeant. 'In these two rows whatever you want it is yours. Your friend doesn't want one with the blood, I can show you those. For you to pick. These are good cars. Every one. If you want my choice you take this BMW.' He slapped the roof again. 'That is my job. Find a good car I am told. I find it. Also, this's a car for us. Two gents in it, that's not unusual. In a Subaru, that's strange. You get whites and coloureds drive a Subaru.'

'Subarus are better,' said Manga. He selected a model two cars down.

'That one had much blood,' said the sergeant.

Manga scanned the interior. 'Doesn't look like it.'

'You cannot see it now. I'm telling you. In the passenger seat that hole, that hole is a bullet hole. Forty-five millimetre, hollow-point. I do not have to say any more.'

'This one,' said Spitz, kicking lightly at the back wheel of the Beemer. He picked up his bag. 'Can you open the boot?'

The sergeant scooted round the car, grinning. 'I have a present in there for you.'

Manga, at the Subaru, started to say something, then stopped. Don't argue, they'd told him. Stick with him. Do what he says. He slammed shut the car door. Spitz glanced up but the sergeant was too busy marvelling at the contents of the boot to pay Manga's attitude any note.

Laid out on a towel was a Ruger small calibre pistol with a silencer. Shiny, like new. A box of .22 Long Rifle cartridges beside it.

'That is what you wanted?'

Spitz nodded.

'I oiled it.'

Spitz nodded again.

Manga came up. 'Captain. Captain, that's a toy.'

'It's a very light gun,' said the sergeant.

'Sure,' said Spitz. 'This is what I use.' He reached in and wrapped the gun in the towel, put the box of bullets into his bag. 'No record on it?'

'Stolen,' said the sergeant. 'Never reported. Not registered either. What're we going to do with it? One day put it in the smelter that will make the gun-free people happier. We got stock piles waiting for that day. One, nobody's gonna miss.'

Spitz placed his holdall in the boot and rummaged in it for an iPod wired to headphones. 'Do you have a bag?' he said to Manga.

'We can get it on the way.' Manga gestured at the gate. 'Meadowlands. Just down the road.'

Spitz slammed the lid shut. 'You have been helpful,' he said to the sergeant.

The sergeant grinned, revealing the gap in his teeth. 'Sharp, sharp. You have a week. Drive safe.'

4

Tami came in with two beers, said, 'I'm reception, né, not a waitress' – plonked the bottles down on the coffee table in Pylon's office right beside where Mace's feet rested. Mace sprawled in an armchair, Pylon perched in the window looking down on Dunkley Square. The cafés filling with Friday drinkers.

'Time you gave up smoking?' said Pylon.

Tami going, 'Like what? Like how's it a problem?'

'Your clothes,' said Pylon. 'The smoke's in your clothes.'

Mace grinned. 'He's kidding, Tami. Working your case.'

'Like I need it.' To Pylon she said, 'Your wife phoned. Wants you to call her back.'

Pylon groaned. 'Talk about working my case' – taking up his cellphone

Mace said, 'Go home, Tami. Get out of here' – watching her head for the stairs with a waggle of fingers goodbye. Had a good arse on her that hadn't started spreading yet.

Mace reached for a beer and took a pull. Pylon at the window gazing up Table Mountain saying, 'Yes, Treasure. I'll pick her up. In half an hour. Relax.'

When he'd disconnected turning to Mace: 'You'd think she'd understand we run a business. That I'm not a chauffeur.'

'Mostly we're chauffeurs,' said Mace, 'when you think about it.'

Pylon said, 'What?' Lifted his bottle of beer from the coffee table. Said, 'Pumla can wait another half an hour. She's at your place anyhow. With Christa. Oumou watching over both of them. But, no, Treasure's steaming.' He drank a short swallow. 'What d'you mean chauffeurs, anyhow.'

'Seems to me,' said Mace, 'that's what security's come down to. Driving scared people around.'

Pylon laughed. 'Good money though.'

'Time we got out.'

'You serious?'

'Reckon.' Mace swallowed a mouthful of beer. And another before he put the bottle back on the coaster, matching the wet ring to the bottom of the bottle. 'Guarding's for kids.

Macho types getting kicks out of belting up a nine mil when they dress.'

'I've not heard this version before.'

'Doesn't mean it hasn't been on my mind.' Mace met his eyes. 'Look at what's happening. What we're doing? All our lives we've been trading, getting shot at, shooting back. The war stops. Whatta we do? Search out a gap where we can get shot at again. Doesn't make sense.'

'It did. Make sense.'

'Not any more. Also I've got this court case on my head.'

'I thought Captain Gonz had sorted it, quashed it.'

Mace shook his head. 'Adjournments. Technical postponements. He tells me no more adjournments're possible. Pressure from the US consul looking after their murdering citizens. Try them, sentence them, get it over with.' Mace took a pull at his beer. 'The consul telling the prosecutors to stop dragging it out.'

Pylon watched people on the square, people hugging each other, relaxing at the end of the week. 'You should've shot them.'

'Paulo and Vittoria?'

'Them, yeah. Saved all this bother. You went soft.'

'Maybe.' Mace fidgeted with a lose thread on the couch arm. 'I thought ... I don't know what I thought. I thought after the killing spree they'd been on, the case would be quick sticks done and dusted.' He pulled out the thread, snapped it. 'Two good scores for Captain Gonsalves notched to his service record. Paulo and Vittoria lost in the prison system. Instead they want to tell the world I tortured them.' He wound the thread round his finger.

'Which you did.'

'To get a confession. How they murdered the Italian homos, Isabella and her sidekick.'

Pylon frowned. 'She was a problem. Isabella was bad news, we should of stayed away from her.'

'She got us the diamonds, remember.'

'She nearly got us killed. All because she lead you by the cock.'

'I fancied her once.' Mace pulled at the thread till his finger hurt.

'Once was once. Your problem you don't let things go.' Pylon shook his head. 'So what's the captain say?'

'He's stuffed too. Colluding. Withholding evidence. Gonz's an unhappy man. Hearing's still set down for a month's time. Any day they could subpoena me.'

'But they haven't yet?'

'No.'

Mace tightened the thread, grimaced.

Pylon said, 'You'll pop your finger, you carry on doing that.'

They drank in silence. Voices from the square drifting up. Pylon broke the quiet. 'So this's why you want to cash in, sell the business? You want to do a runner before the hearing?'

Mace glanced at him, squinted to see his expression against the light. 'You see another option? I'm facing jail time at the end of this. What happens to Oumou and Christa then?'

'The way I see it we've been through this three times already with adjournments. Every time the wheels of justice fall off. Trust to the captain, the man's got a lot to lose.'

'It's not your skin,' said Mace.

'All I'm saying,' – Pylon slid off the window sill, stretched his back – 'is we got to keep the options open, choose the moment to sell out. Now's not it. Know what I mean. You can't put your life on hold because of this court case. Maybe it doesn't get to court. Then what?'

Mace raised his eyebrows, the yeah, yeah in his expression.

'No, hang on. I mean it.' Pylon moved from the window, sat on the couch opposite Mace. 'Listen,' – leaning forward to get Mace's attention – 'there's a way out, in the long term. Come in on the west coast scheme. Golf estates make big bucks.' The west coast scheme one of Pylon's capitalist ventures, something Mace wanted in on anyhow.

'How?' Mace took another swallow. 'With what? Where're Oumou and I going to get spare cash?'

'From me.' Pylon giving him the full eyeball. 'This's our out, my brother. You want it that badly, grab the lifeline. This comes off we can start thinking of selling up. Get out. No more crap and cranola. Liquidate the Cayman account. Live properly. We do it carefully Revenue'll not suspect a thing.'

'And the court case?'

'Forget the court case. Plan positive.'

Mace glancing off out the window at the mountain. The last of the sun against the cliffs, catching the buttresses, the red in the sandstone. 'We sit here, all that money in Cayman, we can't touch it. Our bucks. Hard earned moola.'

'We get the golf estate we can launder it. Some of it. Whatever we want. No problem.'

'It eats me,' said Mace.

Pylon sat back. 'It's a way to sort things out.'

'If I go to jail.'

'I didn't say that. I said forget the court case. We face it if and when.'

Mace looked at his partner. Unwavering conviction in Pylon's eyes.

'Believe me,' said Pylon. 'Mightn't happen. So' – he came forward again – 'let's put that aside, clarify this other matter, about cashing up. I've heard this before from you, this closing down number. Maybe two, three times.'

'Sure.' Mace nodded. 'After Christa got shot. After that bastard pulled that kidnap stunt. After Isabella got killed. I know, I said enough each time. But really, hey, how could we do it really? I needed the bucks. Need them still. Without the money we're in the dwang, Oumou and me.' Mace reached for his beer. 'What I'm saying is, with the court case, I'm stuffed. My family's stuffed.'

They drank in silence. Mace thinking, he did a runner where in the world would they live? Malitia? Go back to Oumou's desert village where they'd met. Medieval Tuaregs and goats. Nothing but Sahara sand, hazed distant mountains. He'd go mad. Nothing to do. No one to talk to. No water, nowhere to swim. And Christa was a city girl. No ways she'd cope. The trouble was Pylon was right. Pylon wasn't going anywhere. This was his life. He had to keep the business until something happened he could wash in the offshore funds. Bit by bit so that no one noticed.

Mace said, 'What about Obed Chocho? He's going to snatch the west coast from you?'

'Major crap,' said Pylon. 'A headache like you can't believe. I have to admit even from prison the man pulls a network. The man who could stuff this up for us. Snatch this deal out of our hands.'

Mace's cellphone rang and he dug it from his pants pocket, connected.

A voice said in his ear, 'Is that Mr Mace Bishop?'

Mace getting that heavy sensation in his chest. The reason he knew he wanted out. He said, 'Who's this?' – watching Pylon launch off the couch, Pylon mouthing at him, 'We'll talk tomorrow.'

Mace held up a hand, wait. Pylon shook his head, drew a finger across his throat. Said, 'Treasure.'

Mace waved him off, smiling, heard the voice say, 'My name is Telman Visser, Mr Bishop. Judge Telman Visser.'

Didn't mean zilch from zucchini to Mace. No Afrikaans in the accent. Cape Town private school tones, quiet, firm. Visser with the 'r' sounded not the usual heavy 'a', Vissa. Mace pictured Bishop's Court: long ranch-style house, tall hedges around it, the judge standing on his lawn gazing up at the mountain. Bird-twitter in the background. The judge not wanting to be overheard by anyone. Man of about any age between late forties and sixties, he reckoned, going by the voice.

Mace said, 'That so.' Waited.

Until the judge on the other end said, 'Mr Bishop are you there?'

'I am,' said Mace. And waited. Mace shrugged. Hearing hadedas squawking loudly, flying right over the judge's head probably.

The judge saying, 'Mr Bishop could we meet? Perhaps at the Michael Stevenson Art Gallery. You know it? In Green Point.'

Mace said, 'There's not many people have this number.'

'Ah.' The hadedas distant, the judge's voice taking on a chuckle. 'Of course. My apologies. A New York colleague referred me to you. Gave me your cellular number. He and his wife were out here for a "surgical safari", I believe he termed it. Last November. Judge and Mrs Steinhauer. He was most impressed with your security service. Also someone locally who preferred to remain anonymous.'

'Intriguing,' said Mace. 'I remember Judge Steinhauer' – picturing the silver-haired judge, a Johnny Cash fan plugged into an iPod for most part of any day. His wife over for a face-lift and a boob job. Not that she needed either at forty-five – ten, fifteen years younger than the judge.

'I have a problem, Mr Bishop. For this I need security. Reliable security.'

'That's what we do,' said Mace, wishing he didn't have to say it. Standing, moving to the window. The sun gone from the face of Table Mountain, the shadow giving it a looming presence.

'Not on the phone, if you don't mind. I prefer dealing with people face to face,' The judge saying. 'Tomorrow morning, perhaps. About ten-thirty, eleven?' A tone of voice that wasn't used to accommodating others.

Mace thinking, Shit. So much for a session at the Point swimming pool. He lost any more training time he wasn't going to keep up with Christa. Have his daughter leave him behind on the Robben Island swim? He wouldn't live it down. Pylon wouldn't let him.

'Perhaps we could do this Tuesday, I'll be back in town then.'

'I need to expedite an arrangement urgently, Mr Bishop. Tomorrow latest. Do you understand?'

Mace thought, had to be a judge would use a word like expedite. Decided, hear the guy out. Could be good business.

'Alright,' he said. 'Ten thirty. Where again?'

The judge repeated the address.

'An art gallery?'

'There's something I want to show you. To make my point.'

The judge rang off.

5

They'd been on the road for two hours. Got through the mine dumps and the industrial belt and into farmlands, the road opening up, quieter, the sun sliding off the western rim hot and red right where they were heading. Cast an orange light over the maize fields. Manga driving, clicked on the headlights. He needed a burger and chips, tomato sauce, a beer to wash it down.

Spitz in the passenger seat listened to his iPod, eyes focused on the landscape. Every forty-five minutes he smoked a menthol. Manga noticed that. Forty-five minutes exactly, Spitz would light up. Like there was an alarm went off only he heard. After the cigarette he took a mouthful of sparkling mineral water. Replaced the bottle in a holder over an aircon vent on the dashboard. Not a word exchanged in two hours.

Manga thought, captain, you're not making me laugh. He reached for the can of Coke in the holder next to Spitz's water. Drained it. Dropped the can over his shoulder. Wasn't for his cellphone, he'd have had no one to talk to. Worse, he'd brought no sounds himself. Bloody going anywhere without Zola was a mistake. And this cousin wasn't going to share his tunes. Weird shit that it was by the vague sound leaking out. Not rap. Not R&B. Not kwaito. Some sort of pop shit.

He leaned across, touched Spitz on the arm. Spitz turned his head, eyes drowsy, hooded.

'Something to eat, captain? Burger and chips? Five kays there's a One Stop coming up.'

Spitz pulled off his headphones. 'Say it again?'

'A One Stop.'

'A One Stop?'

Manga laughed. 'Not Spur or Steers? Not even McDonalds. The One Stop.'

Spitz shook his head. 'What is this?'

'Hey, captain.' Manga glanced at him amused. 'You don't know about One Stops?'

'No.'

'You don't drive? Like this, long distance?'

'I fly. When I work in another city, I fly to it.'

Manga thumped the steering wheel. 'No shit. Not once, in all your life, you've driven across this country? Not even before?'

'No. What for?'

'What for? Captain, hey, captain. To see the place. You know, see where the ancestors hung out. On the grass plains. In the desert. Up in the mountains. The sort of country they knew. The sort of stuff that happens between the cities.'

Spitz shook out a menthol, pressed in the car lighter. 'It does not bother me.'

'Hey?' Manga rolled his tongue round his teeth, considering a sudden realisation. 'You don't know where we're going or what's the job?'

'That is your problem.' Spitz lit his cigarette, blew out a short puff. 'The way I operate is you have to get me to the place, and you tell me what is the target. I do it. Then you take me back home.'

'Guess what, captain?'

Spitz didn't respond.

'Come'n guess what?'

'I cannot see your mind.'

'I don't know bugger all. What I know is we're booked in a

motel another four hours drive away. That means midnight. Tomorrow they're gonna phone us there. Give me directions.'

'That is okay.'

'Maybe for you captain. But me, I like a bit more information.'

Spitz pulled on the menthol. Some way down the road was a blaze of light in the dusk. Had to be Manga's One Stop.

Manga saying, 'This's not my sort of work. I don't chauffeur. I'm doing this as a personal favour to the people who hired us.'

'And for the money.'

'Come again.'

'You are doing it for the money.'

Manga laughed. 'Sure, captain, for the bucks.'

After the One Stop they drove for hours into the night, the burger heavy in Spitz's stomach, a burnt taste in his mouth whenever he belched. He regretted it, should have had the pasta salad. And beer not wine. The wine had gone to acid. He stared into the dark, a darkness so intense he had no shape or size to the landscape they passed through. Occasionally on the curves, the headlights swept the verge revealing rocks and hard scrub and the gleam of litter. Sometimes the red of a creature's eyes. On the horizon lightning danced. Spitz leaned forward to see the stars through the windscreen. The movement made him burp a taste of charcoal; the stars told him nothing.

'This's desert,' said Manga. 'You wanna see the stars?'

Spitz shook his head. 'No. I can see them.'

Manga held a four-battery Maglite in his hand, from time to time playing the beam over the scrub to their right. He had the window down and the air was cool, but Spitz had no complaints. Nor to the smell it brought in, a pungent sharpness of vegetation as fresh as cat piss.

Eyes blazed in Manga's torchlight and were gone.

'Hey, wena, there we go, captain. Yes, yes.' Manga gave a long piercing whistle as he braked and spun the car into a u-turn, brought it to a stop facing the way they'd come.

Spitz braced against the dashboard, said, 'What are you doing?' The words quiet, almost a whisper.

Manga ignored him. Thrust the Maglite into his hands. 'Shine it there. Up ahead. Get the eyes.' Slowly they drove along the gravel edge until the eyes shone up in the beam.

'Yo,' said Manga, pulling the car into the rough, stopping. 'Donkeys, captain. What d'you say? Something to notch up.' Before Spitz could reply, Manga was out rummaging in the boot. Spitz joined him, still carrying the Maglite, shone it on the CZs Manga held in either hand.

'What I say, captain, is you never know. Two is better than one.' He held a gun at Spitz. 'Take it. Come'n. Come'n.'

Spitz did, the weight unfamiliar but easy in his hand.

'Not a shitty .22. Some firepower captain. Nine mil parabellum. That's what we want.' He slammed shut the boot, wrenched the torch from Spitz's grip.

Manga led through the scrub towards the donkeys, flicking the light about, picking up three of them grazing. The animals not moving off as the men approached. He gave the torch back to Spitz.

'Shine it on the head. Behind the eye.'

Spitz held the torch beam on the head of the donkey nearest them. The animal shifted off and in that instant Manga fired, the donkey going down, its body trembling with after-nerves.

Spitz felt the percussion of the shot, the loudness swallowed quickly by the vast darkness. The other donkeys brayed, crashing off, their hooves clinking against the shale.

Manga swore. Shouting first in Zulu then English, 'Follow them. Get them in the light.' And when Spitz didn't, grabbing the Maglite, sweeping the bush to catch an animal's rump disappearing into a gully.

Manga raced after it, stumbling and cursing, scrambling down the erosion. Spitz stood. Heard birds explode from the scrub and beat away. Heard two shots, close together. Waited. Watched the light returning, Manga out of breath.

'I hit it somewhere. One of them.' He shone the light on the dead donkey, a small hole behind the eye, the eye open, glistening. 'Bastards, hey, not so easy to kill.' He raised the light to Spitz's face. 'You didn't fire.'

Spitz held up his hand to block the light. Said, 'I do not shoot animals.'

An hour after they'd checked into the motel, Manga drove out alone, took the bypass round the town and came back down the main street. What occurred to him was the place was a heist job waiting to happen. You could drive a truck smack into one of the banks and no one would know till morning. You could load it and be away before the cops woke up.

He drove slowly, looking for the offices of Jan Niemand, Prokureur/Attorney. Passed another lawyer's office wondering why there was enough work for two legals in a town this size before he found what he wanted. Small building with a gable, fronting on the pavement, middle of the block. Closed shutters at the windows. The lawyer's name neatly scrolled above the door.

Middle of the block didn't appeal to Manga. But he knew a town like this had to have a service lane behind the offices. Which was where he parked outside a gate that had Jan Niemand's signage painted on it. Dogs barked but no lights came on.

He took a can of petrol from the boot and a screwdriver from the toolkit. The Maglite stuck in his belt with a nine mil.

The gate was unlocked. Manga entered a yard. Two garden chairs at a table, a sun umbrella stuck through a hole in the middle. Lawn underfoot. Flower beds down the sides. Someone cared to keep the garden pretty.

Four paces to the back door. He used the screwdriver on the lock: standard single cylinder was like having no lock at all. Inside smelt of drain cleaner. Tea cups on dish cloth, a fridge, a microwave, a toaster. Floorboards creaked at his movement. He paused, listening.

Went through the kitchen into a passage, two rooms on the right, two rooms on the left. Checked each, shining the Maglite round the rooms: reception up front, opposite that an office, behind those back rooms for the paper work: metal filing cabinets against the walls. Manga started right: opened drawers, doused the contents with petrol. Same with the cabinets in the other room. Wooden ceiling, wooden floors under threadbare carpets. The place would blaze. He tossed matches left and right and backed away.

Coming out of the office was an old man in a dressing gown, a hunting rifle gripped in his hands.

Manga shone the light on him. Said, 'Ah, shit man, captain, what're you doing here? Don't you have a home somewhere?'

The man pointed the rifle at him, said something in Afrikaans Manga didn't understand.

Manga said, 'What?' – feeling the heat of the fire, the flames catching at the carpet.

The man said in English, 'Put up your hands.'

'What?' Manga laughed. 'You joking?'

'Put up your hands.' The old man gestured with his rifle. 'I will shoot.'

'Shit, captain.' Before he could shoot, Manga whipped him with the Maglite, the old man collapsing in a whisper. Not only wearing a dressing gown, also had on slippers Manga saw. 'Shit, captain,' Manga said again, backing out quickly, taking the rifle, closing the kitchen door. Weren't even dogs barking. The little town quiet as the desert around it.

Saturday

6

Mace popped a piece of croissant into his mouth, cracked open the newspaper to the story on page three: another four tourists robbed by the mountain mugger. All those rangers running around the mountain, they couldn't catch this prick doing over the tourists. Unbelievable. Waves a knife at some Germans then disappears like he's a spectre. Mace shook his head. One mugger getting away with it again and again. The sort of incompetence encouraged vigilantism. Wasn't too far out of Mace's mind to go up there, sort it out.

'Papa,' Christa said, 'I'm trying to tell you something.'

Mace put the paper down on the breakfast table. 'I'm listening.'

'You're not,' said Christa. 'Come on, Papa.'

'I am,' said Mace, wiped crumbs from his mouth with the back of his hand. 'I heard you the first time. I think I know this person, came to your school. Tell me again.'

Oumou, wearing a blue kikoi, came out of the house with coffee to where they sat eating breakfast beside the pool. Below them the city, Saturday quiet; up on the mountain early tourists rode the cable car to the top pointing at the sights: the harbour, the Waterfront, Robben Island, the curve of the bay along the West Coast.

Oumou said, 'That is a bad story, Christa.' But she smiled as she said it.

'You didn't laugh?' said Mace.

'She did,' said Christa.

'Oui,' said Oumou. 'I have to say so.'

'There you go,' said Mace. 'So let's hear it again.' Cat2 stirred on his lap and he rubbed at the scar-tissue where as a kitten she'd been nailed to a wall. The cat arched against his massage.

'Okay,' said Christa. 'This woman came to tell us about drugs. How she used to shoot up stuff, inject it into her leg so many times that they had to cut it off. Her leg.' She giggled.

'Heavy,' said Mace, leaving the cat and stretching for an almond croissant.

'She's got this cool chrome pole screwed into her knee with a Nike on it, matching the one on her real foot.'

Mace smiled. 'Yellow trainers.'

'How'd you know?'

'I just do.'

Christa glanced at him suspiciously. 'Like how?'

'If it's the same person, that's what she wears. Get on with the story.'

'Okay. So she's telling us about spiking between her toes. She's got this syringe filled with blood and stuff, that's gross and she's showing us.'

Oumou poured coffee from the Bialetti. Smacked at Mace's hand running up her thigh under the kikoi.

'Maman! Papa!' said Christa.

Mace winked at his wife, caught Christa watching them. 'Tell it, C.'

'You're not listening.'

'I am.' Mace squeezed Oumou's knee, returned his hands to breakfast. Smeared honey on the croissant, broke off a piece. He masticated, swilled it down with a mouthful of coffee.

'So she unscrews it. Not unscrews. You know sort of pushes a button behind her knee, that pops off the pole.'

'Prosthesis.'

'That word,' said Christa. 'Pro-thesis.'

'Pros,' said Mace, feeding croissant to Cat2. 'Prosthesis.'

'Anyway,' said Christa, 'like she's standing there on one foot, with her pros... whatever in her hand. Waving it like a wand. And we're going, ah yuk, and she shouts "catch, hey". Throwing her artificial leg down to us. For real. Right at us. Near to me. Everybody's pushing not to touch it.'

'What's she doing?' said Mace. 'The woman on her one leg?'

'I told you,' said Christa. 'She's laughing. It's, like, a big joke.'

Mace helped himself to more coffee and topped Oumou's cup. 'And then Pumla grabbed hold of it?'

'Her and some others,' said Christa.

'But not you?'

'I touched it.' Christa grimaced. 'It was all warm at the knee part.'

'So who took off the trainer?'

'Pummie.' Christa glanced at her father.

Mace grinned, Pylon would like that one: his step-daughter getting in on the act. 'And?'

'The wooden foot had green toenails. That's so gross.'

'It's supposed to be.'

'Mace!' Oumou laughed. 'You are being unkind. This woman is brave to talk about it.'

'Of course,' said Mace. 'I agree she's brave. It's what she does, how she earns a living, being a motivational speaker. It's what people do. You rob banks, you do your time, afterwards people pay big money to hear you speak. Or you get raped, your throat's cut, you're left for dead, you've got a new career.'

'Mace.' Oumou frowned at him.

'What?'

'That is not nice.'

'That's what happens. This chick was a druggie. She gets over it, she gets a new life. Goes to show how people move on. Turn stuff around.' He pointed at Christa. 'We got one right here. A couple of years ago she was paralysed for life.' Mace flashing on the gunshot. Hearing Christa cry out. Seeing her collapse. The blood stain darkening at her stomach. He looked at his daughter looking back at him across the table: her Zen face, her Buddha smile. Mace thought, this is why I've got to get out. Washed down the wish with coffee.

Heard Christa saying, 'Papa! Papa, listen.'

Mace smiling at her.

'Pummie wanted to know why she painted the toenails.'

'What'd she say?'

'She said to remind her of her foot. That she once had a real one.'

'That is sad,' said Oumou.

'She's tough,' said Mace. 'If it's the woman I'm thinking of. Lives with an investigator, ex-cop, we used him once to track down stolen stuff. Chews a lot of mints. Nice guy. Him and his one-legged doll.'

Mace's cellphone rang. He reached for it lying on the table next to the basket of croissants and rolls. The screen displayed 'Pylon'. He thumbed him on. Watched Christa push back her chair and stand. Beautiful, the black costume against her honey skin. The child's body morphing into a young woman. He wasn't sure how he felt about this: her childhood ending.

Said, 'You're interrupting my breakfast.'

Heard Oumou say to Christa, poised on the edge of the swimming pool, 'I must buy clay, cherie: you will come with me?' Saw Christa nod and flash a smile before she plunged into the water. Slipping in like a dolphin, hardly a splash.

Oumou turned from watching Christa gliding through the water, raised her eyebrows at him: who're you talking to?

Mace said, 'Pylon.'

Pylon said, 'I'm driving now, passing Century City. Great view of the mountain opening up. I can tell you I've been sitting for four hours.'

'Some particular reason you're out there instead of at home?'

Mace walked to where he could see the city clearly through a break in the trees. The cascade of the garden suburb down the bowl of the mountain into the concrete centre. The buildings clustered tall and white there, the sea a flat blue beyond.

'Driving behind this brand new black Yengeni. Nice car the ML 350'

'You're thinking of one?'

Pylon not into buying cars at all, happy to use the office Merc.

'Too arriviste.'

Mace smiled, turning from the view to his house: the house Oumou'd wanted of concrete and glass and chrome. Something as far removed from the mud towns of her desert life as she could get.

'I work with clay, Mace,' she'd said. 'In my pottery are my memories. We must live in something modern. Where no one has lived before.'

Once the house was built Mace couldn't imagine living anywhere else. He glanced above the roof at Devil's Peak, deep shadow still in the kloof.

'So where've you been?' Mace waved at Christa to keep swimming. To Pylon said, 'Help me out, I'm pulling teeth here.'

Pylon laughed. 'Outside Mr Chocho's.'

'Doing what?'

'A stakeout.'

'We've registered as investigators? I didn't notice.'

'This's private and confidential,' said Pylon. 'Got nothing to do with us, Complete Security. Got to do with us the property investors.'

'The west coast thing?'

'Precisely.'

'I've been thinking,' said Mace. 'Maybe you lend me something against the Cayman account. An IOU.'

'We can talk about it,' said Pylon. 'Another time. You have to listen to this first.'

'Perhaps turn the music down,' said Mace. The driving sound of the Cowboy Junkies in the background.

'So what do I see?'

'I couldn't guess. Tell me.' Mace watched Oumou clearing the table, Cat2 pawing at her for titbits.

'I see my comrade and consortium partner Popo Dlamini coming out of Mr Chocho's house.'

'And this is interesting?'

'At six in the morning. Very interesting. What I wonder is, does Obed Chocho know? What I also wonder is, how would that brother feel about this brother looking after his wife while he's doing prison?'

'It's nine o'clock,' said Mace. 'Why're you only on the highway now?'

'I told you,' said Pylon. 'Staking out. Had to be sure Mrs Chocho'd been playing hostess. She's driving the Merc I'm following. Must have a date in the city.'

Mace dipped his toe in the water; Pylon's machinations on the empowerment deal were labyrinthine in their complexity. Thorough though.

'Listen,' he said, 'after you're finished playing Easy Rawlins, I'm meeting a prospective client. You got time to be in on that? A judge. Name of Telman Visser.' He heard a blare of hooters and Pylon swear. 'We could talk afterwards.'

Mace said, 'Hey, talk to me. You going to make it or what?'

'Can't,' said Pylon. 'Consortium meeting. I told you, there's major shit on this deal. The seller holding out 'cos he can see paydirt. Young white couple wanting in on the act or major compensation.' A pause, Pylon muttering in Xhosa, 'We're coming off the highway. Check you later.'

Mace disconnected, thinking Pylon was taking strain on this one. Putting in a lot of effort to get them sorted, get them access to the Cayman stash. He flipped closed the cellphone. If only there wasn't the court case. If only. He closed his eyes, shook his head as if to shake out the thought.

With an hour and a half till he met the judge, he could join

Christa in the pool for a dozen laps. Work down the two almond croissants. And the salami roll. He stripped off his T-shirt. Stood poised in his Speedo on the edge of the pool.

Oumou came up, rubbed a hand over his stomach. 'A little bit round,' she said.

7

Pylon, three cars behind the SUV, slid left out of the middle lane into the Woodstock off-ramp, nothing but seventy metres separating him from Mrs Obed Chocho. Lindi, short for Lindiwe to her friends. Friends like Popo. Friends you'd placed some trust in, up to yesterday. Until you heard it through the grapevine that your consortium partner was consorting with the enemy.

A call from a property man, Dave Cruickshank: 'Pylon, old son, you're in with Popo Dlamini on the west coast deal, I heard.'

'You got it.'

'Bidding against the mighty Obed Chocho. The convict.'

'Something like that.'

'Then maybe, my son, you'd want to know that I've seen the lovely Lindi with your man Popo.'

Enough said. Pylon ran the stakeout; turned out Dave was on the nail.

At the traffic lights corner of Lower Church and New Market, he was behind Mrs Chocho, the lovely Lindi on her cellphone, oblivious to the world. Easier following her than a blind woman in a hospital corridor.

With the green, up to Victoria then left. Lindi still on her phone, Pylon wondering where this was heading: what point was there to following her anyhow? Instinct, he believed. The only downside, all the twisty bits she was taking. Mrs C had half an eye to the rearview she had to notice the black Merc driven by the guy in shades. Pylon eased off. Problem was this time of a Saturday morning there wasn't much traffic to hide in.

His cellphone rang. Pumla. 'Mommy wants to know where you are?' she said, using English, almost the only language she spoke these days. Whispering, 'She's in a bad mood.'

'Wonderful,' said Pylon. 'I need that.' Seeing the SUV going right into Roodebloem, no cars turning behind her. No ways she wouldn't notice him. 'Pummie, tell her I'll be home in fifteen, twenty. What's the agenda anyhow?'

'Breakfast,' said Pumla. 'You promised, remember?'

Pylon turned into Roodebloem and pulled against the curb, watched the SUV power up the steep street.

'No problem, we can still do breakfast. Vide e Caffè. The Palms, anywhere she wants.'

'Dad?' Though she wasn't his daughter, she'd known no other father most of her life. She called him that it still tweaked his heartstrings. 'Mom's really mad.'

'Thanks,' he said. 'I'm on my way.' Maybe it had something to do with Treasure being pregnant. Morning sickness. A bit like living with an angry cobra. The deal was: if she fell pregnant they'd also adopt an AIDS orphan.

'I'm the only black man in the country without a child,' he'd complained. 'There're boys of fifteen with more children than me. If we just had one.'

'What about the AIDS orphans?'

'What about them? We're not a charity.'

'You want a child, then we adopt one too.'

'Mr Zuma did that there'd be no AIDS orphans.'

'Exactly.'

Pylon accepted the deal though.

'On our income, our standard of living, it's what we should be doing,' was Treasure's point of view.

Pylon had counter arguments but he didn't advance them. Not to

Treasure. To Mace over a few Windhoeks. But not to Treasure. Never to Treasure. One ran that if the government took HIV seriously there'd be fewer orphans. As a nurse she should know. But the fat cow of a minister told them African potatoes were the answer.

'All I want's a child,' Pylon would say, three or four beers down. 'Not a bloody orphanage.'

He gave Lindiwe Chocho almost to the top of the road, before accelerating after her. Chances were he'd delayed too long. Had to be she was heading into University Estate. Early to be visiting, but Lindiwe clearly made her own arrangements. Then again she could as easily take the Eastern Boulevard either direction. Chances were he'd screwed this one. By the time he reached the highway intersection, the Merc ML 350 wasn't to be seen. At least not on the boulevard. Into town or out of it.

He headed into University Estate, just on the off chance. And there, down the far end of Ritchie Street, Mrs Chocho was getting out of her SUV. Pylon stopped behind a parked car. He reached for binoculars lying on the passenger seat and focused on Lindiwe ringing a gate buzzer. She leaned forward, talking into the intercom, neat in white capris. Moments later the gate opened. Lindiwe and her host embraced. Moments enough for Pylon to recognise the woman: Sheemina February. Attorney Sheemina February. 'Shit!' he said. Then: 'Fuck.' Then: 'Bitch.' Then: 'Bloody bitch.' Keeping the bins focused on the woman. The woman who'd once worked Mace's case. Given him major grief. The woman behind Christa's shooting. Mace's kidnapping. Maybe even behind some club bombings. Ms Teflon. 'Save me Jesus,' he said. Thinking: what's the bitch's connection?

Chocho was mainstream, swung with the big boys. Sheemina February definitely wasn't kosher. A weirdo psycho. In it for the bucks and the blood. Anyone's blood. Strange alliance for Mrs Chocho to be seeing Sheemina February. The two women disappeared into the house.

Pylon rested the binoculars on the steering wheel, puzzled about this development. Of all the things it couldn't be, it couldn't be social. Sheemina February didn't do social. When Sheemina February appeared shit happened. Strange stuff that got people killed.

While he thought about this, his phone buzzed: Treasure.

8

Obed Chocho waved the prison commander to take a seat. On a three-seater couch done out in a floral print. A couch moved up from the warders' common room when Obed Chocho complained he couldn't spend the day on a plastic garden chair.

Wasn't the only piece of furniture the commander had commandeered for his prisoner. Other items included a desk, a side table for his coffee and bowls of peanuts when Obed sprawled out to watch television on the forty-seven centimetre Sony. Also a video player. The DVD player was Obed's. Ditto the mini-tower and speakers, the rack of CDs.

Obed was watching the first series of the Sopranos when the prison commander rapped on the door.

One thing Obed Chocho disliked was being interrupted while he watched the Sopranos. Lindiwe had learnt this with a split lip. Not the first time Obed had backhanded her but the other occasions he'd been tanked. The Sopranos incident he wasn't.

It was ten o'clock in the morning. She was bringing him coffee and marmalade toast in bed, treating him, spoiling him, even considering putting out on a wet winter Sunday. She crossed his line of vision to set down the tray. Crossed back again getting to her side of the bed.

She'd leaned towards him, the neck of her negligee gaping, letting him get a good dose of her breasts. Her nipples extended, longer than any nipples he'd ever seen. So he'd told her. Expecting him to pull her down. Instead he hit her, opened her lip with his wedding ring.

Said, 'What's this I'm watching?'

Lindiwe in tears, blood dripping on her negligee, sniffed the answer.

'Mighty fine,' he said. 'This is nothing you don't know about.'

To the prison commander, he said, 'You know the Sopranos?'

'I've watched them,' the commander said, sitting on the couch, across from Chocho, looking at the shaven-headed man, lying on the bed, propped by two pillows against the metal head. A conventional hospital bed that Chocho'd complained about. He had conjugal visiting rights. How was that supposed to happen on a single bed?

The commander could imagine, especially with Mrs Lindiwe Chocho, but kept his mind off picturing her naked.

Couldn't requisition the bed Chocho wanted either. Well, actually, he hadn't tried. No, that was going too far. The man was a convict: four years for fraud. The commander clicked his tongue. No. To hell with that.

Obed Chocho had been up on other charges: corruption, bribery, extortion, that the prosecution couldn't get to stick but that didn't make Obed Chocho any less guilty in the commander's eyes. So no double bed.

Tough shit. Mr Chocho had it as soft as it got. Own room in the prison's hospital wing. Own loo and shower across the corridor. Ordered in food. Cellphone connectivity. The pressure coming from above: keep Obed happy.

Which he was inclined to do, his job and career being vital components of his life. Prison commander not the final title in his planned trajectory either. He screwed up here it could be. So he played the Chocho thing down the line. When a memo said give Obed Chocho a rehabilitation pass this Sunday afternoon, he did just that.

Said to Obed Chocho, in green tracksuit bottoms and a T-shirt, chilling to his favourite series: 'Can you pause that for a moment?'

Obed frowned. 'What?'

'Pause it.' The commander surprised at his own response, curt, no bullshit. Pleased and edgy about this at the same time. Met Obed's hard stare and held it.

Obed didn't take his eyes off him, raised his right hand holding the remote, pointed it at the television, a question furrowed into his brow: You want to reconsider?

The prison commander waited. On screen Tony in a session with the shrink telling Dr Jennifer Melfi about his life, the camera closing on T's face, that perplexed expression he wore like his favourite clothes. The image froze.

Obed Chocho lowered his arm, didn't say anything, not letting go of the eyeballing.

The prison commander submitted, glanced off at the picture on the wall. This snowed-in village in a valley. Hunters and their dogs coming down from the hills. Some print Mrs Chocho had brought in. Some print they'd bought in a Vienna art gallery that Obed liked. Six months with Obed Chocho wasn't an honour. Two weeks to parole couldn't go fast enough.

'Tomorrow afternoon,' he said, 'the board's given you a rehabilitation pass.'

'Now you tell me,' said Obed, swinging off the bed. 'The day before! Hey, what's that about? Mighty fine, get on with it Obed. Get everybody to drop their lives, come pick you up take you for a drive to the beach. Have an ice cream. Hey, my brother, the day before!'

'That's the way it's done,' said the commander. 'A preparation for parole.' Actually the memo'd come in mid-week but the commander had sat on it.

'Mighty fine,' said Obed. 'Twelve years I spent on the island, my brother. No Sunday afternoon pass. No preparation for parole.

Four months I've been here. A Sunday pass's an insult.'

'After four months you're eligible,' said the prison commander, getting up, planning to keep this conversation short. 'Two o'clock to five o'clock. No alcohol.'

Obed Chocho smacked his right fist into his left palm. 'You're telling me that?'

'I have to.'

'Hey, brother.' Two more palm strikes sharp and hard. 'You're walking a fine line. Know what I mean?'

The prison commander felt the heat prickling on his own palms, was about to say he'd been there too when Obed Chocho's cellphone rang. The commander moved to leave.

Obed Chocho said, 'Wait. Hang on, okay.' Answered with good humour in his tone of voice. 'Ms Sheemina February.' He listened. Laughed. Turned towards the prison commander, said, 'I have the prison commander with me.' Paused. 'No, no, no. He's happy to wait.'

The prison commander stood uncomfortably poised between the couch and the door. Obed Chocho ignored him. Faced the window with its view of a courtyard below, convicts playing volleyball there. The prison commander moved to the desk. Three neat piles: four paperbacks in a stack, Right as Rain on top; an A4 feint-ruled pad with the names Henk and Olivia Smit in pencil; the third pile a printout of sms messages.

Obed Chocho said, 'What's that? Popo? Yes, yes, Dlamini. Sure. I know. It's no problem.'

Glancing down the messages the prison commander reckoned some of them couldn't have pleased Obed Chocho. The ones from this Popo to Lindiwe. The ones from her to Popo. The sort of messages no one should send.

The prison commander smiled, picked up the Pelecanos, flipped to where Obed had dog-eared the page. A third down a character was sniffing white powder from the crook of his thumb. The prison commander believed Obed Chocho would have understood the rush.

His back still to the commander, Chocho was saying, 'I'm out tomorrow afternoon, how about you set up a meeting. What's that?' He listened. Said, 'I've just been told.' He turned to face the prison commander, holding out the phone. 'My attorney.'

The prison commander took the phone, heard Sheemina February say, 'Regulations state a minimum forty-eight hours notice, commander. What's your explanation?'

'I can't help you,' he said. 'Complaints must be addressed to the board.'

'I will,' said Sheemina February. 'What I want to know is when you were told? This morning? Yesterday? Four days ago? When commander?'

'Yesterday.'

'Yesterday. And you wait until this morning? How is Mr Chocho supposed to make arrangements at this late notice?' She paused. 'You'll hear from me, commander, officially. Now let me speak to Mr Chocho.'

The prison commander returned the phone to Obed Chocho. A piece of work that Sheemina February. He'd run in with her before over the Muslim anti-drug vigilantes doing time for their bombings and assassinations. Sheemina February was not somebody he wanted on his case. The way this was going, he'd have to leave no footprints. Give Obed some latitude. He heard Obed say, 'She's with you? Lindiwe? Listening?' The prisoner with his back to the window now, watching the prison commander. Scowling. 'Good, good. I'll call her later. I think first we fix a meeting with the Smits. Tomorrow afternoon. Their place. Wherever they want it. Yes, why not at the property? I can relax there, open a few beers.' Laughing. Looking directly at the prison commander and laughing. The prison commander not happy about Obed Chocho's attitude.

Obed Chocho disconnected. 'You know her?'

'We've met.'

'Mighty fine lady. Maybe if she'd been my lawyer before the trial there'd have been no trial.' Obed dropped onto the couch. 'How long've I got?'

'Two o'clock to five o'clock.'

'You can push it to six?'

The prison commander hesitated. 'There is the question of alcohol. Prisoners on parole may not drink.'

Obed Chocho kept his gaze steady. 'What if Sheemina February gets off your case?'

The prison commander shrugged.

'Lighten up, my brother' said Chocho, stretching his legs. 'I will not be drunk. No one will know if I am away for three hours or four hours. Only you.' He smiled, and stood, came to stand next to the prison commander and put his hand on the man's shoulder. Both men of equal height and build. The only difference, Chocho's shaven head emphasising the two cushions of fat at his neck. Like his head rested on them. He squeezed the commander's shoulder. 'Everything will be mighty fine.'

The prison commander shook loose of the grip, moved towards the door. 'I am sure you want to make some phone calls.'

'Too right, my brother,' said Obed Chocho. 'The world does not stop because you are in prison.'

9

She had the warder's gun. Big lesbo bitch had given up the gun at the sight of the sharpened spoke. She'd wanted to stick it to her. Into that huge belly to see if it exploded like a balloon. But the big lesbo bitch caved. Let her run off into the night.

Christ knew where she was. Vast darkness all around. Not a light twinkling anywhere. She ran, fell, picked herself up, ran, walked into clump scrub that scratched up blood on her hands, tore at her prison jumpsuit. She couldn't hear them tracking her. Believed they would begin with daylight. At dawn she saw the ruined house. A kind of shelter.

For hours she sat in the shade of the doorway watching. She was thirsty. Hungry too, but the thirst burned in her throat. She heard the van before she saw it. Heard it a long way out on the flats. Then the flash of metal in the sun. Then watched it come straight towards her, like they knew where she was.

No point in running. Anything moved on the plain you could see it miles off. She went into the ruin, waited.

The van stopped, the engine cut off. Silence. She imagined them scoping the scene, the big lesbo bitch and the male warder. The van's doors opened, banged shut. The male warder called her name through a loudspeaker: 'Vittoria. Vittoria.'

Up yours, she muttered.

She heard their voices, low.

The big lesbo bitch did her number next. 'Meisie, come out. Vittoria. Stop this nonsense.'

Meisie? What was it with this word, they liked it so much? That it was belittling.

'Come now.'

Come now, meisie She kept dead still.

She imagined they were in line with the front door. That was what it sounded like from the carry of their voices. She heard the warder say, 'She's not here.' The big lesbo bitch reply, 'Where else you think she is?' Silence.

'Vittoria. Come, meisie.'

The male warder said, 'Give me that.' Came on: 'Don't give us shit, alright. Throw out the gun. We not going to stand here all day.'

Instead she stuck the gun round the corner of the building, pulled off two rounds. A shatter of glass. The windscreen. On target. The warder swore. Told her if she didn't chuck the gun out, follow it with her hands in plain sight, they'd shoot the shit out of the ruin until she was dead.

You and whose army, she wanted to shout back but didn't. Two bullets left in the cartridge. One chambered. What'd they have? Maybe five rounds in the warder's gun. Big bloody deal.

She reckoned they hadn't got backup yet. There'd be sirens, helicopters if they had.

So just the two warders with the transit van. Careless assholes hadn't bothered to shackle her. Let her take a pee like she wasn't going to try it on the first opportunity she got. Stupid dorks. Thinking she couldn't screw them over.

'I'm coming out,' she shouted. Stuck a hand up, waggled her fingers. Her hand framed in what was once a window.

No response to that. Just the stuck record: 'Throw the gun out.'

She stood up, framed by the window. Her hand holding the gun hidden from view.

There they were standing beside the van like this wasn't a shootout.

'Come'n, meisie,' said the big lesbo bitch. 'Be a good girlie. Stop this shit. We's all gonna get into kak otherwise.'

'Hands.' said the warder through the loudspeaker. 'Lemme see your hands.'

'Fuck you,' she said, brought up the pistol put a shot smack into the loudspeaker. Saw the warder fall. She ducked down. Sat on the floor in the bird crap, listening to the wounded man groaning.

The big lesbo bitch shouted, 'That's up to shit, meisie. Yous for it now. No chance yous gonna see your home again. No chance in heaven or hell. Better stop the tricks now.'

Five shots zinged through the window, slammed into the mud bricks, earth chips falling on her.

She got below the window, knelt to the side. Counted one, two, three, slipped into view. Saw the big lesbo bitch kneeling beside the man, not even looking in her direction. She shot. Watched the lead zap home. Looked like a neck shot. The big lesbo bitch laid out.

And a bullet left.

She punched the air. Said to herself, 'Go out there, girl, drive away.'

She went out there. Walked straight to the van. The big lesbo bitch shot her in the back.

10

The two men checked out of the motel mid-morning, the shorter one settling the bill. The other man waiting to one side, smoking a menthol.

Earlier he'd walked into the veld, not far, a stone's throw beyond the motel's perimeter fence and stood staring at rock outcrops to the north. About him the yellow sweep of clump grass and low scrub and thorn. Blackened stones underfoot and sheep turds. Above him a large bird circled on the rising thermals. He wondered what type of bird it was. Where this place was. It belonged to no country he knew.

He'd smoked two cigarettes in succession, flicking the filters away in an arc, then walked back slowly to his room and sat on the double bed with his back against the headboard and his feet in silk socks neatly crossed. His shoes, brogues, were on the floor beside the bed. From where he sat he could see himself in the wall mirror above the vanity table. He stared at his reflection without expression or recognition. In his ears Stuart Staples sang about strangling a girlfriend.

At ten thirty Manga rapped at his half-open door, looked in. 'Ready to leave, captain?'

Spitz swung his legs off the bed, tied up his laces. 'They have phoned yet?'

Manga shook his head. 'Nah.' Grinned suddenly. 'That worry you?'

Spitz didn't reply. Picked up his holdall and walked out the door.

Manga glanced round the room: half the bed still neatly made, a heap of crushed butts in the ashtray on the side table. The room he'd left was devastated: pillows flung around the floor, the bed rumpled as if he'd screwed a dozen women, a slop of tea stain across the sheets. The difference, he believed, was uptight Spitz-the-Trigger maybe obsessing on the day's business.

They drove in silence to a Wimpy off the main road, two trucks and a few cars pulled up outside.

'Breakfast?' said Manga.

'Here?' Spitz gestured at the roadhouse. 'At this place? Is this what you eat? Fast food?'

'Not only. Also sushi, Thai, Italian, Cajun. Captain' – Manga half turned towards Spitz – 'this's Colesberg, middle of nowhere Karoo, there is no sushi here. Not even umpokoqo?'

'I do not eat porridge.'

'So no problem. This's a good fry. The best. Two eggs, bacon, sausage, tomato, that American stuff, hash browns. White toast. Filter coffee. You can look out at the desert. Watch the cars go by. Captain, this's breakfast, okay?'

They took a booth in the window, ordered the full-house. Neither of them speaking: Manga tapping his cellphone on the table, Spitz staring at two truckers outside joking. Beyoncé or some other jelly baby warbling on the sound system. The waitress put down two cups of coffee. Spitz knew it would be watery, stale. He tasted it. Twisted his mouth at the thin bitterness.

Manga, watching, laughed. Poured a sachet of sugar into his mouth and crunched the granules. 'Sweeten it, captain. Isn't espresso.' He emptied two sachets into his cup, and stirred. Lifted the cup but before he drank said, 'Tell me captain, why a man like you doesn't hunt, hey?' He sipped at his coffee. 'This interests me.'

'You mean shoot at donkeys?'

'I mean hunt.'

'Settlers hunt. White men hunt.'

Manga waved his hand. 'We're finished with that shit. The great white hunter shit. Black men hunt. Businessmen. Lawyers. Judges. Politicians. Like they play golf, they hunt.'

'I have noticed,' said Spitz.

'But you don't. Hey, captain, why not?'

Spitz examined the fried breakfast the waitress slid before him. The eggs cooked both sides, the bacon thick, the skin peeling off the tomato. 'What for, hunting?' he said. 'Where is the reason?'

'To get excited,' Manga made a hollow fist, gave a few masturbatory pumps – 'by the chasing.'

'By standing in the back of a Land Rover.' Spitz sliced into the eggs, the yolks were solid, the white rubbery. He wondered if he could eat it.

'Sure. It doesn't matter. What you want is the kick. The magic moment.' Manga held an imaginary rifle to his shoulder. 'When you stare down the barrel and you know that if you pull the trigger the animal is dead. This magic moment. Pow! Hey, captain. That is the kick.' He lowered his arms. 'When you see the kill. When you see the animal die. Is this not another magic moment? Hey, captain. I know why these big men hunt. It is like sex. They get excited.' He pricked a sausage with his fork and released a spurt of fat. Gathered a mouthful of sausage and egg and bacon, and grinned at Spitz. 'I am right?'

Before Spitz could answer, Manga's cellphone rang, some rap shit. Manga swallowed quickly. 'Mornings, captain.'

Spitz kept eating, watching the tension in Manga's shoulders, the tightness of his grip on the small phone. The nodding of his head. 'It was no problem.' Then a change in his voice: 'We must come to Cape Town now?'

Spitz guessed it was Obed Chocho. Could tell by Manga's frown and spluttering that there'd been a change of plan. A change of plan wasn't good. He wasn't contracted for a change of plan.

The understanding was one job. He wiped his lips with a paper serviette and held out his hand to Manga, his fingers beckoning for the phone.

'Captain,' said Manga, 'here is Spitz.'

'Spitz,' said Obed Chocho. 'I have some extra work that's unexpected. The same price, the same percentage. Help me out here.'

Spitz stayed silent, thinking about it.

'The other job can be done anytime. This is more serious.'

'Plus five thousand,' said Spitz.

He heard Obed Chocho blow out a lungful of air. Could hear a television playing, a signature tune he thought he recognised. 'Mighty fine. Okay mighty fine. Plus five thousand.'

Spitz gave the phone back to Manga. They wanted him in Cape Town they could've flown him. This was a shit story shaping up. Heard Manga say, 'About six o'clock. We gotta drive seven, eight hours.'

That was it, seven, eight hours on the road. Maybe five grand had been too cheap. More like double that.

Manga disconnected, took a swallow of coffee. 'I don't like a change of plan. That's when things get stuffed up.'

'Many times,' said Spitz. 'What are the details?'

'Search me, captain. You don't get details from Mr Chocho. You get instructions.'

11

Mace thought a better meeting place would've been Dutch's. A table on the pavement watching gay Cape Town flounce about De Waterkant's cobbled streets. Always something happening among the chi-chi renovations. What he liked too was the motor show, more expensive hardware parked in the streets than any other quarter of the city. Even the Clifton coke and tequila strip couldn't compete. And his Spider caught the boys' eyes.

At a place like Dutch's, you felt part of the city life. Also more relaxing than an art gallery. Art galleries made Mace nervous. Like when Oumou had pottery exhibitions, he stood there with a permanent grin that made his jaws ache and drank too much.

'Darling meet the artist's husband.'

Jesus, enough to make your skin crawl.

Mace parked the red Alfa Spider in De Smit, hoping the handbrake would hold on the incline. Took a brick he kept for these occasions from the boot and jammed it behind a back wheel. He left the top down. Any chancer tried to steal the radio he'd know about it.

Surprising thing was, not a car guard to be seen. Just a block from pink city, yet empty. Nothing going on. Had to be one of the few streets left in town where some Congolese doctor or Angolan teacher didn't tell you he would guard your car with his life.

Not many cars in the street either. The A-Class Merc, Mace guessed, belonged to the judge. Not a quaint street either, blank walls of office blocks either side, only the windows of the gallery breaking the monotony. Would appeal to Oumou's concrete and glass ideas of architecture but didn't get him excited. Mace pushed through a heavy glass door into a small foyer. One lift, a security desk to the side. The guard looked up from his screen, indicated an open door on the left.

'Maybe I don't want the gallery,' Mace said.

The guard shrugged. 'The judge tells me he's waiting for you.'

Mace stopped. 'You don't know me.'

'Old-style red Alfa Spider, the judge tells me that's your car. I don't know this Alfa Spider, but I know old style.' The guard gave a white tooth smile. 'Still a nice car.'

'You know the judge?'

'Why not. He comes here to the artist openings. Plenty times.'

The guard swung the monitor for Mace to see his car filling the screen.

Mace laughed. 'Just keep watching it.'

Inside the gallery Mace nodded at a woman behind the reception desk, tapping at a laptop. She looked up quizzically.

'Just having a look,' said Mace.

'The judge's in the next room,' she said, pointing at an opening behind him. 'That way.'

'Right.' Mace turned, frowning. Anywhere else this would be a set-up.

He stepped into a large room, the walls a stark white, a minimalist exhibition of big pictures each the size of the Spider's bonnet symmetrically arranged. Two black benches end to end in the middle of the room. Mace's trail sandals squeaked on the wooden floor.

The judge sat in a hi-tech wheelchair facing a picture. 'Mr Bishop,' he said and moved a lever on the arm and the chair whined as it turned. 'I appreciate this.'

Early fifties, Mace reckoned, big shouldered and fit, probably still worked a schedule at some gym. He walked over and shook Judge Telman Visser's outstretched hand.

'I wanted you to have a look at this photograph,' the judge said, 'well, it's not a single photograph, a series, but its intention is singular. I have bought it. Probably to hang in my chambers. I buy most of my art from Michael, you know the gallery owner, Michael Stevenson' – not a question, although Mace shook his head, the judge hardly pausing – 'including, you'll be pleased to hear, a pair of hands he acquired for me, fine porcelain hands clasped in anguish. The detail is exquisite, so poignant. But you know this. You probably saw them being made.'

Mace nodded, unsure what the judge meant.

'Your wife is good. Very good. I'd like to meet her sometime.'

Mace eased, realising the judge was talking about the hands from Oumou's obsessive period when the bowls and the plates and the jugs, the useful things, were abandoned for hundreds of hands.

Hands modelled on his own hands. His hands she'd held against her breasts, and said, 'These hands I did not think I would feel on my body again.' Said that after he'd been kidnapped by Sheemina February's hitman, Mikey Rheeder. 'Every hour I thought you were dead.' The hands that she turned into artworks. As she did with so much of the pain in her life.

'You did some homework,' said Mace, his eyes still on the judge.

Judge Visser smiled. 'I do that,' he said. 'I like to be sure of the facts. But don't worry, Mr Bishop, I don't know how many traffic fines you have outstanding and I don't know how much money you owe on your house. Although I do know it is very modern, very angular, at least from the street.'

The judge had a small black bag in his lap, leather undoubtedly, the sort of handbag that had almost become a fashion accessory but never quite made it. The thought occurred to Mace that maybe Telman Visser was gay.

'If you're interested,' the judge was saying, 'mostly I got positive responses: family man, doesn't drink to excess, doesn't smoke, keen swimmer, good at his job. On the right side in the struggle, even trained in the guerrilla camps. I know you met your wife in Malitia. I know she is a ceramicist trained in Paris. I know you were gun-running in Malitia. Although I am not sure if arms trader is an advantage on a CV. To some people it might be off-putting. I am neutral. If there was a downside it was that you shoot too quickly. That you're ruthless, even. I don't know, is that a downside? Probably, in the eyes of the law these days. But I wouldn't hold it against you. Oh yes, I know about your court case too. A nasty business.'

Mace thought, enough of the crap, judge, let's cut to the detail. Said, 'That's reassuring.'

'And, a colleague tells me you have a weakness for unconventional methods. Like threatening to hang people. He found the incident amusing. Then again, once upon a time, he, and others I know, had a penchant for hanging people. Personally I am against capital punishment.'

The judge manoeuvred his chair to face the photograph. 'Have a look at this.'

Mace did. It was a large composite made up of smaller squares: five down, five across. The foreground almost at the photographer's feet, at the top a distant horizon. Each photograph linked to the adjacent pictures like pieces of a puzzle.

'The photographer,' said the judge, 'is a man called David Goldblatt. You've heard of him?'

Mace shook his head.

'Excellent photographer. Done some extraordinary work. I have three of his photographs. Four counting this one.' With his left hand, the judge wheeled closer to the photograph. 'What's important, from your point of view, is what's happening in the middle.'

Wasn't much happening in the photograph as far as Mace was concerned. Nobody hanging around. No cars. No trace of a house. What it seemed to be was the slope of a hill, grass, rocks, clumps of bushes down to a road then the plain sliding off to the horizon. Looked like bushveld. Thorn trees. Good kudu country.

The judge pulled back slightly. 'Here, on this fence beside the road is the important detail.'

Mace leaned forward. The fence was adorned with wreaths and crosses.

'Those were placed there by farmers,' said the judge, 'as a protest at the farm killings. Perhaps you didn't know that last year alone a hundred and fifty farmers and their wives, if the women were unlucky enough to be around when the killers came in, were murdered. For no reason. No one was robbed, except of guns, food, liquor. Always the women were raped. In many cases the people were shot execution-style. They kneel. They feel a gun at the back of their heads. End of story. They are the lucky ones. In most cases people are tortured. Husbands and wives. No one is arrested. No one is even suspected. The killers come out of the night and disappear back into the darkness. They may as well be ghosts. The farm labourers do not see anything, they do not even hear anything.'

'I've read about it,' said Mace.

The judge backed his wheelchair away. He pointed at a bench. 'Please sit down so that we can be eye to eye.'

Mace obliged and the judge positioned himself a metre off. 'That,' he gestured at the photograph behind his back, 'makes a powerful statement. More powerful than the farmer's protest. We have become used to crosses beside the road. The country is littered with them. But that photograph speaks of the aloneness, the emptiness, the indifference of the landscape. That is about our history. All those farmers were white. The descendants of settlers. People who took away the land from the indigenous people. And now the land is reclaiming itself.' He stared at Mace, a slight smile on his lips. 'Am I being fanciful? I don't think so.'

The judge stroked his clasp-bag. 'I had a privileged childhood on that farm. Running wild with our dogs across my own huge playground. Such days in my own worlds. The magical worlds we make as boys, not so, Mr Bishop? For children there is no better place than a farm. An adventure wonderland.' He paused to look at the photograph. 'My father and his wife live on the farm,' he said. 'My father's elderly. In his eighties. She's slightly younger. My grandparents are buried there, and my great-grandparents. There are older graves which are probably my forebears. My father believes that if it was good enough for the previous generation to die on the farm then it is good enough for him. My grandparents died naturally. I am afraid that my father will die at the end of a gun. Some black men will get into the house one night…' He let the sentence hang but his stare stayed on Mace's face, searching in his eyes for sympathy.

Mace sat forward, clasping his hands between his knees. Was going to ask about the judge's mother, then thought, no, don't get involved. 'We don't do that sort of security, judge. Not our line of business.'

'I know. I know,' the judge waved his hand as if at a fly. 'I know what you do. Big names. Top business people. Celebrities. Minor royalty. Surgical safaris. I know this. The people fly in, you babysit them, off they go again. The wild city doesn't get in their face.' He smiled, somewhat snidely Mace thought. 'It's not a big strain on you.'

'The long and short of it.'

'I'm not asking you to babysit. What I'm asking for is professional advice. You go out there, assess the situation, tell me what sort of security devices must go in. Maybe recommend a guard from your staff. I don't know. We can work out a separate contract. Something.'

The judge stopped, his face serious. Mace thought, hey, the man's worried.

'All I'm requesting is an opinion. Your recommendations. No commitment beyond that.'

Mace sat up, stretched the muscles in his back. Why not do it? What was it going to take? Three, four days tops including travelling time. Get out into the wide open spaces. Had to be better than overnighting in Berlin. Had to be better than overnighting anywhere. He could take Christa. Father and daughter time. Said, 'Okay, I can do that. I'm not sure about contracting a guard from my staff, that's a different story. But I'll check out the place for you.'

Judge Telman Visser exhaled a sigh of relief. 'I'm obliged. Thank you. You take a great weight off my mind, Mr Bishop. A considerable burden. I will be able to rest easy. You've knitted up what Shakespeare called the "ravelled sleave of care". Do you know the quote?'

Mace shrugged, not giving away that he did or didn't.

'Macbeth. Probably my favourite Shakespeare. And a great film version by Polanski I can recommend.'

He stretched out his hand. Mace shook it: firm, strong, may even have been a hint of Masonic pressure and rub that he'd not noticed the first time. If it had been there the first time.

'Now. When can you do this? The sooner the better as far as I'm concerned.'

'Can't help you there,' said Mace. 'Probably not until late next week. The weekend.'

'I see.' The judge frowned. 'That's pushing it. I'd hoped for sooner.'

'I'm in Berlin tomorrow, judge. Back Monday night. Tuesday, Wednesday, I'm duty bound. Wednesday night back to Berlin. Friday I'm home again. Friday's the earliest I could go. And what're we talking, a five, six hour drive? That's not fun after a long flight.'

'Charter flight could get you within an hour's drive.'

'If you're picking up the tab.'

'Of course.'

'What if I want to take my daughter with me? Get her out onto a farm. Something she's not experienced, that adventure wonderland.'

'I've heard about your daughter,' said the judge. 'A horrible experience for you.'

'She's over it.'

Judge Visser unzipped his clasp bag. 'I'm not sure this would be the best occasion to have her with you.' He brought out a business card. 'Maybe some other time I can arrange for you to stay at one of the hunting lodges. We hire them out. You could take your wife and daughter for a week. Be our guests.' He offered the card to Mace. 'Do you have a card?'

'Sure.' Mace took one from his wallet.

'I'll get back to you on Tuesday,' said the judge. 'With the arrangements.'

Mace stood.

'Thank you, Mr Bishop.' The judge raised his hand. 'I appreciate this.'

As Mace turned to leave, he noticed the judge swing his chair back to face the photograph.

12

Obed Chocho, lying on his bed, the screen of the television paused on Tony Soprano's scheming face, thought about what his wife had told him. What Popo Dlamini had told her. That the money backing the other consortium on the land deal was German. Which he did not like. He wondered what Tony would do in this sort of situation.

Except Tony wouldn't be in this sort of situation. Wouldn't be in jail. Wouldn't have his wife screwing her arse off. Opening her legs to a prick like Dlamini. Carmela wouldn't do that. Wouldn't dream of doing that.

Carmela wouldn't take a man into Tony's bedroom and fuck him stupid on Tony's bed. She had respect. She wasn't going to let some young flash paw at her flesh. Stick his dick in her. Suck her tits.

Tony could trust Carmela. Obed didn't trust Lindiwe. Turned out he was right not to.

Obed Chocho groaned. 'Mighty fine. Mighty fine.' Hit his hand against the iron railing of the bed head until it hurt. Didn't stop the image of Lindiwe, shiny with sweat, moaning and grinding beneath Popo Dlamini, thrusting her breasts up for his lips to slide around her long nipples. Didn't stop the twitch in Obed Chocho's groin but shot him off the bed.

Almost made him get Lindiwe back on the phone. Tell her again: I'm not joking. It's over. I catch you anywhere near him, you better watch out.

When she'd phoned he'd let her get to the point of anxiety without saying a thing. Hearing her become nervous over his silence. Blurting out the shit from Dlamini about the German backer with long long euros. The sort of bucks that would get to the greedy mlungu Smits holding out for the big lotto win. White shit dealing white shit, muscling in to take his land. Going to cut a deal with the other consortium that would sweep him off the table. Like he was dirt. To be spat on. Ignored. Oh no. Mighty fine, oh no.

Only his wife crying, saying, 'That's what he told me. 'True's God, help me, that's what he said.' Only Lindiwe's snivelling snapped him back to her.

'I hear one more time you've seen him, hear me, one more time, then mighty fine, he is dead. No more smses how you want to hump each other.' He heard her gasp. 'You talk to him. You phone him. You send him any message I'm going to know. You got that mighty fine?'

She whimpered.

He shouted, 'You got that mighty fine?'

Her reply so soft through the sobbing he had to get her to say it again. 'Yes, Obed.'

'Hear me, Lindiwe,' he said, 'listen hard. I know what's going on. I know mighty fine. You are over with him. You are finished. No more. I sit here, I get your smses "Oh baby, come duze tonight", you think I like that. My wife screwing this arsehole. Over now, okay. Finish and klaar.'

He waited. Lindiwe going you are my darling, you are my sweetheart, I love you, I never loved him, until Obed said, 'Mighty fine, enough. Tomorrow you pick me up in the afternoon, this is forgotten. Like it didn't happen. We are together. No one laughing behind me about who Obed Chocho's wife is jumping. Obed Chocho the convict moegoe. No more bullshit like that, alright?'

He got her promise. Let her sobbing continue until it became sniffling. Said, 'Tomorrow you get here two o'clock. No African time shit. Two pee em. Now, let me speak to Sheemina.'

Sheemina February said in his ear, 'The German's name is Rudolf Klett. He is a businessman based in Berlin. At the moment that's all I know.'

'Find out more,' said Obed Chocho.

'Oh yes sir, right away sir,' said Sheemina February. 'Anything else, sir?'

'No. Nothing.' He disconnected, his palms sweating at her sarcasm. Might be the best bloody lawyer in town but two things about Sheemina February put him on edge: one was her tongue. The other thing, she was a bushie. You couldn't trust a coloured.

Calmed down, the image gone of Lindiwe's hips banging against Popo Dlamini, Obed Chocho stretched out again on the bed. Stared at Tony Soprano's scheming face. A German? These guys bringing in a German backer. He snorted. Well, to hell with them. They didn't know what sort of fight this was. That's how Tony would handle it. Change the game. Obed aimed the remote, pressed play.

13

Top down, Mace drove slowly along Somerset Road wondering about Judge Telman Visser, his sense of the dramatic. For heaven's sake, like a photograph was going to impress someone. A strip of highway with some wreaths on it. And for that he'd pay over a hundred thousand bucks. The judge had more money than sense.

But he had sense too, doing his homework. Checking up on the sort of people he hired. Probably the judge did know the Bishop household's bank account. Judges had contacts; they could get things done. Find out stuff.

Not that knowing how much was in his bank account was a big deal, Mace reckoned. It wouldn't tell you anything more than how often Mace Bishop was in overdraft. And he wasn't bothered about the judge knowing that. Because that became an explanation for the mean and lean attitude when payment was due.

Issue was, the real issue was, time this bullshit came to an end. This client soft-soaping. He thought about that: soft-soaping. Pictured Judge Visser in a bubble bath, himself an attendant with a loofah on a stick about to scrub the judge's back. Not a pretty picture. But what guarding came down to, you looked at it that way.

Time to quit the scene as he'd told Pylon. Get out of security, sell the business. Sorting other people's crap wasn't doing it anymore. Had been okay for a time. Even fun, even lucrative. But enough. The more he thought about it, the more Pylon's west coast scheme became an out. Pylon got that to work they'd be steaming. No more Judge Vissers. No more surgical safaris. No more neurotic celebs. Could even make the future look a bright place, you took it in that light.

Mace stopped at the traffic robots on Buitengracht. A hot March sun on his shoulders, hotter than normal without the south-easter pumping across the city.

A *Big Issue* vendor thrust a magazine at him. 'Hey, boss my larney, sweet 'n sporty.' Dropped the mag into Mace's lap.

'I've bought one of those,' said Mace, handing it back.

'Ten bucks,' said the vendor. 'Present for a friend.'

'I already did that.'

'Present for another friend.' The vendor gave him a two-jerk nod of the head. 'Howsit with a smoke?'

'I don't,' said Mace, irritated now that he couldn't wait at the traffic light, gaze up at the mountain, be okay about the day undisturbed. 'Give me a break, hey, china.'

The vendor pulled a sour face. Mace watched him in the rearview mirror getting nowhere with other drivers. Someone finally giving him a cigarette. As the lights changed, Mace's cellphone rang. Pylon.

'You coming in?' Pylon wanted to know.

'Wasn't that the arrangement?'

'I'm just asking.'

'Man, what's with the rattiness.' Mace laughed. 'Treasure on your case?'

'Ah, just get here.' Pylon disconnected.

Sometimes Mace wondered who was pregnant: Pylon or Treasure.

He cut down Wale past the cathedral and the Slave Lodge, the streets easy except for coach loads of tourists grouping to wander through the Company's Gardens. Japanese strolling about like they weren't taking pictures from the middle of a street. He gave one man a toot and smiled at the apologies. Yeah, yeah, have a nice day, pal.

Up a deserted Plein Street back of parliament, the government quarter so quiet, Mace thought, you'd think there wasn't one. Come to that, wasn't much busier during a weekday either, even with parliament sitting. He turned into Dunkley Square and parked opposite their offices, a Victorian in the middle of a terrace.

Almost midday, no one about. The late-night cafés still shut, windows of the houses and apartments curtained. Some tables outside Maria's: the only customer, Pylon, at the only table under an umbrella.

'Today some sort of holiday I forgot?' said Mace, flopping into a chair opposite his partner. 'The town's still asleep.'

'On a day like this at the beach,' said Pylon. 'Or in the shopping malls. What's anybody want to be in town for?'

Mace ordered a Coke float, stressing lots of ice cream in the Coke.

Pylon snorted. 'That's a kiddy drink. You want a milkshake have a Dom Pedro. At least it's whisky.'

'Hey,' said Mace, tapping his car keys on the table. 'Look at me. I'm not your wife, savvy? This is your friend and business partner sitting here. Treasure's riding you, I don't want to know. Pregnant woman aren't a joy.'

'No kidding.' Pylon called back the waiter and ordered himself a Dom Pedro with whisky not Kahlua. Looked across at Mace and shook his head. 'That's the part I don't get: why this isn't a happy thing? Why she's not sweetness and light?

'We're in the Palms okay having breakfast. She likes the Palms. It's off the street, inside, all the expensive home shops packed together. She can go feel the bed linen, stare at all that black wood shit from Bali, hey I don't know, choose bathroom tiles, get people to show her a million colours of paint. For Treasure this is heaven. Pumla and me, we go along with it. I go along with it on account of Treasure's a bit edgy over where I've been all morning. But that's alright, I talked her through it.

'So we order breakfast: eggs Florentine with the spinach garnish. You know it? Treasure's best. She's got a cappuccino, lots of froth. Everything's humming. Out of the blue she says, we got to get the orphan child first before ours is born.

'I'm what? That's not how we planned it. A year later's how we planned it. Let's get over one baby before we take on the next. Because with the orphan she wants a baby. No pulling in a two- or three-year-old, definitely not anything older. Because Treasure's theory is nurture beats nature. We disagree here, for me it's in the genes. But for the sake of a happy home I go with nurture.

'So now, starting Monday, we're visiting the AIDS adoption centres. Or wherever the government's hiding the kids. Except here's a thing: Treasure doesn't want a Zulu. They got Zulu babies stacked up five deep because that's where the bug's bitten hardest. Also there're more Zulus than anyone else. But no we can't have a Zulu. You're going to tell me now about nurture and nature. The reason she doesn't want a Zulu is that the males are bastards; the woman are like cows. Take any shit the men dish out. But no, hey, this is not racist. This is fact. Now, you tell me you can pick a Zulu from a Sotho when the kids lying there a week or two old? No ways.

'We have some words here until Pumla kicks me under the

table and I wise up. Okay, no Zulus. Next thing the breakfast doesn't taste right, not the eggs, the spinach. It's overcooked. I'm about to say, can't be. You overcook spinach it disappears, when I catch Pumla's eye. So we don't go there. It's not that there's much spinach. The stuff's a garnish, save me Jesus.'

The drinks arrived, Pylon taking a quick pull through the straw deep into the mixture to get the whisky.

Mace spooned up ice cream. 'Pumla's smart.'

'It's her mother. They're born like razor blades.'

'You hear about Pumla catching the druggie's peg leg?'

Pylon frowned.

'Ex-druggie.'

'What crap's this?'

'Fact. Down the line.'

'Uh huh.'

Mace told the story, up to the green toenails.

Pylon laughed. 'She's good that kid. Not too much in the world that scares her. Like her mama. Packaged dynamite. This's what we're talking.' Pylon relaxed in his chair, then came forward again, lowering his sunglasses to stare at Mace over the top. 'Never guess who I saw this morning?'

'The pope in shorts?'

'Sheemina February.'

Mace stirred ice cream into the Coke, sucking the rising head noisily through the straw. 'I've seen her around. You mention it now, probably more than usual in the last two weeks. Before that I hadn't seen her for a long stretch. Even wondered if she'd left town.'

'You don't think she's tagging you again?'

'What for?'

'Old time's sake.'

Mace thought about it. Couldn't see an angle. 'Nah. It's coincidence.'

'Interesting, though. It's at her place that Mrs Lindiwe Chocho rocked up.'

'Her Bantry Bay place.'

'A new place she has in town. University Estate.'

'Still the property mogul.'

Pylon tapped his finger on Mace's hand. 'You listening to me?'

Mace nodded.

'Good. It's to her, Sheemina February, that Lindiwe went after shagging Popo Dlamini all night.'

'You can see why Lindiwe needs a lawyer.'

'Mace.' Pylon, pushed his shades up his nose. 'Sheemina February's not mainstream. She's coloured. There're black lawyers would've creamed to handle the lovely Lindi, a name like that. So if she's gone outside the tribe it's because her husband said so.'

He reached for his cellphone lying on the table. 'Where we're in the shit is on account of she got to Popo.'

'Meaning?' Mace glanced up from his Coke float, met Pylon's gaze.

'Meaning…' Pylon gave some attention to his drink. 'I like Popo, he's sharp. Brought us – our consortium – a strong link into government. Even against Obed Chocho. With Popo's contacts we were in the deal. Fighting. Especially you add Klett's backing. That's talking hard cash. Euros. Outside investment. Foreign investment. Not some local bank putting up the capital. You want to know who owns the country after these black empowerment deals? The banks. Brothers and sisters can't trade in an AK for a seat on the board. Got to have something else. You know the president, that's helpful. Some moola that's better.'

Pylon dialled, put the phone to his ear. Mace stretched, tipping back his chair. The square had movement. People stirring for a late breakfast or an early lunch. He heard Pylon say, 'Popo, my friend, we've got to talk.' One person he didn't envy was Popo Dlamini being braced by Pylon. Sleeping with the enemy wasn't something Pylon appreciated.

The noon gun boomed across the town, and Mace checked his watch, thinking, every time he heard it he did that. Automatically, like he was conditioned. You heard the gun, you knew it was twelve, still you had to check your watch.

Pylon closed his phone. 'Bloody gun. It goes off I have to apologise, sorry, say again.' He placed the phone on the table. 'I've got him. Tomorrow. Twelve o'clock. At his golf estate. The one other side of Pollsmoor Prison. You ever been there?'

'Come on,' said Mace. 'We've got clients staying there right now. Maybe you're letting the land deal thing take up too much time.'

'That a criticism?'

'Hardly. I'm looking at it as a life raft.'

Pylon squinted at him. 'It can be.'

'Except I've got no cash. Except for Cayman.'

'How about this?' said Pylon. 'I'll back you five hundred K.'

'Against what security?'

'Cayman.'

Mace thought about it. 'Why not? Or diamonds. I've still got diamonds.' Two, three hundred thousands worth in a safe-deposit box stashed from the Angolan gun run.

'Whatever.'

'One catch: Oumou.'

'No problem. You tell her I'm shifting it sideways to you, at ten per cent when the profit's totalled. Save me Jesus, what could be easier?'

Mace said, 'I'll run it past her.'

'Why not? Hey' – he leaned towards Mace – 'this afternoon I'm seeing the Smits, you know, the whiteys holding out for a stake of the action. I come to a deal with them, some mutual arrangement and we're home. Everything's sweet. On Monday you fly in our man Klett and the scheme's a done deal. Obed Chocho's left weeping in the dust.'

'We hope,' said Mace. 'Right now what we got to talk about is a judge called Telman Visser.'

'I know that name,' said Pylon.

'Sure. What he wants is farm security for his parents.'

'We don't do that.'

'I told him.'

'So?'

'So he wants an assessment.'

'Where's this?'

'Hell knows. Out there.' Mace waved behind his back. 'Takes six, seven hours to drive. I told him, okay, normal fee I'd do it. He says best to fly in.'

'At his cost.'

'Of course. Rather I'm thinking of heading out next weekend with Christa. Give the kid a joyride.'

'I got it.' Pylon clicked his fingers. 'He's the judge sentenced Obed Chocho.'

'Physically challenged guy in a zooty wheelchair?'

'Don't know that. I remember he handed down six years, knocked the breath out of comrade OC.'

'What, knowing he'd only sit a tenth of that?'

'Having to sit at all. Com Chocho couldn't figure out why fraud was a problem. Com Chocho reckons he personally's owed big time for the suffering of two centuries of colonialism and apartheid.' Pylon finished his Dom Pedro. 'A judge puts away such a nice man can't be all bad.'

14

Spitz smoked a menthol every forty-five minutes, crushed out the butt in the ashtray, took a drink from his bottle of mineral water. The mineral water in a holder over the air-con vent kept nice and cool. Tindersticks crooning their deadly anthems in his ears had chilled his anger at the long drive. The moment would come he could reclaim on this waste of his time.

He relaxed, let the empty scrub roll by, wondering at the ruined homesteads scattered on the plains, the stone blockhouses at river crossings. Mostly the only living movement was sheep.

For an hour he watched mountains come closer: turning from blue to brown. How people lived with this vastness he couldn't imagine? By the look of them, the few they passed walking from nowhere to nowhere, the space had shrivelled them. Small and wrinkled people, had to be Bushmen he believed. Or their remnants.

Manga drank Coke, the empty cans rolling about in the well behind his seat. He wasn't freaked about the driving, actually enjoyed the easy speed of the G-string. A Subaru would've been better, more fun, but this was okay, he was happy on the road.

He called a few friends, spent maybe an hour talking till the cellphone battery beeped its death throes. He plugged the phone into a recharger, turned his attention to the shimmering land.

He'd driven this distance about five or six times, the last northwards from a heist in Cape Town. Four of them in the car hyped on adrenaline, dagga, pills, and quarts of beer. A million in the boot. Their driving all over the road. Amazing they'd not brought out every cop along the way. Amazing they even got home without an accident.

He grinned to himself, stared down the long road. Once he thought about the old man in a dressing gown waving around the big rifle. Not scared at all. Had to be admired for not being scared at all. The sort of Afrikaner, Manga'd heard tell, inhabited the dry regions. Leftover types.

He drove on for half an hour drumming a refrain against the steering wheel, something from Boom Shaka, regretting every moment he'd forgotten his player. Eventually Manga tapped Spitz on the shoulder. 'Captain. Hey captain, we can both listen to that.'

Spitz slipped back the headphones, said, 'What is the matter?'

'Your music.' Manga pointed at the iPod lying in Spitz's lap. 'Plug it in, we can both hear it. Some kwaito, hey!'

'My music is not kwaito.'

Manga grinned. 'Come'n, man, stop kidding me, get the tunes.'

'There is nothing on here.'

Manga glanced sideways. 'No kwaito.'

'No kwaito.'

He shook his head. 'Everybody listens to kwaito.'

Spitz made to wire himself again. Manga reached out and stopped his arm.

'Hey, hey. You move too fast. So tell me what's the music. Lemme hear it.'

Spitz stared at him. 'This is not your scene.'

'What's my scene? Captain you don't know what's my scene. Let's have it. Open up. Gimme some names.'

Spitz reached for his mineral water, swallowed a mouthful. 'You have heard of M Ward?' He got a negative from Manga. 'Steve Earle? Woven Hand? Jesse Sykes?'

'Niks.'

'Like I said to you, it is another scene.'

'It's music. Music's music. Spin it DJ Trigger.'

Spitz tensed, waved his finger. 'Not that name, okay? Not that name.'

Manga took both hands off the wheel, held them up in surrender. 'No problem.' Gripped the wheel again, the car arrow-straight on the road.

Spitz replaced the water bottle in the holder. 'Understand me?'

'Hey, captain, leave it. Move on.'

Spitz let kilometres go by, then moved on. Scanned his iPod, selected David Eugene Edwards with Sixteen Horsepower, got the leads plugged into the car's sound system, bringing up the slow guitar thrum of 'Hutterite Mile' and Edwards' ancient voice. Sat back, the swamp gospel filling him.

A minute into it, Manga held up his thumb. 'Okay, that's sharp, captain.'

Spitz pursed his lips. Gave a quick nod.

Manga kept to it for two tracks. At the end of 'Outlaw Song' said, 'Uh uh. Not my scene. Something else, captain.' He made a fist, pumped his arm. 'More vooma.'

'I have no music with vooma,' said Spitz. 'I have badlands songs. Motel blues. Lamentations.'

He tried Johnny Cash singing about a guy getting hot for a thirteen year old. Next Jim Kalin's tale of a girl caught on a high mountain. Her screams under the driving chords and banjo pluck.

Manga pulled the plug. 'Stick with it, captain,' he said. 'I'm not there. I'm nowhere in that country.'

Spitz smiled. He pointed at the landscape. 'What country do you think this is?'

'For Boers,' said Manga. He ran his tongue over his teeth, let a couple of kays run past before he tried a new line. 'Tonight, we get some chicks?' giving Spitz a sideways glance, seeing the man's unmoving profile. 'In the township I know a place, they have virgin specials. Little girls. Tight.'

'No,' said Spitz.

'No! Captain, your mama's so far away she doesn't exist.'

'I have no girlfriend.'

'So what's it, man? You don't like girls?'

'I like women.'

'No problem. We get you a woman.'

'Tonight a movie would be better.'

'Hey, captain, captain. On the town. Okay, porno. Porno's good.'

'No, a movie. In a cinema. Big screen, Sensurround.'

'Huh!'

'In my collection I have three hundred DVDs.'

Manga shook his head. 'Three hundred! What for? You've seen it once, you've seen it.'

'Some movies I have seen ten times.'

Manga whistled.

'Thelma and Louise, I have watched fifteen times.'

'Why?'

'To see them die. In the end they die like heroes.' He raised his right hand, floating it on an upward trajectory.

'Captain,' said Manga. 'You're crazy moegoe.'

Two hours later, coming off the Karoo plateau into the vinelands of the Hex River Valley, Manga's phone rang, the CLI reading: Sheemina February. He connected.

She said, 'Everything going smoothly?'

'Except we don't know what everything is.' He lodged the cellphone between chin and shoulder, needing both hands on the wheel for the curves down the pass. 'Unless you tell us.'

'I'm about to, Manga. Here are the wishes of Mr Obed Chocho.'

'I'm listening,' said Manga.

'First, where are you?'

He told her.

'Excellent. You've been driving hard.' A tone in there that bristled Manga: a patronising bitch. She said, 'That's going to take you, what, another hour and a half?'

'I expect,' said Manga.

'Good timing then. There're rooms for you in the City Lodge, the one off the N2. You know the city?'

'Enough.'

'Not far from the Lodge's a steakhouse. Have a shower, have a steak, relax. The job's tonight at nine o'clock. Not earlier, not later. You with me, Manga?

'Sure,' he said, wondering who this bitch was Obed Chocho'd hired for his dirty work.

'I'll sms the address. It's on a golf estate near Pollsmoor Prison. You probably know it, the prison.'

Manga let it go, not rising to the sarcasm.

Sheemina February pausing slightly then going on. 'There's two entrances, security at both. Electrified fence all round. The man you have to see is called Popo Dlamini. Tell Spitz no cock-ups.' She disconnected.

Manga told Spitz the gist of it, including the bit about no cock-ups.

'She said those words?'

'Exactly.'

Spitz let it go without comment. 'And that was her message? You know this Popo? You can recognise him?'

'Nah, captain, never heard of him.'

Spitz broke a new pack of menthols. 'So what am I supposed to do? Ask the brother for his ID first?'

15

'Non,' said Oumou. 'This is not a good idea. Borrowing money.'

Mace, spruced from a swimming session at the gym, overnight bag packed for Berlin, selected a wine bottle from the rack, about to stick in the cork screw. 'This's a screw top!'

'Oui.' Oumou set out ciabatta and a dish of caprese on the table, the basil still pungent in the kitchen.

'Supposed to be a cork.'

'This is what the man gave me.' She cut thick slices of bread. 'I ask him for a good wine, this is his choice.'

Mace looked at the label. Diemersfontein pinotage. In a screw top? One minute it has to be a cork so the wine can breathe. Lying on its side in a cool place. Next it's in a screw top like cheap wine, standing upright.

'At Woolies?'

'Oui. Of course.'

'The man actually recommended it?'

Oumou put down the breadknife. 'Non. He says if I want a bad wine, this is good. Tastes terrible of chocolate and coffee. The man hates it. He says they sell so much because everybody is a fool. No one can tell what is rubbish if he says it is nice.'

Mace said, 'I just asked.' He cracked the seal and unscrewed the cap. Sniffed the nose, couldn't smell coffee or chocolate. He poured the wine thick and dark into their glasses. 'Nice colour.'

'The man said if you tip the glass it is like bull's blood.'

'Bloody wonderful.'

'I am telling you his words.'

Mace took a swig, held it in his mouth as someone had told him you had to. He swallowed. 'Guy's right. First time I've ever tasted what somebody's said. You listen to the experts they go on about pencil shavings, a hint of farmyard, you have no idea what that is when you drink it. This Woolies man I understand. I can taste coffee. Chocolate even.' Mace refilled his glass. 'What d'you think?'

Oumou sipped. 'Yes, there is chocolate.' She sat and spooned caprese onto her plate, tilting the dish to fill the spoon with dressing, drizzling this over her portion. 'Come. You must eat before you go.'

'We could sit outside,' said Mace.

'The girls are at the pool. Leave them to talk.'

'They're both going to this party tonight? Christa and Pumla?'

'Of course.'

'Treasure's okay about that?'

Oumou forked mozzarella and basil onto her bread. 'Oui. Bien sûr. Treasure is okay about that.'

'Know what?' Mace said, taking down another mouthful of wine that tasted more like the toasting of the coffee beans than coffee now that he thought about it, 'I still love your accent.'

Oumou flushed, not in her cheeks, on her neck, the colour deepening to a rich brown. Brought to Mace's mind the colour of her nipples.

'Non,' she said. 'You cannot slip over this one with your words. I am serious, no? Before we have borrowed from Pylon that was okay. It was desperate. Now we are not desperate. We have money from the bank, we do not need to take money from Pylon.'

'That's the thing. We're not taking any.'

'You said it is five hundred thousand.'

'It is. But he's not giving it to us. Not as money. It's shares. Shares in the scheme. That's their value only we don't have to pay for them now. When the development's finished, they divide the profit, we get our share and give Pylon a hundred grand. Doesn't cost us anything, technically.' Mace forked up salad. 'Closest to a free lunch you can get. Pylon thinks for that investment we might earn maybe a million.'

'With his money.'

'Sure it is. He's doing us a favour.'

'But if there are problems, the money could be lost.'

'Problems. What sort of problems?'

'Any kind. It is a risk, no? It is like gambling.'

'Not really. Not with land. With land you can't lose. The price always goes up.' Mace tore a slice of bread and dipped a piece in the caprese, soaking up vinaigrette. 'They're angling to buy this stretch of land up the west coast.' He chewed at the bread. 'To build a golf estate on it.' He swallowed and chased the mouthful with wine.

'Who is this?'

'A consortium. A group of people Pylon knows. Plus a friend of ours in Berlin, the man I'm going to collect, Rudi Klett, he's the main backer. He's the real money behind the scheme. Most of the land's in what they call a letter of purpose. An agreement to sell at a certain price. When they've got everyone's okay then they buy. Right now just one owner's holding out for a higher price. Or wants to be in it. Or something, I don't know. It's Pylon's thing. I don't always listen when he's talking about this deal. Anyhow, this afternoon Pylon's going to make another offer, see what they say.'

Mace filled his glass, held the bottle poised above Oumou's. 'Some more?' She shook her head.

'It would be better if we didn't take Pylon's money.'

'Sure. But where do we get five hundred grand?'

'From the bank.'

'Even if they gave it, it'd cost too much. This way it doesn't cost us anything.'

She reached across the table and put her hand on his. 'It's not five hundred thousand, no. It's a million, that is what Pylon is giving.'

Mace thought about this. 'If you look at it that way I suppose you're right.'

'Even from a good friend you cannot take so much money.' She released his hand.

Mace looked at her, holding her eyes. 'We need something like this. Some security. Something we can invest.'

'We have the house.'

'Twenty per cent of the house. The rest belongs to the bank.'

'But one day not.'

The thing about her eyes, Mace felt, was looking into them, looking deeply into them, was like falling into the past. Then they weren't Oumou's eyes, they were the eyes of all the women who'd lived in the desert for thousands of years. All her forebears staring back at him. Brown pools of sadness. Eyes that Christa had too.

'Why don't we think about it? Till Monday when I'm back?'

Oumou pushed the dish with the last of the caprese towards him, indicated for him to finish it. 'Maybe if I talk to Treasure.'

Mace couldn't see Treasure buying this arrangement. Not with one in the oven and an orphan to go. He soaked up the remains of the sauce, wiping the bread round the dish. 'Before you do that, think about it. We'll talk more next week. When Rudi's here.' Mace finished his wine in a swallow. 'I've got to rush. Back Monday night for supper.'

They embraced, then he went out to say goodbye to the girls, Oumou watching him from the sliding door. Christa leapt up to hug her father like he was going for good. She heard Mace say, 'No drugs, okay?'

And Christa say, 'Ah, Dad, we don't do that.' And Pumla echoing her.

Oumou thought, sometimes Mace got too edgy over Christa. Overprotective. Because he believed he'd failed her once and couldn't live with that. Even now she was walking again, he couldn't let it go. Smsing her after school to know where she was. And Christa was good about it, understanding, maybe even pleased he did it, but Oumou worried that one day the attention might be too much. Push her away from him.

She smiled at Mace approaching her. Held out her hand to take his.

'Those girls,' he said, 'they frighten me. Well, not them but the world we live in.'

16

'This job,' said Spitz, 'it is a cock-up. I do not work on cock-ups.'

Manga said, 'The tunnel or the mountain?'

Spitz looked at the mountains closed about them. 'How long is the tunnel?'

'Twelve kays.'

'That is a long way to be inside the mountain. It is better to take the passage over the mountain.'

'Captain, there's no time. You wanna check out this place first, we've gotta take the tunnel.'

'In Switzerland a car catches fire in a tunnel and then everybody dies. This accident happens all the time.'

Spitz toggled Manga's cellphone to open the sms again: 25 Gary Player Close. He said, 'A golf estate has got two hundred houses, maybe more that are close together. They have security. This is not a place where we can drive into. Not a place we can wander about in the dark trying to find number twenty-five.'

They went into the tunnel, Spitz focused on the car ahead. On the red taillights that brightened and dimmed as the driver toed the brake when there was no need.

'Why is this man driving like this, doing that braking?'

Manga shrugged. 'He's nervous. Probably doesn't like tunnels. Relax, captain, fifteen, twenty minutes we're outta here.'

The tunnel stank of petrol fumes. The blue swirl of exhaust so dense in the headlights it reflected the beams. Manga switched the air conditioning to interior. Didn't stop the stench of fumes. He forced a cough. 'Worse than cigarette smoke.'

Spitz sat rigid, the tinny sound of guitars leaking from the headphones in his lap. What he didn't like was the casualness. No attention to detail. An address in a golf estate wasn't a help at all. When a job got changed there was always shit to pay.

He said, 'Tell this woman February we want a map.'

'You tell her,' said Manga. 'I'm driving.'

Spitz dug his cellphone from his pocket, pressed keys to unlock the pad but got no signal. 'If you catch fire how are you supposed to phone?'

Manga pointed at an emergency phone set on the tunnel wall. 'They got them all along here, every hundred metres.'

Spitz snorted.

They drove in silence for the remaining distance coming out of the tunnel onto a double-lane highway that curved across a bridge, the valley far below.

'Where is this place? This golf estate?' said Spitz.

'Down the peninsula.' Manga waved at the mountains ranged against the horizon. 'Where the mountains curve. In that corner. I know this place. We don't need a map.'

Spitz keyed in Sheemina February's number. She answered on the third ring, saying his name.

'Ja, this is Spitz,' he said. 'I require some more details about this job tonight.'

'There isn't anything more you need.'

'For me I think there is.'

'Like what?'

'In a golf estate there are maybe two hundred houses. With no directions, no map, we must find one. You want us to drive up to security to ask them for directions?'

'Exactly. You're expected.'

'This is a joke.'

'Popo's told security he's expecting a delivery. Nine o'clock.'

Spitz let this sink in, wondering if he'd heard correctly. 'I do not understand. Come again.'

'Nine o'clock, Spitz.' She spoke slowly enunciating each word. 'Popo is expecting a delivery. The security know this. They will let you in. Tell you where to find his house. How much more simple do you want it?'

Spitz laughed. 'No more simple than that.'

'Excellent. Nothing has to be complicated in this world, Spitz. Just takes a little planning. A little attention to detail. I do attention to detail. You do the service delivery.'

Spitz thought here was a woman he could work with. 'In a moment you were going to tell me this arrangement?'

'If you asked.' He could hear Sheemina February clinking ice in a glass. 'If you had some other way I wouldn't have interfered.'

He was about to disconnect. 'Oh Spitz, one more thing. Go in the main gate and out one of the others. I would, if I were you.'

17

The city below stood bright as bones in the afternoon sunshine, some shadows starting across the tower blocks, the sea taking on a deeper blue. Had to be paradise on a windless day. Better to be grilling fillets of yellowtail on the gas Weber, Mace thought, than taking a flight to Berlin.

Bloody Rudi Klett so jumped up these days wanted men in black with him all the time. Then again two exploded cars, three attempted kidnappings, some 9mm rounds smacking into the wall behind your head probably enough to convince you protection was needed.

Mace went down Molteno slowly, his foot tapping lightly on the brakes. He'd have preferred the hardtop off but wasn't going to leave the Spider in the airport parking lot like an open invitation, help yourself.

Strange thing was no matter how many times he did this drive to the airport, and he did it once a month, sometimes more, he got onto De Waal under Devil's Peak and into the turns, the Spider's engine a low basso accelerating, and he'd catch a thrill like flying into Malitia on an arms deal, a crate of guns in the transport's belly. Same excitement. That moment when anything can happen.

Not that he missed the gun-running, not the actual transactions, but the times around them in strange and foreign places had fed his restlessness. Like waking to the muezzin's call in Sana'a as if God had torn back the sky, demanding vengeance. The calls answered mosque to mosque across the city. A city where men strapped up with guns before putting a foot in the street. A good city to do business in. The memory brought a smile.

Mace pushed up the speed coming over the curve behind the hospital touching one twenty down the straight, into the S-bend that funnelled him onto the highway. Gave the Spider more juice drifting right behind a minibus taxi and flashed his headlights. The taxi stayed solid. Mace flicked the lights again, tempted to hoot.

Except his cellphone rang: Pylon, loud on the hands-free, launching straight in with 'These are two bastards, the Smits.'

Mace changed lanes to get past the taxi on the left. Glared a black look at the call-man squeezed against the sliding door. The man grinned, gave him the finger. Up yours too, Mace said.

'Hey what?' said Pylon.

'Taxi,' said Mace, as if that explained all, which it did. 'How so they're bastards?'

'We're talking twenty, thirty somethings. Young smart people: the wife's a lawyer, the husband's a fund manager. Saab cabriolet that she drove. The place they want to meet is Den Anker for a Belgian beer. You know how much Belgian beer costs? Three blackies per three fifty mil. They both have two, and I'm paying. I say to her I didn't know many women into beer. She tells me no, she's not. Only Belgian. A brew called Leffe blond. Very nice, I have to say.'

'How'd you know it was a cabriolet?'

'I followed them afterwards.'

Mace laughed. 'Part of your new PI routine?'

'Just getting the information.'

'So where to?'

'Clifton apartment, below Victoria. Very zhoozsh. Has to be a couple of million. Maybe kiddies, but sharp rich kiddies. Not only playing with daddies' money I would say. Probably quite a lot of their own too, which is why they're holding out.'

'Still holding out?'

'I had to bring them in. Yes, they'll sell but what they want is shares. Okay, we don't have to pay out initially, that's good, except the cake just got smaller.'

'And if the other bidder sweetens the deal?'

'Obed Chocho?'

'Him, yeah.'

'What if? Not what if, he's going to. Same deal I'd say with frills. The difference is, at the end they're in with a crook.'

'They don't know that, unless they read the news. Don't know you're not a crook either.'

'I told them I wasn't.'

'Oh smart move.'

Pylon laughed. 'I'm holding one more card. Rudi Klett. They talk to Rudi and he'll bring them over. Obed Chocho's got a sweet tongue, but you've got Rudi whispering in your ear the world changes. Everything you see has the colour of money. Because it is money. Euros, dollars, sterling. With Chocho everything's on paper.'

'Government letterhead some of it.'

'This is true. But you're streetwise that's not going to fool you.'

'For your sake I hope so,' said Mace, taking the slip road onto the airport approach.

'Just bring me Rudi Klett,' said Pylon.

Mace parked under shade-cloth opposite the international departure and arrivals halls. Checked in, got stamped through customs, bought a can of Coke, took a seat near the boarding gate. A Coke float would've been good but too complicated for the waitress. Especially take-away.

He thought some more about Pylon's offer, believed he would take him up, keep the arrangement secret from Oumou and Treasure. No point in stressing them. 'Cos if it stressed Oumou it would stress Treasure. Yet what a difference it would make. Not only a tidy sum down the line but an out. Goodbye Complete Security. Goodbye guarding the neurotics. Nothing wrong with that. And if Pylon offered, he offered because he wanted to. Wanted out too. Would be almost an insult not accepting.

Half an hour later in the boarding queue, Mace's phone rang: the name Rudi Klett on the screen. Mace stepped out of the queue to get some privacy.

'We are going to breakfast tomorrow,' said Rudi. 'I will meet you at your hotel.'

'Sure,' said Mace. 'Were am I staying?'

'Kempinski. I remember this is your favourite. For you and Isabella.' Rudi Klett gave a laugh.

'She's dead,' said Mace. 'Didn't you know?'

The silence answered the question. 'No. This is very abrupt.'

'Shot by her husband. Here in Cape Town actually about three years ago.'

'She was married to a South African?'

'Long story,' said Mace. 'But no, an American.'

'I will change the hotel.'

'No need. If I stop going to all the places I went with Isabella, I'm going to have to stay home.'

'Very well,' said Rudi Klett. 'We will remember her with champagne. And how is the beautiful Oumou?'

'Beautiful.'

'And my Christa?'

'Fully recovered.'

'Good, good. You know, my daughter is gone. We do not talk anymore, not even a card for my birthday. She thinks I am a merchant of death. A Mephistopheles buying the souls of African presidents. Do you think I am taking your president to hell?' He laughed. The hard wicked laugh Mace remembered. The sort of laugh Mephistopheles would make at the hour of collection. 'We will talk tomorrow, ja. Catch up.' And the laugh again. Still loud in Mace's head when he rejoined the queue.

18

At nine, Manga stopped at the security boom to the golf estate. Main entrance. He told the guard he had a package for Popo Dlamini. The guard checked a clipboard, handed it to Manga to fill in his details. Manga wrote his name as Manfred Khumalo, gave his company as One Time Delivery, mixed up the numbers of the car's registration plate. The guard told him first right, second left, go down counting to the fifth house on the right. Bottom of the close. Manga said thanks, was about to say something else but stopped himself. Gave back the clipboard.

He pulled off slowly, leaving his window down.

'You almost made a mistake,' said Spitz.

'What?'

'By calling the man captain.'

'But I didn't.'

'It was very close.'

'Close doesn't matter. Saying it matters.'

The streets were lit, but the streetlights too dim to reveal anything about the car. At a few of the houses people sat out to enjoy the evening. Their voices and laughter carrying to the two men.

'You fancy living on a golf estate, captain? With all the larneys.' Manga took the first right, the indicator flashing and clicking in the dashboard. Loud, insistent.

'No,' said Spitz.

'A cousin I know does. Cousin like me. Ordinary guy. Has this flashy house, upstairs, downstairs, three bathrooms.'

'Sure,' said Spitz.

'Estate's called Blue Hills, in Midrand. You ever heard of it?' He glanced at Spitz. In the darkness couldn't say if he responded. 'He tells people he won the Lotto, and they believe him, strues. I won a million rand, he tells people. Maybe so. Maybe he got in there before everything cost two million rand. What I can't add up is I know how much I get, I know how much he gets, and my house is in Soweto.'

'Maybe he did win the Lotto.'

'Maybe. Maybe it's something else, captain. You know, like a retainer. Cousin's maybe an impimpi. Hotline to the fathers. I get that feeling sometimes on a job that the cops're waiting.' Manga leaned forward. 'Passing first left.'

'There are people like those,' said Spitz.

'Other thing. You got money you don't show it. No fancy stuff. Cars, houses, jewellery. No, no no no, no. No, captain, you keep a low profile.

'The turn is coming,' said Spitz. On his lap he had an envelope and under it the Ruger, the can screwed on. The iPod in his pocket, the earphones round his neck. Wearing his brogues, black chinos, green golf shirt. 'Go to the bottom, turn round and pull up so I am next to the curb.' He worked his fingers into black leather gloves.

Manga saluted. 'Yes, captain.'

'And switch off the car.'

'Hey?'

'Off,' said Spitz. He saw the house, number twenty-five, set back about twenty metres from the street. No fencing, low shrubs either side the path to the entrance porch. Open shutters at the windows, the curtains drawn. Lights at two windows and a light in the porch.

Manga said, 'Not a good idea, captain. Having the engine off.'

'Off,' said Spitz. 'If you keep on the engine there will be faces at every window in the street.' He racked the pistol. 'Only when I tell you, must you switch on.'

Manga made the turn in the close and came back to twenty-five, killed the engine. As far as he could tell, no one in the street. All the houses fronted onto it. Which was useful. 'Feel free, captain,' he said.

Spitz got out. Scanned the street up and down, walked to the front door. He pressed the intercom, heard a bell chime. A woman opened the door. Not a detail he was expecting.

'A delivery,' he said. 'For Mr Dlamini.'

'I'll give it to him.' The woman held out her right hand for the envelope. In her left a glass of wine.

'He must sign for it. That is my instruction.'

The woman frowned. 'That's bullshit. I'll give it to him. I'll sign.'

'Sorry ma'am.' Spitz kept hold of the envelope with both hands.

The woman swore. Shouted out, 'Popo. Popo. You need to get this.'

Popo called back that he was coming.

The woman moved away from the door and Spitz stepped into the house, with his elbow pushing the door closed behind him. He followed her into the lounge. She stood there beside a coffee table, watching him, about two metres away, sipping at her wine. He could see the room opened onto a patio, and a man out there grilling meat over charcoal. The man flipped two steaks, took a drink from a bottle of beer. He came into the lounge carrying the meat tongs. Relaxed in shorts, bare feet.

Spitz said, 'Mr Dlamini?'

Popo Dlamini said, 'That's me.'

'Please to sign on the paper, sir.'

Spitz fired as the man moved towards him. Brought his arm up to shoulder height, popped Popo Dlamini between the eyes. Popo Dlamini dropping backwards against a couch. Spitz swung left to shoot the woman and caught a glass of wine in his face. The woman jumping him. He kneed her crotch and pulled away, shot her once in the chest. Again in the face. Too close for comfort. He had blood on his golf shirt and splashes of wine. The stains looked the same.

Spitz left the house, closing the front door with his hand bunched in his T-shirt. Lights had come on in one of the houses, a curtain shifted and a man looked out. Spitz got into the car. Manga had the engine on idle.

'The engine is running,' said Spitz.

'For sure, captain. After three bloody shots.' Manga eased off sedately from the curb, the man at the window still peering out.

'You could not hear the shots.'

'If you were listening for them, you could hear them. Pop. Pop pop.'

Spitz hauled off his T-shirt, reached for another on the backseat. 'I was contracted for one,' he said. 'Nobody told me about two.'

'Two what?'

'One, two.'

'Right.' Manga caught the drift. 'Collateral. Shit happens.'

'Shit does not happen,' said Spitz. 'My fee is for the hit. Anybody can add up: one and one is two: double fees. Obed Chocho owes me for another one.'

Manga slowed down at the security gate. 'You dressed for this?'

Spitz adjusted the collar on the clean golf shirt. 'No problem.'

Manga said to the security guard, 'We came in at the top. One Time Delivery.'

The guard didn't leave the security kiosk, waved them through.

Manga took the forest road, playing cool, wishing Boom Shaka was booming through the sound system. Wishing too for a brandy and Coke, chased with a Black Label. Sitting in the dimness of the bar at the City Lodge, sport on the TV, men and women getting pissed left and right. Talking Kaizer Chiefs or Mamelodi Sundown, keeping an eye open for the good-time sisters, the young ones. He could do with that: a young one without tits. No fuzz. Smooth. Like after a job you get a virgin. Good for HIV. That gasp they make when you go in. Oh wena, baby. This wasn't gonna happen here. One thing he knew: driving Spitz didn't add up to the best time of his life.

Spitz on the cell to Sheemina February said, 'There was not enough detail that you gave me.'

'How's that?' she said, not asking anything about the job.

'I am charging my rates for the head. Not for the job.'

'I'm not with you, Spitz. What're you on about?'

'The woman.'

'There was a woman?'

Spitz thought, you are lying to me. Said, 'Yes. A surprise for me and for her. But maybe it wasn't a surprise for you.'

A pause. Sheemina February coming in with, 'Tomorrow, tomorrow we can talk about it. Nothing to get steamed about, Spitz.'

Before Spitz could reply, she disconnected.

Manga said, 'Not good.'

'The problem in this business,' said Spitz, 'is you never know what is the true story. For most of the time I do not care. I do not care now. Only I get angry when someone wants a job done without paying.'

He searched in his pocket for his iPod. Felt round his neck for his headphones, the wires dangling. Spitz thought, Nein, donner! Said, 'I have lost my music.'

'Oh shit, captain,' said Manga.

'All that music.'

Manga glanced at Spitz, shook his head. 'No, captain, don't even think it. You'n me, neither one's going back.'

Sunday

19

Lufthansa 301 came out of dense cloud at one thousand feet, lined up with Frankfurt's north runway. Pitch black at six ten in the a.m., five minutes ahead of schedule. Rain sluicing down. Wonderful, Mace thought. An hour later he was in the air again on the Berlin connection, a Turkish Mädchen offering rolls and coffee. Which he accepted, his stomach gurgling. One thing: the coffee was as good as airlines could get it; the rolls fresh.

This early on a Sunday morning only a few dozen people scattered around the cabin. Mace in a row to himself, grateful for the space after the cramp of the overnight long haul, shifted to the window seat, looked down on grey cloud that broke once revealing rectangles of brown farmland furrowed with snow.

By seven forty-five he'd cleared Tegel and was in a taxi on the Stadtring, listening to tyres hiss against the wet road, thinking, the last time he'd met Isabella in Berlin was January 1989. Same sort of conditions only colder. Dirty snow then stamped on the pavements and lumpy under hedges.

She'd turned a gun deal around for him. Afterwards, in the Kempinski, they'd screwed in the shower because the shower had black marble tiles that she found sexy. He hadn't thought about Isabella for weeks, maybe a month. Her memory a sudden ache in his chest.

He wondered if there'd be a time he'd no longer think of Isabella. He couldn't imagine this would be. Only had to hear REM singing about the end of the world as they knew it, to see Isabella at the Café Adler coming in with the chorus. Her playful voice: and I feel fine. Isabella, sitting other side of the table, two empty espresso cups between them, saying, 'Maybe I can oblige. Once again.' And getting him the hardware just like that after a couple of phone calls. Talk about feeling fine. Across the road Check Point Charlie grim as it ever was. The two of them randy with triumph and laughter.

He had to smile. Made the heartache of missing her even worse in a way. Maybe later he'd find a record shop, listen to the song again.

At ten, after he'd showered in a shower with cream tiles, changed into a black polo neck and black jeans, Mace met Rudi Klett downstairs in the Kempinski's breakfast room. Rudi Klett with the sleeves of his jacket hitched up to expose his forearms. A black Armani jacket, wool. Even in the desert Rudi Klett had worn jackets with the sleeves hiked to his elbow. Linen jackets in acknowledgement of the heat. Rudi Klett without a jacket was not a Rudi Klett Mace had ever seen.

'You have a gun?' Rudi Klett said when they'd greeted and done the hug and the backslap and Mace sat opposite him while a waiter spread a napkin across his lap.

'How am I supposed to have a gun, Rudi?' said Mace. 'I've flown across the world. You can't carry a gun on an aeroplane.'

'Bah,' said Rudi Klett, 'that is nonsense. I have special permission for my fellows to do this. In the security business you must have such allowances too. Not so? There is no way to protect anybody otherwise.'

'We manage. Nobody's been shot yet.'

'Yes of course but there is always a first time. Therefore as a precaution I have a present for you.' Mace felt a package pushed against his shoe. 'Bring it to the airport tomorrow. I promise there will be no problem at the check-in. In South Africa we walk straight through customs because who is going to have a gun coming off a plane? Obviously no one. Also it is a present you will want to keep. A P8. The army's choice. An example of the excellence of German manufacture. We thank you Herr Heckler and Herr Koch. Regrettably I have to say it is second-hand but never fired out of anger. Or with fear. Something a connoisseur will appreciate, am I not correct?'

'The gun or the sentiment?'

Rudi Klett smiled. 'Ah, my old friend Mace Bishop does not change.'

The waiter shuffled to gain their attention. Mace glanced up at him, but the waiter's face was bland as if he'd not heard a word they'd said. They both ordered continental breakfasts; Mace anticipating a fine array of hams and cheese.

At the buffet bar, Rudi Klett said, 'In South Africa there might be some interest in my name with the authorities. Which would be an inconvenience, you would agree? So I shall be travelling as Herr Wolfgang Schneider, a businessman from Siemens head office, Berlin. This is no problem, only a precaution.'

Mace didn't respond, from the old days used to Rudi Klett's anonymous way of flitting about the world. In the old days he'd never travelled on the same passport twice. And clearly Klett enjoyed the thrill. Still, you had to believe the money was big for Klett to put himself on the line if it involved so much cloak and dagger.

'The last time I was in your country,' said Rudi Klett, his plate stacked with meat, cheese, a melon slice, a bunch of grapes, 'was some years ago to facilitate the business with the frigates and the submarines. You should have stayed in the business, Mace. Not the small arms. That is pocket money. The big deals. You could have been useful, you and Pylon. We trusted you in the olden days. With these others we had to talk to we did not know them, we could not trust them.'

'We were small fry,' said Mace.

'So what do small fry do, you have to lick the right backsides, and then you are not small fry anymore. But no, this is not the way of Mace Bishop and Pylon Buso. You had no ambition, Mace. Look at what you do now? Bodyguards. Instead of sitting at home with lots of money in the Cayman, you are here in Berlin to look after me. With this arms deal you could have made life easy for me, for your government, for yourself. No more worries for the rest of your life.'

'But you're worried,' said Mace, lining a roll with parma ham and smearing a film of honey over the meat.

'Cautious, my friend. Cautious.' Rudi Klett cut his melon into cubes and sank his fork into the flesh. 'Because I have to sign the documents personally for the development with Pylon, I have to come to South Africa. It is not a good time for me to come to South Africa. You know there is a presidential enquiry into the arms deal about the frigates and they want to talk to me. If they know I am in the country they will stop me from leaving. But.' Delicately, unhurried, he lifted the fork and closed his mouth about the cube of melon. Dabbed at the corners of his lips with a serviette. 'But I like to live dangerously.'

'My problem,' said Rudi Klett, 'is that I know everything about that arms deal. I watched the money. I know where it went. Who has got it. Sometimes this is an asset. Sometimes this is a liability. In your country it is a liability. In your country if I am killed I am just another victim of crime. A poor tourist, shot for his euros in the street. Anywhere I can be killed and it is just your crime problem. Something random. Something most unfortunate. This is so convenient a cover-up, you would agree?

'I do not want to talk to your president's commission. There are many other people in your country who do not want me to talk to your president's commission. Especially the president. They know how I feel about keeping everything kosher but they cannot take the risk. At home I have a request I received for an interview. This is a letter from a judge, the chairman of the president's commission. They will send someone here to Berlin to have a little discussion with me. If I would oblige. You have heard of this person, Judge Telman Visser?'

Mace nodded, swallowed the food in his mouth. 'Actually,' he said, 'I've met him.'

'Ah so. Tell me?' Rudi Klett wrapped a strip of gruyere in ham and bit off half of it.

'I don't know much. I only met him yesterday. Briefly.'

Through the mouthful Rudi Klett said, 'Is he government?'

'Difficult to say.' Mace shrugged. 'He gave a big government man six years for corruption, so maybe not.'

Rudi Klett looked up from his food. 'How do you know him?'

'He came to us because he's spooked about the farm murders. He wants security for his parents.'

'This is natural.'

'Of course, they're old. He's worried. The way things are there're fifteen, twenty, farm murders a month. You're living with that sort of statistic you're going to have someone calling sometime.'

'The South African civil war.'

'It's good for the security business.'

Rudi Klett laughed his hard Machiavellian laugh, reached out and clapped Mace on the shoulder. 'Only arms traders can be so cynical.' He broke a roll. Lifted a curl of butter from a silver dish and dabbed it on a piece. 'So, then, your friend the judge is a good man to head a commission, you would agree?'

'Probably.'

Rudi Klett popped the piece of roll into his mouth. 'With all these names and numbers in my head and many people that want this information to disappear forever, your judge is a good man for me to stay away from.' He chewed and swallowed.

'Not difficult,' said Mace, 'he's in a wheelchair.'

Rudi Klett raised his eyebrows but made no comment.

When they'd finished eating and the waiter had brought them second espressos, Rudi Klett told Mace that he'd been sorry to hear about Isabella. In turn, Mace briefly told him the story, leaving out the drug deal and the gun deal, keeping it simple to a love triangle. Hubby shoots wife to get out of the marriage so he can marry his squeeze, hopes the murder will be lost in the general mayhem.

'My point,' said Rudi Klett. 'You want to kill anybody you take them to South Africa. Bam. Sounds like it's part of the background noise.'

'Except not this time,' said Mace. 'The guy's sitting. Life. Which means what, ten, fifteen years? When he comes out the brother, Isabella's brother's, got a contract on him. Wants him whacked as part of the background noise.'

'That is what I like, a little bit of revenge.' Rudi Klett stood, pointed at the package underneath the table. 'Don't forget the present.'

Mace retrieved it and the two men shook hands.

'Tonight,' said Rudi Klett, 'do not make arrangements. I will show you something that will interest you. Shall we say eight o'clock? Yes? Until then enjoy Berlin. You will find the city has put on make-up but underneath we are the same whores.' He laughed, and Mace watched him walk out, draping his coat around his shoulders in the European way. Always reminded Mace of Count Dracula.

20

Fifteen minutes late for his appointment with Popo Dlamini, Pylon drove through the ornate entrance, stopped the Merc at the security gatehouse of the golf estate. He recognised one of the guards on duty. Couldn't remember his name though.

'Mr Buso,' the man greeted him. 'Didn't know you were a white ball addict?'

Pylon shook his head. 'You didn't know because I'm not.' He slipped his shades down his nose, looked at the security man over the top. 'You worked for us, yeah?'

'Couple of years back'

'And this is more exciting?'

'Free golf. Get to see the rich and famous too, and I don't have to take so much of their crap.'

'Tell me about it.'

He handed Pylon a clipboard: name, host, vehicle registration, time in, time out. Said, 'Who're you seeing?'

Pylon told him Popo Dlamini.

While Pylon filled in the daily sheet, the security man put through a call to Popo Dlamini.

'No answer,' he said, taking back the clipboard.

Pylon checked his watch. 'Must be there. I'm not that late.'

'Probably he's out, talking to a neighbour,' the security man said. 'This is the crap we have to deal with. People know they have an appointment, so they leave the house and sit in the club bar or chat up women on the fairway. Makes them important when we come looking for them. Black guys are the worst.'

Pylon let it go. Probably this was why the man didn't work for them any longer. Said, 'What's his address? I'll find him.'

The security man hesitated. 'Someone's gotta take you. Hang on, there's personnel in the office.'

'Hey,' said Pylon, 'I'm late already.'

The security man nodded, not happy about this but giving the address anyhow. Said, 'I'll try him again.' He pressed a button to raise the boom.

'Do that,' said Pylon. 'Before you're finished I'll be knocking on his door.'

Pylon drove in, following directions, passed golfers trundling home in their golf carts, couples gardening, children riding bikes and skateboards like here they weren't at risk of being snatched away by paedophiles. Probably they weren't. This was Treasure's dream location, so up close to the mountain you could hear the francolins calling. Way better than a security complex in her estimation. After the new baby and the AIDS orphan she'd let him know that the dream location wasn't far behind.

'How about a unit in my golf estate?' Pylon had responded.

'Up the west coast?'

'Forty-five minutes out of town.'

She'd given him the you've-got-to-be-joking glare. 'Hayi! At two o'clock in the morning it's forty-five minutes maybe. Any other time of the day it's double that. And where's Pumla supposed to school? We're supposed to change her school? I don't think so.'

Not the end of the conversation. Treasure had gone through to the kitchen and come right back. 'Much better to take the profit and buy into somewhere established. That's the option, okay? Somewhere the kids are safe.'

He turned into Gary Player Close went to the bottom and came back, parking outside number twenty-five. Place looked like nobody had woken up yet. Curtains closed. Pylon switched off, sat a moment scoping the street. You looked closely it seemed Popo Dlamini's neighbours were as dozy. Not much sign of life in their houses. And so quiet he could hear Popo Dlamini's phone ringing.

Wouldn't Treasure love this. The mountains so clear you felt you could touch them. No more cluster clatter. The neighbours had a row you wouldn't hear it in your bedroom. He got out of the Merc and flicked the remote locking. The car beeped. Probably in this sort of street that wasn't necessary.

Pylon went round his car and down the short path to the door, almost trod on an iPod. Neat device. The sort of thing he'd been meaning to get. He picked it up, flicked through the menu: scrolling a list of music, a lot he recognised. If this was Popo Dlamini's they had more than business in common. He pressed the doorbell, heard it chime inside the house, competing with the phone. Then the phone stopped. Nobody'd answered it though. He rang the bell again. No movement inside. The phone rang once more and Pylon reckoned if the security boys were any good they'd be down within two, three minutes. Before then he tried Popo Dlamini's cellphone. He could hear that going off, too. Fainter, maybe in a bedroom. The call went to voicemail and Pylon disconnected. He tried the door. Locked.

Was standing there, considering taking the path to the front of the house when the security guard from the main gate cycled up.

'Regulations,' he said to Pylon, more out of breath than Pylon thought he should've been. 'A call goes unanswered we've gotta find out why.'

'Fair enough,' said Pylon, still holding the iPod. 'Best we try round the other side.'

'Once more,' said the security man, going through the routine of pressing the doorbell, knocking on the door.

'Regulations,' said Pylon.

The security man grimaced. 'We don't do it they shit on us. The white major, our boss, is like manic.' He also jiggled the door handle. 'So okay let's try the other door.'

Pylon followed him round the house to a patio, open to a section of green rough and then the fairway. No golfers visible, only a pair of hadedas spiking through the grass, the sun glinting off the blue burnish of their backs.

On the patio, a table laid out with plates, a bowl of salad, bread rolls. Two candles burnt out. On the grid of the portable braai, charred steaks over a heap of white ash and the smell of the fire still noticeable. The sliding door from the house to the patio wide open.

Pylon thought, save me Jesus, going hard on the security guard's heels through the clutter of garden furniture into the house. Took a moment for his eyes to adjust to the gloom and the sight of Popo Dlamini collapsed against a couch with a third eye in his forehead, a track of blood down his face, that'd pooled on his chest. Other side of the couch a female body, her short skirt rucked up on her stomach, exposing a white tanga and long legs. He saw a wine glass smashed on the floor in the entrance to the room, a loop of wine spilt across the back of the couch. Like the glass had been thrown.

The security guard said, 'Oh shit!' – started jabbering on his radio to the security office. 'There's a murder/suicide, number twenty-five.'

Unlikely, thought Pylon, seeing a shell on the floor and peering for a closer look. .22 Long Rifle. Ordinary stuff, not even hyper-velocity. Not a hollow point. You used this sort of ammo, you had to know what you were doing.

The security guard was clutching his arm, saying, 'We've gotta stay outside, Mr Buso. Please.'

Pylon shook him off. 'Sure, sure, let's go.' The security guard turning to leave while Pylon stepped over to the female body. The woman was lying front down, her head skewed sideways, her right cheek and eye a mess of gore.

The guard shouting at him from the door, 'Come on, get out, get out.'

Even through the blood, Pylon recognising Lindiwe Chocho. He didn't say anything, slipped the iPod into his jeans pocket and joined the guard outside.

As cops and paramedics and ambulances screeched in, Pylon

called their friendly cop: Captain Gonsalves. The very man in shit with Mace over the natural born killers, Paulo and Vittoria. From time to time Complete Security contributed to the good captain's retirement fund. In return for favours. What they called among the three of them a working relationship.

The phone went to ten rings before Gonsalves answered, Pylon about to hang up. 'What's it?' said the policeman. 'This's a Sunday dammit.'

'Little story about a murder,' said Pylon. 'Two murders actually.'

'That you Buso? Where's the Bishop fella?'

'Around.'

'But you're in the shit again?'

'Not exactly.' In a sentence Pylon gave the guts and glitter of the side interest. 'The one body lying there belongs to a brother I know, Popo Dlamini. The other body lying there belongs to the wife of someone I don't know, man called Obed Chocho.'

'Politician or something?' said Gonsalves. 'Done for fraud or theft?'

'That's the wonderful man. High-up type. Can talk to the president.'

'So what're you telling me? It's a hit?'

'Chocho's still in prison, has to be. Not only that. We're talking a pro. Uses a .22 probably silenced. You can't hear that gun if you're not listening for it. This is neat. Efficient. This shooter doesn't want back-splatter over the curtains. He fires a head shot the bullet stays in the brain. Nice and contained. Except for the lovely Lindi. Her face is a bit mucked up. And I couldn't see but there's probably a body shot.'

'You're saying what? She jumped him.'

'Probably closer than she should've been. I don't know. You're the expert.'

'This is outta my area,' said Gonsalves. 'What you expect me to do?'

Pylon could hear he was chewing. No doubt had the phone

tucked under his chin while he peeled a cigarette and balled the tobacco in the palm of his hand.

'Keep a watching brief. Let me know from time to time what's going on.'

'You reckon Chocho did them?'

'Wouldn't you?'

A pause filled with the suck and sluck of Gonsalves working a tobacco plug round his mouth.

'What're we talking here?'

'I can make a contribution. Say five hundred bucks.'

'That's cheap. Double it.'

'Hell no. To just tell what happens? You're crazy. Six tops.'

'Seven-fifty.'

Pylon sighed. 'You're a hard man Captain Gonsalves.'

'You think I like it that my retirement package's gonna have me being night-time desk security in some office block? After forty-two years on the force. Hey, you think I enjoy that?'

'The service,' said Pylon. 'There's no force in it anymore.'

'Bloody right,' said Gonsalves. 'Another thing, tell the Bishop fella he can relax. The court case isn't gonna happen. Seems Paulo got on the wrong side of his prison pals, they cut his head off. Vittoria she tried to escape in transit, got shot for her troubles.' He disconnected.

The cops insisted Pylon made a statement there and then. He sat on the patio dictating to a sergeant why he'd come to see Popo Dlamini in the first place, stating the nature of their business association as property investment, leaving out that he knew the name of the dead woman. They'd find out soon enough. No doubt then come asking more questions or they wouldn't depending on what story they decided best dovetailed the facts.

Nor did he mention the iPod. Had no reason for this except instinct. Cause the iPod could be anybody's: Popo Dlamini's,

Lindi Chocho's, some kid from the estate. Didn't have to've been dropped by the killer on his way out. What sort of killer would go in dangling accessories? Anyhow, Pylon argued to himself, his prints were all over it. Probably if forensics did the work right they'd find a print on it that wasn't his. Only thing, Pylon was convinced they wouldn't do the work right but he knew somebody who would. The print info could always be slipped back into the system via Gonsalves should the process of justice get so far as arresting somebody.

Which Pylon doubted it would. Professional contract hits had a low arrest rate. You hired someone at a taxi rank, you all got nailed soon enough. A careful man with a .22 might die a natural death. Even if he dropped the odd iPod.

The other reason Pylon stayed quiet was curiosity about the tunes. Those he'd recognised put the iPod's owner in a different category. A category not far from his own. They'd be out in familiar territory.

It was going two before Pylon got away but he wasn't fazed by that. Given him a chance to see that some top brass were called out for this one. Popo Dlamini pulled connections Pylon hadn't expected. Among them a man with a smile who read Pylon's statement and asked him what he thought was going on here?

Pylon put the smiler down as national intelligence. Two surprises: the pinkness of the guy's skin. And his being an Afrikaner. With a smile like that he had to have a load of dirt on someone to still be hanging in there.

Pylon told him the truth, that what he thought was going on was a hit.

Smiler said, 'Interesting observation. From someone in the business.' The smile broadening lopsided into his right cheek. 'Next question's, why?'

Pylon matched smiler's smile. 'One thing I learnt in the

business, all the shit comes from here' – he tapped his chest. 'Affairs of the heart.'

'Strues,' said smiler. 'We should have a beer sometime, talk about it.'

'You got my details,' said Pylon, pointing at the statement. 'Now I have to go. I've got a wife who's not taking this well. An hour I told her and back for lunch.'

Smiler added a nod to his smile. When Pylon turned the corner of the house, he glanced back to see the agency's man still watching him. One of those types who didn't smile with their eyes.

21

Obed Chocho was maudlin. Unexpectedly down. Stricken when he should've been mighty fine.

After the call from Sheemina February he'd known a grief that kept him awake, tossing. Had him up drinking the better half of a bottle of Glenmorangie. The sort of whisky that should celebrate the good, not dull the bad.

At the end of the fourth double it was Lindiwe's fault. For disrespecting him. Disregarding him. Opening her legs to Popo Dlamini, thinking nothing of it. Straight afterwards, opening her legs for him, letting him, her husband, slide in among her lover's sperm. The bitch.

He'd warned her. Clearly in so many words: 'You talk to him. You phone him. You send him any message I'm going to know. You do not want that to happen.'

Deadly serious he'd been when he said it. This was no joking matter, no funny business. This was about loyalty. Honour. Reputation. He was her husband. So it was over with Popo Dlamini. Stay away, he'd told her. You are making me out a moegoe.

Still she doesn't listen. Still she goes running to the bastard last night. Mighty fine, the bitch, she had it coming.

But it wasn't that easy. After four doubles Obed Chocho was in tears, weeping for his dead wife. He finished the last whisky, hurled the glass at the wall, the shattering like a gunshot in the quiet of the prison hospital. No one came to check.

Obed Chocho threw himself face down on his bed, smothered his head in the pillow to stop his howls. Great sobs racking his body, misery heaving and gasping in his chest. He gave himself to this: let the shuddering quieten itself and fell into exhausted sleep whispering no more Lindiwe. No more taking one of her long nipples between his teeth.

When the prison commander knocked on Obed Chocho's door at two o'clock on Sunday afternoon, the prisoner was sharp and waiting. Trademark suit, white shirt unbuttoned to show chest and a gold chain.

Obed Chocho checked his watch. 'It's two.'

The prison commander nodded.

'At two I should be through the gates, my brother. Not waiting here to be taken down.' He picked up his cellphone from the bed. 'This is my time we're on now.'

'It's your lawyer's come to fetch you.'

'I hope so,' said Obed Chocho. 'Business before pleasure.'

The prison commander blocked the doorway. 'The regulation is five o'clock, you're back. I'm giving you till six. You come back later I'm the one in the shit.'

Obed Chocho grunted, waving the man out of the door way. 'Mighty fine. That's mighty fine, no one's going to be in the shit.'

The prison commander stepped aside and followed the prisoner down to the visitors' reception room. Watched Obed Chocho shake hands with Sheemina February, the lawyer almost as stunning as the man's wife. Only the lawyer had something else about her: a ruthlessness the prison commander thought. Because of the black glove on her left hand, the flash in her eyes that saw and dismissed him in the instant. The briskness of her exit. So abrupt she left a presence behind, a lingering malevolence.

In Sheemina February's high-riding X5, Obed Chocho said, 'Are they found yet?'

The lawyer fired the ignition, slipped the gear into reverse. 'Yes. A little earlier than I'd thought but what can you do? Sometimes there're wild cards in the hand. Anyhow, earlier, later doesn't make much difference in the end.'

Obed Chocho thought of the medics lifting Lindiwe's body onto a stretcher, carrying it out covered by a sheet out to the ambulance. He wondered where she'd taken the bullet. In the head was Spitz-the-Trigger's style. She wouldn't have known fear. Would've gone from this world to the next without a pause.

'How'd you intended it?'

Sheemina February pulled the SUV round in a U to face the gates. 'I thought putting the broken-hearted hubby on the scene would've been good. Would've stirred the press.' She glanced at him. 'Are you broken hearted?'

Obed Chocho kept his head turned away from her, facing the road. 'I was. I'm dealing with it, okay, leave it.'

She left it, steering slowly out of the prison and turning towards the highway.

Obed Chocho settled himself on the seat, easing down the backrest. 'How long to the Smits' place?'

'You're going to sleep?'

'Why not? It's a way isn't it?

'Forty-five minutes.'

'Mighty fine. Get us there.'

He was finished with talking but Sheemina February wasn't.

'Obed, there's another matter: Spitz.'

'What's his problem?'

'Money. He wants more of it.'

'To hell with him.'

'That's not so easy.'

'So what's his case?'

Obed Chocho brought the seat up. He needed a drink. Whisky would be preferable but he'd settle for something long and cold. 'Tell me there's a six-pack of beer in the back.'

Without a flicker of a smile, no hint of humour in her voice, Sheemina February said, 'Behind your seat is a cooler box. Help yourself.'

Obed Chocho slapped her thigh. 'That's mighty fine, my sister, mighty fine. A woman who knows my preferences.' He reached back and broke free a Black Label can, tore the ring-pull, putting his mouth over the opening to draw up the foam.

Sheemina February waited until he'd wiped the back of his hand across his mouth before she said, 'Don't do that again. I'm you're lawyer. That's how we keep it. That's how I know your preferences.'

Obed Chocho took another hit of beer. 'What're you saying?' He looked at her: her profile sharp and outlined against the side window. Her jaw tight, her mouth closed. Her lips bright as the flesh of plums. Her eyes secret behind the designer shades. Very elegant. His sort of woman. Not the sort of woman he wanted lip from. 'What're you saying?'

She didn't answer. Let a minute pass. Let him drink another mouthful.

He broke her silence. 'Lighten up, lady, okay? I'm mighty fine. Everything's mighty fine.'

'What I'm saying,' said Sheemina February, 'is the beer's not free. On my invoice under incidentals you'll see there one six-pack listed.'

'Hey,' said Obed Chocho, 'you're on a good number with me. Keep it in mind.'

Sheemina February smiled but the sight of it didn't fill Obed

Chocho's heart with joy. Nor her words: 'Oh I do, Mr Chocho, all the time.'

He drank the rest of the beer without pause. 'So Spitz is moaning. That's what Spitz does, he moans. People who know Spitz say he's a pain in the arse.'

'He wants double payment.'

'What for?'

'He believes he was contracted for one hit, ended up two. One plus one.'

'That was my wife. He wasn't contracted to kill her.' Obed Chocho broke open another can of beer.

'Technically, not his problem.'

'Mighty fine. The trigger man goes in to do a job, someone else is there he shoots her too. Who asked him to do that? No one. No one said shoot everybody in the house. Take no prisoners. Like here is a licence to kill. Go ahead, be my guest. Massacre everybody.' He drank deeply. 'He didn't have to kill her. She shouldn't have been there.'

'I'm not going to answer that.'

'Why not? Why not? He didn't have to kill her.'

Obed Chocho felt the tears start, the emotion clogging in his throat. One thing he didn't want was for Sheemina February to see him distraught. He swallowed more beer.

'You want to do denial, you do it Obed. Just don't do it on me.'

Obed Chocho groaned, turning away from her to still the sobs, bring himself under control.

'I'm going to pay Spitz, Obed. Keep it simple. We don't want problems from him and Manga. When it's over, what you do then is your business. For now I'm paying him.'

Obed Chocho blew his nose into a handkerchief. Stuffed it back in his pocket. 'Mighty fine. You're the lawyer, sister. You handle it.'

The lawyer didn't reply, kept the car humming down the highway.

Half an hour later Obed Chocho stood on the stoep of the old farmhouse and looked at the sea. The water still with kelp heads resting on it. A path of broken shells leading from the house to a curve of beach. Headlands of white boulders either end.

'Mighty fine view,' he said to the two Smits, Henk and Olivia, standing between him and Sheemina February.

'It's our weekend park-off,' said Olivia. 'We love it. You can see Cape Town and the mountain from the top of the rise back there' – she pointed off to the left – 'but otherwise it's like nineteenth century.'

'With indoor plumbing,' said Henk, laughing.

'But no electricity,' said Sheemina February.

'We could've got it put in,' said Henk. 'For a price, but then we couldn't see the point. If you put in electricity you're going to bring work here. The idea wasn't to do that.'

'Gas and candles're all you need,' said Olivia. She stuck her hands in the pockets of her cut-off jeans, looking, to Obed Chocho's way of thinking, far too easy in the situation.

The conversation died. Obed Chocho thought spoilt white kids in their trendy gear, Raybans stuck in their hair, dark blue Saab cabriolet parked on the gravel patch at the back of the house. The house furnished shabby chic. And an apartment in Bantry Bay, Sheemina had found out.

Where'd two kids not thirty, okay maybe thirty get this kind of money? Not a question he had to ask himself because he had the answer: white privilege. Centuries of it. People like Henk and Olivia made him want to spit.

He stared at the horizon, realising the smudge in the haze was the northern tip of Robben Island.

'That the island?'

'You get a perfect view from the rise,' said Olivia.

'Mighty fine, I'm sure.'

'On a clear day, through the bins, you can see people. It's that close.'

Sheemina February said, 'Mr Chocho spent time there. In the old days.'

Olivia Smit frowned, said, 'Wow.'

Henk Smit said, 'Oh interesting.'

Olivia saying, 'Did you know Mr Mandela, Madiba?'

'They'd taken him off already, when I got there,' said Obed Chocho. 'But I know the Old Man.'

Olivia said, 'That's a privilege.'

Obed Chocho made no further comment but turned to face the Smits. Smiling at them. 'Business,' he said.

They nodded.

'Mighty fine. The story's you bought this five years ago? For what? Five hundred grand? Five hundred and fifty? Six hundred?'

'It was a good deal,' said Henk, taking the answer no further.

'We needed diversity in our portfolio,' said Olivia. 'More property, specifically. The West Coast was obvious. Where else is there for the city to grow?'

'We're offering to double your money.'

'Uh ha,' said Henk.

'Five years that's a good return.'

'It's fair.'

'Market related,' put in Olivia.

'So where's the problem?'

'No problem,' said Henk. 'We'll sell at that price for a buy-in. We like your development. Only thing we've got to do is structure this.'

'We do it all the time,' said Olivia. 'Paperwork.'

Obed Chocho said, 'You got any beer?' He'd had three in the car but could do with another. And one beyond that to wrap the deal.

While Olivia went to fetch the bottles and glasses, Obed Chocho said, 'You understand what's going on here? This is a BEE project. Black. Economic. Empowerment. Totally. To push this through we can't be seen otherwise.'

Henk nodded. 'Of course. We appreciate that.'

'Not about getting our slice of the cake. About getting back the cake.'

'I hear you,' said Henk. 'I don't see it quite that way but I hear you.'

'How do you see it, Henk?' said Sheemina February.

'I can talk straight?'

'We're adults.'

Henk drew in a long breath. 'Okay. What I see happening is some people getting rich on the back of a political situation. Getting very rich. Mostly it's the same people. So happens I don't have a problem here. This is capitalism: the acquisition of wealth. It's what we do, Olivia and me, most waking moments of our day. No reason others shouldn't.'

'What's that?' said Olivia, setting down the bottles on the table.

'Make money.' Henk moved to uncap the beer. Olivia laughed but neither Obed Chocho nor Sheemina February cracked a smile. 'Glass or bottle?'

Sheemina February said, glass; Obed Chocho said, bottle. He was thinking that these were punk whiteys wasting his time. His valuable time talking their stupid politics like there'd been no change of government. He took the beer Henk offered. 'You think I'm greedy? That's why I'm in jail.'

'I don't know you,' said Henk. He handed Sheemina February a glass of beer and she took it in her good hand. 'Personally I don't know what you're like. I'm talking generally. Theoretically. The reason you're in jail, that's old news. Doesn't bother us.'

'But if you come down to it,' said Sheemina February, 'what you're saying is that Mr Chocho is greedy.'

'Mr Chocho's a businessman,' said Olivia. 'He lives in a nice house, he drives high-ticket cars. He has certain tastes. We all do that. So what?'

Sheemina February sat down at a chair beside the table. 'You've done your homework.'

Olivia inclined her head.

Obed Chocho standing on the edge of the stoep felt a pressure build in his temples. To get this far and be stopped by two young mlungus whose forebears had stolen the land in the first place. To be insulted. To be called greedy. These arseholes judging him. He swallowed a mouthful of beer, said, 'You think I am corrupt? That I took bribes?' His voice quiet, containing violence.

Olivia was about to respond when Henk put his hand on her arm. She let him talk.

'For myself I'm not concerned about that arms deal business. Neither of us are. What we see here is a way to make some money. We want to invest' – he gestured at the beach and behind the house – 'this property. For that we want a share of the profit. Open to negotiation of course.' Henk shut up. He and his wife watching Obed Chocho.

Sheemina February watching Obed Chocho too. The pulse point throbbing on his forehead. One hand gripping the beer bottle, the other latched onto the stoep railing.

He turned to face the couple, went towards them, stopped a pace off. The woman and the man meeting his gaze. Obed Chocho held out his hand. He laughed. 'My brother, my sister. I like you. So mighty fine we have a deal. Shake.' He took Henk through the brother's handshake, but kept it Western for Olivia. 'We will negotiate like greedy people.' Laughing again, letting them see he was relaxed. 'Put your proposal in writing. We will work something out.'

In the car driving away, the Smits standing arm in arm at the back door of the farmhouse, waving, Sheemina February said, 'That was too easy.'

'Of course,' said Obed Chocho. 'But I can't deal with that shit. You're the lawyer, fix the details.'

'They're sharp.'

'Mighty fine,' he said. 'Blunten them.'

'What?' She glanced at him. 'That's not a word.'

'Now it is. You know what I mean.'

Sheemina February took the coast road: one side the shining sea, the other mile on mile of Tuscan complexes stacking up against the Blouberg highrise beachfront. Obed Chocho stared at the sea, wondering why nobody had found out yet that the woman's body was his wife? How was he supposed to mourn before that?

'Where're we going?' he said, suspecting he knew the answer.

'Your house. Where else? You've done your business, you're going home to spend the rest of the free time with your wife.'

'And when she's not there?'

'You phone around trying to track her down. Find out what's going on with her.' Sheemina February checked the time on the dashboard clock. 'It's four. I'd have thought by now the cops would be on it. All they had to do was check his cellphone for a couple of clues.'

'Mighty fine, okay. Mighty fine.' Obed Chocho sat hunched and silent, not even concerned about another beer, until they turned into his street and saw an unmarked double-cab parked against the curb outside his house.

'Cops,' said Sheemina February. 'About bloody time.' She pulled up behind the van. A heavy brass got out, came up to the window on the passenger side.

The heavy brass said, 'Mr Chocho?'

'Yes,' said Obed Chocho, opening the car door.

The heavy brass stepped back. 'I've got bad news, sir. We have a body. We believe it's your wife. Sir, could you come with me. To make an identification.'

'You believe? You don't know?' Obed Chocho started ranting. 'My wife's at home. In there, in our house. What's the problem that you can't make a few decent phone calls first. Before you come with this stuff. Hey, you think it's mighty fine to tell someone in the street, hello, man, your wife's dead?'

'Sir,' said the heavy brass, 'Mr Chocho, please.'

But Obed Chocho was bending at the intercom mounted on a pole beside the driveway gates, stabbing the button, shouting into the mic, 'Lindiwe, Lindiwe, open up.'

'We've done that,' said the heavy brass to Sheemina February. 'Rang the home phone. It goes to voicemail. We've rung Mrs Chocho's phone too, it rings in her handbag. That's why we think…'

'I'm Mr Chocho's lawyer,' said Sheemina February. 'We'll follow you.'

'Ah, no,' said the cop. 'He needs to come with me. Regulations. Under the circumstances.'

'He's on a four-hour pass. The time's not up yet. We'll be right behind you.'

The heavy brass sucked his moustache, considering, glancing across at Obed Chocho straightening up at the intercom post. 'Stay close.' He turned on his heel, saying, 'Mr Chocho, let's go, sir.'

Following the cop van down the highway to the mortuary Sheemina February said, 'Don't overdo it Obed. Keep it contained. Grief looks better that way.'

Obed Chocho said nothing.

'The other thing we've got to sort out,' she said, 'is Rudi Klett. He's flying in tomorrow. The sooner Spitz handles it the better.'

A few minutes later, she took the Woodstock off-ramp, Obed Chocho still hadn't answered her.

'Should I talk to him?'

No response.

'Obed!' She got no movement out of him. 'Obed, listen to me. Should I talk to him?'

At the traffic lights, they stopped behind the double-cab. The heavy brass watching them in his rearview mirror.

'Obed, there is another option. I can let the president's men know. Or your friend Judge Telman Visser even, if you're feeling kindhearted. They all want to talk to Rudi Klett in their way. Which option? Take your pick. We do the president a favour, mmm?. Afterwards, let him know he owes you, oh good and faithful servant.' She laughed, the hard sarcastic laugh that riled Obed Chocho. 'What's it going to be?'

'Ja, mighty fine,' said Obed Chocho.

'Spitz?'

No response.

'Spitz it is then.' She parked behind the police double-cab.

Obed Chocho looked up at Devil's Peak, then across the wide street at the mortuary: brown face-brick with a gable. The sort of building you don't notice among other buildings you didn't notice in an empty part of town this hour of a Sunday afternoon. He thought of Lindiwe lying on a gurney in there. Her lovely face with a bullet hole in it, given how Spitz worked. He wasn't sure how he'd be when he saw her.

22

Spitz, stretched out on the bed in front of the television in his hotel room, answered the call from Sheemina February.

'You're getting your money,' she said.

'Sharp,' said Spitz, and waited.

So did Sheemina February. The only sound Spitz heard from the phone was a car pass slowly wherever Sheemina February was. It could be, he thought, that she was bringing the money to him?

Eventually she said, 'That's it? Sharp?'

Spitz liked the irritation in her voice. Smiled at how he'd riled her. 'Sure.'

She let it go and he imagined her mentally shifting the issue aside. Putting it in storage for later use. The sign of a revenger in Spitz's book. The sort of person who preferred salads and cold meat. As he did.

'Tomorrow it'll be in your account.'

So she wasn't driving it over personally. 'I will check it.'

'I'm sure you will. And if it's not?'

'You have said it will be. That is fine. I trust you on your word.'

'You don't know me, Spitz.'

'We have talked together.'

'And what? You're a psychologist? Just by talking to someone you get a profile?'

'Sure.'

Spitz brought up the remote to turn down the sound on the television, reckoning there was something else on Sheemina February's mind that she was letting this conversation draw out.

'There's another job for you,' she said.

Again he had to smile. 'I know that one.'

'What do you mean you know?'

'That is the one I'm contracted to undertake.'

'Later,' said Sheemina February, 'next weekend. This one's tomorrow.'

'Oh yes?' said Spitz. He fired a menthol. On the television Humphrey Bogart told Ingrid Bergman 'Here's looking at you kid.' Spitz wondered if you watched television everyday for a month how many times you'd see Casablanca. In six months of random watching this was the second time. The other time had also been in a hotel bedroom between jobs.

'Not difficult,' Sheemina February was saying. 'I've got pictures of the man who's not the target. The one with him is. No collateral, okay?' They're flying in tomorrow.' She gave him the flight details.

Spitz inhaled, and let the smoke ooze back out. Ingrid Bergman was in the plane taxiing for takeoff.

'Another thing, I thought you might like to know that was Mrs Lindiwe Chocho you blotted last night.'

The dame, as Bogie would call her.

'I did wonder about that woman,' said Spitz.

'You wondered?'

'Sure.'

'Like to tell me why?'

Spitz swung his feet off the bed. 'I do not have anything to tell you.'

'But you will anyhow.'

Spitz made a face in the mirror. He thought he might like Sheemina February. 'There is a feeling you get about a job. A feeling of what is right and what is not right.'

'That so?'

'If a job comes suddenly then I must wonder why?'

'This's a sudden job.'

'But you are phoning me. Before it was Mr Chocho on the phone.'

'He can't call you,' Sheemina February said, 'he's over the road in the morgue. Identifying his dead wife.'

'That way he knows the job is done.'

'He's upset, Spitz. Grieving.'

'This collateral does happen sometimes.' He opened the curtains to a view across a motorway at the mountains. 'He has to tell me. In the beginning. Who is the target, who are the friends.'

'Like I'm telling you now,' said Sheemina February. 'One smack. Not the guy in the pictures.'

'These pictures, you have them with you?' said Spitz.

'Yes.'

'Then I will fetch them.'

'Tomorrow. They'll be delivered.'

'With another gun?'

'There's a problem with the one you've got?'

'It has shot two people.'

'It can shoot another one.'

Spitz shrugged at his reflection in the window. 'For me I do not like that sort of arrangement.'

Sheemina February laughed. 'What arrangement? That the cops will connect them. Since they put black brothers and sisters in there the system's gone kaput. Forensics is sitting on a backlist two years long. You get unlucky and they put these two together, the files will be buried under stacks taller than a giraffe. This is not a problem, Spitz.'

'It is to be your funeral,' he said.

'No, Mr Trigger, not mine. Think again.'

'The man next to the man in the pictures.'

'Clever boy.'

Spitz thought, why not go straight in, she was cockteasing anyhow. 'I am thirsty,' he said. 'I can buy you a drink.'

'I don't think so,' said Sheemina February. 'Why spoil it.'

'What is the thing we have to spoil?'

'Lots, Spitz. I've this image of you. From your brogues to your short dreads.'

Spitz let the curtain fall closed. So the lady knew stuff. 'Only one drink? I will pay for it.'

'I've got a client to comfort, Mr Trigger. This is no time for socialising.'

On the television the credits were rolling. He'd missed the takeoff, the look of unrequited love on Bogie's face.

'There could be afterwards?'

'Till the weekend, you're on your own. Enjoy the city.'

'I mean after you have taken Mr Chocho back to the prison?'

'Then I'm going home to bed.'

'We could meet anywhere you like?'

'Forget it, Spitz. I don't need any other nonsense.'

He liked her more and more. The sort of woman he could talk to. Not freaked by life.

'Please,' he said. 'Show me your town. Tonight. Or on any night? Or you could take me up the mountain. That is something that I must do.'

'Forget it, Mr Trigger. I don't do tourists. What you do is tomorrow you do the job. Friday you drive away for the main contract. In between you can go up the mountain. With the other tourists.'

'No. There is a problem with the car.'

'What sort?'

'We have to leave it.'

'Why?'

'For the police to find.'

'I don't get it.'

'This was the arrangement with them. After a week it is in their computer system that it was stolen.'

She paused, Spitz imagined her frowning as she worked it out. Then: 'You'll get a replacement. And another gun. How's that? Very professional.'

'Show me your town,' said Spitz. 'One drink on the town.'

'No,' she said. 'I'm surprised at you.'

The softness of Sheemina February's voice stirring movement in his groin.

'Why are you surprised with me?'

'I thought you were the consummate professional.'

'I am such a person.'

'Wanting to seduce the client.'

'I want to buy you a drink. I think you are a nice lady.'

'Sure, Spitz. But I think not. So leave it.'

Spitz frowned. Weren't many women, weren't any women, who spoke to him like that.

'Tomorrow night. And Saturday night on the farm. Those're your obligations. Nice talking to you, Spitz.'

She disconnected and Spitz decided that one thing he'd do before he left the city was have Sheemina February.

He dropped into a chair. The continuity announcer on the television was promising Play it Again, Sam up next. Spitz didn't know if he could watch a Woody Allen. He would rather smoke menthols, listen to bad songs, fantasise about Sheemina February.

23

As Judge Telman Visser powered his wheelchair out of the shower room, up the ramp to the gym's entrance, his personal trainer came trotting up. A young man, sweat stained.

'See you out, judge?' he said, dropping to a walk beside the wheelchair.

'That's kind of you,' said Judge Telman Visser smiling up at the face that for the last hour had talked him through bench presses and weights and a rowing regime that had worked his heart until he thought it might pop. A face he could exercise with. A face he found engaging.

An engaging young man all round, saying to him, 'There's another murder happened on the golf estate where my ma's employed. At Tokai.'

Employed. Not works. A young man bettering himself.

'Oh,' said Judge Visser, 'I hadn't heard.' He paused to take in a light the colour of chardonnay that washed the Constantia valley to the mountain, pale and hazed.

'Nothing on the news yet. My mom told me.'

'Really,' said the judge. 'I'm not sure I even knew about the first one.'

'Man shot his wife,' said the young man. 'You must have a lot of that in court.'

'You'd be surprised,' said the judge. 'A lot of it doesn't come to trial. But enough does.'

'This oldie got fifteen years. I mean really an oldie. Like sixty-five or something. He said he did it to stop his wife suffering.'

'Non est ad astra mollis e terris via.'

'Excuse me?'

'Seneca.' As they left the building and started down the path to the car park, the judge steered towards his car in the bay reserved for the handicapped. 'From the earth to the stars, there is no easy way.'

'I suppose,' said the trainer. Unsure, frowning.

Judge Visser glanced at the puzzlement on the brown face. 'Life's a bitch,' he said, which made the young man laugh.

'Fifteen years is a bit harsh though.'

'I wouldn't want to comment,' said the judge. 'Without knowing the facts.' He aimed his remote at the car and unlocked it, hydraulic pumps kicking in to open the hatch door, lower the ramp.

'This is just the coolest car,' said the trainer. 'Every time I see it I can't believe what they've done.'

'It cost,' said the judge. 'And while it works, it's wonderful. I don't want to think about something breaking down. I'd be truly buggered.' He lined up on the ramp, looked at the eager face of his personal trainer. 'That other murder, did your mother say who was killed.'

'Uh-uh. She's not nearby. You know, grapevine stuff among the staff. But she did hear they were black.'

'Oh well,' said the judge, 'c'est la vie' – reaching out to squeeze the young man's arm. A strong arm, firmly muscled. Arms that he'd let lift him into his wheelchair from time to time.

'Right,' said the trainer.

'Such is life.' The judge released his grip and rode the wheelchair up the ramp into the car. He dropped his kit bag on the passenger seat and pressed the remote to lift the ramp and close the door. His wheelchair clicked into position behind the steering wheel. The judge pressed a button to lower the side window where his trainer was waiting to say goodbye.

'Do you like kudu?' Judge Visser asked. 'Occasionally we shoot one on the farm. Fresh kudu is better than any meat you've ever tasted. Perhaps you'd like to come with me to the farm? For a break? A couple of days, next time I go.'

'Oh wow,' said the trainer.

Sometimes the judge thought of him more as a boy than a young man. A boy with unbound enthusiasm for life.

'That'd be cool.'

'Alright then, the next trip I make,' said the judge. 'Should we say in a month?'

'Brilliant,' said the trainer. 'Let me know, I'll take off some time.'

The judge smiled as he drove away: that would be an entertaining few days.

At home, with a large scotch to hand, Judge Visser phoned his father. The old man was worked up.

'I just heard,' he said, 'Niemand's dead. Burnt to death, the stupid fellow.'

'What?' said the judge. 'Old Jan?'

'No one else called Niemand I know,' said Marius Visser.

'Burnt to death.' The judge taking a mouthful of the scotch.

'Speak Afrikaans. That's what I said. In his office.'

'When?' The judge switching to his home language.

'Friday night.'

'Christ,' said the judge.

'I will have no blasphemy,' said Marius Visser, going silent but the judge had no intention of apologising. His father starting again, 'You know she kicked him out, that bloody wife of his, Betsy. She told him to smoke his cigars outside, not in her house, not in her bedroom, not in her bed. A month ago he told me he moved out. To hell with the woman, he said, if he wanted to smoke he was going to smoke.'

'I didn't know,' said the judge. 'You never said anything about that.'

'I wouldn't. I'm only telling you because he's dead. Stupid fool.'

'And Betsy?'

'I phoned her. She's not talking or crying. I can't talk to someone on the phone who doesn't answer back. The children are there with her. I can't talk to them either, they're crying. The daughters and the son. What a bloody mess.'

The children, thought the judge, were his age. The youngest probably in her forties. The two daughters married to farmers. The son a lawyer in another town.

'In the old days,' his father was saying, 'the fire engine would have got there. Probably saved the building and Jan. This time they couldn't get the engine started. Bloody darkies. You give them a pencil they break it. What're they going to do with a fire engine?'

Judge Visser cut in, 'Jan was…'

'Toast,' his father said. 'The latest word I hear on the TV. To you and me burnt meat. Charcoal.'

'They couldn't get him out?'

'A bloody raging fire, Telman. Everything burned. All his papers. My bloody will. The farm documents. Bloody everything. No one could get into the building the fire was so fierce.'

'Christ,' said the judge.

'Ag, Telman,' said Marius Visser. 'Not the Lord's name, please.'

The judge stared at the reflection of himself in the window, the garden now dark. A man in a wheelchair, a phone to his ear, a glass of whisky in his right hand. He found the sight troubling. Raising an anger in him. At himself. At his father.

His father was saying the funeral would be on Friday, maybe it would be a good thing if he could come up.

'I can't make it,' said Judge Visser. 'I'm on a commission.'

'What commission?' said Marius Visser.

'It doesn't matter. The arms deal scandal. We have hearings all next week.'

'I didn't expect you to come.' Which to Judge Visser meant the opposite. 'But on the weekend, you could.' He paused. 'Maybe

Betsy Niemand is a hard woman but we can show some respect. Christian compassion. For the whole family, Telman.'

'It's impossible,' said the judge. 'Not next weekend.' He could imagine his father's temper rising at this obstruction.

'You are a judge, Telman. In my time that meant something. People respected you. If you said something they listened. And you could bloody well have the court go into recess for a day. Two days. A week. If that was what you decided.'

'No, Pa,' said Judge Visser. 'Pa, listen to me. I cannot come to the farm this weekend.'

'Don't patronise me, Telman. I don't ask anything of you,' said Marius Visser. 'But I'm asking this: pay your respects.'

At the anger in his father's voice, Judge Telman Visser smiled and relaxed. He eased his grip of the phone, tapped a finger dance on the rim of his whisky glass. 'I will write to Betsy Niemand,' he said. 'And send flowers with my condolences.' He heard his father curse, the swear word muffled as Marius Visser covered the mouthpiece with his hand. 'Vervloekte seun.'

In English the judge said, 'This weekend you will have a visitor, though.'

'What's this?' his father said. 'What visitor?'

'A security adviser,' said the judge, reverting to his father's language. 'His name's Mace Bishop.'

'No, Telman. Not this weekend. That's impossible. With all this other business going on.'

'He can sleep in the guest cottage,' said the judge.

'And who's going to feed him?'

'Farmer's hospitality. What is one more mouth?'

'Tell him to bring his own food.'

'You need to talk to him, Pa,' said Judge Visser. 'Tell him everything that's been going on. About the fences pushed over. He's a good man. The best in the business.'

'An Englishman?'

'He speaks English, yes.'

'Bah.' The sound exploded in the judge's ear. 'What does an Englishman know of farm murders?'

Judge Visser switched languages. 'I'll let you have the exact arrangements later in the week.'

'You talk too much English,' said his father. 'You sound like a bloody Englishman.' The line went dead.

Judge Telman Visser thumbed off his phone and took a sip at the whisky. He stared through his reflection into the night. At the bottom of the driveway he could see a light winking as a breeze moved the foliage.

The problem with his father, he thought, was that he was his father. A problem that haunted his earliest memories.

Judge Visser propelled his wheelchair to the liquor cabinet and poured a shot two fingers deep into his glass. In his study waited a file on the arms scandal. A depressing account of self-enrichment. The avarice of the powerful. And the Machiavellian guile with which they'd been hooked by men like one Rudi Klett. Rudi Klett would have stories to tell about the worst of human nature. Perhaps he should have suggested a meal to the engaging young trainer. Enjoyed instead the better side of human nature and passed a pleasurable evening that might have opened up other possibilities.

His telephone rang and for a moment he wondered if it was his father. Unlikely. The old man was not given to remorse. He considered, too, letting the answering machine take the call. Having to talk to anyone other than the engaging young trainer seemed a hassle too far.

On the sixth ring he took it.

The voice was a woman's: sophisticated, firm, instantly recognisable. She said, 'This is Sheemina February, Judge Visser. As you know Obed Chocho is my client.'

'Indeed,' he said.

Since they'd last spoken he'd found out certain things about Sheemina February. That once she'd represented the Muslim organisation, People Against Gangsters and Drugs. That she'd blocked a controversial development in the city when the bones of slaves were excavated on the site. She'd taken up the cause and cost the developer millions. Also got half the city in an uproar that the remains of their ancestors were being disrespected. He'd sympathised with her fight. But he couldn't imagine how she'd become the lawyer of someone like Obed Chocho. Surely Chocho would have someone from the Black Lawyers Forum. Had had some black lawyer. That he'd replaced a blood brother with a coloured sister intrigued Judge Telman Visser.

'Judge Visser?' said Sheemina February. 'Are you there?'

'Yes,' he said.

'Judge Visser,' said Sheemina February, 'I am applying for my client to be released on compassionate grounds.'

'I'm not a parole officer,' said the judge. 'I don't see what this has to do with me.'

'I know,' she said. 'My apologies for disturbing you at home on a Sunday. But I believe I have exceptional cause.'

'Go on.'

'My client is due for parole next weekend. On Friday actually. But he has...' She paused. 'His wife has been murdered. Under the circumstances I am petitioning for his early release.'

'I'm sorry,' said Judge Visser. 'But I still don't see... This is surely a matter for the prison authorities.'

'Of course,' said Sheemina February. 'I have consulted with the prison commander and he has no objection. The same with the chairman of the parole board.'

'Then?'

'The petition needs a judge's authorisation. As the judge who sentenced Mr Chocho, as the judicial officer most intimate with his case and character, I believed you would be sympathetic.'

She paused and Judge Visser felt the manipulation in the moment's silence: the undertow of her words. He marvelled at her timing as she came in just as he was about to speak.

'Mr Chocho is severely distressed, as you can understand. He has been sedated. Obviously in his condition he could not leave the prison tonight.'

'I see,' said the judge.

'If you cannot…' said Sheemina February, 'then you cannot…'

'No, no,' said Judge Visser. 'That's alright.' And himself left a gap before saying, 'Tell me, how was his wife killed?'

'She was shot. Police believe during a robbery.'

'At their home?'

'No. She was visiting a colleague.'

'Dreadful,' he said. 'Will you wait a moment.'

Judge Telman Visser put the phone down and sank a good finger of his whisky in a single swallow. If the man was to be released in five days, there could be no harm in letting him go early. What signal could it send the public but one of judicial compassion. Would he make the same call for common convicts? Probably not. But Obed Chocho was not a common convict. He picked up the phone.

'Miss February, tomorrow morning at my chambers.'

'I do appreciate this, judge,' said Sheemina February. 'I owe you a favour.'

'No,' said Judge Telman Visser, 'your reference the other day has proved useful.'

'I'm pleased. He's a good man, Mace Bishop,' said Sheemina February. 'Ideal in the situation.' And rang off.

The name reminded Judge Visser that he still didn't have the man's agreement. Without replacing the handset, the judge dialled the cellphone of Mace Bishop. He got voicemail. The message he left said please to call him urgently. Next he tried Mace Bishop's home number. The person who answered said she was Christa Bishop.

He gave her his name: Judge Telman Visser. He said he knew her father was out of the country but that the soon as he got home he was to phone, no matter what the time.

'Please,' he said. 'This is most important. Most urgent.'

When he'd put the phone down, Judge Telman Visser realised his heart was pounding. He was slightly breathless. He gripped the arms of the wheelchair and brought his breathing under control.

24

'What's this about, Rudi?' said Mace from the front passenger seat as Rudi Klett gave his driver an address in the Grunewald. The driver a big goon, shaven head, pierced ears.

'You've got the gun with you?' said Rudi Klett from the back.

'Listen,' said Mace, 'I'm not into fun and games. What I'm here for is in-flight security. Strictly.'

'Ah come, my friend. Where is the old Mace ready for all adventures? Where is the swashbuckler, huh? Tell me what else would you do in Berlin tonight? Find a babe? Here look' – he pointed at the whores on the wet Kurfürstendamm – 'round the corner from your hotel. The best. Top class. That is convenient, not so?'

'Thanks,' said Mace.

'Not the same as Isabella, but some replacement.'

Isabella had been much on Mace's mind. He'd wandered maudlin through the streets, had lunch in the Café Adler gazing at tourists scurrying around what little was left of Check Point Charlie, wandered then through Mitte, the cold war gloom banished under the glass and fashion of the new until he found a music shop off the Unter den Linden where he could listen to the

REM song. And now had the chorus lines on a loop through his brain. Not that it bothered him. Sort of went with the feeling he had about whatever was on Rudi Klett's agenda. The end of the world as he knew it.

'This will be illuminating for you,' Rudi Klett was saying. 'That I can promise. You will learn things, Mace. Things about your country. Your leaders. Afterwards you will thank me. Honestly, you will.'

'Then what's it about?'

'A surprise. Nothing dramatic.'

'But I've got to have a gun.'

'For show.' Rudi Klett leaned forward to tap the driver on the shoulder. 'Not so Wolfie?'

Wolfie said 'Genau.'

They drove up the Kurfürstendamm and round the Concrete Cadillac sculpture on Rathenauplatz, taking the Koenigsallee into a part of the city Mace didn't know. Bigger houses. A thickening forest. After twenty minutes Wolfie swung into the driveway of a large house, ivy covering the walls, every window lit. He stopped at the front door.

'Here lives Herr Dr Konrad Schultz when he is in our wonderful city,' said Rudi Klett. 'Otherwise his family home is in Hamburg. Sometimes he has his girlfriend with him, except not tonight. Tonight he is alone. I have told him I have a South African contact with me and we are coming to see him for a chat. For this reason he believes it is about more orders, a weapons system for the ships your navy has bought. Really, tonight he is going to pay me commissions. You see he is a man who owes me much money. For a long time he has been in my debt. Now it is time for him to lessen his burden. To persuade him about this necessity, Wolfie has a gun and you have a gun, Mace. When he opens the door you are both going to point your guns at him.'

'No,' said Mace. 'That's not the deal.'

Wolfie reached into his coat and unholstered a .38 Colt Python revolver. He cocked it.

'Mace, my friend,' said Rudi Klett halfway out of the car, 'I do not want to kill this man. He owes me much money. I do not even want to hurt him. We are having a little fun, that is all. At his expense. So please, humour me.'

Mace said, 'Jesus, Rudi' – nevertheless drawing the P8. But not racking the slide or getting anywhere near ready for shooting. He joined the two men waiting at the front door.

'Good man, my friend. Like the old times.'

After the second press of the buzzer, Mace could hear Herr Dr Konrad Schultz coming to open the door, calling out something in German. Rudi Klett responding then adding in English that it was freezing outside.

When Dr Schultz opened the door, Wolfie rushed in knocking the man sideways, slamming him against the wall, pushing the short barrel of the Python into the flab of Konrad Schultz's cheek. Mace stood outside, his gun arm half raised pointing at Schultz's stomach, Rudi Klett nudging him forward.

'What is this, Herr Klett?' said Schultz, the words barely audible, the man wide-eyed with fright.

'Money, Herr Dr,' said Rudi Klett, closing the front door. 'Some payment of the fees you owe me so that I can show some gratitude to my friends. My friends who made everything possible. Shall we go to your study?'

They followed Schultz down a short hallway, Wolfie with the gun against the Herr Dr's head, his other hand clamped into the Herr Dr's jacket. Mace next, more bit player than actor in Rudi Klett's staging. Rudi Klett bringing up the rear with a running commentary on the paintings hanging shoulder height like it was an art gallery along both walls of the hallway. Rudi Klett saying he was impressed the first time he'd visited but the collection had got even better since then. Some serious money the Herr Dr had been investing in artworks. A wise policy. Pay cash directly to the artist or the gallery, keep the paintings out of sight, nobody was going to ask any questions. Ten years later you sold some stock, who was to know? Not inland revenue.

Mace thought, if Rudi Klett ever met the judge they could talk arms and art for hours.

In the study, Rudi Klett told Konrad Schultz to log into a bank account Schultz kept with Deutschebank. Schultz hesitated.

'Herr Dr,' said Rudi Klett, 'it is better if you oblige. This man here, not Wolfie, my shy South African friend, he was in the camps of the liberation movement. He would search out the spies. His technique for aiding them confess was to break their fingers. It is a technique he will use here tonight. One by one, he will smash your fingers using the butt of his handgun. In the camps I saw him use a hammer. But the gun will be as good. Not so Mr Bishop?'

Mace nodded, wishing to hell Klett had kept his name out of it. And with no intention of doing any finger breaking.

'To do this he will tie you to the chair because otherwise you will fall over with the pain. He will gag your mouth. In the end you will do what I want but you will also have a broken hand. For this you will require hospitalisation. Many weeks of agony.'

Rudi Klett paused to fill in the bank account number on the screen. 'You see I can put in the number for you.' He stood back.

'So, if you are wise you will do what I ask. Moreover, what I am asking is my due. There is nothing I am asking that we couldn't do as gentlemen, if you had done it the first time as you promised.'

'Please,' said Herr Dr Konrad Schultz, 'there is no action I can do from this account. The money is gone already.'

'Ah so,' said Rudi Klett. 'Gone to the right place? Or gone, lost?

'Paid,' said Schultz, 'already.'

'In the last hour, you've done this?'

Herr Dr Schultz nodded vigorously. 'Why not? This was

our agreement. Of course I would honour it. This was the arrangement.'

'Then show me and we will say goodnight.'

'Come, Herr Klett, how can I do that? Then we are going against the protocols. You are saying you do not trust me.'

'I have no problem with saying that,' said Rudi Klett. 'Throughout the world I have found that those who trust sometimes do not wake up. While they sleep so trusting their throats are cut.' He drew his forefinger across his throat. 'Psish. So Herr Dr Schultz I am light on trust. Therefore let us see the account.'

'Impossible to do so. The protocols say the account must be closed afterwards. Voosh. The account is closed, it is off the system.'

He stared up at Rudi Klett standing to his right. Wolfie two paces behind the Herr Dr, Mace circling the room: pretending interest in the floor-to-ceiling bookshelves, some of the shelves given to photo frames of a woman with young children, formal portraits of older people, knick-knacks: an arrowhead of bone, lead rounds, bullets. The desk faced a shuttered window, dull lights in the garden beyond.

'For everyone's precautions these are the formalities,' Schultz was saying.

'No problem,' said Rudi Klett, 'there are other ways to check.' He pulled out a cellphone from his coat pocket, made a call, talking easily straight to the point. Took less than thirty seconds before he disconnected. 'They will ring back in a moment. With the internet the world is a small place.'

To Mace, Rudi Klett said, 'The thing I wanted to show you was interesting. Something that would be very interesting to our friend Pylon with all his feelings for money. You will see now that among the Herr Dr's beneficiaries is a bank account with the Lloyds Bank in London. This account has the name of a business, Chancery House. You know Chancery Court in Dickens?'

Mace shook his head.

'Charles Dickens, the English writer?'

'I've heard of Dickens,' said Mace, 'just not this Chancery Court.'

'In the book Bleak House?'

Again Mace shook his head, came to stand other side of the Herr Dr so that he could see the computer screen.

'No matter. For the bank account Chancery House there are five people who can use this account. Important people in your government. Ja, okay, so two are not in your government anymore. They were when the arms deal was made, and they are still important people. Because they were so helpful to the Germans and the Swedes and the French and the Brits and the Americans, Herr Dr Konrad Schultz says he has sent them a little present. A big little present.'

Rudi Klett's phone rang.

'That is what he has told us as we will see now. Not so Herr Dr?' He answered the phone.

The Herr Dr attempted to stand but Rudi Klett put a hand on Schultz's shoulder and pushed him back down. Rudi Klett said only four words, 'That is a pity.' He disconnected.

Herr Dr Konrad Schultz said, 'Please. There is a reason.'

'There is always a reason,' said Rudi Klett. 'My reason is because you have not done the right thing, Herr Dr.' He nodded at Wolfie.

Wolfie raised his arm and shot Herr Dr Konrad Schultz in the back, a clot of gore tearing out of the Herr Dr's chest, exploding over the computer screen. Schultz fell face forward on the keyboard.

Mace jumped at the retort, thought, Jesus Christ what was Rudi's case. Smelling cordite and blood. Thinking, I could've done without the drama Klett. For Chrissakes.

'Sorry for this,' said Rudi Klett. 'Sometimes these matters do not go the way you want. Then you have to make examples. You agree? The way we did in the old days, that is still the best.'

25

Sheemina February came out of her bedroom barefoot, wrapped in a white towel. She had showered. Her hair hung wet, her left hand unsheathed tucked strands behind her ear. She poured herself a white wine. Stood at the kitchen counter listening to the quiet. The hiss of the sea against the rocks, the calls of gulls invisible in the darkness. Then silence. The quiet of her lair. No sirens, no street noise, no angry voices shouting in the night.

Two nights and she'd had enough of the city. The constant growl of its disquiet. She drank off half the glass, refilled it. Moved to her desk, brought up on her laptop a folder with photographs of Mace Bishop. Mostly her own efforts, also several of Mace naked in a shower cubicle that she'd commissioned. Photographs that'd cost nothing other than gentle persuasion.

'You want to get off the paedophilia charge?' was the way she'd put it to a client. 'Here's how? Turn your camera to proper use.' The client had seen sense. Snapped Mace in the gym changeroom the same afternoon. For his trouble the paed's police file went missing. Case withdrawn.

Sheemina February stared at the photographs: Mace's body looking as toned as the photograph she carried in a plastic sleeve. Firm, broad shoulders, stomach with a faint six-pack moulding. In the shower series his arms up lathering his hair, the stretch and bulge of his biceps pumped in the movement. Her gaze went down to his penis, stubby and withdrawn poking out over the lopsided sac. She could imagine the coarse hair. Felt the thrill in her fingers, caught her breath. Leant forward, her toes burrowing into the thick flokati.

'One day, Mace Bishop,' she said. 'One day' – flicked through the screens to some photos of Mace with Oumou and Christa. Brought up one: quite the family outing, the parents either side their child holding her hands. Cute. The setting a walk in the reservoir park one Saturday afternoon after the girl had got her legs back. The hand-holding not only about mommy's and daddy's love but about keeping their darling upright. She zoomed in on Mace for a head and shoulders. His expression tight. A face people pulled when they got a tax demand. Or the sort of face you might make when the person in the passenger seat next to you took a .22 Long Rifle load in the head. Especially when you were the security for the person in the passenger seat. She made a print. It'd help ensure Spitz didn't shoot the wrong target.

'You don't know what I'm doing for you,' she said to the portrait. The portrait almost life-size. Held it at arm's length. What it'd be like if he were standing on the rug opposite her. She in a white towel, naked underneath. She rubbed the image, felt a sudden pain tighten across her chest. Sheemina February let the print-out drop. The head of Mace Bishop coming to rest on a couch, staring up at her.

'Have I got things in store for you,' she said, the ache easing.

Bent to the computer, selected another photograph from the reservoir series, Mace more relaxed, smiling, actually looking straight into the camera. She'd been walking towards them.

For half an hour had watched them playing with the girl on the swings. Waited for them to head back to their car. When they did she'd wrapped a scarf round her head and lower face, Muslim style. Headed directly towards them in a long black dress, stylish, not quite an abaya but near enough that most wouldn't notice the difference.

As they'd passed she'd overheard Mace say, 'More and more women doing that these days. Covering up.'

And Oumou's reply. 'Because they do not know what it is like for women in the Islamic countries.'

Mace saying, 'Underneath she's probably wearing a tanga.'

A remark that'd stung Sheemina February, made her want to round on him.

Oumou said, 'Non, I do not want to imagine that.'

'What's a tanga, Maman?' – the girl pestering.

Sheemina February flushed to think of it. The bastard making fun of her. His bitch getting in on the act. She put back some wine, relaxed her shoulders, massaged beneath her left breast. Then fingered the touchpad to zoom up another head and shoulders of Mace, printed this. Retrieved the one from the couch, slid both into an envelope. Sometimes she wondered why she took so much trouble. Spitz hit both men what'd be the difference?

Actually too much of a difference. That'd be too easy. She flipped the envelope onto the desk, sat on the couch to finish her wine. Legs tucked beneath her, Sheemina February stared out at the night, remembered the camp: Membesh. The camp where freedom fighters trained. Where she went to join the guerrilla army.

Where these two men called her story: we don't believe you. You're a spy. Nobody could get here the way you did. Walking through the bush, crossing borders. Catching buses. A young girl like you, alone. Shaking their heads despite her nodding. The three of them sweating in a hot room. Having tied her to a chair, her hands flat on the table. The questions coming at her over and over. Tell us. Tell us. Tell us. Her tears. Her sobbing. Her story always the same. Their insistence: it's not the truth. Her constant: why don't you believe me? The two of them sitting back looking at her. Matter of fact. Not angry. Resigned. The black guy doing the introductions: I'm Pylon, this's Mace. Explaining: no point in introducing ourselves before but now we feel it's important, okay, sister? Now we've got to do stuff that's painful. The white guy Mace nodding along like he was disappointed. Pylon going off to a metal cupboard, coming back with a mallet. Mace describing the process they'd go through, showing her the coin they'd flip to get matters underway. Before he did saying, anything you want to tell us first? Her anguish. Her pleas. Her distress. Nothing persuading them from their course. The two men waiting for her, then Mace saying, we flip for the best of three, heads up. Winner does the hard stuff. He won. He smashed her hand.

The memory jolted her upright. 'Bastards.' The agony on her face. 'Bastards.' In a sweep of her arm, Sheemina February hurled her wine glass through the open door into the night. Sat staring at her crab hand. Flexed her fingers, stiff as claws. Could have cried for that young woman. That young woman still a girl really.

Monday

26

Pylon drove up to the golf estate's security gate, relieved to see his former employee on duty. Let down his window, said, 'Don't you get time off?'

The guard frowned, unfriendly, mumbling something about standing in.

Pylon lifted his shades to squint at the man in the harsh morning light. 'You get a bitching out?'

'Big time.'

'What for?'

'Letting you in without clearance.'

'That's harsh.'

The guard looked away. Pylon marking his unease and thinking there wasn't a hope in hell he'd do him a favour now.

'The house still a crime scene?'

'Uh huh, taped up.'

'And a cop standing sentry?'

'No.'

'Listen.' Pylon looked up at the anxious man in the gate house. 'I need a favour.'

The guard shook his head. 'Forget it. No chance.'

'You don't know what it is?'

'I don't have to.'

'Five minutes, okay. That's all it'll take.'

'No ways.'

Pylon took his hands off the steering wheel, held them out the window, palms open. 'Look. No bullshit. All I need is to see his CD collection. What sort of music he was into.'

'Why?'

'Something I'm working on. Five minutes. In, out, before the cops get there. Assuming they're coming back.'

'There's major shit about this.'

'I know. It's why I'm here.'

The guard hesitated. Clicking a pen against the counter top faster than a rave beat. Pylon sensing the issue here: part going against regulations, part what's in it for me? Said, 'I can ease your pain.'

The guard sighed, glanced away at the mountain. 'One large.'

Pylon pursed his mouth, about to cut the sum in half but the guard jumped in first.

'No deals, okay. I don't need this kinda crap. I do it for one thousand or I don't do it at all.'

Pylon nodded, taking out his wallet. 'Okay' – justifying it to himself that he owed the guy for the earlier favour as well.

'Not here,' said the guard.

Pylon in his Merc followed the guard on his bike to the house. The golf estate as quiet as a Sunday. Maybe quieter. Nobody on the fairways. Gardeners weeding among the border shrubbery and the greens manager out plugging holes, but not a resident visible. As they stopped at the crime scene, Pylon saw a curtain flicker across the road, a white face appearing. He waved in greeting and the face disappeared.

The two men ducked under the crime tape and the guard unlocked the front door, going in ahead of Pylon. Inside a mess: fingerprint dust on every surface. Chalk marks of the bodies on the carpets. More blood where the woman had fallen than where Popo Dlamini had gone down.

'One grand,' said the guard, holding out his hand.

Pylon palmed him ten one hundred buck notes.

'Just sort out what you want,' said the guard. 'Fast.'

Pylon was going to say relax but shrugged instead. Headed over to a wall unit on the far side of the room. On it kitsch ornaments in porcelain and wire, and a single rack of CDs above a mini-tower sound system. On a tray next to the player a bottle of red wine with the level one measure down. As Pylon remembered it there'd been a broken wine glass on the floor, a damp stain on the carpet. The wine was a cabernet. Good estate. The lady'd had cultivated tastes. But then the lady, having been who the lady had been, she would've taken high-end for granted.

He scanned the CDs. Best of Makeba, Masekela, Abdullah Ibrahim, a Youssou N'dour, an Ismaël Lo, some female soft voice stuff, the first Tracy Chapman, Brenda Fassie's Memeza, a clutch of symphonies. Collections of mood music. Nothing that he was looking for.

Lying open on a shelf an empty box of Zola's Khokhovula. Pylon picked it up: he guessed this had to be more Lindiwe's style than Popo's. The cover showed the kwaito star's screaming face, his hand slammed into a pane of glass, the glass spider-webbed from the impact. Pylon powered on the system and found the disc in the tray. He pressed play. The sound was turned low but high enough to get the guard jumping.

'No, no,' he shouted, pushing Pylon aside in his haste to switch off the system.

'That's what must've been playing,' said Pylon. 'Kwaito to die for.'

'We're outta here,' said the guard. 'Now.'

Pylon shrugged. 'I'm done.'

Sunday night, Pylon had spent three hours listening to the music on the iPod. Or rather, some of the music on the iPod. Specifically the playlists titled: Killer Country I, II and III. No hardship here.

Many of the artists he recognised. Cash, Giant Sand, Emmylou Harris, Tindersticks, Sixteen Horsepower. The guitar wonder of Steve Earle. Also the mournful voice of Jesse Sykes and the Sweet Hereafter and some Calexico tracks.

This was familiar territory. So was the new stuff: love songs and madness songs and murder songs and maudlin motel songs for long dark nights. Songs by the Cowboy Junkies, and the Handsome Family, and M Ward, and the Willard Grant Conspiracy that gave him the rittles: a cold gooseflesh shiver like people doing a jig on his grave.

Listening to it Pylon thought the iPod's owner was someone he could talk to. Someone out in the same badlands. But he couldn't see it being Popo Dlamini. Popo Dlamini didn't have any of this poetry in his soul. It could be a neighbour dropped the iPod coming back from his jog. Or it was Lindiwe Chocho's? Or someone who'd knocked on Popo Dlamini's door.

A neighbour he couldn't see. A neighbour would've gone looking for it. Nor could he place it as Lindiwe Chocho's. She was into kwaito. Someone who did kwaito wasn't going to do killer country. So maybe, just maybe it was the someone who'd knocked on Popo Dlamini's door. The courier. Aka the shooter with the .22 and the Long Rifle loads.

He could believe this. It was the sort of music to kill by.

But first he'd had to cross off Popo Dlamini from his list. And simultaneously the lovely Lindi. And with the neighbour theory junked, Pylon reckoned that the chances were these songs haunted the mind of Mr Death. A neat ordered mind that loaded specific themes into each of the playlists. A mind that collected stories and arranged them. That gave the playlists a descriptive title.

As he drove away from the golf estate, taking the road through the forest and the leafy suburbs before he joined the highway into the city, Pylon wondered if the hit was about Popo or Lindiwe or both of them. Was it business or revenge? Land or love?

He jacked the iPod into the car's player and brought up Billy Bob Thornton singing about love, the guy's oily voice oozing the 'forever and ever and ever', as sincere as a motel bedroom. Sunfilter curtains and brandy afternoons.

When his cellphone rang Pylon jerked back to the slow crawl of traffic towards the university. He pressed on the hands free and a voice said, 'My name is Judge Telman Visser, Mr Buso. I wonder if you could give an urgent message to your colleague, Mr Bishop.'

Pylon turned down the music. 'He's out of the country.'

'I know. I spoke to him on Saturday. He told me he would be back today.'

'He is. This evening. Six, seven something like that.'

'Please, Mr Buso, it is essential that I speak to him as soon as he has landed.'

'He's got a phone.'

'I have left messages on his phone. I left a message last night. He didn't return my call either then or this morning. I have left a message at his home. Now I'm leaving one with you.'

'No problem,' said Pylon. 'What's it?'

'It's critical that he contact me.'

The judge paused.

Pylon said, 'About?'

'Tell him to phone me.'

'That's it? That's the message?' But the judge had disconnected. 'Funny message,' said Pylon aloud, turning up a Johnny Cash song that reeked of a dirty old man doing bad things to a budding teenager. A girl Pumla's or Christa's age. A song that unsettled him. Despite the great man's voice.

Still he rode with it. That and the next about Emmylou's poisonous love and the next about Billy Bob Thornton's private madness and the next about a lone man's loneliness, the drive bringing him in above the city on a day so crisp the air smelt of salt and fish. He swung down Hatfield into Dunkley Square and a parking space outside the terrace row. Lounging against Complete Security's office gate was Captain Gonsalves, chewing, a rolled-up newspaper under his arm.

'I'm not staying,' said Gonsalves as Pylon came up. He moved a plug of tobacco from cheek to cheek, a yellow glisten at the corners of his mouth.

Pylon noticed shreds of cigarette paper littered on the pavement. Flecks of tobacco on the captain's tie. 'You should quit,' he said.

'I have.'

'Chewing it's not quitting it.'

'Hey,' said Gonsalves, 'I don't need your shit. This sorta shit I get from my wife.'

Pylon went for his wallet, counted out five hundreds and handed it to the policeman. 'So what's happening?'

'Zip, nada, niks, nothing, bugger all. Total blank out.'

'Come on.'

'No kidding.'

'Like it didn't happen?'

'It happened. Officially botched robbery. Don't you read the papers?' He offered the newspaper to Pylon. 'Everything's in there. 'Cept her name, pending telling the next of kin.'

'So why'm I paying you five hundred bucks when I could've paid four singles to the man at the robot.'

'Because what it doesn't say is that the file is tight in the commissioner's office. Or that the investigating officer was told, nice work, Jack, let's move on now.'

'It was a hit?'

'Doesn't seem like it.'

Pylon stared at him. Gonsalves exposing his ivory peg teeth.

'That's it? That's all? The investigating officer's shrugging off.'

'I would. My commissioner took a file off my desk I wouldn't stop him. One less I'm not gonna solve. Know what I mean. One less I don't have to put on the stack.'

'Save me Jesus,' said Pylon.

'No grief, okay,' said Gonsalves. 'We've all got headaches. You want to know my headache, I'm sitting with thirty-two murders in my basket. That's over the last month. Most stations every detective's got the same number give or take. It's a war, my friend.' He pushed himself off the gate. 'So smile. You're alive. It's a beautiful day. Hey, how often we see the mountain this clear?' Captain Gonsalves gave a yellow grin, patted Pylon on the shoulder as he sauntered off.

'Anything more let me know,' Pylon called after him. Without turning round, the policeman held up his hand.

Pylon sighed. Halfway through the morning and fifteen hundred bucks down. For what? Zilch. Except he knew the hitman liked some killer music. He unlatched the gate to see young Tami the receptionist standing at the front door, worried. A stunner too. Which Treasure had had something to say about.

He greeted her in Xhosa. Tami not even going through the ritual hullo, telling him two people were waiting, had been waiting for thirty minutes. The Smits.

Pylon thought, maybe there was a god.

Until Henk Smit told him, 'We felt it the right thing to tell you personally, we're not going with your deal.' Olivia, serious faced, nodding agreement. The two of them sitting on the sofa in his office facing him perched on the coffee table.

'It wouldn't make good business sense,' said Olivia. 'We've run the figures, there's a bigger margin on Mr Chocho's scheme.'

'On paper,' said Pylon.

'Admittedly.' Henk took a slurp from a bottle of mineral water. 'But?'

'But he's better positioned. Better connected. To swing it.'

'Ah!' Pylon stood in exasperation. 'The man's a fraudster. As of the moment a convict. He is not going to want you as part of his scheme.'

'We don't think that's true.'

'You are going to lose your investment. Believe me.'

The Smits glanced at one another. Henk said, 'Why should we trust you more? You're an arms dealer.'

'Was. Was an arms dealer.' Pylon sat down on the coffee table again. Faced them. 'Listen. There's no reason for you to trust me more. But think of this. We will take you on as part of the consortium. Is Obed Chocho doing that? I would doubt it.'

Olivia shook her head. 'We're sleeping partners.'

'Hidden partners more like it.'

'Sleeping, hidden doesn't matter.'

'It matters. If no one can see you, you'll disappear. When it's convenient for him, poof, you're history.'

Henk snorted. 'He's going to do what? Kill us?'

Pylon looked at them, didn't say anything, didn't raise his eyebrows, nod his head, make any gesture.

'Ag, don't be ridiculous. We're not in a crime novel.'

Pylon flipped open the newspaper Gonsalves had given him. Held it out, pointing at the story headlined: Botched Robbery on Golf Estate. Two killed.

'The story names one of the victims, Popo Dlamini. Popo was part of our consortium but I think he had a deal going with Obed Chocho.'

'Oh, come on,' said Henk.

'No, no, wait, listen okay. The woman who was shot in his house is Obed Chocho's wife, Lindiwe. She and Popo were having it off.'

'How do you know that?' said Olivia.

'That's tabloid stuff,' said Henk.

'Isn't it,' said Pylon. He glanced at Olivia. 'Let's just say I know it. Tomorrow her name will be in the papers.'

'You're telling us Obed Chocho from jail got a hitman to take out his wife.'

'Put it together,' said Pylon.

Henk Smit stood. 'Forget it, my friend. No ways. Doesn't happen like that. Never in a million years. This is Cape Town. Not LA Confidential.'

Pylon got up from the coffee table. 'Alright. Here's a suggestion. Tonight our backer's flying in. Tomorrow you can talk to him. Before you go with Obed Chocho, talk to our man. See how the project's structured. Sure, the profit's bigger on the Chocho's scheme. I'll admit it, you'll make more money. If you make any money at all.'

'Nice try,' said Henk.

'A cautionary,' said Pylon.

'One thing,' said Olivia. 'If this is a black empowerment deal, it's not going to fly with white faces.'

'We've got another card,' said Pylon. 'Community organisations.' He named a few. 'We're bringing them in as shareholders. So the money doesn't only go to the bling blacks. It's called real trickle down.'

What he needed to do was bring in Treasure. Ten minutes and she'd have them signing on the line. Probably also making out personal cheques to Treasure's NGOs of choice.

'Like I said,' said Henk. 'Nice try.'

'It's genuine,' said Pylon. 'I can give you names and addresses. Audits. We're talking organisations of long standing. Reputable operations. Into HIV/AIDS, housing projects, anti-rape and child abuse. All the stuff on our conscience.'

'We'd have to see it,' said Olivia.

'No problem.'

They shook hands and Pylon saw them out, not convinced he'd done anything but buy time. When Treasure played the guilt card she got results. Commitments. When he played it, people suspected an angle.

He went upstairs to his office. What people never allowed was that you'd changed. Still, the charity tie-in just had to be a winner.

Pylon phoned the others on the consortium. The wavering Smits the second bit of bad news he'd had to give them in two days. Mostly they took it on the chin. Resigned. Sighing heavily. What they all needed was Rudi Klett to convince them everything was green fields and blue skies.

27

The prison commander looked through the peephole at convict Obed Chocho. Chocho's holdall packed and upright on the bed. A stack of books on the coffee table, no evidence of the DVDs or CDs. Chocho suited, sitting on the couch staring at the wall. At the place on the wall where he'd hung the picture of the hunters in the snow. The print not hanging there anymore.

What the prison commander couldn't see was the broken picture glass that Obed Chocho had smashed with the heel of a shoe. Or the remains of the picture that had been ripped from the frame and torn into shreds. This debris lay at the base of the wall out of the prison commander's line of sight.

The prison commander glanced at his watch: eleven o'clock. Obed Chocho had been sitting in that position for almost an hour and a half. According to the warders, Obed Chocho had not eaten breakfast. He had been taken a mug of coffee but not touched it. The mug could be seen on the table next to the books.

According to the prison doctor, Obed Chocho was fine. Or 'mighty fine' as he'd said to the doctor when the doctor asked. His blood pressure was marginally up but nothing to worry about. His pulse strong, his lungs clear. No symptoms floating in his eyes, no infection in his ears.

As far as the prison commander knew, the only time Obed Chocho had spoken during the morning was his response to the doctor. At nine-thirty he'd been seen answering his cellphone but he'd not said hello or goodbye or anything in between. His phone had rung often throughout the morning but he'd not taken any other calls.

The prison commander held Obed Chocho's parole release authority in his hand. In the downstairs reception room waited the lawyer Sheemina February. A fragrant Sheemina February. An unsmiling Sheemina February, her lipstick a harsh gash of plum red. She'd handed the release form with Judge Telman Visser's signature to the prison commander and said, 'Let's do this without any fuss.' His idea too, although he resented agreeing with her.

The prison commander tapped on Obed Chocho's door and opened it. As much as Obed Chocho was a bastard, he was a grieving husband and this weighed with the prison commander.

'Mr Chocho,' he said, 'you're free to go. Your lawyer's downstairs.'

Obed Chocho looked up at him, cleared his throat. 'My brother,' he said, his voice grating. He coughed, started again: 'My brother, I'm donating this' – he waved a hand at the television, video and DVD players, the mini-sound system, the pile of books – 'to the prison.'

The prison commander nodded. 'It will be appreciated.' He noticed then the smashed frame against the wall, the shards of broken glass, but said nothing.

Obed Chocho lifted his bag from the bed and followed the prison commander downstairs to the reception room. Sheemina February stood waiting for him, making no move towards him. Not smiling or greeting him. And he neither smiled nor greeted her. At the door the prison commander held out his hand but Obed Chocho ignored the gesture, saying 'Mighty fine, my brother, mighty fine', and pushing past, heading through the doors to the car park. Sheemina February watched the big man until he was through the doors.

'Thank you, prison commander,' she said, holding out her ungloved hand. 'You have been most cooperative.'

'He's depressed,' said the prison commander, feeling the strength in the hand that shook his.

'Understandably so,' said the lawyer, stepping sharply after her client.

In the car, Sheemina February said, 'Don't do that to me again in public. I am not your woman. I'm your lawyer. You are my client. This is worth remembering.'

She drove out of the prison compound and onto the highway and still Obed Chocho had not answered her. He stared at the houses lining the motorway: small cramped places in patchy gardens. Occasionally a smallholding littered with junk between them. His thoughts were of going home to a house without Lindiwe. Where everything in the house would remind him of Lindiwe. He had another concern: when news of the killing of Lindiwe reached her family they would send a delegation. When they heard that Lindiwe was killed with Popo Dlamini they would suspect the reason. Matters would become tense. Sheemina February broke into his thoughts.

'Obed,' she was saying, 'let's start this again.'

Obed Chocho said, 'Does Lindiwe's family know?'

'Good morning, Obed,' said Sheemina February. 'This would be the proper way to start.'

'Mighty fine, mighty fine,' he said, 'do they know?'

'Good morning, Obed.'

He looked at her, at her profile, her eyes steadfastly on the road, a rage building in his chest. Who was this woman?

'Don't do it,' she said, without glancing at him. 'Don't dare raise your voice at me, don't even think of it. I'm not patronising you. I know you're going through hell but there's stuff to be handled, Obed. Business.'

Obed Chocho let out his breath in a whoosh. Closed his eyes behind his dark glasses and controlled his breathing. The woman was right. He had to stay in the frame. Eventually he said, 'Alright. Mighty fine, my sister, what's the business?'

'To answer your first question,' said Sheemina February. 'Yes, her family have been told. They want to see you. I suggested this afternoon in my offices.'

'They will cause trouble.'

'What trouble?'

'They will think I killed her.'

'Really?'

'Someone will have dreamed about it.'

'The murder?'

'Of course. We can use Spitz and Manga,' said Obed Chocho. 'For security.'

'I don't think so.'

'They're hanging around, costing me my money.'

'A,' said Sheemina February, 'you do not want to be associated with those two. B, they have a job later today.'

'From tomorrow,' said Obed Chocho. 'No one will know. They stay in my house, that is where I need them. So there's no surprises when I get home at night. Please arrange this.'

'You've got to be joking.'

'No, why not? I am paying them. Tuesday, Wednesday, Thursday, I'm paying them to sit at a swimming pool drinking my money. So, mighty fine, instead they can be useful by sitting in my house. I have a swimming pool. Beer. Dish television. Music. Servants to make the beds, cook the meals. This is like room service. For Spitz and Manga what is the difference to a hotel?'

'And for the ceremony, when you slaughter the bull? What do you do with them then?'

Obed Chocho turned to face her, he allowed a smile. 'You know my culture?'

'I know you have to appease the ancestors. Have a cleansing ceremony. Wipe out the blemish of jail.'

'We will slaughter on Saturday. By then Spitz and Manga will be gone.'

'It's not a good idea, Obed, having Spitz and Manga hanging around.'

'It's mighty fine,' said Obed Chocho. 'No problem.'

Sheemina February shook her head but said nothing more.

The highway opened to three lanes as they took the Tygerberg hill, and she kept the needle on one thirty, flashing slower traffic out of the way. At the top, on the long right sweep, Obed Chocho caught the view hazed by smoke and fumes over the low suburbs to the peninsula and ahead of them the distant city buildings and the mountain. At the sight he forgot his grief and thought, my city, the boy's back in town.

'Talking about Spitz and Manga,' said Sheemina February.

'Yes, what?' he said, coming reluctantly away from the brief rush of swagger.

'Spitz wants another gun for the farm shooting. And they need a car.' She held up a hand. 'I know what you're going to say, I've said it to him already. But he has a point. So I can organise it, or you can organise it.'

She kept the car's speed constant down the hill and onto the straight past the malls of Canal Walk.

'I can,' said Obed Chocho, remembering the times Lindiwe had dragged him there shopping, and lapsed again into moodiness.

They drove in silence until nearer to the city, Sheemina February said, 'The judge sends his condolences.'

Obed Chocho heard her distantly. 'Huh? Who?'

'Judge Visser. He'd read about Lindiwe's murder. He sends his condolences.'

Obed Chocho remembered the judge on his bench in court C staring at him, handing down six years. Six years! Like this was for real.

'Sure. Mighty fine.'

'Amazing, I thought.' Sheemina February paused but Obed Chocho wasn't going to play along and kept shut up. 'The man who sentenced you, sending his condolences. Can't imagine it happening many places in the world.'

'He's alright.'

'Sentencing you to six years! That was alright?'

Obed Chocho didn't respond.

'That was harsh, Obed. That wasn't about what you'd done. That was about sending a message. That was about politics. About making Obed Chocho the scapegoat.'

Obed Chocho didn't respond. That sentence had allowed him to ditch his lawyers in favour of Sheemina February.

'Someone's got the judge by the curlies.'

'I don't think so.'

'I do. Someone important. In the cabinet maybe.'

Obed Chocho laughed. 'You think I'm that important? Mighty fine, you think that.'

'I do. That's why the judge sends condolences.'

Obed Chocho flicked his hand dismissively. 'Believe it if you want to.'

Sheemina February took the elevated freeway between the harbour and the city, catching the lights on green until halfway up Buitengracht. At Wale she turned left.

'Another thing. Judge Telman Visser's heading a commission.'

'I read newspapers.'

'He'd want to talk to Rudi Klett.'

Obed Chocho shrugged, ignoring the upturned hands of a

streetkid dancing at his side window. Ignoring his lawyer's remark.

'I was wondering,' said Sheemina February, 'about the connections. The links to Rudi Klett.' The lights changed and she turned right into Queen Victoria back of the court where Obed Chocho had been sentenced to six years. A block from where Judge Visser had his chambers.

'Where're we going?' said Obed Chocho.

'My offices. Up near the museum.' She fished in the ashtray for a remote control. 'Some people in government wouldn't want him to talk to Rudi Klett. Would they? They'd want a tame commission. Like all our commissions.'

Obed Chocho didn't answer. Stared out at the Company Gardens, at tourists and children being told its history, at young people lying on the lawns, at a woman in an overcoat talking to herself. At the statues and the cannons and the columned portico of the National Gallery. Why hadn't he ever walked in the gardens with Lindiwe? He snapped his mind away.

'What about the Smits?' he said.

'I spoke to them. They've left three messages on your phone. When you didn't answer they phoned me.'

'And?'

Sheemina February aimed the remote at the gates under a block of apartments. 'They want in and they've done the paperwork. It's in my office.' The gates opened and she drove in.

'Mighty fine,' said Obed Chocho, feeling anything but.

28

They went sightseeing, Manga and Spitz. Drove to the Waterfront and browsed the high-ticket clothing shops, Robert Daniel, Hugo Boss, Fabiani, at the Spitz store Spitz trying on Bally moccasins, a pair of which he considered buying when the money came through. Afterwards wandered the malls, licking Italian sugarcone ice creams.

'Captain,' Manga said as they drifted outside to watch a Nigerian fire-eater going through a fast routine, 'maybe I'm living in the wrong city.' Manga tossed five bucks into the man's pot. 'Other hand, you couldn't pull a job here. Too much going on.'

They sauntered further, past camping shops and restaurants, tourist traps selling carved ostrich eggs and beaded wire baskets to where a banjo band in get-ups of blue and white played the local beat beneath a pepper tree. Too shrill for Spitz but he liked the vibe. Manga dropped five bucks into an open banjo case.

They took the lane between Hildebrand's and the Green Dolphin jazz bar that opened on a plaza dotted with soapstone sculptures and a view across the harbour to the loading quays. A red clocktower caught their eye and they headed for it over a swingbridge.

The sight before them impressed Spitz: Paulaner's, a German-style beer garden selling weissbier in tall glasses. He led Manga towards it.

'A beer and maybe white sausage and pretzel, if we are in luck.'

They sat beneath an umbrella, ordered large weissbiers. Spitz flicked through the menu, salivating.

'Amazing. Here is my favourite,' he said, finding white sausage on it. 'Try them. With sweet mustard, they are very good.'

Manga rolled his tongue over his teeth, tapped a cigarette from a pack. Eyed Spitz. 'How d'you know this?'

'For six months I lived in Bavaria. Sometimes we went to a beerhall on the lakes. I remember sitting there, outside at benches, and across, in the distance, there was the Alps.'

'You were in exile?'

Spitz lit a menthol and exhaled a plume. 'No. I was not in exile. I have done some training in East Germany, Berlin. Afterwards to West Berlin and by car to Hamburg down the corridor. Then for a while in Munich. In those months I listened to country music. The German where I stayed had only country and western music.

In the beginning I thought it was stupid, these sad cowboy songs. But when you listen to them you hear something different. Now I like country rock. I like the stories. They are my company.' Spitz stared wistfully across at the tourists clustered round the clock tower. 'When we are back in Jozi I can make another playlist.'

The weissbiers arrived and Spitz ordered the white sausage in German, carried away by the atmosphere, the Bavarian get-up of the serving staff. The waitress smiled at him. 'I'm from here,' she said. 'Cape Flats. But I know what that is.' She spun away with a swirl of her skirt: both men glimpsing her legs.

'Oh captain,' said Manga. 'Gimme some of that.'

'Gesundheit,' Spitz said, holding his glass out, the base towards Manga.

Manga leant forward to click, Spitz instructing him to use the heavy base. 'Bavarian-style,' he said.

They drank the beer quickly and ordered seconds when the sausages arrived, getting another sight of the waitress's legs. Spitz told Manga to skin the sausage, peeling off the sheath like a used condom. Manga grimacing as he dropped it on a side plate.

'Germans have got funny ideas,' he said. But he liked the sausage with the mustard.

'Better than a Big Mac,' said Spitz.

'Right at this minute,' said Manga, 'but maybe not later.'

As Spitz bit into his second sausage his cell rang. He glanced at the screen, swallowed quickly. 'My girlfriend.'

'You kept her quiet, captain,' said Manga through a mouthful.

Spitz lowered his tone to say hello to Sheemina February.

She laughed. 'I like your voice, Spitz,' she said.

'We are having a drink,' said Spitz. 'Perhaps you could come here and join us.'

'I don't think so.'

'Even lawyers must eat some food.'

'We prefer our client's blood.'

Spitz guffawed. 'I like that one.'

'But you won't like this,' she said. 'Tomorrow you're checking out of the hotel and staying at Obed Chocho's for a couple of nights. Until Friday.'

'No,' said Spitz. 'That is not the arrangement. I do not do this sort of business.'

'I know. You're just going to have to bend your rules, okay. You'll get en suite bedrooms each. Plenty of servants running round to feed you, take your drinks out to the pool. Staying at Mr Chocho's the same as staying at a hotel. He'll be there too. In and out.'

'Mr Chocho is out of prison?'

'Compassionate early release.'

'I do not like this idea.'

'Neither do I particularly. But this is how it's going to be.' She paused. 'He's hurting, Spitz, but he won't take it out on you. He needs you. Remember that.'

'This way is not my style.'

'I've told you I appreciate that. My hands are tied. Do the job tonight, check out of the hotel tomorrow at ten and we take it from there. After tonight you'll be his main man. Oh yes, Spitz. I've couriered the photographs. Look carefully at them. Don't kill the wrong man.'

She disconnected and Spitz told Manga what Sheemina February had laid out.

Manga finished his beer. 'Captain,' he said, 'this is not good news.'

29

Mace was pissed off all the flight to Cape Town.

Pissed off that there were voicemail messages from Judge Telman Visser. Pissed off when he got into the car beside Wolfie in the cold wet dark outside the Kempinski, Rudi Klett in the back cheerfully good morning him like the Herr Dr Konrad Schultz interlude hadn't happened, pissed off when Rudi Klett walked the P8 through check-in at Tegel, pissed off when the only in-flight movie he hadn't seen was Shrek 2.

Pissed off at Rudi Klett running endless Sudokus on his PDA.

Pissed off at the loop of the REM song in his mind. An hour from Cape Town, calmed down to a point he even wanted to talk to Rudi Klett, Mace said, 'What was that all about, last night? I didn't need that, Rudi. I try to stay out of those situations.'

Rudi Klett took off his glasses, glanced at Mace. 'I am the same. Believe me.' He switched off the PDA, reached for a watered whisky on his tray. 'Those sort of situations are not pleasant. I avoid them, too. Usually, these days, people are more cooperative. But the Herr Dr I had been told was a problem. Above his station in life. Like me he is an intermediary. Like me he feeds at the trough. But not like me he worked the margins also. You know what I mean by this?'

Mace nodded. 'Sure.'

Rudi Klett sipped his whisky. 'He would keep the money for too long so he could earn interest. If you say the deadline is Thursday, he waits to Monday to make the deposit. Because why? On Friday when you want to know where is the money he says the transaction has gone through but the bank clearance takes a day. On Monday when you phone he says, ah, because of the weekend everything slows down. On Tuesday you have the money so no problem, but in the meantime he has made some thousands that could have been yours.

'Many people have told him, Herr Dr you are making a mistake. In this business time is honour. If you say Thursday then next Tuesday is not acceptable. I am told that Schultz is yesterday's man. He gives you any trouble, Herr Klett, I am told, take him out of the loop. This is meant literally. So I do everyone a favour.'

'Except me.'

'Na ja. You are unlucky. I am sorry, Mace. Forgive me.'

Mace thought, typical Klett, forgive me over and done with but let it go. Said, 'Tell me about Chancery Court.'

'Ah ha.' Rudi Klett grinned. 'That is a story. In the Dickens book it is where a legal case was heard. Something to do with an inheritance. This case goes on and on until there is no money left in the estate so the lawyers can't get paid anymore, so the case is dismissed. I think who chose the name for the business had a sense of humour.'

'I don't see it.'

'You know, it is about... what is that English word? Ja, obfuscation. It is about making everything complicated. Chancery Court is a good business I am told. Lots of money goes through the account. But if you phone the office of Chancery Court, no one answers. The phone rings and rings in this little room they have in London.'

'And so?'

'So I thought it would be interesting for you to know this.' Rudi Klett took another swallow of whisky. 'Once you were in the business of trading arms. Your old friends now trade armaments. The money is different. There are big kickbacks. Maybe what I was doing was offering temptation to you.'

'I don't need it,' said Mace.

Rudi Klett shrugged. 'Good. Then it is academic.'

The two men fell silent, Mace thinking maybe it might have been a better option than security, to carry on selling guns. The commissions were major. He'd have had no financial worries. Not like now. The house would be paid for and no final demands from the bank for missed payments. A whole different scenario. Then again Oumou's law had been simple: her or the guns. No choice. But there were always side deals. Things she didn't need to know about.

Rudi Klett touched his arm. 'In the future, if you want to change your mind, let me know. People remember you still. Not only in your country. All over. They ask about Mace and Pylon. They want to know what you are doing. How you are. So if you have a change of heart…'

'It's not going to happen,' said Mace.

'The beautiful Oumou.'

'That's right.'

'Well, you have that saying, needs must when the devil is driving. Something like that. What I am saying is you can always be in touch.'

30

Late afternoon, Cape Town International was chaos. Drivers pulling strange manoeuvres with no warning. People crossing the approach road blind to the traffic. Manga and Spitz drove round once to get the layout, came back through the parking lot looking for an old-model Alfa Spider, not a difficult car to spot. There it was gleaming red two rows back in the first section, outside the international hall.

'Sharp car,' said Manga, driving them past to an empty bay diagonally opposite, reversing in. 'Me, personally, I'd take the new model. More vooma. Cars've moved on, the new Spider's got stuff they weren't even dreaming about when they made that one.' He switched off.

'No,' said Spitz. 'We are too close.'

'Hey, captain,' said Manga, 'what's too close? We're hidden. Five cars between us. They're not gonna see two gents sitting here. They'll come out, put their bags in the boot and drive off. Even if they see us it's two gents sitting in a car.'

'That is exactly right,' said Spitz, striking up a menthol. 'The man is security. He will check out things like that.'

Manga fired the ignition. 'Your call, captain. Where to?'

Spitz pointed down the row. 'At the bottom.'

Lying in his lap were two colour prints of Mace Bishop. Zoom detail and ink-jet prints that were not the best. But good enough. No chance of making the wrong hit. Unless he got in the way.

Manga did a three-point to get into a bay at the end of the row, the angle too steep to see the Spider. Said, 'This suit you, captain?'

'I like it.'

'Can't see bugger all.'

'There is no need for you. I have to see,' said Spitz.

They had two plans: Plan A and Plan B. Both plans based on the assumption that Mace Bishop would take his client into town.

'Have to, captain,' Manga had said. 'Obviously. Get the cousin to his hotel. The hotel's in town. Why'd they go out in the other direction?'

'It is what I would do,' Spitz had said. 'I would have another arrangement.'

'Wena, my cousin!' Manga had raised his hands in exasperation. 'You have a sad mind, captain. Sometimes you gotta trust people to act normally.'

Spitz didn't believe that but decided this time the odds were in his favour. Any doubt, Sheemina February would've said something. The woman was a jackal, quick and sly. So he went with the scheme.

Plan A happened at the first traffic light leaving the airport: Manga would draw up alongside the Spider and Spitz in the back would put one into the target as they pulled away, Manga turning left while Mace Bishop and his dead client headed straight on towards town. Might even be a couple of minutes before the Bishop guy noticed anything was wrong. Strapped in, the hit wasn't going to fall over in a hurry. The catch here was they caught the light on red.

Failing this Plan B kicked in where the road split to join the highway. The Spider would take the city ramp, Manga coming up on the inside lane, Spitz doing the job at the split. Simple 'pop and peel' in Manga's jargon.

'Now I check why you use the .22,' he'd said to Spitz when Spitz outlined the tactic. 'Causes no shit with the driver.'

Spitz'd looked at Manga as if he was a major moegoe not to have snapped on this before. A look that worked under Manga's skin. But Manga said nothing.

Spitz held up the printouts of Mace Bishop.

'Make sure you don't hit the wrong one, hey, captain,' said Manga. He kept a straight face, twisting sideways to see if this put a crack up tight-arse Spitz. It didn't.

Spitz stubbed out his menthol. 'I am going into the terminal.' He opened the car door.

'And I'm supposed to do what?' Manga's voice high-pitched. 'Wait here?'

'Yes,' said Spitz. 'You can chill, my brother' – smiling to himself at Manga running his mouth about not being an on-tap chauffeur.

'What you need is a peak cap,' Spitz said, closing the door, heading off through the warm air to the arrivals hall. Wasn't the best time for a job: the sun falling fast behind the mountain, the light fading. Another twenty minutes, half an hour he'd be shooting at a shadow. But he had other matters on his mind.

The matter on Spitz's mind was his bank balance. Finding out if Sheemina February's word was good. He believed it would be. Then again belief, Spitz knew, was about the world you hoped for, not the one you lived in.

Inside, the arrivals board told him the Lufthansa flight was down thirty-five minutes. Next ten minutes the passengers would start dribbling through.

He found an ATM, put in his bank card and entered his code. Pressed through to his current account: the balance up by ninety-five large. Meant she'd paid for Chocho's wife. A smart move. He transferred the total to an interest account, and closed the menu, withdrawing his card. Then sauntered over to the crowd waiting at the barriers, thinking, no ways Obed Chocho's wife hadn't been part of the intended target. Maybe Obed Chocho wasn't too happy but no ways she'd been collateral. What'd gone down was what the coloured chick had wanted to go down.

Spitz saw the two men: the one pushing a luggage trolley; Mace Bishop as good as his pictures, not a smile to be seen, his eyes running a sweep through the people close up against the barrier. Also noticed how his jacket snagged at his hip and the butt there of a weapon. Had to have a contact to get that through the system.

The German was talking, relaxed, no problems in the world.

Spitz followed them out the building to the parking ticket paypoints. Cleared his own ticket right after Mace Bishop paid for his. The target saying something about dinner as the two men went off.

Spitz tracked them one row to the right. Saw them stop at the Spider, Mace Bishop doing a full three sixty scope and clocking him without concern. Spitz hurried on but not too fast to cause the Bishop guy any anxiety. Ahead he saw Manga slide off the bonnet of the G-string and stand at the driver's door. The sort of movement any security was going to notice. He motioned him into the car.

Manga had the engine started when Spitz got in at the back. Spitz spitting.

'Why are you sitting up on the car?' he said. 'That was not a clever thing. Why not use a sign saying what we do.' Spitz set the Ruger on the seat and fished the silencer from his pocket: screwed the can to the barrel.

'Be cool, captain,' said Manga. 'Keep the shakes out of your hands.'

Spitz ignored this. 'He has got a gun, the security. If he fires back you might need the thirty-eight.'

'I've got it,' said Manga catching Spitz's eye in the rearview mirror.

Spitz shifted over behind the driver's seat, the gun lying easy against his thigh. He missed the airy croon of Jesse Sykes at a moment like this.

Manga edged the car forward, said, 'Come on, cousin, let's go, let's roll.' The Spider stayed parked. 'Why'sn't he moving?'

'We must just wait with patience. In the parking bay.'

'I can't see him from there, captain. I gotta be forward to see him.' Manga rolling the car back and forth like a kiddies ride at a fairground.

Spitz said, 'You are getting an audience for us.' A family group up the row, packing luggage into a SUV, staring at them.

'No problem,' said Manga, 'we're moving. Hot to trot, let's shake.'

31

The worst part, Mace knew, was stepping into the hall, all the people facing you. Aunties and uncles and kids and grannies and lovers swirling about. The moment he'd choose would be then, in the chaos. Plop. The target goes down, people scream. In those ten seconds you're walking away, crossing to the drop-and-kiss zone outside, driving off.

Typically with high-profile people he'd have Pylon in the crowd, maybe one other staffer hanging loose for safety's sake.

With Rudi Klett he was relying on low profile. Wasn't so much the risk of a hitman lurking among the aunties as the prosecutors angling up with a warrant of arrest. Snappy dressers was who he scanned the hall for as they walked into the exposure. No one stuck out but maybe it was a mistake not having backup anyhow.

He kept Rudi Klett moving, not hurrying, keeping it brisk through the families, the conference greeters, the tourist couriers and outside towards the parking ticket paypoints. Rudi Klett not letting up for a moment on Mace and Pylon joining him for dinner. Why didn't they get Pylon on the cell right now?

'In a moment,' said Mace, 'okay.' Digging in his pocket for money. Aware of a man beside him feeding change into the machine.

Rudi Klett saying, 'Oumou can come too. Why not? And Pylon's wife. We can arrange babysitters for Christa. I would like this, Mace. I would enjoy us having a good meal together. Something to make up for last night.'

The man behind them now so close Mace could smell his aftershave.

Rudi Klett saying, 'This would save Oumou preparing a supper. My first night for a long time in your city, this would be a way to celebrate old times, Mace. Not so? If the hotel restaurant is not to your recommendation, then somewhere else. Wherever you choose.'

Mace slowed to keep himself between the man and Rudi Klett until the man brushed past and away. A man without any luggage, no overnight bag, no briefcase. But a man walking away which was how Mace wanted it.

He guided Rudi Klett towards the Spider.

'No,' said Rudi Klett, seeing the car. 'I do not believe it. You have still got this car? So retro. For Mace Bishop, a '69 Spider in the new century. I do not believe it. If you had said an Alfa I would have said, yes, why not that is a good car. The 147 especially. This would suit the Mace Bishop image. The image of what you do. Security. Protection. Confidence. Fast. Sleek. Discreet. But the old Spider. Like in The Graduate. No, Mace, this is too much.'

'I prefer it,' said Mace. 'It's different.'

'There is no joking about that.'

Mace opened the boot, let Rudi Klett heft in his own luggage. Security didn't extend to valet service.

'But this is the hard top,' said Rudi Klett, drumming his fingers on the car's roof. 'For an evening such as this we should have the top down. Enjoy the warm air. The smell.'

'The petrol fumes, you mean.'

'No, Cape Town has a smell. It's own smell, like wet bushes.'

'You can smell that?'

'I remember it from before. On the mountain.' He pointed behind Mace at the peninsula mountain chain dark now against the sky. A faint light etching its outline. 'Look at the mountain so beautiful. Magnificent. Not like Berlin. In Berlin everything is old and heavy and grey. Do you feel it like that?'

'This time, especially,' said Mace. His cellphone beeped an sms. Another message from Judge Telman Visser. Mace ignored it, wondering what Rudi Klett would say if he knew the judge was a phone call away.

The men got into the car and Rudi Klett wound down his window.

'Who else still has a window winder in their car? I don't know anyone with a car this old.'

'It's a talking point.'

Mace pulled the P8 from his belt, clipped it in a holder he'd had fitted on the door. Easy to reach for, easy to bring up the gun in any hijacker's face. Shoot his nose off before he even sensed a change of play.

In this city you needed it. No point in driving around with a gun if it was stuck in the glove box or the boot. He knew people who kept their weapon in the boot. People who lost both car and gun to the hijacker. Mace would say to them: 'When you bought the gun you must've considered shooting someone? Being in a situation where you had to kill?' They'd look at him with their mouths open, horrified.

'I like it,' said Rudi Klett. 'Very comforting.'

Mace brought out his cellphone, thumbed through to Pylon. 'What time you want to make dinner?'

Rudi Klett checked his watch. 'Say eight-thirty.'

Mace nodded, Pylon answering in a tone even more pissed off than Mace had been earlier. Rattling through a list of the day's wrongs from the cop clampdown on Lindiwe's murder to the Smits pulling out in favour of Obed Chocho. Ending with Treasure being on his case about when was he coming home for supper. Sometimes, he said, he could understand why men ran away from their pregnant wives.

Mace let it wash over him, even the murder bit. 'Rudi's paying for dinner. Eight-thirty. onewaterfront. And Treasure's invited.'

Pylon groaned. 'This's going to please her. I can hear it: what's she going to wear? Where do we get a babysitter? Why's it always at the last minute.'

'Shit happens,' said Mace. 'Get one of the guys to sit. Best babysitters in the city.'

'They're employed for the celebs,' said Pylon. 'Not to mind our kids.'

'Part of the job description.'

Rudi Klett said loudly, grinning, 'This is your financial backer offering dinner, Mr Buso. Please not to mess him around.'

'Tell Klett he picks his moments,' said Pylon.

'He says you're going to land him in the crap,' Mace said to Rudi Klett.

'Occupational hazard.'

'Alright,' said Pylon. 'We'll be there.'

Mace disconnected. 'One more. To Oumou.'

She answered, light and whisky in her voice. 'You are going to say we have a dinner date with Rudi,' she said before Mace had said anything.

'I am.'

'Good. Because I have made no supper.'

'And Christa?'

'Is with Pumla. They have one of your security there to babysit.'

'That's not what Pylon told me.'

'Pylon does not know everything.'

Mace laughed. 'You and Treasure have a bet on this?'

'Of course. I know Herr Rudi Klett remember.'

Mace said she was the most wonderful woman in the world.

She said she knew that too. She also said there was a judge looking for him. Judge Telman Visser. Who'd phoned not ten minutes earlier.

When he disconnected Rudi Klett said, 'Oumou has it organised?'

'She has.' Mace put the key into the ignition and the engine fired on the turn. 'In the desert she would do things and I'd wonder why. And then four, five days later something would happen that she'd anticipated. Uncanny stuff. Like Oumou's in this different world. Past, present and future all mixed up.'

'Very useful.'

'No kidding.'

Mace reversed the Spider out of the parking bay and headed for the exit. At the bottom of the row he noticed a black car nose forward. By the time they reached the exit booms the black car filled his rearview mirror: a new-model BMW with the lights on dim, only a driver in it. And not the man he'd marked at the ticket paypoint.

Mace inserted his ticket to open the booms, drove through.

32

Manga let the Spider turn into the exit lane before he left the parking bay, driving past the family at their SUV, everyone of them giving him and Spitz the once-over.

Spitz said, 'Wave to our club of fans.'

'Don't sweat it, captain,' said Manga, turning into the exit lane, slowing for a Ford Focus to nose between them and the Spider, fifty, sixty metres ahead.

'That is okay for you is it? They see two black men in a BMW with one driving, the other in the back, they will think this is very strange?'

'They're whiteys. Whiteys think everything we do is strange. Probably think you're a cabinet minister.'

'Without any security forces? With no vehicles to back up?'

'Or new elite.'

'I can ask the same questions. White people are not stupid.'

'Most are.'

'Then you are stupid. When white people see two black men in a BM car, they think there is trouble.'

''Cos they're paranoid.'

Spitz had to laugh, the sound coming out like a bark. He pulled on his gloves.

'What'ja need those for, captain?' Manga shaking his head, frowning.

'They are how I do the job,' said Spitz.

The Spider turned towards the exit booms, and Manga nudged up close behind the Focus to move it along, muttering, 'Come on, guys. Let's roll it. Let's tap the pedal.'

The four exits were occupied, no chance of getting out at the same time as the Spider. Manga went in behind it.

'Why are you doing this?' said Spitz. 'He can see you in the mirror.'

'So what?'

'He is watching you. The man is not a fool. Later he will think about we two. He will remember the black men in the car. The one behind the other. He will give the police details.'

'What details?' The Spider eased off and Manga rolled forward, inserted his ticket into the receiver. The boom went down behind the Spider and up immediately. 'In this light. A black face wearing shades. You're not even gonna see me. And maybe you didn't notice, anyhow, gotta be about a million of those faces in this city. Captain, you're stressing.'

Which riled Spitz but he kept it down.

The Focus was ahead of them again, driving slowly. At the intersection the traffic lights on red, the Spider in the fast lane, a car in front of it. The Focus went right behind the Spider.

'Heita,' said Manga, coming up slowly on the Spider's left, giving Spitz a clear shot. Less than two metres. 'Plan A, one time.'

Spitz shifted to the centre of the seat, readied the Ruger. When they pulled opposite, he'd sight and squeeze.

The lights changed and the car ahead of the Spider fish-tailed off burning rubber. The Spider accelerating behind it, the opportunity quickly lost to pop and peel.

'Bloody bushies,' said Manga. 'A coloured gets a car he thinks he's Michael Schumacher.' He went through the gears keeping with the game, before them now a clear kilometre of two-lane feeder road to the highway on-ramps. Plan B with no complications.

Spitz said nothing, watching the Spider pull ahead in the fast lane, Manga holding steady a car's length behind and to the left, the Focus parallel to the right, a kid in the back of the Focus levelling a bright orange gun at him. The gun held sideways like the kid had seen hoods do it on CSI.

Spitz raised his left hand in surrender, the Ruger lightly in his right. The kid shot him once and ducked down.

Manga caught the movement of Spitz's hand. 'What's happening, captain?'

'There is a boy in the Focus playing that he is shooting me,' said Spitz.

Manga snorted. 'Kids see too much shit on TV. Okay, you ready for this?'

'If there was sun it would be better.'

Spitz pushed the window-down button, felt the car picking up speed, pulling ahead of the Focus, his line of sight coming onto the back of the Spider, riding to the open passenger window, the passenger turning to look at him.

'Now, captain, now,' shouted Manga, holding the car straight before swinging left, taking the gear down, putting foot, the BM coming alive with a jerk and tyre screech.

33

Rudi Klett, his window down, his arm leaning on the door, was shouting above the tyre noise, 'I came in that time, Christa was a little one, must have been when, what year, 1996?'

'She was five.' Mace checked the rearview: the Focus behind them, headlights on dim, the BMW on the inside lane, sitting squat in the blind spot of his wing mirror.

'Louder.'

Mace thinking this was crazy, having to shout at one another. He held up a hand, showed Rudi Klett five fingers barely visible in the gloom. 'Five years old. Maybe we should wind up the windows, switch the aircon on?'

Rudi Klett shook his head, not put off at having to shout. 'Wait one minute.' Taking deep breaths. 'Still the same smell.'

Mace thought, you've got to be kidding.

'In '96, there was a wonderful feeling with everyone. So much excitement and promise of building houses so that no one lived in a shack anymore.'

'Didn't happen as you'll soon see,' said Mace.

'Some of the big boys saying, no what did they want with a navy and jet fighters? Who was going to invade South Africa? So I have to tell them this is an uncertain world of course you must have an insurance policy. You don't know what is going to happen. The wise man has cover. A good thing the Old Man listens to what I'm saying. The message is passed on and even the critics change their tune. Everybody sees the light. Hallelujah.'

Mace pointed ahead at the on-ramp to the highway. 'We go up on that curve and you'll see squatter land. Some of them double storey. Double-storey tin shacks!'

'Ah so.' Rudi Klett turned his head at the sound of a car coming up on the left.

Mace bellowing, 'I've been in some of them. You get inside and its Home and Décor, what the magazines are calling township chic. Unbelievable.' He sensed the BM taking the off-ramp east, caught a flash of its headlights in the wing mirror. 'Only problem is fires.' He pointed again at the squatter shacks below. 'There's a fire in that lot, the fire fighters haven't got a chance of getting the engines there. Every time a candle blows over, there's a fire. People burn. Not the sort of death you'd want.'

Coming off the approach, Mace lined up the Spider to merge between two long-haul juggernauts, the noise deafening, the traffic on the highway fast and free. He clocked in at one twenty, tiny between the rigs, the chrome radiator of the Mack behind on his bumper. Not a situation Mace relished. In his right wing he watched minibus taxis belting up and go booming past, and squeezed more juice from the Spider, throwing it right to overtake the front truck, the needle climbing to one thirty, thirty-five, the Spider beginning to feel light on the road. Mace kept it steady in the drum and tear of the road roar, lights flicking at him from behind, the Spider hauling past the horse and trailer. Then he was ahead, the noise receding.

'Wind up your window,' he shouted, winding up his own. 'It's crazy out there.' When Rudi Klett made no move, Mace glanced at him to see Rudi Klett leaning away, his head slumped forward. 'Hey, Rudi.' He tugged at him. 'What's the matter. Wind up your window.' The body of Rudi Klett flopped towards him, only checked by the safety belt.

Mace saw the blood then. Not much, a small red stain above the pocket of Rudi Klett's golf shirt.

'Rudi. Jesus Christ. Rudi talk to me. Stay with me.' Mace groped for Rudi Klett's wrist and found a pulse still fluttering there. He pushed the Spider back up to one thirty, thinking he could make the nearest hospital in maybe ten minutes or stop and check out the wound? Deciding on the hospital, telling Rudi Klett to hang in that he'd get to medics in no time flat. Then phoned Pylon.

'How'm I supposed to understand this woman?' was Pylon's opening.

Mace said, 'Klett's been shot.'

A beat, then: 'What?' Then: 'Dead?'

'There's a pulse,' said Mace.

'Where're you?'

'Coming up to the cooling towers. Heading for Groote Schuur.'

'What's it?' Pylon said.

'Head shot. Left side. Don't know where exactly or how bad. Not much blood though.'

He heard Pylon blow out breath. 'I'll phone it in. Just get there. Fast.'

Mace disconnected, felt again for Rudi Klett's pulse and pressed down his fingers to find a faint throb. 'Rudi,' he shouted. 'Rudi, can you hear me?' Getting no response, keeping his eyes on the traffic thickening now with flows coming in from Bridgetown and Athlone. He rode the needle higher, seeing the temperature climb too with the speed. All he needed now was the radiator to blow.

Mace eased the accelerator back to one twenty over the Black River rise, planning to make his break left across the lanes at the last moment. His cell rang: Pylon. Mace keyed on the hands-free, said, 'I'm in the corner towards the Parkway bridge. What's that two minutes if I run the lights?'

'Run the lights,' said Pylon. 'They're waiting. Klett still with us?'

'Hanging in I hope.'

'Talking?'

'Not a chance. Can't hear his breathing, shallow pulse. I'm going over the bridge. Jesus, the bastards won't let me across.' Mace flicking his lights, leaning on his hooter.

Under the noise he heard Pylon say, 'I told them he's a German VIP caught a stray bullet down the N2. Nobody's fazed. Medics say it happens all the time.'

'Keep with me,' said Mace, taking a gap between two cars onto the hard shoulder to pass inside a surfer's rust-bucket kombi and onto the off-ramp.

Pylon saying, 'I'm staying right here.'

'Light's red,' said Mace and came up right of the cars stopped at the intersection, swinging right again into the traffic. Caused a bewildered moment and a cacophony, hooters and brakes and one bang of a collision. 'I'm through,' he said.

'Sounds bad,' said Pylon.

'Running the next red,' said Mace, this time with a clear passage down the wrong side of the street. He pushed the Spider against maximum revs through the next light, braking hard at the hospital entrance. 'Here now.'

'With you in ten,' said Pylon.

Mace chased an ambulance to Casualty, squealing in behind it. Even before he was switched off, medics had the passenger door open, were unstrapping Rudi Klett and dragging him out on to a gurney.

Mace and Pylon sat in a reception room down from the operating theatres. The prognosis on Rudi Klett not sunny. His condition critical, a bullet stuck behind his ear.

Mace phoned Oumou.

'I'm alright,' he told her, comforted by the anxiety in her voice. 'Just a bit hyper.'

She told him he needed coffee. With sugar. Lots of sugar.

'Here?' He laughed. 'You don't get coffee here. They call it that but it's not.' Again he assured her that he was fine.

'I am not hearing this in your voice,' she said. 'I can hear something different.'

He didn't respond.

'Mace,' Oumou said. 'Cheri, are you with Pylon?'

'Sure. He's here,' said Mace, feeling suddenly fatigued. Thinking the Rudi Klett jaunt had been bad news all round. Thinking this was exactly the sort of reason to get out of guarding. Who needed this in his life?

'Then what is the matter?'

'I don't know,' said Mace. 'I don't know what happened. One minute we're talking the next he's shot. I can't understand it. No one knew he was coming.'

'This is shock,' said Oumou.

Mace snorted. 'Klett's not the first person been shot next to me. This's not shock, Oumou, this is worry. That I buggered up a simple job.'

'No. That is wrong. This is bad luck.'

'I don't know. A stray bullet's pushing bad luck.'

'It is possible. From a person shooting out of the squatter shacks.'

'Maybe, maybe not. The doctors believe it.'

'You are tired, no?' She paused.

Mace didn't deny it.

'Why don't you leave it to Pylon? Come home. I will fetch Christa from Treasure's.'

'There's stuff we've got to sort out. Security arrangements.'

'This is what he can do.'

'I'll see,' said Mace. 'I'll call you later.'

'In an hour. Or we will fetch you.'

Mace smiled, disconnecting. He liked the idea she was concerned. His phone rang: Judge Telman Visser's name on the screen. Mace clicked him to voicemail.

At a dispensing machine in the corridor he bought two cans of Coke and lifted five sachets of sugar from a holder on a tray with teabags and a jar of instant coffee. He tore the ends off the sachets one at a time, poured the contents into his mouth, crunching the granules. Washed the last one down with a mouthful of Coke. The other can he took to Pylon in the reception room.

Pylon, finished talking to a doctor, said, 'He reckons it's dicey.'

'They get the bullet?'

'Yeah. No sweat the doc said.' Pylon pulled the ring on the can. 'Found it lying there right behind his ear. That wasn't the hard part.' He sipped at the Coke. 'The hard part's stabilising him. The doc says a lot of brain damage.'

Mace nodded. 'The bullet ran around? Went in the top and down.'

'Probably a light calibre.'

'I'd say, if it's a hit.'

They sat down on plastic chairs opposite the theatre door.

'But it doesn't have to be. Something coming over from the township would've gone in like that. Bounced around his skull.'

Mace finished his Coke. 'A tired bullet.'

'Why not?'

'No reason why not. Any other time I'd say probably. Except the man in there is Rudi Klett.'

'Problemo,' said Pylon.

They sat in silence until Pylon said he'd arranged for security. Two of their best guys. And went quiet again until Mace said, 'Klett was weird in Berlin' and told Pylon of the business with Herr Dr Konrad Schultz.

'Like I'm standing there thinking what am I doing here with you? He's going in to plug the Herr Dr from the start. So why am I along for this? He tells me so I can see the sort of commissions being paid traders these days. What's that about? We're out of that shit.'

Pylon said, 'Klett's a dealer.'

'No kidding. He's got some government commission on his arse. He's got the big politicos anxious that he's got stuff on them. Top government, he tells me. The last place on earth he wants to be is here. People are out for him. He's travelling under a different name. So what's he here for, I want to know? Not to put his signature on some small-change land deal.'

'Hundred million's not small change.'

'The sort of figures Klett talks, it's small change, believe me. Klett's into something else. Someone else knew he was going to be here. What flight. Who he was with. All the little details.'

'Scary.'

'Damn right.'

Mace got their empty cans and walked across the room to dump them in a bin. What he wanted was to go home, take a shower, lie down on the cool sheets of his bed and get Oumou to massage the hard knots in his shoulders. What he didn't want was to be sitting in the bright fluorescent light waiting to hear if Rudi Klett was dead yet.

Pylon said, 'Best to get a story to the paper.'

'Saying what?'

'Tourist survives stray bullet.'

'Assuming he does?'

'Either way, doesn't matter. It was a hit, someone's going to rock up asking about the tourist. The man wants his payment, he has to have Rudi Klett dead.' Pylon toyed with his cellphone.

'You do it,' said Mace. 'I'm going home.'

'There's other stuff,' Pylon said.

'Like what stuff?'

'Like Popo Dlamini. Lindiwe Chocho.'

Mace rubbed his hand over his face. 'Tomorrow, okay. I've got to crash.'

Pylon put a hand on Mace's shoulder. 'And some good news.'

'Such as?'

'Such as your case with the American couple is off. According to the captain.'

'What?' Mace stared at his partner. 'For real?'

'Yeah, for real. Both of them dead. She trying to escape. He in a prison gang thing.'

Mace let out a long whoosh of breath. 'Wonder of wonders. There's a relief.' Gave Pylon a wide grin. 'You could've let me know earlier.'

'I meant to. Except stuff kept happening.'

Mace came out of the hospital into the warm darkness carrying the stench of antiseptic on his clothes. The smell embedded in his nostrils. Wasn't for Rudi, he'd sing.

He opened his car door, thinking, shit, he hadn't locked it. Felt down the side for the clip where he'd attached the P8, his fingers sliding lightly over the metal. Out loud he thanked the gods. He checked the boot: the bags untouched. Had to be some kind of miracle.

Getting in behind the wheel, Mace noticed a smear of blood across the passenger seat: a faint glisten from the arc light in the parking lot.

'Bloody Rudi Klett.' Everywhere he went, afterwards there was blood.

The end of the world as we know it. Mace shook his head as if to dislodge the lyrics still on their endless loop through his mind.

The Spider fired at the turn and Mace drove up the dark street beside the hospital taking the slip road onto the highway. This hour of a Monday night the traffic into the city moving light and fast. On the bend he lined up for the De Waal Drive split, tapping a devil's tattoo on the steering wheel.

If it was a hit, it'd been a long time coming. If it was a hit, some seriously strange links must've played out behind the scenes. The sort of linkages that worried Mace. Meant they'd have to jack up security, for sure. Sweep their offices. Their homes. Check out the staff profiles. Heavy stuff that made him sigh.

He kept the Spider to the speed limit, drifting easily through the curves, the city bright below him, the mountain dark above.

If Rudi Klett stayed alive and the morning news touched the hitman where it hurt most, all kinds of shit could unravel in the coming days. Nothing Pylon couldn't handle. Alone. Mace smiled at the thought of Pylon taking this news.

Because why? Because after the crap Rudi Klett had dealt him,

Mace believed he deserved chill time. Like a few days on a farm. So he'd tell the judge he'd drive up on Friday. And would be taking Christa. Whatever the judge's problem was of having Christa along, the judge would have to lump it. For Chrissakes he was doing him a favour.

Roads opening up. Long scrub vistas. Huge skies. The idea of doing some serious Karoo travelling was appealing. Top down through the small towns. It would be a gas. And Christa with him.

This lightened his mood. Had him making a tuneless whistle up Orange along the back of the reservoir to Molteno, at the top into Glencoe coming slowly to his gate. Fifty metres off Mace pressed the remote, watched the gate roll back and stop halfway. There'd been little problems with the mechanism over the two years they'd had it. Like the chain rode off the ratchets, it could be a pain in the arse. He stopped and got out, left the car idling.

The two men came at him from the shadows, almost hesitant, the one whispering something, even sounded like his name. Mace turned at the movement, starting a pace towards them. The one held a knife, carrying it low against his thigh. The other an automatic. The one with the knife doing the whispering, telling him to lie down.

Mace said, 'No, china, you got the wrong corpse.'

The gunman screamed at him, 'Down, down, down' – jamming the pistol in his ear. A quick movement, sharp and trained.

'Make like he says, my bru,' said the whisperer, not getting any closer. 'No shit, no grit. Pellie's dangerous.'

Mace smelt booze breath and the stench of sweat on the gunman, a big black with a web of veins in his eyewhites. One eye swollen.

'Relax, guys, okay.' He kept his eyes on the knife-wielder though, this one coloured, thin and jumpy. A twitch in his cheek.

'Everyone's loose, my bru. Except you.'

Mace schemed, a roll to the car door, come up with the H&K, he could take them.

Knowing if Oumou didn't hear the alarm bleep for the garage door opening, she'd come out. The last thing he wanted. Only problem: the gap to the car was major, he wouldn't make it fast enough. He took a pace forwards.

The big black hit him. A short punch with the gun, slamming it hard into Mace's head. Mace going down on his knees, putting out a hand to stop from falling over. The big black following with a kick between the shoulder blades that sprawled Mace on the cobble paving.

The coloured jumped him then, landing on his back. 'See, my bru, comply or die' – pricking the knifepoint at Mace's neck. At the cord of his artery. 'Make nice and we's away.' The coloured laughed, running his free hand into Mace's pockets coming up with a wallet of credit cards, a clip of notes. 'There's a good larney giving to the poor and needy.' The coloured patting him down for a money belt, saying, 'Where's the cell, my bru? You talk, we walk.' Saying to the black, 'Check the car.'

Mace, tasted blood, his head pushed hard against the cobbles, watched the black lean into the Spider. Heard him mutter in Xhosa.

The coloured cut in: 'Hey, English, my bru, talk a language.'

The black said, 'Nokia 3410.'

The coloured shifted, kneeling on Mace, digging the knifepoint into Mace's neck until the skin broke, blood beading at the cut. Mace tensed.

'Larney, larney, larney. My bru that is a cheap phone. For a Mr Gentleman up here onna mountain, you behind the times. A small-change man.'

The coloured stood.

'But we's grateful for a contribution. My pellie and me. So we's gonna say goodnight my larney but first we wanna see you crawl like a motormac. Underneath the car, hey, my bru. Poke inna engine.'

Mace spat blood, said, 'You're dead, chinas. Both of you.'

The coloured snapped back. 'Don't tune me grief, my larney.' And sliced quickly to open skin behind Mace's ear.

Mace pushed up at the pain. The men kicking him down, kicking him while he slithered leopard-crawl under the Spider, the exhaust pipe burning across his back. When the kicks stopped, Mace heard the men laughing, heard them running off onto the mountain. For a moment he lay there, eyes closed, smelling hot oil and burnt flesh.

Mace, more troubled than angry, sat on the edge of the bath, showered, a towel wrapped round his waist, Oumou swabbing an antiseptic solution into his cuts and scratches.

'It's the Klett bullshit,' he said. 'Has to be. Got me freaked out. It's scary.' He paused. 'It's why I fell for the trick. I'm not thinking straight. I'm distracted. Two arsehole rubbishes pull a stunt like that and I fall for it. The story I warn everyone about. I don't even consider this is what's happening to me' – flinching as Oumou smeared ointment on the burn across his back.

'I tell people, the gate gets stuck someone's jammed the track. All it takes is a stone. So sit tight. Drive off. Don't get out the car. What do I do? I get out of the car and some useless piece of shit puts a gun in my ear. Eina.' He pulled back.

Oumou squeezed his arm. 'You must keep still.'

'Being sliced's not as sore.'

'Of course because it is macho.' She dabbed at the cut behind his ear. 'This one is deeper. Maybe you need a doctor for a stitch?'

'Not at this time of night. Pinch it closed. Tape it.'

'This is macho.'

'Hey,' he turned and slid his hands round her, linking his fingers above the swell of her bum. 'What's with the lip?' Opened her wrap and caressed her belly with his cheeks, the rasp of stubble loud in his ear.

Oumou took his head in her hands. 'Mon copain,' she said, 'so many times I have seen you dripping with your blood. Always it frightens me.'

Mace stood, pulled loose the fold of the wrap above Oumou's breasts, and held her.

'This is like it was in Malitia,' she said. 'Any time we could be dead. Even our home is not safe.'

Mace knew it, knew there were no words to reassure her differently. Knew he'd been suckered like a tourist. Mr Security made out a prick. He held Oumou to quiet a surge of anger and stepped out of the bath, walking her to the bed, the two of them falling in a tangle of limbs.

Tuesday

34

In the night the wind came up. Dawn, the city woke to a cloth low on the mountain, grit in the air, an incessant howl across the houses and through the streets.

Mace took an early walk on the scrub slopes opposite his house, leaning into the wind that poured over Devil's Peak, scoured the amphitheatre. Behind a rock not two hundred metres away he found his wallet, driving licence, credit cards scattered about. Small compensation.

He crouched there out of the wind, sheltered by the rock. Noticed then the bottle neck that'd been a white pipe. Stubbed out cigarette butts. A half-jack of brandy.

They'd sat there he realised and watched him. Watched him crawl out from under the car, remove the stone, drive into the garage. Watched the gates roll closed, the garage door come down. Two men armed with guns and a knife watching his house from this rock.

Two men who'd crushed Mandrax tablets into a stash of dagga, lit the white pipe, passed it between them while Oumou was cleaning his cuts and bruises. Mace touched the tenderness on his cheek where he'd been hit. Grimaced at the pain.

All that time they'd sat here: finished the pipe, drunk a half of brandy, smoked cigarettes. Sitting here in the dark above the city like all was right with the world.

Two more thugs wild on the mountain. Like the mugger rolling tourists up on the plateau. Fourteen hits in two weeks. Someday vigilantes would do something about it. Hurl the bastard down Skeleton Gorge. Shoot him. Stash his body in an old mine shaft. Time was coming someone would start justice for the people.

He looked down at his house: he could see Christa swimming lengths, the movement of Oumou in the kitchen. Maybe the men had been here for days, watching. Mace clenched the wallet in his fist. It was all too easy: the trusting carelessness of people's suburban lives.

He shifted his gaze to the city and out across the northern urban sprawl. In the hospital lay Rudi Klett shot in the head. Somewhere was the man who'd shot him. And somewhere, probably under a bridge or a flyover, were the two men with his cellphone and his small change. Luckily they'd missed the P8 Rudi Klett had thought would take care of all contenders.

Mace sighed. Sometimes it didn't matter how careful you'd been, you hadn't been careful enough.

He walked down the slope, entered the house through the garage. In the kitchen Oumou was talking on the landline mobile.

'One moment, he is here,' she said, covering the mouthpiece. To Mace she said, 'He says he is a judge. Yesterday he phoned as well.'

Mace took the phone.

'You're a difficult man to get hold of,' said Judge Telman Visser. 'I have left voice messages and smses on your cellphone. I have left messages with your daughter and your wife and your colleague. I have expressed an urgency. But you haven't phoned me back.'

'My cellphone was stolen,' said Mace. 'I was mugged.'

'Hardly a good advert. Were you hurt?'

'Cuts and bruises.'

'I'm sorry.' The judge paused. 'The thing is this, Mr Bishop. I need to confirm your visit to the farm.'

'I'll have to get back to you on that,' said Mace.

'You will be able to go?'

'I'm not sure.'

The judge hesitated. 'I see. I thought it was arranged…'

'Ninety-five per cent.'

'And now?'

'Maybe sixty per cent.' Mace grinned at a frowning Oumou, enjoying stringing out the judge.

'Mr Bishop, please, it needs to be this weekend for a number of reasons. I can't postpone it. It has become even more urgent.'

'Judge,' said Mace. 'I'll get back to you. This afternoon.'

'Please, Mr Bishop,' said the judge. 'I'm counting on you.'

Mace wondered what the reasons were. What since Saturday had ratcheted the trip up a notch? But he had other things on his mind: Rudi Klett being primary.

After the judge had rung off, Mace phoned the hospital. No change in Rudi Klett's condition: critical but stable. He got hold of Pylon next, his partner already driving into Dunkley Square.

'We've got to talk,' said Pylon.

'Later,' said Mace. 'I need an hour's swim.'

'Uh uh. No, Mace. We must talk first. This is major stuff. Like there's something going on.'

Mace walked onto the patio outside the kitchen, watched his

daughter climb out of the pool, lithe, supple, snatching off her swimming cap, shaking free her hair. When'd she changed from the child who'd been chubbier?

'Give me half an hour,' he said to Pylon, turned back to Oumou in the kitchen. 'Last night,' he said, 'after we'd spoken, you went to Treasure to fetch Christa didn't you?'

'Oui.' Oumou bit the end off a croissant. 'It took half an hour that was all.' She poured Mace coffee, held out a plate of croissants. 'By quarter past eight we were at home.'

'It's dark now by quarter past eight,' said Mace. 'They could've got you.'

'Who is this?' Oumou swallowed, licked the butteriness off her fingers.

Mace looked at her. 'The men who got me. They could've got you and Christa.'

Oumou gave a Gallic shrug. 'This is true.'

'Last night you weren't so relaxed.'

'What can we do? Tell me? What is another way? From Malitia we run to Cape Town for the safety?' She came over to Mace, took his hand. 'There is nowhere to run now. This is how people live in the world. In many of the places in the world. We can live here with it.'

'I don't know,' said Mace. He looked over at Christa drying herself on the edge of the pool. Unconcerned about the whip of the wind.

Oumou let go of his hand. 'All that we can do is to be careful.'

Famous last words, thought Mace. Said, 'Sometimes it doesn't help.'

He dropped Christa off at school, Christa wanting to know all the way there about the bruise on his cheek, the plaster keeping closed the slice on his neck. At first Mace joked about walking into doors, shaving nicks, even slipping on a cake of soap in the shower.

Christa said, 'Yeah, right' – scratching about in her bag, not paying him that much attention.

'You don't believe me?'

She shook her head, her hair swirling.

'The truth?'

'Papa,' she said, 'your truth'll be another story. I know.'

'I was mugged.'

Christa stopped the bag search. Turned to her father. 'In Berlin?'

Mace loved the look of concern. The frown, the clear worry in her eyes. He opted for more of the truth. 'At our front gate, last night, by two men.'

She gasped. 'With a knife?'

'And a gun. But it's okay, alright, C. Just a random thing because I should've known. When the gate doesn't slide you know there's a problem. I should've realised there was a problem. I wasn't thinking. So, a wake-up call for all of us.' He reached over and squeezed her arm. 'No panic.'

Mace pulled up at the school but Christa made no move to get out of the car. 'I want to learn to shoot a gun,' she said.

'That's what it's come to,' Mace said to Pylon ten minutes later, sitting opposite him at the long table in what they half-jokingly called their boardroom. He'd set the context, described his mugging. 'She wants a gun. My daughter wants to shoot. Shooting means killing.'

'She wouldn't've thought about that.'

'Maybe. Maybe not.'

'A kid says that after what you've told her, she hasn't thought about it. She hasn't had a chance to think about it. She's just saying it. Pumla says things like that all the time. One day she saw my gun, the first thing she said was "Cool, can I shoot it?" Treasure goes ballistic. What'm I doing bringing guns into the house. Letting Pumla see it. Whadda, whadda, whadda. This is my

179

job, I say. I have to carry a gun. Nothing new here but Treasure plays the gun-free card. Fewer guns, less crime. I don't go near that argument. Pumla's listening to all this. A couple of hours later she comes to me, she wants to see the gun. I show it to her on the promise she doesn't tell her mother. Afterwards, that's it, the gun doesn't come up again. I'm talking about probably a year ago when this happened. What I'm saying is kids don't think. Stuff happens in the moment and then it's gone.'

'I don't know,' said Mace. 'It's more like they store it away.'

Pylon slid a copy of the morning paper across the table to Mace, folded back to the page three story on Rudi Klett, named as Wolfgang Schneider. Not a long story but enough to let the shooter know that his job needed finishing.

'It's going to cause some trouble somewhere,' said Pylon.

'They might sit it out.'

'I don't think so. What I think,' said Pylon, 'is that Obed Chocho's riding this. I've been putting the pieces together.'

Mace gazed out the window at the small yard behind the house, Tami, sheltering from the wind in a corner taking a smoke break. 'I thought Tami didn't smoke.'

'She doesn't,' said Pylon, leaning back to look. When he saw her smoking he opened the window. 'That'll kill you.'

'I'm giving up,' Tami said.

'By smoking?'

'My last day. Okay?'

Pylon closed the window. 'I better get Treasure onto her.' He turned back to Mace. 'Look.' Then started at the Popo/Lindiwe affair: how Popo must've told Obed Chocho about Rudi Klett causing Obed Chocho to order up a hit on the German to secure the development contract also do some government people a favour then thinking why stop at that when he could also get Popo out of his life, and, by accident or design it didn't matter which, took out Lindiwe too. Which would have repercussions with Lindiwe's family who wouldn't read it as anything other than a jealous husband's revenge and want compensation. But Obed Chocho was a man of resources and would handle that too. It all stood to reason. Why else, said Pylon, had the Smits defected to the Chocho camp? Why had the police closed the file on the Popo/Lindiwe killing? Why was a .22 gun used in both hits if it wasn't by the same shooter? That calibre not generally what your street-hired gunmen favoured.

'Doesn't explain,' said Mace, 'how a hitman would've known who Rudi Klett was?'

'Maybe he didn't have to,' said Pylon. 'Maybe all he had to know was what you looked like.'

'Assuming all along that you knew where I'd gone to in the world. And who was coming back with me.'

'Assuming,' said Pylon. 'That's the missing bit.' He stood and went to the window. Tami was no longer in the back yard. 'I heard too Obed Chocho's out on compassionate parole. He's laughing. His bid'll go through the process faster than the pages can be stamped.'

Mace thought, so much for that million-buck nest egg.

'What stinks is I can't see how to touch him.'

'Get his cellphone records.'

'I thought about that.'

'And?'

'It's happening.'

'Watch Rudi Klett.'

'I'm going to do that,' said Pylon. 'Right now. Coming?'

Mace shook his head. 'I've got things to do. Get a new cellphone. Go swimming.'

35

Obed Chocho smacked the newspaper with the flat of his hand. Held it in Spitz's face. Spitz giving the full eye to Sheemina February. The woman as stunning as her voice. Sheemina February staring back at him unfazed.

'He is not dead.'

Spitz took the newspaper and read the report about Wolfgang Schneider's critical condition.

'He is going to be dead in a short while.'

'He is,' said Obed Chocho. 'Because you're going back to make sure.'

'It would be better to wait.'

'Wait!' Obed Chocho looked from Sheemina February to Manga and back to Spitz. Sheemina February might've smiled, that slight derisive twitch of her lips. Manga seemed to be sucking a lemon by the sour purse of his lips. Spitz, though, Spitz wasn't troubled, dropping the newspaper onto a chair as if there was no big deal about this stuff-up. As if he wasn't talking to the husband of the woman he'd shot. Obed Chocho burst out again. 'Wait? What d'you mean, wait?'

Spitz took a step back from Obed Chocho's spit range. 'Later today, otherwise tomorrow, he will die.'

'Oh, mighty fine, my brother. You can lie here drinking my beer while you wait. Take a break. Maybe go for a swim. Ask the servants to bring out a plate of chicken nuggets for lunch. Mighty fine. Enjoy yourself, mighty fine.'

Spitz wondered why he'd let himself be dragged into this. With a type like Obed Chocho. Someone as unhinged as this man. Sweating even when there was no heat to sweat in. When the wind was blowing crazily.

'This afternoon,' said Obed Chocho, 'if he is still alive I want him dead.'

'That will be difficult,' said Spitz, catching Manga's worried frown as he said it, and Sheemina February's dancing eyes. 'It is against my methods.'

'Hey, my brother!' said Obed Chocho. 'Do I hear you correctly? It is against your methods. To pull a trigger, that is your methods? So, mighty fine, that is what you will do.'

'No.' Spitz shook his head. 'Not in a hospital. There are too many dangers.'

'You're afraid?'

'Of course.'

'The great Spitz-the-Trigger is afraid?'

'Let me explain. In that situation if I am caught, you are caught,' said Spitz. 'The first thing I will tell the police is Obed Chocho has ordered the job.'

Obed Chocho barked a laugh. 'Mighty fine. Your word over mine, my brother?'

'I have some evidence.'

'What evidence?'

'I have telephone calls recorded.'

'That wasn't a good idea, Spitz,' said Sheemina February.

Spitz focused on her. 'There is always an insurance policy. You will have one too I am sure.'

Manga shifted his weight from foot to foot and Spitz noticed the movement but kept his eyes on Sheemina February. He felt she was still playing with him. Enjoying the game if the amusement on her face meant anything.

'Alright,' said Spitz. 'At four o'clock I will phone the hospital. If the man is not dead we will take some action.'

'It better happen,' said Obed Chocho. 'Otherwise no payment, my brother.'

'And for Saturday?' said Manga, his voice sounding like a little boy's.

'One thing at a time,' said Sheemina February.

At five o'clock Spitz and Manga drove into the hospital parking lot. Manga found a bay two rows back from the entrance with the view across the Flats to the mountains of False Bay. Salt hazing the distance. He lowered the chair back a few notches, and switched on the radio to some larney-voiced sports jockey gabbing about cricket. Manga hated cricket.

'All yours, captain,' he said. 'Work your magic.'

'What you have to understand,' said Spitz, not moving, 'is why we are staying at his house.'

'Why's that?' Manga turned off the know-all on the radio.

'Because he is worried he will be killed. He is afraid his wife's family will send someone to shoot him. We are there as his bodyguards.'

Manga considered this. 'Nah ways. Which of us is gonna stop a bullet for him? Not me, captain.'

'And not me either.'

'So?'

'I am saying this is the way his mind thinks.'

'Isn't gonna happen. Someone wants to shoot the shit outta Obed Chocho I'll let them.'

'Perhaps it will not be so easy when there are crossfire bullets,' said Spitz. He got out of the car, the wind whipping the door from his grasp, smacking it into the next vehicle, scoring a blue scratch across the paintwork. Spitz jerked the door free and leaned in to retrieve a small overnight bag.

'Ah shit,' said Manga. 'Those people come back and see damage, it's obvious who did it.' He fired the engine once Spitz slammed the door closed. As he pulled off Manga lowered his window. 'Hey, captain. Have fun. Don't shoot any nurses, we need them.'

Spitz stared at him blank faced. 'Where are you going?'

'Over there,' said Manga, pointing at an empty bay.

'No stupid tricks,' said Spitz, turning towards the hospital entrance. He carried the bag in his left hand, leaned into the wind that buffeted off the building. At the reception desk he asked for a Mr Schneider in intensive care, indicating the bag, telling the receptionist they were the man's personal effects.

'You can't go into ICU,' said the receptionist.

'I understand,' said Spitz. 'I have been asked to leave these with the ward sister in charge.'

'We'll get them to her, sir.'

'No, I must do it. At the request of the embassy.' He dug in his jacket pocket, brought out a wallet as if to show some identity, lay this on the counter beneath his hand. 'I will not be a moment.'

People were queuing behind him, someone pushing at his elbow, saying, 'Excuse me, please this is urgent, please'. The receptionist gave in, told Spitz, up in the lift to the second floor, then right down the corridor, left at the end. At the doors ring for a nurse.

Spitz gave a nod, walked towards the bank of lifts, a man not in a hurry, the heels of his brogues clicking on the linoleum flooring. He waited with six others: two elderly people holding onto one another, a mother and child, a young woman carrying flowers, a man about his own age in a dressing gown with a bandage swathing his head.

The lift doors opened, a group of people got out, visitors mostly except for a man on crutches. He greeted the man with the bandaged head, Spitz skirting round the two to enter the lift. He caught their exchange: the man with the bandage saying there was nowhere to smoke where the wind wasn't howling.

The doors closed. At the first floor the mother and child got out, standing in the foyer bewildered. The elderly woman said, 'The clinic's down the corridor, if you're looking for it?' 'On the right,' added her husband. The mother turned right, not acknowledging the advice. 'How rude,' said the elderly woman. The man with the bandage sniggered.

At the second floor only Spitz stepped out, not hesitating,

heading right as the receptionist had told him. He heard the lift doors close. A sign indicated the direction to the intensive care unit.

The corridor was about fifty metres long: empty except for two aides pushing a gurney coming towards him. Spitz stood aside, nodding, as they passed, the woman on the gurney looked more dead than alive.

He went to the corner, turned into a reception area. Spitz had hoped for a more cautious approach, an opportunity to check out the situation. He hesitated. The only people here were two men. Security written large all over them. They sat on chairs facing the ICU doors, the one playing games on his cellphone; the other plugged into an iPod, flipping through a magazine. Spitz took a seat opposite them, settling the bag on his lap.

The man listening to the music took the iPod from his shirt pocket, switched it off. Spitz noticed a blue iPod like the one he'd lost. The man said, 'You've got to ring the bell.'

'It is fine,' said Spitz. 'They told me to wait here.'

The security shrugged, went back to his music. Spitz heard the opening thrum of 'When A Man Comes Around', thought it had to be his iPod. Who was this guy?

36

Judge Telman Visser sat in his chambers staring out across the Company Gardens at parliament. Above the city, cloud poured over the face of the mountain. The noise of the wind rattled in the building. After thirty years in Cape Town, the wind still tore at his nerves. Had torn at his nerves all day.

On the screen of his laptop an email from Sheemina February. A short, courteous one-liner thanking him for being so understanding in signing the parole release. An email timed an hour earlier at five fifteen.

Not many attorneys were this polite. Not any attorneys in his experience.

He'd heard more tales of her reputation during the day, intriguing anecdotes.

What she was doing with Obed Chocho was the question. Or rather, perhaps, what Obed Chocho was doing with her.

But her email was only a distraction. Not having heard from Mace Bishop weighed most with Judge Telman Visser. Settling Bishop's trip to the farm for the weekend ate at his nerves more than the wind. He tapped his cellphone against the arm of his wheelchair. To phone the man would be wrong. Tactically wrong. Obsessive even. It might decide Bishop that he was dealing with a neurotic and that might cool him. The last thing Judge Visser wanted was tracking down another security consultant this late. Too much hassle. Bishop had been recommended, Bishop was the man.

'Do you have the balls, Telman,' he asked himself aloud. 'To wait fifteen, sixteen hours.'

Waiting was what lawyers were trained for. He could wait but it would not be easy. He needed amusement. He flicked through his cellphone contacts to the name of his personal trainer.

'I know this is late,' he said when the young man answered, 'but could you fit me in at, say, seven. For a quick session.'

The young man said sure but the judge heard the reluctance in his voice. He needed sweetening.

'I'd appreciate it. And, oh, how about supper afterwards? On me.'

That changed the tone of the young man's response.

At least it will keep my mind on other things, thought the judge. And might even be pleasurable. With a thin smile Judge Telman Visser deleted Sheemina February's email, closed the laptop. A pretty face was what he needed most at the moment.

Wednesday

37

Pylon hung up on his fingerprint contact, said to Mace, 'No match.' He dangled the iPod by the headphone wires. 'Apart from mine, one other set of prints.'

'We could do a door to door.'

'We could.'

'But what's in it?'

'Nothing really. Somebody may get a lost iPod back.'

'Exactly. And if somebody's lost it they've probably bought another one already. Claimed on insurance.'

'So why bother?'

'Other hand, the cops might've picked up the fingerprints inside.'

'Except they've closed the case.'

'And even if there was a match all you can say is the killer liked some heartbreak music.' Mace got up from the couch and stretched. 'I should've done a beach swim, if it wasn't for the wind. Now I need coffee.'

'Tami can make it.'

Mace turned at the doorway. 'She's not here to get us coffees.'

'I made for her yesterday.'

'Big deal.'

The two men stared at one another, Pylon conceding defeat. 'Mlungu liberal bullshit. This sort of attitude's destroying our culture.' He came round his desk still swinging the iPod, his mind moved on to the Popo Dlamini case. 'You can imagine being a cop. Facing all these sort of dead ends.'

'Give it to that PI with the long hair. Let him figure it out.'

'Mullet Mendes?'

'Why not?'

'Mullet's too smoked up.'

They went downstairs and into the kitchen. Mace took coffee from the cupboard, unscrewed the Bialetti, knocking the grounds into a rubbish bin. He filled the base with water, tamped down the French roast in the filter basket, screwing the parts together again.

Pylon put his nose in the air like a dog, sniffing. 'What's that smell? Save me Jesus! It's bloody cigarette smoke.' He shouted down the passage. 'Tami!'

Mace fired the gas hob, set down the coffee pot. 'Leave it.'

'Hey?' said Pylon. 'We told her, this's a non-smoking environment.'

'She's trying to quit.'

'Not hard enough.' He yelled her name again. Tami answered from the courtyard. Pylon leapt at the backdoor. 'You're supposed to've stopped.'

Tami crushed the butt under foot, bent down to pick it up. 'I'm trying, okay.' She headed for the door. Pylon stepped hurriedly back.

'Well try harder.'

'I've got one father I don't need two,' she hurled back over her shoulder.

'You hear that,' said Pylon. 'She doesn't think I've got Pumla. I don't need another daughter.'

'Take her a cup of coffee,' said Mace, digging his new cellphone out of his pocket, putting a stop to its sharp ring tone.

'More liberal bullshit.'

'Hello, judge,' said Mace. 'You're wanting to know if I've made a decision yet but I haven't.'

Mace listened to the judge going on about how critical it was becoming. How he, Mace, had been highly recommended and it was too late to seek an alternative at this stage. That he now felt he was being let down.

'I told you, judge, up front, I had other priorities,' said Mace.

The judge sighed, apologised for his outburst. It was his concern getting the better of him.

Mace said, 'Look, I'll make a decision this morning. Let you know this afternoon. If it's not me it'll be one of our guys.' He thumbed him off. 'The judge's not a happy camper.'

'Only the great Mace Bishop will do.'

'Something like that.' The coffee came to the boil. Mace switched off the gas, letting the brew settle before he poured it into three espresso cups, Pylon shaking his head.

'Women just walk over you.'

'Why not?' He gave a cup to Pylon. 'Take it to her.'

'Me? No ways.'

'Take it,' said Mace, heading upstairs with their cups.

When Pylon came up he said, 'I wouldn't want to be her father.' He held up an A4 sheet with the message REMEMBER TO COLLECT CLIENTS AT THE AIRPORT TOMORROW AT 12 NOON printed on it in eighteen point.

'She's kicking a drug,' said Mace. 'You weren't much fun doing it either.' He took a swig of coffee, pointed at the message. 'But she's efficient. I might've forgotten that. Left the clients stranded.'

'I wouldn't have.'

'Good for you. Now why don't you phone the hospital. Get an update.'

'I did,' said Pylon. 'This morning from home. Stable but critical.'

'So what do you think: do I tell the judge yes or no?'

'Go,' said Pylon. 'What's the issue?'

'Rudi Klett.'

'How? We've got a roster going. It's okay.'

'Unless he gets plugged again.'

'Isn't going to happen,' said Pylon, blowing over the surface of his coffee before he sipped it. 'Yesterday, though, this snappy dresser wanders in. I think, oh yes, here we go. He's carrying a small bag, you know, for toiletries, change of underwear, that sort of bag. He sits down so I tell him he has to ring for the sister, he says no he was told to wait. So he waits with the bag on his lap. Keeps looking at his watch but then he's been told to wait so he's anxious. I assume whoever he's waiting for has been in surgery and is being brought up to ICU. Twenty minutes later, he clicks his tongue, mumbles something, walks off. I assume to track down what's happening. We never see him again, and I was there for another hour, hour and a half.'

'An assessor?'

'In retrospect, could be. I told the guys anybody drifts in like that, they get them out.'

'I'm going to phone,' said Mace, keying the hospital number into the pad of a desk phone. He got through to ICU. They asked who he was and when he'd told them they told him Wolfgang Schneider was dead. 'For Chrissakes,' said Mace. 'When?'

About an hour earlier. A haemorrhage in his brain.

'And no one's phoned us?'

They were getting round to it he was told. Trying to find the man's next-of-kin.

'We're the contacts,' said Mace. 'You're supposed to phone us.'

'Save me Jesus,' said Pylon when Mace hung up. 'Wonderful hospital service we've got.'

'Don't know what I feel about his dying,' said Mace. 'He was a bastard. A likeable bastard but still a bastard. Especially what he put me through on Sunday.'

'It's sad,' said Pylon. 'We go back.'

'Sure, there were times.'

'Then he gets popped sitting next to you.'

'Thanks for that.'

They sat in silence finishing their coffees. Eventually Mace said, 'I suppose I should tell the judge I'll take up his offer.'

38

Beside the pool at Obed Chocho's house, Spitz and Manga stretched out on loungers. Jammed in a bucket of ice were a clutch of beers, Black Labels mostly but also Amstels. Spitz smoking menthols; Manga rolling a short stop of dagga.

They were sheltered from the wind by a wall of dressed stone with a gurgling fountain feature built into it, the water issuing from a seraph's mouth. Obed Chocho had a liking for statuary. Concrete small-sized imitations of the Greek classics scattered about the garden: the Venus, the victory, some maidens and the discus thrower.

Spitz and Manga had been there since lunch, their empty plates cleared away a few hours back by a young woman who'd flitted about the place all morning with a vacuum cleaner and a dust rag. Manga had come on to the girl, trailing after her, suggesting one or two alternatives that made her giggle until Obed Chocho told him to lay off before he got his dick amputated. The girl was a niece from some dusty village: not for plucking.

After lunch Obed Chocho had gone out telling Spitz and Manga to stay put. They could drink all the beer they wanted but they didn't leave the property. And Manga to keep his body parts to himself. Anyone came round, they should dissuade them from calling back.

'What about my money?' Spitz had said.

'You'll get it,' said Obed Chocho, slamming out the front door.

This hadn't amused Spitz. Nor was he amused by being told what to do. And not having his tunes greatly riled him. Maybe sprawled in the lounger with a long menthol between his fingers, his eyes behind shades, he looked cool but he wasn't. In his gut churned a bile that he could've spat all over Obed Chocho as easy as piss on him.

'Luck, my brother, mighty fine luck,' had been Obed Chocho's reaction to the news of Rudi Klett's death.

At which Spitz shot back. 'A bullet fired into his head when he is in a moving car and I am in a moving car is not because of luck.'

At which Obed Chocho scowled but made no retort.

Replaying this, Spitz watched Manga light the joint and take a deep pull, holding in the smoke. Gradually he let it trickle out. 'Yo, bru.' He offered the joint to Spitz. 'Chill, captain?'

Spitz shook his head.

Manga shrugged, went through the process again. He tapped a head of ash onto the paving, squinted at Spitz.

'Yesterday,' he said, 'at the hospital, you didn't have the gun, did you?'

Spitz smiled. 'No, I am not crazy.'

Manga laughed. 'You're a cool dude, captain.'

'There was nothing cool,' said Spitz. 'We were talking about the short odds. It was logical.'

What wasn't logical and what Spitz decided not to tell Manga was that he'd recognised as his the iPod feeding tunes into the ears of the security guard outside the intensive care unit. That made no sense. But then Spitz also knew that very little made any sense when it came to the cops and crime scene investigations.

In the evening, Spitz drove a green VW following Manga in the car they'd had for almost a week, heading for the airport to dump it. When they got there Manga entered the covered parking, found a space near where they'd waited two days earlier. He felt leaving the G-string in the same bay was a nice touch. Funny, actually. He locked the car, tossed the keys onto the roof of a covered walkway.

Spitz circled once, picked him up at the drop-and-go outside departures. They changed places: Manga driving, Spitz in the passenger seat.

Manga had to tell Spitz where he'd left the car. 'For a joke,' he said.

'Where is the joke,' said Spitz, 'if only you know about it?'

'So do you?' said Manga.

'No. For me that's not funny,' said Spitz.

After the airport they drove to the V&A for a weissbier. It was dark now, and too windy to sit outside. While Manga ordered, Spitz walked onto the swingbridge, waiting until he was alone before dropping the Ruger into the canal. Then he phoned Sheemina February.

'We are having a drink on the town,' he said. 'Perhaps you would like to join us.'

'I don't think so, Spitz,' she said. 'Let's keep it professional. That's how I prefer it. How's the car?'

'Mighty fine,' said Spitz, pleased to hear Sheemina February laugh at his choice of words.

'And the gun?'

'I would say perfect for the job.' Spitz paused. 'Please. Come and have a drink. We could have a good time.'

'I've heard that from a lot of men. The good times never rolled though.'

'They will when you are with me.'

'Keep your head clear, Spitz. You don't want to mess up.'

'There is no chance.'

Sheemina February gave her short throaty laugh again. 'Goodbye, Spitz, maybe we'll call on you again one day' – and she disconnected, and when Spitz dialled straight back he got her voicemail. He turned towards the beer hall, cursing. A couple approaching across the bridge moved closer together. Spitz caught the movement, snorted his derision.

39

Sheemina February held the phone in her gloved hand and smiled. Amused to be hit on by a hitman. Not her type but sweet in his way. Women would fall for him, she could imagine. Charmed by the formal English and the strange Germanic accent. A nice guy. At heart.

She stared at her reflection in the plate glass window, the black void of the sea beyond. No lights on the water. No passing ships. With the wind, no night fishermen dangling hooks in the kelp holes.

The figure in the glass stood still. A silhouette, slim. Relaxed in a man's shirt worn loose over jeans. Barefoot on a white flokati. For five minutes she didn't move. Emptied her mind until it was dark and quiet. From speakers embedded in the ceiling, Yo Yo Ma played the tangos of Piazzolla so softly they might have been in her head.

The music brought her back. She turned abruptly into the room, strode across to the kitchen counter. Pulled the wine from the ice bucket, refilled her glass. With a serviette, wiped lipstick from the glass's rim: a plum smear on the white linen. She raised the glass and drank, left a fresh imprint of her lower lip.

Sheemina February sat down on a couch, swung up her legs, stretched along its length. So much better the Bantry Bay apartment to her town house. A place to be truly at home: her lair on the cliff. Hers and hers alone. Never had she invited anyone into it. Never would she.

She reached for the envelope on the coffee table, drew out a document: a list of phone calls to and from the cellphone of Mace Bishop. Judge Telman Visser such splendid bait. Possibly it would be worth getting their transcripts. For the record. How wonderful that Mace Bishop was slowly being reeled back into her life. That already she had been his guardian angel.

'You don't know what you owe me, Mr Bishop,' she said aloud.

There were other lists. Lists of conversations held at Complete Security. Conversations between Mace Bishop and Pylon Buso. Summaries of each conversation gave her enough to know what was on the minds of the two men. A couple of summaries she highlighted. She'd need the transcripts.

She set the lists aside, shook a batch of colour photographs from the envelope.

Mace Bishop in his little red Noddy car, top down in Somerset Road. A wide grin on his face. Enjoying himself. Sheemina February couldn't resist the grin, had to smile.

Another of the security man leaving the gallery where he'd met Judge Telman Visser. The judge's car in the background, the number plate clearly visible. The photograph caught Mace stepping onto the pavement: energetic, brisk, a hand adjusting his sunglasses. What she liked were his sandals. Robust. Hi-tech trail sandals. Very outdoor.

The last pictures had been taken earlier that morning. Grainy but clear enough. Mace standing with his back to the photographer facing the blurred city. The gleam of the swimming pool in the foreground.

Another of Mace at the edge of the pool in his Speedo. His swimmer's physique. Strong arms, broad shoulders, the torso still narrowing to the waist but thicker than in the photograph she carried. The one she'd taken herself at the gym pool some years back.

The problem with this photograph was his approaching wife.

Sheemina February got up, searched through a drawer for scissors, snipped the woman out of the frame. She crumpled the discard into a wastebin.

From the table took a box file of photographs and returned to the couch. She riffled through them, found others of Mace in a Speedo. Mace three years younger. A trimmer figure but weathering well.

Among them a picture of Mace Bishop chained to a bolt in the wall took her fancy. Mace lying on a foam mattress, manacled at the ankle. The security man comatose, imprisoned in a cellar at her mercy. Until the careless Mikey Rheeder screwed it up.

This time would be different, she reckoned.

She lingered over the photographs of Mace. Good-looking guy. Vicious as a viper. But the type she went for. Like her late ex. Mo Siq. Especially when she had good reason and she had good reason.

'I can't wait to meet again,' she said to his image. Rubbed her thumb over his face, leaving a smear. 'On my terms. In my territory.' Again the pain spiking her chest. She massaged below her breasts. The ache fading.

Sheemina February put away the box file of photographs, stuck the list of transcripts into her briefcase. Yo Yo Ma came to an end, she changed him for the real thing, the accordion player. Wound up the sound, poured the remains of the wine into her glass. She stretched out again on the couch. Wondered how well Mace Bishop tangoed. Pictured an empty hall, the two of them dancing.

Thursday

40

Mace swam, a slow crawl, his body working, his mind void. Swimming on automatic, the way he liked it. Time out of himself when no thoughts intruded. Not the present, not the past. Just the body Mace Bishop alone in the sea, the sea a green haze about him, bubbles streaming off his hands with every stroke, his eyes tracking across the sand floor. Swimming through dappled light.

When he'd gone in he'd thought to do this more often, a sea swim. Not many around. Some early walkers on the beach but the sea to himself. Unlike the pool with people training, others clustered about the edges. Here he was alone. Alone in himself and in the water.

He swam the bay between the mountains: Clovelly to Fish

Hoek. Measured, easy. Breathed in below the arch of his left arm, let out his lungs in a pop and boil. In, out, the rhythm settled for a long haul. Going like this he could swim all day. His last thought before his mind became reptile, instinctive.

An hour later Mace took a call on the beach, drying himself, pumped up that he'd gone the distance, even though the knife wounds smarted from the salt. He had the lungs, he had the muscle, he could do the Robben Island swim. Show Christa that her pa was still an iron man.

'Judge,' he said, 'this is early.'

Judge Telman Visser said something inaudible, then: 'I need an answer, Mr Bishop, and I need it early.'

Mace stared at the quiet sea, perfect after the days of wind, only a breeze feathering the surface. He wished he were back there swimming through the liquid light, not listening to the griping of Judge Visser. 'Fair enough,' he said, moving away from a gaggle of morning bathers towards the water's edge.

'And so?' The judge staccato, demanding.

'As it happens, matters have changed. I can do your farm this weekend.'

'I'm pleased to hear that. Good. Only thing, Mr Bishop, it's not my farm. As I told you, it's my father's.'

'Yours to inherit?'

The judge said 'ummm', and Mace wondered at that.

'Plan is,' said Mace, 'I'm driving up tomorrow with my daughter. Be there Saturday morning. Overnight Saturday, leaving Sunday.'

'I don't think that's a good idea,' said Judge Visser. 'Your daughter being there. After the threats we've had, it's too dangerous. Farm attacks are random.'

'It'll be fine, judge.' Mace glanced up at the mountainside, at people moving about on their decks: a woman going through tai chi positions full frontal to the hard sun.

'You're putting her at risk. I know what happened to her, that kidnapping, I'm surprised at your attitude.'

'No risk,' said Mace. 'Someone's going to attack, they're not going to do it when there's visitors around.'

The judge didn't answer, said eventually, 'She's your daughter, Mr Bishop. You know best.'

'I do,' said Mace, picking up on the criticism, still watching the methodical tai chi woman. Was she naked? 'What happened to Christa before was thanks to someone in your profession. A lawyer. One Sheemina February. You ever come across her?'

'I've heard of her,' said Judge Visser.

'A bitch,' said Mace. 'A manipulator.'

'I know the type.'

Mace left off his fascination with the tai chi woman, started back towards his towel and clothes. 'She was into retribution. Personal stuff. This is a simple job. Having my daughter along for the ride's no big deal.'

'I've had my say, Mr Bishop.' Mace heard the judge sigh. 'You must do what you think best.'

With that he told Mace he'd fax directions and a map, and the telephone number on the farm.

Mace hung up wondering why Judge Visser had such an anti on his taking Christa. More tricky was going to be convincing Oumou to let their daughter take a day off school. He scanned the mountain homes for the tai chi woman, saw her standing motionless on one leg leaning forward, reckoned she had to be naked. The idea of it arousing.

At home he played Oumou down the line, the two of them in her studio. Told her about the farm and the client and how he planned to drive there, make a long weekend of it. How it'd been decades since he'd been in the Karoo, and although it wasn't desert as she knew it, wasn't sand and dunes, it was almost desert, long plains of stone and shale and scrub and koppies. The sort of landscape you couldn't imagine until you saw it. How he'd love for her to get a sense of it. And Christa. It being part of her country, after all, a place she wouldn't be able to imagine by looking at the mountains of the peninsula, the forests and the vineyards. It would blow her mind. Be important for her to see it. So many kids grew up with no idea of what their country looked like. For example, Pumla. What did she know of where Pylon and Treasure were born? Of her own roots.

'You should ask Christa, oui,' said Oumou.

'And you?' said Mace. 'I want you to see it.' He unsheathed the short sword hanging in its scabbard on the wall. A dull metal blade. A leather handle with a red patina, inlaid beads, a brass decorative knob. A smooth cool feel in your hand. The blade well balanced.

'Non,' said Oumou, 'it is impossible. I have too much to make.'

Which Mace knew. He tested the blade against the palm of his hand. The sort of blade that could do a lot of damage. Probably in its time had done a lot of damage.

'In ten days is the exhibition. How can I have a holiday?'

Which Mace had supposed might be the case. He slid the sword back into the leather scabbard. An old sword. One of Oumou's treasures.

'That is why you should take Christa.'

'And have her miss a day of school?'

'Bah! What is one day for her. It would be good for her. For you both.'

'And you?'

'I can have a chance to do a lot of work in quiet and peace.'

Mace came up behind her, slipped his hands under the bib of her dungarees to clasp her breasts, Oumou not for a moment taking her hands off the clay moulding on the wheel.

'You don't mind?' he said, teasing her nipples, the image of the naked tai chi woman flashing behind his eyes.

'Non. Of course not. For you and Christa all you do together is swim. How can you talk to her? You are together but you cannot say important things, no? Now you can sit in the car for a long time and talk about everything.'

'Scary,' said Mace, sliding a hand down into her crotch.

'Not so scary.' Oumou slowed the wheel. 'But, oui, there is a lot for you to know about Christa. And that she wants to know about her papa.'

Mace frowned, suddenly unsure if he'd engineered the trip with his daughter or if he'd fallen into some long-planned scheme of Oumou's.

'Why don't you ask Christa?' said Oumou. 'Make it her day.' She reached up and drew Mace down to her, leaving a smear of clay on his cheek. 'You will have a good time.' She pulled his hand out of her lap. 'You want to do this now?'

'Why not?' said Mace.

'Here?'

'Why not?' said Mace.

Later, as he drove down Molteno into the breathless city, he wondered if sometimes Oumou didn't know more about what was going on than he did. Even in his own mind.

41

Pylon met Henk and Olivia Smit in a reception lounge of the downtown offices of Smit & Desai Financial Advisors. While he waited stood looking at a view over the harbour, at the expensive apartments fringing the marina and the malls beyond. To the right a sight of the working harbour, an oil rig berthed there, swarming with maintenance crews.

From here too he could see the curve of the bay disappearing up the west coast. Couldn't see as far as the land he'd hoped to develop but almost. The sight brought a metal taste to his mouth.

Not only because of Rudi Klett's murder but because of Obed Chocho. Because Chocho was riding over everyone.

Which was what he told Henk and Olivia Smit.

'Wait,' said Henk. 'Hold it, okay. Before you start, I have to tell you we're not about to reconsider. Your deal was good but Obed Chocho's is better. Nothing personal about it. Just hard figures.'

'You're not listening to me,' said Pylon. 'I'm telling you Chocho's hanging you out.'

'Meaning?'

'Stringing you. Dishing up what you want to hear. Come the time he's going to cut you free without a tiny cent.'

Henk interrupted him. 'Oh, come on.'

Olivia said, 'Let him finish.'

Pylon glanced from Henk to Olivia, their faces non-committal. 'Why I'm here is to give you more information. Information which you should know before you go any further.'

'We've put down our cards,' said Henk. 'You can't tempt us.'

Pylon smiled. 'I'm not going to. We've pulled out. Had to pull out, I should say.'

'Why?' said Olivia. Where she sat on a leather couch beside her husband, she kept running her hands down her skirt, smoothing the creases. Such a delicate, fragile woman, Pylon thought, to be in finance.

'Because our backer was shot.'

Olivia stopped in mid-iron. Henk said, 'Hell, man!'

'Driving into the city on Monday night, he was assassinated. The best we can work it out the shooter came alongside and popped him where the road splits at the freeway. He died in hospital yesterday.'

'Hell,' Henk said again.

'That's horrible,' said Olivia.

'You're sure it was an assassination?' said Henk. 'Not something random.'

'We've discounted that.'

'I can't believe it. That's pulp. That's what happens in the movies and books.'

'Real life, too,' said Pylon. 'I told you about Lindiwe Chocho.'

'Not the way the papers reported it,' said Olivia.

'Course not,' said Pylon. 'Because they weren't told. The papers don't know everything. Didn't know, for instance, that Popo Dlamini was passing on information to Obed Chocho about when our backer was flying in from Berlin. Unfortunately we didn't know Popo Dlamini was doing this until too late.'

'Bullshit,' said Henk. 'I don't believe it.'

'Wait,' said Olivia, putting a hand on her husband's arm. 'You're telling us Mr Chocho had him killed, your backer?'

'Let me put it this way,' said Pylon. 'From what I know of Obed Chocho, and I know a lot over a long time, then it's not impossible. I've got no proof. Just circumstantial evidence and some inside information.'

'So you're telling us what?' said Olivia.

'To be careful,' said Pylon. 'Don't go in with him. Sell at his price and walk away. Stay alive.' Pylon stood up, stared at the young investment analysts. Doubt in Henk's eyes; Olivia troubled, believing him. 'A quick story to fill you in.'

Olivia and Henk stood.

'This happened in the camps. Twenty years ago. The bad one, Quattro, in Angola. You want to hear it?' He waited for them to nod. 'Okay. What happened at Quattro is people were brought there, people they thought were impimpis, betrayers. Some of those people died in that camp. Died because they were tortured to death. Raped. Beaten. Starved. Driven mad because they weren't given water. They could see it there in a glass on the floor but they were tied up and couldn't reach it. Or they could feel it dripping on their heads, smack, smack, smack. The lucky ones were shot. Gun to the head. Bam.'

'Stop,' said Olivia. 'Stop.' She had her hands on her face, covering her mouth.

'For a year,' said Pylon, 'Obed Chocho was one of the commanders at Quattro.'

Henk folded his arms tightly across his chest. 'How d'you know that?'

Pylon smiled, a wan smile that hardly moved his lips. 'I was there. I saw him.'

'He killed people?' Olivia had lowered her hands and now held them flat against one another as if in prayer.

'You don't have to take my word for it,' said Pylon. 'There're records. But the president's got the paperwork under lock and key. And, yes, that's what I'm telling you.'

Which was what he told Mace as they drove to the airport to pick up two clients flying in from London. Return business, husband and wife motivational speakers who'd done a surgical safari the previous year. Wanted a little peace of mind while in Cape Town. Nothing heavy, more a chauffeur with clout than a bald bouncer. Complete Security's speciality. Five men, two women, all police services finishing school. Any one of them could've done the meet-and-greet, except with return business Mace and Pylon preferred to do the honours in person. Helped shine the image. So here they were on the highway in the big Merc pushing the clock.

'But they're not going to listen,' said Pylon. 'They're not the type. Only thing now is how badly they'll get burned.'

'If not killed.'

'A possibility. Except I don't reckon Obed'll go there. More likely to take their bucks and leave them steaming. What he'd call righteous returns.'

As they took the exit to the airport, Mace said, 'That's where Rudi got done' – pointed at the outgoing lanes – 'still can't get round it that I didn't realise till we were on the highway. One maybe two kays away. Hey? How can it happen?'

'It does,' said Pylon. 'After the Smits I took a drive to Obed Chocho's place. Don't ask why, okay. I don't know. I just did. Two hours to kill I thought I'd go and sit there, see if anything was going on.'

'Pylon Buso, private dick.'

'Just listen alright.'

Mace slowed on the approach to the arrivals building. 'I'm going to park in a drop zone.' He checked his watch. 'They're probably through already.'

'No panic,' said Pylon. 'You want to hear this?'

'Sure, sure,' Mace stopped to let passengers wheel baggage trolleys over the pedestrian crossing then angled the car into a no-parking bay.

'I sat down the road from Obed Chocho's. I've been there about forty minutes, nothing going on and I'm thinking about how I did this just five days ago checking out Lindiwe and Popo Dlamini. I'm about to leave when the gates open and Obed drives out in his macho black Yengeni. The same one I followed when Lindiwe was driving it. Problem: follow or stay? Something says stay even as I switch on. So I switch off. Sit there watching Obed Chocho drive away. Not five minutes the gate opens again, here comes a nice new Audi with two gents. This time I think, follow them. So I do.'

'Tell me inside,' said Mace. 'Our clients'll be waiting for us.'

He and Pylon got out, hurried into the terminal, Pylon saying, 'I don't even remember what they look like?'

'Chic,' said Pylon. 'T-shirt and black linen jacket on him. Her: white linen blouse, jersey knotted round her neck. Lots of white hair on both.'

They scanned the crowds.

'Here's the rest,' said Pylon, 'short and sweet. Where I followed them to was the Waterfront. The guy in the passenger seat with the short dreads was the guy who wandered into ICU the other day. No mistaking him.'

'Jesus,' said Mace.

'Exactly,' said Pylon.

'And the car?'

'Hired. Yesterday in the name of Obed Chocho. One extra driver by name of Manga Khumalo. Strange thing: last Saturday night a courier signed himself out of the golf estate where Popo Dlamini lived as Manfred Khumalo. Coincidence, or what?'

'Curious.' Mace saw an arm waving in the thick of the crowd, the twin heads of white hair. 'That's them' – he said, angling off towards the mid-fifties couple: tanned people, tall and slim, dressed exactly as he said they would be.

42

Spitz stood in front of the mirror gazing at his feet in the Bally moccasins. He moved his toes, watched the black leather ripple. Soft and silky. Cool shoes. Shoes to walk into JB's on a Saturday morning as if you're walking on air. Have the babes nudging one another. Tinkling their lattes, running their eyes full time in your direction.

He walked a few paces, watching the movement in the mirror, the cuff of his jeans riding up slightly to expose the low cut of the shoes. Po-et-ry.

Manga, sprawled in a chair, said, 'Captain, just buy them. No more catwalk stuff.'

'With shoes,' said Spitz, 'you have to be very careful. Even good shoes can sometimes be the wrong type.'

'For what?'

'For the job.'

Manga snorted. 'And these are the right type?'

'Yes. They are light and they are quiet.'

'For the job we've gotta do, you need this,' said Manga, thrusting out his trainers. 'The tough ones. Go anywhere, go anytime.'

Spitz twirled on his left heel to come face to face with the shop attendant. 'I will take them,' he said.

The attendant beamed at him. 'If sir'll sit, I'll slip them off for sir.'

'No, that is alright,' said Spitz. 'My other shoes you can put in the box. These shoes I will wear.'

'Very good, sir,' said the attendant. He turned to Manga. 'We can't interest sir in some proper shoes?'

Manga shook his head.

'That's a pity sir,' said the attendant, sweeping Spitz's brogues off the floor. 'Nice shoes, sir,' he said to Spitz. 'Sir has taste.'

Manga glared at the attendant poncing off, head high. 'Shit, captain,' he said. 'These coloureds are fulla shit.'

Was still pissed off with the shop jockey when they drove out of the V&A following Spitz's directions along the waterfront cutting back beside the golf course towards the traffic circle that spat them onto Somerset.

'Now you can drive slowly,' said Spitz. Manga noticed the scatterings of prossies on the corners. He groaned, 'No, captain, no way, not these.'

'Coloureds' – Spitz grinned at him – 'for me they give the best head.' He tapped his two front teeth. 'Those ones without these teeth to get in the way.'

They cruised the length of the street once, u-turned at Glengariff coming back fast on the other side, Spitz making a selection, saying, 'That is our girlfriend, that one with the red skirt. That is our baby. Go to her.'

'You maybe,' said Manga. 'I don't do coloured.'

Spitz laughed. 'My friend is racist.'

'Hola, captain, it's about preferences. The way I see it. Me, I prefer young. I told you.'

'She is young. Eighteen years old. No more than that.'

'I like younger. And no coloured.'

'This is Cape Town. Everyone is coloured.' He pointed out the window at sky, mountain, sea. 'Tomorrow we are gone. Maybe we should go up the mountain afterwards?'

'I don't do mountains,' said Manga. 'Even flat ones.'

'Because of you I cannot go up the mountain? Is that what you are saying?'

'Do your thing, captain. But if you wanna go up the mountain you go alone.'

'I ask you please. At this moment we must enjoy the city.' Spitz waved at the girl in the short red skirt. 'Stop the car.' He lowered the window as they pulled alongside. 'Hello, baby,' he said, 'how about we can have some fun?' To Spitz the girl looked the image of Sheemina February. Only younger.

The prossie strutted, half turning away, giving them the lower curve of a cheek hanging out the red dress. 'What you want, gents?'

Manga whistled, changing his tune. 'Come for a ride, my cherry.'

'With you gents, not a chance.'

'Come'n,' said Manga, 'we're good.'

Spitz held up two pink fifties.

The girl-woman snorted. 'Nah, sweetie gents, what d'you want for that little.'

'Gates of heaven,' said Manga, leaning across Spitz to waggle his tongue at the prossie.

Spitz got out, opened the back door. 'Please,' he said. 'What is your name?'

'Cherildeen, sweetie.' She changed hips, the dress riding higher on her bum. Still half turned away from Spitz and Manga, looking back at them over her shoulder: wet red lips. 'You put another pinkie to it I'll mos blow yous both.' She grinned at them, gap toothed. 'Seventy-five, drive alive. Come again twenty ten.'

'You like football?' said Manga.

Cherildeen stuck her tongue into her cheek. 'Anything with balls, hey sweetie gents.' She brushed past Spitz to get into the car, feeling at his crotch. 'I like you, sweetie big boy.' He eased himself in next to her.

Manga, eyes riveted to the rearview mirror, said, 'What d'you think I am, captain? A Spitz special chauffeur?'

'Your turn'll come, sweetie,' said Cherildeen, already working to undo Spitz's belt and flies. She got him loose and gasped. 'Oh what a pallie. You wanna wait until you've got a sea view or you want me to mos do it now.' She slid down to give him a lick. Like she would an ice cream.

'Now,' said Manga. 'This isn't a tourist trip.'

'My friend is from Jozi,' said Spitz, putting his hands in the frizz of the prostitute's hair. 'You can give him the sea view.'

She did Spitz on the drive to the car park at Mouille Point lighthouse. He got a sea view, even a sight of Robben Island before she sucked him off. Swallowing. She came up, dabbing her mouth with a tissue, her lipstick smeared. While Spitz zipped, she unclicked a purse, reapplied a glossy red.

'A girl's gotta look girlie, hey sweetie,' she said, taking the three fifties.

Spitz nodded, got out of the car.

While she blew Manga, Spitz leaned on the railing watching two surfers riding a small break off the rocks. He smoked a menthol. Enjoyed the sun on his back. The salty air. The squabbling seagulls. Reckoned maybe this day was enjoyable. When Manga was finished they could take another beer and white sausage at the Paulaner. See a movie. Tomorrow ride off, Saturday do the job. Sunday lunchtime he could walk into JB's to flash the moccasins. Putting it all together: for a week's work a good return and interesting scenery. He crushed out the menthol as Manga started shouting. Turned to see Manga dragging the prossie from the car. Manga's belt undone, his jeans unzipped; the prossie flailing at him, getting free and hobbling off on her high heels. Spitz watched. Manga chased her, landed a few kicks, danced round her like an ostrich, holding his jeans up with one hand, trying to swipe at her with the other. The prossie jumped a children's roundabout did a complete circle with Manga galloping alongside calling her bitch, poes, whore, umqwayizi, moffie, his jeans slipped down on his bum, flashing his black arse at a nearby granny. The prossie said something Spitz couldn't hear. Manga stopped, hiked his jeans. The prossie leapt off the roundabout, gave him the finger, wide grin on her dial. She got a bitch, poes, whore from Manga. Spitz saw the granny get in on the act, yelling at Manga he wasn't in a kaffir township now. Manga told the granny to suck her tit. He zipped up, tucking his shirt in as he walked back to Spitz. Manga spitting, saying, 'Shit, captain, shit, man she's not a prossie. That's a guy. With a cock and balls squeezed between her legs.'

Spitz stared at Manga. Stared at the prossie Cherildeen in her short skirt hurrying away in the distance, forced a laugh.

'Sometimes,' he said, 'with coloureds you cannot tell.'

Friday

43

'This is so cool.' Christa in jeans and T-shirt stuck her arms in the air as Mace accelerated the Spider onto the N1. No doubting that. Top down into tangy air, eight-thirty in the morning, all the good citizens going about their jobs: on the left loaders working the harbour's container yard, to the right a slow crawl of commuters on the incoming lanes. Behind them the bright mountain, ahead blue sky forever. It didn't get better.

Mace had to smile, actually felt like laughing. He leaned across, squeezed his daughter's knee. She swatted his hand. For a moment they looked at one another grinning.

To hell with it all, Mace reckoned, for three days he was out of it. On the road, baby.

He pushed more juice into the Spider taking her to one twenty down the Woodstock straights, out, out past factory land, under flyovers, out past the office parks, the malls, the ranch-house suburbs and over the Panorama hill out out heading for the mountains.

'Tunnel or over the top?' he shouted on the long glide across the valley towards the pass.

'Over the top,' Christa yelled back, her hair blown wild, so young-miss behind her sunglasses.

Mace took the mountain pass, no other cars behind or ahead. He roared the engine on the straights, geared down for the corners working the car like this was fun. At the top he pulled over onto a view point at a gravel clearing.

'I've got to pee, I've got to pee,' said Christa. hopping out of the car.

'Take your pick,' said Mace, 'behind any rock you like.'

Christa, legs clamped, bending against the urge, looked dubious. 'What if there's snakes and scorpions?'

Mace laughed at the sight of her. 'Take a chance.'

'Ahh, Papa, I've got to go.'

'Next to the car,' said Mace. 'No one's going to see you.' He threw his arms wide. 'There's no one to see you.'

He caught the movement of her pulling down her jeans, crouching, heard the hiss of her release. It made him want to pee. He found a bush a short way off that half hid him from the road.

He heard Christa call out: 'It's so easy for you.' And shouted back, 'Well, you wanted to be a girl.'

Before they left the view point, they stood together not talking, gazing into the valley and at the distant mountain, flat as an ironing board. The quiet held them: only sunbird twitter among the proteas until a baboon barked. They looked up, saw the troop coming down the slopes towards them. Some big buggers in the lead.

Mace said, 'Time to go.' Christa racing him to the car.

The pass down was still in shadow mostly, the mountains rising high and green either side and up against the summit, grey crags and shale.

Where the pass bottomed out they swept into the long curves beside a river, the road gently cambered and wide, the Spider humming. Came out of the mountains, crossed the Worcester floodplains into the Hex River Valley with the sun beginning to scorch. Along the roadside stood vendors, women and young men, holding up boxes of grapes, shouting at the sports car as Mace and Christa bore down and on. Sometimes Christa waved, sometimes she looked back at their poverty, her hand half raised.

At the end of the valley the pass took them onto the escarpment, the long plains of scrub and the silence of heat. Mace pulled into a picnic spot, cut the engine. For some minutes they sat getting used to being still, their ears popping from the road noise.

'It's so quiet,' said Christa, 'except for the flies' – swatting at their irritation.

'It's what I remember,' said Mace, 'just the whine of insects.'

He brought out two Cokes from a cooler pack. They leant against the Spider's bonnet, sipping, staring at blue hills in the distance.

Obed Chocho, dangling a car key and remote, said to Spitz and Manga at breakfast on the patio, 'This is yours.'

Manga said, 'And the VW, captain?'

'I'll have those keys.'

Manga dug the keys for the hire car from his pocket, tossed them onto the table.

Obed Chocho let them lie. From the breakfast tray took a bowl of muesli, heaping on yoghurt. 'This's another G-string. Especially for you. More vooma. Nice white colour. Nobody sees a white car.'

'There must be no blood in it,' said Spitz.

Obed Chocho stared at him. 'It's clean.'

'It was hijacked.' Spitz peeled an apple, keeping the skin curling unbroken.

'Go'n have a look.'

'It's okay, captain,' said Manga.

Still standing, Obed Chocho spooned muesli into his mouth and said without swallowing, 'No, go'n have a look.'

Spitz quartered the apple, and halved the quarters. Speared a slice with his knife and ate it. 'Blood is not a good sign.'

'My brother.' Obed Chocho pulled out a plastic chair and sat opposite Spitz. 'My brother listen to me. You find blood in it, mighty fine, I'll lick it clean.' He kept his eyes on Spitz but Spitz didn't meet them. 'There's no problem here. You do the job. Drive home to Jozi, lose the car.' He took another mouthful of muesli, glanced across at Manga. 'When're you going?'

Manga juggled the key and remote. 'After breakfast.'

'Mighty fine,' said Obed Chocho, 'that's now.'

'I am not finished,' said Spitz. On his plate seven slices of apple. He took one on the knife, raised it to his mouth. Bit into the crisp flesh. 'For this drive we have all day.'

Obed Chocho pointed his spoon at Spitz's shoes. 'You been shopping. Expensive.'

Spitz bit into another piece of apple. Didn't answer, gazed off into the garden at the concrete statuary, bright in the early sun. He felt Obed Chocho tapping him on the knee with his spoon.

'I can hurt you Mr Spitz-the-Trigger,' he was saying. Tapping his spoon with each word. 'Pour shit on your reputation. One-time big-time bugger-up. Single word, Mr Triggerman, and no more work. Forever. You hear me, my brother. You are mighty fine in deep shit with one word from my lips. No more work. No more money. No more fine and dandy shoes. Finish.' Obed Chocho made a gun with his right hand and shot himself in the temple. 'Kapow. You give me any shit with this job and that's the story. One word and mighty fine Spitz is the living dead. Like a zombie. Take my meaning?'

Spitz placed his knife on the plate next to the six remaining slices of apple. He stood, his chair scrapping on the patio tiles. 'That would not be a good idea, Mr Chocho,' he said, bowing slightly in the German manner, walking off indoors.

'Don't threaten me, my brother,' Obed Chocho shouted after him. 'I can hurt you mighty fine. I can make you disappear outta this world.' To Manga he said, 'Go, comrade. Take him away. Quickly. Any more sight of that brother and I will kill him.'

Mace couldn't see the link. One minute they were talking about the wool stuck on the barbed wire fence, the next Christa was asking about his parents, her grandparents.

'I don't have any,' he said. 'So you don't have any either. On my side. Not on your ma's side either, actually. They're both dead.' Trying to make light of it.

'I know about them,' she said. 'But what about yours?'

'I'm not kidding. I don't have any.'

She laughed. 'You've got to have.'

'Sure,' he said, 'I've got to have somewhere but I don't know where they'd be. Or who they are.'

She went thoughtful. 'No. Really?'

'Really.'

'You don't want to know?'

'Once. But that was long ago. Then I stopped thinking about it.'

'So who looked after you?'

'An orphanage.'

She grimaced.

'In Johannesburg. St Thomas's Orphanage for Boys. Horrible place. Smelt of toe jam.'

Christa picked at another tuft of wool snagged on the fence, rubbed it between her fingers. 'That's weird,' she said, offering him the wool.

He took it, feeling the oily fleece under his thumb, strands coming away. 'It wasn't nice.'

'And you didn't know your mom at all?'

'The story is she threw me away. Someone found me in a rubbish bin.' Mace saw Christa's eyes water. 'I'm joking. That's what they used to tell me but it probably wasn't like that at all.'

'It happens in stories.'

'Not all stories.'

They walked back to the car and Mace put up the hood.

'Sometimes,' said Christa, 'I pretend you're not my papa. That there's another man in Maman's village that's my real dad.'

'Why?' said Mace. 'Why'd you want to think that?'

'So I'm like Pumla.'

'Really?' said Mace.

'No,' said Christa coming up to him, holding her arm against his. 'We're different colours.'

'Pumla's black like Treasure.'

'So?'

'So you're not dark, not the same colour as your ma. Has to prove something, doesn't it?'

Christa thought about it, grinning at him. 'One girl calls me latte.'

'And you do what?'

'I don't freak out about it. I call her vanilla ice.'

Mace laughed. 'Yeah, well. Nothing wrong with latte. It's all the rage.'

They drove off, Christa plugging herself into her iPod and Mace thinking he might do the same to the tunes of killer country in the iPod that Pylon had thrust on him. But before he settled in for the ride, his phone rang: Judge Telman Visser.

'You checking on me, judge?' said Mace.

'Yes, if you put it that bluntly,' said the judge, a laugh in his voice. 'No, to put it politely, but so that I can advise my father.'

Mace nodded to himself, not amused. 'All as we agreed. Right now I'm staring at the Karoo.'

'With your daughter?'

'You got it.'

'I wish you hadn't, Mr Bishop. I wish you'd listened to me.'

'Why, judge? What's the big deal?'

'Unnecessary exposure, I think is the term.'

'You don't mind risking my life.'

'Security's your business, Mr Bishop. And you know how to take care of yourself.'

Mace thought, bugger you china, said, 'Meaning I don't know how to take care of my daughter.'

'I didn't say that.' He paused but Mace didn't come in. 'Nevertheless, enjoy your stay.'

'We will,' said Mace, and disconnected.

He was about to wind up the first of the Killer songs, Johnny Cash with 'The Man Comes Around', when his phone rang again: Pylon.

'Listen to this,' Pylon said, 'two guys in a white BM have just gone into the tunnel. Drove out of Obed Chocho's place forty minutes ago.'

'Where PI Buso was on a stakeout.'

'It just so happens. I'm going to sms the registration. Belonged to a scrapped Toyota. I got pictures too.'

'Tell the cops.'

'I have, for what it's worth.'

'There's a law-abiding citizen.'

'Don't take the piss,' said Pylon. 'You never know what's going to come in useful. And just so's you're on the nail, the short dreads brother's the one from the hospital.'

'Why'd I guess that,' said Mace.

'Captain,' said Manga. 'There's a Merc behind us, big black job, black dude at the steering.'

Spitz lowered his sun visor to check in the vanity mirror, the mirror and the back of the visor sprayed with dried blood. 'Aah, this is shit.' He shouted it, staring at his own face behind the blood.

'What?' said Manga. 'What the…?' – looking up at the stains on the visor.

'I told him,' said Spitz, 'there must be no blood in the car.' Spitz thumping the dashboard with his fist. 'No blood.'

'Okay, captain, okay,' said Manga. 'I'll pull in at a garage, we can clean that mess, okay. Relax.' Leaning over and flipping the visor up, glancing in the rearview to see the black Merc one car back. 'What we gonna do about this guy? In the Merc?'

'I told him,' said Spitz, 'there must be no blood.'

'Right, that's right,' said Manga. 'We'll get it cleaned.'

Couple of blocks later at a suburban shopping mall, Manga pulled into a petrol station. Spitz was out, cracking a menthol from a packet before Manga had switched off. Manga waved away the petrol attendants, tearing a length of paper towel from a dispenser. To Spitz he said, 'Just cool it. Okay, captain, be together.' The Merc he noticed cruised past, the driver not giving them a moment's attention.

When the visor was clean, Manga said, 'That suit you, captain?'

Spitz looked in, still unhappy. 'He said he would lick it clean. That is what he should have done.'

'Come on,' said Manga, 'we've gotta go.'

They got into the car and Manga took off gently, Spitz striking up another menthol. 'Blood in a car is no good.'

Manga kept shut-up.

They turned out of the suburb and headed for the highway in steady traffic. At the on-ramp, Manga moved into the fast lane, nodded at the car's response. One thing about a Beemer, it had guts in its early life. He put foot. Five kilometres later, he glanced in the rearview mirror to see a black Merc locked in behind them. The black Merc with the black dude in his dark glasses.

Manga said, 'What's this, captain? What's this brother's problem?' He pointed at the rearview mirror. 'Behind us. That guy again.'

Spitz lowered the sun visor using the tips of his fingers, angled it to get the car in the vanity mirror.

'What's he want? What's he following for?'

Spitz turned to get a better look, and the Merc driver made a gun of his hand, pointed it at them. Spitz thought, the second time in an hour someone had done that. Then he recognised their follower.

'He was at the hospital. He was probably a security.'

'So what's he doing here?'

Spitz shrugged, straightened himself in the seat. 'Maybe he is the sheriff to see us out of town. Like in the Western movies.'

'Funny, captain.' Manga pulled his thirty-eight from the holder in the door, laid it in his lap. 'Security guards don't drive big Mercs. They don't follow people.'

Spitz crushed his cigarette, flicked the butt out the window. Ahead were the mountains. 'Go through the tunnel,' he said. 'Then we will see.'

When the Merc turned off at the approach to the tollgate, Manga whooped. 'Maybe we're ritzed, captain. Maybe it was nothing.'

'It was the security,' said Spitz. 'Do not get too happy.'

Mace listened through the song list: Don't Let Me Go, I'll Follow You Down, The Wound That Never Heals. Watched the road slipping under the bonnet of the Spider as they crossed the brown unfolding landscape, and thought about Rudi Klett. About the hit job in Berlin, about the shooter taking out the German not twenty hours later. A case of what goes round, comes round. Like some sort of justice. Some sort of moral universe.

Some sort of bullshit story more likely, he reckoned, giving Emmylou Harris's Snake Song a couple of repeats for the sake of her voice and the melancholy. If this was a hitman's iPod then he was a shooter with a taste in music Mace appreciated.

The thing about Rudi Klett was about who'd known he was on the flight. Also about how they'd got to know. If it wasn't one of Klett's spook enemies, had to be something to do with Pylon's golf estate scheme. Which meant the office was wired again. Because he and Pylon'd got casual about getting in the sweepers regularly. Which meant not a moment went by when someone wasn't working out an angle to wire the office just on the off-chance.

You had to consider the connections though: a hitman taking out Lindiwe Chocho and a main player on Pylon's syndicate, popping their German backer, then turning up on the road heading north. Somewhere behind them. And what to be done about it? Bloody nothing. Time was in the camps he and Pylon might've, would've reacted differently. Pulped the man's hand to find out what was happening. But Pylon'd let this one slip, was sniffing at the dirt, not even talking about getting involved. Why? Because maybe it was too much effort. The way Mace felt too.

Mace felt Christa tapping him on the arm, unplugged an earphone from his ear.

She said, 'What was it like being an orphan?'

He laughed. 'You've been thinking about that all this time?'

'Not all the time.'

'You're sweet.' He reached over to caress her cheek with the backs of his fingers.

'So, tell me.'

'Lonely. Sometimes I wanted to hurt people. Sometimes I did.'

'Like how?'

'Like hitting them. When I was little. Once I tried to stab a priest.'

'Papa!'

'With a pencil. Not something I'm proud of.'

Christa said nothing. Mace could hear Johnny Cash singing in the earphone over his shoulder a story about shooting a man for no reason, just aiming at him from the cover of some rocks and squeezing off a shot. Taking him down. Going on the run, getting caught, now heading for the electric chair. Killer country music.

Christa said, 'Papa, have you killed someone?'

Mace heard Johnny Cash say, 'I hung my head, I hung my head.' He took his eyes off the road, turned to his daughter. She wasn't looking at him, didn't turn to meet his glance, kept her gaze straight on.

'I've had to,' he said. 'Ja, when we were fighting a war.'

She thought about this. 'With a gun?'

'Sure. With a gun.'

'The one you've got?'

'No, not with that one. I haven't shot anyone with that.' Not that he hadn't wanted to. The two Yanks that had killed Isabella he could've shot with no blow-back. No hanging his head in shame.

'Why, papa?'

'Why what?'

'Why did you have to?'

'Because otherwise they would've shot me. Simple as that. Shot me and Pylon, actually. In a war it's what happens, you shoot people. In this case it didn't have to be but that's how it turned out. If they'd played it straight it wouldn't have happened. They would've paid, we would've given them what they wanted. We would all have gone away happy. But no. They got greedy. Wanted to keep their money. And they reckoned there's just two of us, there's five of them so what the hell they can take us down easily. So while I'm counting the money and not looking at what's going on, one of the five thinks now's the time to do it, and shoots at me. Bam. Bam. Twice. From I don't know, maybe four, five metres away. Missed by a mile. Then there's this moment's silence, this silence where you can't hear anything, absolutely nothing, no insects, no birds, complete quiet before he lets the whole clip run. A bloody Czech Skorpion, but it must've been the first time he'd shot it because the bullets went every which way. Now the others start shooting. Pylon starts shooting. I've fallen on the ground and start shooting. For I don't know how long, not long, thirty seconds, a minute, no more than that because we're all out in the open, in this clearing in a forest, with nothing to hide behind, so it couldn't have been for long but for whatever time it was, it was crazy shooting. Felt like an age but it couldn't have been. These things always seem longer than they are. I don't know. Say, thirty seconds. Anyhow when it stopped we were the lucky ones. Perhaps we shot better than them. I don't know. It's just when the shooting stopped, three of them are dead. The other two made it to their truck and drove off.'

Christa said nothing. Mace glanced at her but she was staring out at the scrub and flat-topped koppies rising in the distance. He caught his own shaded eyes in the rearview mirror, raised his eyebrows, wondering what it was his daughter made of his life.

'You still want to shoot?'

She took her time about replying. Said, yes.

They stopped for a fast food lunch at a joint attached to a petrol station in the middle of nowhere. Parked the Spider in what small shade the building cast.

Christa frowned, hesitant. 'We're going to eat here?' – looking around at some long-haul trucks, goats browsing among car wrecks in the veld, five ragged children sitting in the dust watching her.

'Sure,' said Mace. 'Toasted cheese and tomato sarmies and a Coke float, more ice cream than Coke.'

She followed him inside to a table in the window, the children still watching her.

'They're looking at me,' she said after they'd ordered.

Mace called the waitress back, asked her to send out three packets of deep-fry chips to the kids. The woman shrugged. 'They eat better than me.'

Mace eyed her wide backside and thought not. He shielded his mouth with his hand, whispered to Christa, 'They're probably her kids.'

Christa looked at the group. The eldest, about her own age, got up, went round the back of the building and the others followed. They were barefoot, white scratches on their legs. Mace watched his daughter: the intensity of her gaze, her shoulders easing when the children were gone.

'You can relax now,' he said.

She held her nose. 'We're going to stink of cooking oil.'

Mace laughed. 'The hazards of travel. Hey!' – he pulled the iPod out of his pocket, unpopped his earphones. 'Plug yourself in and listen to some serious music' – searching through the playlist for Lilium's 'Lover'.

Christa listened all the way through, so loud he could hear the slide guitar. At the end she said, 'He killed her, didn't he? Up on the mountain.'

'Sounds like it,' said Mace. 'But what about the music?'

'It's okay,' said Christa. 'For country.'

Mace leaned back mock-horrified. 'Where's your soul, girl?'

'Papa,' she said after the waitress had clattered down their toasted sandwiches, slopped their drinks, 'when those soldiers shot at you, was that because of guns?'

Mace bit into a quarter of toast, chewed. 'Why d'you ask?'

'Pumla said you and Pylon sold guns.'

Mace nodded. Not exactly the sort of conversation he wanted to get into. 'Uh huh. That's what we did.'

'Like gun-runners?'

'Gun-runners.' Mace laughed. 'What d'you know about gun-runners?'

'Lots.'

'Tell me.'

'That they're not nice.'

'I'm not nice?'

She spooned ice cream from the glass, not looking at him.

'Okay. What else?'

'This DVD. In life skills class they showed us this DVD of men selling rifles to children.'

'Life skills?'

'You know like I told you that woman with the one leg told us about drugs? That's life skills. Last time a woman told us about gun-runners. She had this DVD where children shot people in villages. Shot women and little babies.'

'She showed that to you? To your class?'

'I cried,' said Christa.

'I didn't do that,' said Mace. 'Okay. Pylon and I didn't do that. We didn't sell guns to children. Also it was a long time ago. Before you were born. What we did was sell guns to soldiers because they were fighting wars. Wars to free their people.' He moved to sit next to her, put his arm around her. 'We gave up selling guns, C. We protect people now.'

'It felt like I was being shot again,' she said.

Mace clenched his jaw, an old anger twisting in his stomach. He tightened his hug, drawing Christa to him.

They sat for a time looking out at the children playing with a soccer ball, kicking it between themselves and to the truck drivers. Occasionally cars pulled into the petrol station but mostly the petrol jockey sat smoking in the sun, a ghetto blaster at his feet tuned to a hip-hop station. Mostly no one stopped here, mostly the big horse and trailers came blaring through non-stop with three long toots on the horn. Somewhere, at the back, among the thorn acacias and the kapok bush, Mace knew would be a group of small brick-and-tin houses. Dogs lying at the doors. Women inside cooking. Litter, bottles, metal scrap scattered about. He'd seen it everywhere. Variations of it. It made him jumpy.

'Let's go,' he said, standing. 'Let's hit the road.'

'Doesn't mean I don't want to learn to shoot,' said Christa.

Manga and Spitz sat down at the table while the waitress removed the glasses and plates.

Spitz watched the man and his daughter get into the red Alfa Spider and pull off. He recognised the man, the car too. More specifically he noticed the blue iPod the guy'd been attaching to his earphones.

Manga said, 'They don't do burgers.' He flicked at the menu with his fingers. 'Yo, captain, what sort of place doesn't do burgers? Cheese. Cheese 'n tomato. Bacon and peanut butter. Toasted or plain. But no burgers. They've got chips. I can smell chips. The place stinks of fry oil.'

Spitz remembered what Sheemina February had said, 'I've got pictures of the man who's not the target. The one with him is. No collateral, okay?' The same man wiring into a blue iPod. Like the one he'd lost. Like the one the security had at the hospital. The security in the big Merc.

Manga was saying, 'Anywhere you go in the country whites want toasted cheese and tomato. If it's not a burger place, it's cheese and tomato. What's with them they always wanted cheese and tomato when they drove across the country?'

Spitz said, 'Do you recognise that car?' – pointing at the Spider accelerating onto the road.

'It's an Alfa,' said Manga, squinting against the light. 'Hey, captain, like the one at the airport.'

'I think so,' said Spitz. 'And the driver has a blue iPod. The same as mine was.'

'Coincidence,' said Manga. 'Has to be more'n one red sports car. Certainly there's plenty of blue iPods.' He turned back to the menu. 'They've got beer.' Grinned at the waitress, 'Hey, mama, bacon and peanut butter, toasted. Brown bread, for health. A Black Label. What you say, captain?'

Spitz didn't say anything. What Spitz didn't like was coincidence.

Nor did Mace. The white BMW had passed them an hour back going fast and reckless not even slowing to check for oncoming cars as they overtook on a blind rise. Mace had leaned on the hooter in anger and the driver'd given him the finger. Otherwise he wouldn't have paid attention. But a white BM with two black brothers caused him to check the registration plate against Pylon's sms. Same car. And as he and Christa pulled into the motel at sunset, the Willard Grant Conspiracy loud on the sound system, there it was too, parked outside the row of rooms. Coincidence. But Mace didn't like it. He almost drove off to find somewhere else to spend the night. Except why? They were bloody booked in. He phoned Pylon.

'They're here,' he said. 'Merino Inn Motel. You can tell the cops.'

'What a pleasure,' Pylon said. Then: 'Hey, Mace, it's a helluva coincidence, don't you think?'

'Helluva.' Mace disconnected and stared at his daughter coming out of the bathroom looking more like eighteen than thirteen. 'We're only going to eat at the local steak house,' he said.

She pulled a face.

44

'Please,' said Sheemina February, pushing the contracts across the table to Obed Chocho with her gloved hand. 'I need you to sign them now.'

'They can wait. Come, what is the hurry?' He left the paperwork lying in the middle of the table just beyond his reach, stretching over to pour more Cap Classique into her flute.

The bottle was two thirds down. 'Celebrations first.' He filled his own glass. 'Empowerment.'

Sheemina February raised her glass. Again he leant across to clink the toast.

'Empowerment.'

'Salud, Obed,' she said, feeling the bubbles burst against her upper lip as she sipped.

It was their second toast. He'd come in loud, swaggering down the corridor to the boardroom. Following her, booze and cigarette smoke oozing from him, brandishing the bottle of méthode champagnoise. Any partners working late stayed behind closed doors.

In the boardroom, Sheemina February took long-stem flutes from a cabinet. 'Signing contracts does not need champagne.'

'These do.' Obed Chocho pulled the cork with a violent twist, the fizz exploding over the glasses. He snorted a laugh. 'Mighty fine, mighty fine.'

The first toast: standing opposite one another.

'To success.' Obed Chocho, making to clink her glass, but she drew back.

'Perhaps we should be cautious. Not tempt the gods.'

'To success.'

And she had shrugged. Their glasses touched. She'd sipped cautiously at the wine. He took the bubbly in a swallow.

'Here are the contracts,' she'd said, moving to the far side of the boardroom table, taking the papers from a manila folder. Sitting.

He'd drunk off another glass before he sat.

'You must drink. Honour our venture.'

She'd taken a swallow, pushed the contracts into the middle of the table. He'd filled their glasses, proposed the second toast. The contracts lay between them.

'Empowerment.'

He was watching her, grinning, leaning back in his chair.

She held out a pen. 'The contracts, Obed.'

'Why do you wear that glove? Take it off. Show me what you're hiding.'

'No.'

He reached for the pen and caught her hand, her good hand. 'Show me. We are business partners. We have no secrets.' He tightened his grip.

'Let go.'

'Show me.'

'I said, let go.' She wrenched her hand free.

'Do not play with me.'

'You've been drinking, Obed. You are in violation of your parole on that count. On another you are breaking the hours of restriction.'

'To sign the contracts.'

'We agreed you'd be here at three o'clock this afternoon. I have been waiting since then. For five hours.'

'I had business.'

'Nothing more important than these papers.'

'Business.'

'Drinking with your friends.' She picked up the pen and held it out again. 'Stop wasting my time. Sign and I'll drive you home.'

He took the pen. 'Because of you my wife is dead.'

'What!' She came forward, her hands on the table pushing the papers at him, a bemused smile on her lips. 'Oh come on. Get real.'

Obed Chocho wagged the pen like an admonishing finger. 'Because of you.'

'No, Obed, not because of me. Because of you. Because you wanted Popo Dlamini killed. Phone Spitz. Phone Manga. Make the arrangements. Perhaps you've forgotten that.'

'I did not say kill her.'

'Nor did I. But you knew if she was with him, she'd die. You knew that. You didn't try to stop her.'

'I did.'

'Well it didn't work.'

Obed Chocho drank off the rest of his glass, and refilled it. 'You are a hard bitch.'

'I am your lawyer, Obed. I am looking after your interests.'

'Oh mighty fine. And whose name is this?' He pointed at her name on the contracts. 'The name of my business partner. The lady with the gloved hand.'

'Sign, Obed.'

He laughed at her, imitating her voice. 'Sign, Obed. So that I can be rich.'

'So that everything is legal.'

She flipped the contracts through to their final pages. Obed Chocho scrawled his signature.

'Drive me home,' he said. 'Work for your money.'

'I intend to,' said Sheemina February, filing the papers back into the manila folder. She held out her gloved hand, her fingers rigid. 'The pen, Mr Chocho. If you don't mind.'

Saturday

45

The white BMW was parked where it had been. No sign of the black dudes. Mace hefted his bag into the boot of the Spider, thinking, bloody cops. What was so difficult here? He flipped open his phone and called Pylon, watching Christa come out of their room carrying her shoulder bag by the strap. Standing there in her knee-length jeans and red T-shirt, Diesel shades stuck in her hair, asking what she should do with the key. Heard the call going through to voicemail, said to her, 'Leave it in the door', and put a message on Pylon's phone that the cops hadn't followed up.

He looked back at the BMW: a brother now leaning against the car, drinking from a mug, his eyes on them. Not the short dreads man.

Christa flung her bag into the boot, rabbiting away about the heat so early in the morning.

'It's going to get worse,' said Mace, folding back the top. He got in beside her. Started the Spider, let it idle to running temperature, aware of the man watching them. 'Take about a hour to get there.'

When the car was cooked, he headed past the lounger at the white BMW. The guy barefoot in the dust, wearing shorts and a creased T-shirt, beaming at them. Called out something Mace couldn't catch.

Christa waved, said to Mace, 'He's a happy man.'

Mace said, 'Don't you believe it' – wondering if Pylon would get any joy out of the cops second time round.

They skirted the town, drove north on a secondary road, no traffic except a farmer in a double cab heading for market and a family walking next to a donkey cart, going north into an empty landscape. Scrub and white-thorn acacias and plains of dry grass.

'Where's their home?' Christa shouted against the tyre drum.

'Probably that's it, their cart,' Mace yelled back. 'They're cart-people. They move around.'

Other side the Seekoei River, he slowed down picking up the judge's markers: a plot of three graves on the left, the ruins of a house back among poplars on the right. Couple of hundred metres farther a rusted shell of a car that'd been out of production for sixty years more or less. Next gate on the right would have two whitewashed rocks either side of it, turn in there. Remember to close the gate. Sign on the fence said trespassers would be shot.

The gravel track beyond had a high middle ridge overgrown with rank weed. The scratch and scrape against the Spider's chassis gave Mace the rittles. Christa too, her hands clamped over her ears as the car bucked and bumped.

'We should've had a 4x4, Papa,' she shouted.

'No kidding,' Mace said.

About three, four kilometres from the gate to the farmhouse, the judge had said. Across the stone flats, round a koppie, in a stand of bluegums a kilometre off they'd see the house on the slopes looking towards the river. Might be called Seekoei River but hadn't been a hippo there in probably two hundred years, the judge had said. On the stoep though were some bones and teeth that'd been found in the river bank.

Mace eased the Spider along the track so slowly they could have walked faster. You were thinking security, you'd think the approach alone might put off any but the determined. Farm murderers fancied getting out in a hurry. And no way you could do that without a high-wheeled rider. Mace wondered if the judge wasn't overplaying the problem here.

They came round the hill mostly in first gear, the temp gauge riding higher than Mace was happy about and no chance of gearing more than second tops. To the west of the hill the view opened up over black rock krantzes dropping to a slash of riverine bush. Beyond that thorn acacias, savannah grasslands, yellow in the morning light. A nice sight, except Christa screamed and Mace saw two Dobermans and a Rottweiler tearing up the track, the dogs silent, showing teeth.

No time to bring up the hood. He kept the car moving towards the house among the eucalyptus trees. If they stopped, the dogs would have them: the Dobermans circling the car now, making snapping feints. The Rotty lumbering up, barking.

Mace brought out Rudi Klett's P8 and worked the slide, thinking to put a round in the air. But before he could two shots went off in the trees, shotgun twelve bore, Mace reckoned. The dogs backed off: the Dobermans still circling, the Rottweiler following red-eyed. Up ahead a thin man stepped into the open, feeding shells into the chambers, the shotgun broken over his arm. Mace brought the car up to him.

'Mr Bishop,' said the man, lanky in denims that sagged at the crotch, 'you've come out here for nothing, my friend. I told Telman, this is not a good time. We have other matters to think about.'

Mace cut the engine, got out of the car. 'Nice gun, the Mossberg.'

'It has its uses.' The man locked in the barrels.

'Like keeping the dogs in line.'

'One of the few things they'll listen to except my voice. If they can hear my shouting.'

Mace pointed at the shotgun. 'With those things I go for the side by side, myself. Looks more scary. May I' – holding out his hand to take the gun. 'You're Mr Marius Visser, Telman Visser's father?'

'Justice Visser. Judges stay judges.' Justice Marius Visser hesitated before letting Mace take the weapon. The dogs growled.

'Lovely,' said Mace getting the weight and balance of the shotgun, lifting it to his shoulder, steadying the barrels on a Doberman. The dog didn't like it. Crouched, baring its teeth. 'My preference's a Remington. The classic SPR. Something about the spread of the barrels I suppose.'

'You know about guns?'

'A little.'

Justice Visser nodded. 'Like I said, there's no purpose for you here.'

'That's not your son's idea.'

The farmer snorted. 'I don't listen to him. Most of the time I don't have a son.'

Mace let this go, looked past the old man, saw a woman come onto the stoep and wave. 'That your wife?'

'It is.'

Both younger than Judge Visser had said. The woman a lot younger than the justice. More like the son's age.

She called, 'Bring them in Marius. For coffee.'

They sat on the stoep: Salome taking Christa through the bone collection; the old man and Mace staring at the view down to the river, out across cattle country beyond. Except old man Visser didn't run more than a small herd anymore, he told Mace. Too much hassle. Heartwater. Botulism. Brucellosis. TB. Ticks. Worms. A long list of trouble. What he did run was an orchard of apricots down on the river's flood plains. A production of fruit that was beyond describing. Through all the talk, Mace noted the Mossberg wasn't far from the judge's reach. The dogs lying on the steps of the stoep.

After coffee Mace called the old man's bluff, said they'd be leaving, Marius getting a set to his jaw and Salome going, 'Ag no, what's this nonsense! Nee, man, Marius tell them to stay.'

And Justice Marius Visser, moving off the stoep, saying, 'Ja, wife, ja, okay' and to Mace, 'You will find me in the shed.'

While Christa got their overnight bags from the Spider, Salome said to Mace, 'We were expecting you. Don't worry about him.'

She took them into the lounge, down a dark passage to a bedroom. On every wall the heads of kudu, eland, hartebeest, springbok, jackals, caracal cats, warthog, otters. Skins instead of rugs on the floor.

Christa said, 'Did Mr Visser shoot them all?'

Salome laughed. 'No, sweetie, not any of them. Most of these animals you can't find here anymore.'

'It's creepy,' said Christa, 'all these dead things.'

'I'm used to it,' said Salome. 'On my father's farm it was the same.' She held out her hand to Christa. 'Come, I have eggs to collect from the hens. You can help me.'

Christa looked dubious.

'It's what your mother used to do,' said Mace.

Mace found the old man in the shed, tending a mampoer still. A heavy mustiness in the air, the only light coming in the open door barely brightened the gloom.

'This's what I use the apricots for, those I don't sell,' said the justice. He handed Mace a shot glass of clear fluid. 'The best you'll find between here and the Marico.'

The still looked ancient to Mace. Like Marius Visser's pastime wasn't anything new on the farm. He took a sip at the juice. It hit his stomach with fire but the apricot taste lingered, a faint sweetness under the burn. Mace spluttered. Rotgut at mid-morning gave him the sweats.

'Good, hey?'

'Strong,' said Mace, clucking his tongue to get some feeling back. 'Usually this stuff doesn't taste of anything but alcohol.'

'Because it's kak. Good mampoer's got to have smell and tang.'

Justice Marius Visser took a bottle from a cupboard and topped up Mace's glass, poured one for himself. He directed Mace towards a circle of old wingbacks, the fabric worn down to the thread in most of them. Dark stains between the wings where men had rested their heads over the years. Visser took a chair facing the door, placed the Mossberg beside him. The Rottweiler collapsed at his feet. The Dobermans, Mace reckoned, had to be looking after Mrs Visser. Which suited him. Mace sat at an angle to the old man and the door. He wondered if maybe he shouldn't have left the P8 in the Spider.

They sat in silence until Marius Visser said, 'What happened to your face?'

Mace touched at the plaster that covered the knife slit on his neck. 'A mugging.'

The justice snorted. 'You need security, my friend.'

'Appears so.'

'Get out of the city. In the small towns there're no problems.'

Mace raised an eyebrow but let it go, took another sip at the moonshine.

The two men fell silent until Marius Visser said, 'That's your daughter, the girl?'

Mace nodded.

'She's coloured.'

Mace shrugged, thinking if the justice wanted to get a rise out of him he'd have to try harder.

'If she's your girl what about the car?'

'What about it?'

'A bit moffie.'

'I'm not queer,' said Mace.

The justice took his shot glass in one throw and refilled it, holding the bottle for Mace. Mace followed him. The test here hardly subtle. The old man leaned over to fill his glass.

'I'm not into black,' said Marius Visser. 'I'm a white chocolate man. That black's better is bullshit. I've had black. A bit swampy otherwise seemed the same as white to me.'

Mace made no comment.

They sat in silence again. Mace could hear the voices of Salome and Christa in the distance. Nothing distinguishable but the excitement in Christa's tone.

Justice Visser took the level in his shot glass down to half. Mace left his standing on the side table between them.

'I see your little red ninnie car coming round the koppie this morning,' said Marius Visser, 'I thought you had to be one of Telman's bum chums. He's sending his moffie mafia, I thought.' He glanced at Mace. 'You know my son, Mr Bishop?'

'We met once. We've spoken on the phone.'

'Your thoughts?'

'He seemed concerned about you.'

'Bah!' The sound exploded from Marius Visser so forcefully Mace felt the blast. 'From his mother's death thirty years ago I don't hear a word from Telman. Suddenly nine months back he phones. We talk. What do you want I ask him? Nothing, he says.

To talk to you. You're my father. I tell him he's out of my will. Has been out for twenty-nine years, his talking to me's not going to change anything. He says he doesn't want the farm. That was Telman's problem: no contact with the land. I think, ja, son, what scheme are you pulling. Salome says, loosen up. Talk to him, things change. It starts happening that every two weeks he calls. Once he comes here to see us. Nogal! In his chair. That was difficult for him and for me. But, ja… We get through it. After that a couple of times Salome makes me phone him. Like last Sunday. I phone him because my friend's died. I ask him to come to the funeral. But no. I ask him to come this weekend. But no. Instead you rock up because he's on about farm murders.'

'You're carrying that Mossberg around,' said Mace.

'Precaution.'

'Why?'

Justice Marius Visser smiled. 'What'd Telman say about me.'

'Nothing much. That you'd been a judge.'

'A hanging judge. He tell you that?'

Mace shook his head.

'Sixty-three executions. Sixty-three rapists, murderers, scum bastards out of this world. Take away two whites that makes sixty-one blacks. That's a lot of people might have a grievance. Telman starts with this nonsense about farm murders I think maybe we're not talking random violence we're talking revenge.'

Mace said, 'He wants me to put a man out here.'

'No way.' Justice Marius Visser shook his head. 'No way in hell, my friend.'

'The only other option is fences, lights, sensors, radio contact.'

'I'm not going to live like that.'

'I didn't think so,' said Mace.

The old man finished his glass, reached for the bottle. 'Drink up.'

'Uh uh,' said Mace, placing a hand over his glass.

Marius Visser frowned, unscrewing the bottle's cap. 'No? A

bloody moffie drinker!' He refilled his own glass, raising it in a mock toast. 'Telman give you his wheelchair story?'

'We only spoke business.'

'Ask him one day he'll tell you. Tell you why he hates his pa.'

'So much he followed the same profession? Got appointed to the bench?'

'Out of spite, Mr Bishop. Getting back. Showing he was as good as me, even from a wheelchair.'

Mace took another mouthful of mampoer not sure where this was going or if he wanted to hear it.

'Because his pa, me, I put him in that wheelchair.'

Here it comes, Mace thought, watching Marius Visser kill another shot glass of mampoer.

'Coming back to the farm one day, late, driving into the sun, I rolled the car. Telman was a boy, ten years old. He goes flying. No safety belt so he goes flying. Snap, snap, his spine broken in two places. From that day he hated me.'

'Shit happens.'

'The shit wasn't finished happening. Twelve years later my wife, Telman's mother, kills herself. With tablets. Telman blames me.'

Mace took the rest of his mampoer. Said, 'Maybe I should look around a bit.'

In the afternoon he and Christa took a walk down to the river to see a Bushman painting. But mostly for Mace to get away from Marius Visser. The man in his face about the death penalty, abortion, child rape, gun laws, hijackers, criminals' rights, TV violence, bad language, some theory that blacks had a smaller brain without the hardwiring that allowed for a sense of forward planning.

'You give a darkie a bonus, what does he do? Gives the job the finger, goes home and sits under a tree till the money's gone. Like there's no tomorrow, my friend.'

Mace'd wondered how he'd get through the rest of the

day and evening until Salome suggested the rock art. Saying, 'Whyn't you and Christa take a walk there. Marius rests in the afternoon anyhow.'

She'd drawn them a map, Marius Visser going on about how it was difficult to find and badly faded.

'Piss on it,' he'd said.

Salome saying, 'Language, Marius.'

'Brings out the colour.'

'That's why it's faded, all your family splashing it.'

And Marius Visser had stomped his Mossberg off to bed.

The path led Mace and Christa down a break in the krantz, the black rocks rising either side of them like an entrance to a primal world. Mace noticed the Dobermans had stayed back with Salome on the stoep, the Rotty following to the slope then stopping. Not that he wanted the dogs. He had the P8 in his backpack.

Where the path bottomed out it joined a sand track and they followed this into the apricot orchard, the fruit long harvested, the leaves turning brittle. A quiet among the trees, no birds, no insects. At the end of the orchard, a gate opened onto a path that cut through the riverine bush to a clearing above the river. More a pool than river flow, the surface scummed with algae. Where sun shafted through the wattle and willow, swirled clouds of mosquitoes silver in the light. A bad smell everywhere. As if beneath the undergrowth small dead animals lay rotting.

Mace got the feeling they were being watched, that prickle on his arms.

Christa said, 'I don't like it here, Papa.' She took his hand.

They stood, listened to the quiet. No weavers chatter, no piping frogs. Mace with the hair up on the back of his neck, squinting into the foliage. Situations like this you had to go by your ears. As he and Pylon had in the gun-running days. Situations like this? Walking with his daughter on a farm ... What was to fear? Unless you spooked yourself.

'Come on,' he said, heading across the clearing to where the path went on through the bush. 'This's the way the map says.'

'We don't have to,' said Christa.

Mace looked over his shoulder. 'Go back and tell them we couldn't find it. Hey, are we going to do that?'

Christa smiled. 'No.'

'So then.'

They went on through the matted growth, Mace flailing with a stick at spider webs that snagged across the path. Big Golden Orbs running up the threads. Still the lines caught against their faces, sticky, binding.

Out on the open ground below the krantz, they stopped to rub the webs from their skin.

'How're we getting back?' said Christa.

'They way we've come.'

She looked off at the bush, her face tight.

Mace said, 'There's nothing there.'

'It's so dark materials.'

'What?'

'You know. Poisoned.'

He didn't know but felt no need to pursue it. Christa's world, Mace reckoned, was often filled with weird stuff. All that reading when she'd been flat on her back facing a life paralysed.

They walked on, the path faint and disappearing, running out on a slippage of hard shale. The Vissers had mentioned this. Mace scanned the krantz for any breaks and gaps.

'Bit of a climb,' he said, pointing at what seemed a cave. They scrambled up and between the rocks, emerging onto a ledge, behind it the overhang hardly big enough for two to crouch under. They waddled towards the back on their haunches and found the drawing: a thin red figure with horns. In his hand a stick. Appeared to be issuing from a fissure in the rock the way the Bushman had depicted him. Not a big figure, the span of Mace's hand from finger tip to thumb tip. You didn't know it was there, you'd miss it.

Mace said, 'Hardly a picture' – wondering how the Visser males had ever got enough angle to piss on it. He shimmied off to the ledge, found a place to sit with his feet dangling.

Below, the land folded out towards the horizon: a hot stillness settled on it. He recalled one of the killer country groups on the iPod singing about the loom of the land. All the menace packed into the word.

'Hey, C,' he called turning to his daughter, 'check this view.'

'Coming,' she said.

When she hadn't ten minutes later, he said, 'Leave it now.'

She joined him and they sat on the krantz that was without birdsong or birds, gazed over the cut of the river and the long savannah flats beyond.

'He's still here,' said Christa eventually.

'Who's this?'

'The man with the horns.'

'Yeah?' said Mace.

'Down there,' said Christa. 'At the pool, he was watching us.'

46

Spitz and Manga spent the day beside the motel pool on plastic loungers under thatched umbrellas. Both of them keeping out of the sun, slathering on upper UV-factor sunblock.

'Too much sun, captain, you go black like a Mozambican you're in deep shit,' was Manga's advice. 'Nobody wants to be shiny black. Or you're dead, captain. Dead as a Somali trader in a township.'

Manga went off twice for burgers and Cokes from the Wimpy, bringing Spitz back a chef's special salad instead of a double cheese and chips the second time.

Spitz spent the hours with an old Halliwell's he found in the reception's courtesy bookshelf, putting together a roster of movies for when he got home. Chill out for a week with his collection. For starters: Dog Day Afternoon, Blade Runner, Blood Simple, Panic.

Towards four he told Manga he planned to take a rest, Manga saying, 'Captain, seven we're gonna eat at the Wimpy. Eight wheels are rolling.'

Spitz shrugged. 'It is your schedule.'

'Ms February's,' said Manga. 'According to the lady's sms.' He held up his cellphone.

'She left you a message?'

'All the details.'

Spitz slipped on his moccasins, walked off towards his room, thinking, Why must she have the contact with Manga?

Manga called out. 'Hey, captain, not those moegoe shoes on your feet tonight. You want some proper shoes ask me.' Spitz walking away from Manga's laughter, feeling his phone vibrating in his pocket. Sheemina February.

'I have the message from Manga,' he said.

'Good. But that's not why I'm phoning, Spitz.' He could hear the sound of the sea, waves breaking, behind her voice.

'Where are you standing?' he said.

She laughed. 'Doesn't matter, Mr Triggerman. What matters is this: that man in the photograph I gave you will be at the farm. He is not part of the contract. If he gets hurt that is fine, but he must not die. You understand me.'

Spitz unlocked his room door, went in out of the glare. 'Who is this man you protect?'

'Never mind. Oblige me, alright. I have my reasons.'

'To me they are very strange.'

'Humour me, Spitz. It will be worth your while.'

He tried the earlier question. 'Where are you standing?'

And heard her sigh. 'Sometimes you can be very irritating.' The line disconnected.

Spitz shrugged at his reflection in the motel room mirror. If the man was no problem he would stay alive. Although nothing could be guaranteed.

By eight they were driving into the night, Spitz wanting to know the destination when Manga turned the BM onto a secondary road, nothing but blackness up ahead.

'Forty-two kays down the drag,' said Manga, clicking the odometer to zero. 'Make it half an hour. Ten minutes for the job. Forty, forty-five minutes we are back on the road, captain, straight arrow for Jozi.' Manga thumped the steering wheel. 'Tomorrow you can see a movie at the Zone.'

'I have not thought about it.'

'Shit, captain, why don't I believe you?'

The thing Spitz had thought about was finishing with Manga. No more captain. No more burger-breath.

At forty kays Manga slowed down said, 'Grab a flashlight, captain. On the right you're looking for a car wreck, then two white stones at a gate.'

They found the car wreck and the gate, turned onto the farm track, taking the rough slowly.

'There will be dogs?' said Spitz.

'Probably,' said Manga. 'For you to shoot.'

'With this weapon?' Spitz held up the Ruger 10-shot with the can screwed on that'd been lying in his lap since they'd left town. 'In the darkness? How will I do that?'

'That's your problem,' said Manga. 'You use that small shit for people, it can work on dogs.'

'People are standing still,' said Spitz. 'I don't shoot animals.'

'I dunno, captain. You've got another idea?'

Spitz shook his head. 'This job it is a cock-up. From the blood in the car to now it is a cock-up.'

When they rounded the koppie and saw the lights of the farm house in the distance Manga stopped, lined up the Beemer for a hasty exit. He cut the engine, leaving the keys in the ignition. They sat listening: no dog bark, only the screech of crickets.

'Let's go,' said Manga, sliding a nine mil into his belt.

Spitz sat tight. 'I work alone.'

'Not on this one. Mama's orders.'

Spitz didn't budge. 'They know my conditions.'

'Captain,' said Manga, opening his door, 'this is the way it's gonna be, okay. You go in. You do the job. I stay outside taking a smoke. It's the same as you're working alone, except I'm not waiting in the car.'

'This is a cock-up,' said Spitz.

Manga got out of the car, leant back in. 'You've said. So how about we cut the crap 'n do the job.'

Spitz held himself, a pulse starting in his neck. Watched Manga standing at the front of the car, staring back, grinning. And got the feeling he'd had before that Manga was running another agenda. Maybe Sheemina February too. 'Goodbye, Spitz, nice talking to you.' Some strange set-up he couldn't see. Spitz thought about the money, opened the car door. He took out his gloves, put them on.

'You lead, captain,' said Manga. 'You're the triggerman in the fancy shoes.'

Spitz didn't rise to it. Brushed past Manga, so the guy stumbled back a pace, off balance.

They walked one behind the other down the long track, Spitz in his lace-up brogues, stepping carefully over the shale and broken ground. A dikkop started up at their approach, flew off calling and the two men stopped, listened until long after the bird was quiet, Spitz scanning the shadows for any dogs. They went on, able now to see the outline of the house against the trees. Ten paces farther Spitz stopped again, crouched, lowering onto his right knee. Manga bumping against him, bent down.

'What's it?' Looking ahead, saying 'Wena' at the sight of the Rottweiler coming on.

Saying, 'Shoot, captain, shoot.'

Spitz steadied himself, raised the pistol in both hands, waited until the dog was two metres out to put the sharp lead of the rimfire into the animal's chest. Which dropped it.

Manga exhaled a whoosh. 'Man, captain, you take your time.'

The Dobermans hit Manga from behind, taking him down beneath them with a grunt, their jaws working at his neck, a low growl in their throats, tearing at clothing and skin to get a choke hold.

Manga gasping, 'Help me, captain. Help me' – kicking out at the dogs.

Spitz waited until the dogs were still, Manga pinned beneath them. 'Do not move,' he said, stepping towards the nearest, from a metre putting a round in the animal's head, swivelling left to knock off dog two. Such close ups, the slugs raced round the tiny skulls, finding no way out.

Spitz helped Manga to his feet. Manga panting, bleeding from teeth punctures, his T-shirt bloody and torn.

'Sshh,' said Spitz, watching the house, the door opened, a woman stood there. She whistled for the dogs, called their names. Said something back into the house and closed the door.

Manga reached for the pistol in his belt. 'Any more dogs I don't care.'

'I do not think so,' said Spitz. 'They would have barked for her.'

Manga fingered his wounds, yelping at the pain. Some of them bleeding. He held his shirt against them to stop the blood. 'Captain,' he said, 'captain, you coulda shot me.'

Spitz gave a German shrug. 'With your gun, yes, maybe that is likely. With this the chance is doubtful.'

'But possible.'

'Sure. Perhaps it can happen.'

'Captain,' said Manga, 'your problem is you don't care.'

They crept closer to the house, approaching from the front

until they could hear through an open window the voice of a man talking, a woman interrupting him, saying 'Marius, please that's enough. Leave it.' Another voice cut in too low to hear what was said.

Spitz scoped the surroundings, saw the red Alfa Spider parked near the shed. He touched Manga's arm, pointed at the car.

Manga grinned. 'The larney with the lovely daughter.'

47

Justice Marius Visser was saying, 'Bring back hanging, simple as that. For murder. For rape. For paedophiles. Maybe even for aggravated assault. Ja, even. The more you've got it onna books the better. Sending out the right signals. We mean business, chommies. You get outta control we're gonna kill you.'

Marius Visser taking another half a shot of his apricot mampoer, a good number under the belt already. He leaned across the table towards Mace.

'Hanging doesn't stop anyone except who you hang. But that's what you want. Stops him, the bastard. Makes him think about what he's done.'

'Marius, the girl.'

Justice Marius Visser looked at Christa across the table, Christa looking back at him Zen-faced. He waved his hand at his wife. 'She's big enough.'

Salome glanced at Mace but he kept his eyes down, focused on mopping up gravy from his plate with a slice of bread.

'I went to every one.' The justice hammering the table with his fist the way he'd brought down the gavel at a sentencing. 'For the bastards to see me. Not one I had second thoughts about. Even the whites. They're hanging there by their necks I thought good riddance.'

'Marius, please, that's enough. Leave it.'

Mace saying, 'We've had a hectic day. And got a long drive tomorrow.' Pushing back his chair. 'What you say, C?'

'There's pudding, man,' said Marius Visser. 'Siddown.' Thumping the table again as the front door banged open.

Mace saw a black guy with a silenced .22 enter. Neat short dreads hairstyle, impassive face. The gun on Marius Visser. Behind the gunman a brother he recognised, the lounger at the BMW. Standing in the doorway with a nine, held up at shoulder height. Grinning like this was major fun.

He heard Salome gasp.

Heard Marius Visser yell, 'Kaffertjies', the shooter taking him out with a head shot, even as the justice lunged for his Mossberg. The shooter swivelling left to Salome putting a single load in her forehead. The Ruger coming on, aimed at Mace.

Heard the hitman say, 'No problems. Stay standing still.'

Mr Nine Mil stepping in, blood on his T-shirt. 'Heita, peoples. Sorry to disturb.' The man bleeding from neck wounds.

The hitman saying, 'Tie them up.'

Mr Nine Mil bringing his pistol onto Christa. 'You crazy, captain. There's a little chickie here can to save us from HIV. Hey, sweetheart?' Mace watching the man come up to Christa, pull her face into his crotch, the muzzle of his gun laid against her temple. Christa rigid with fright. Drops of blood falling into her hair.

'Leave her.' Mace rising, his chair crashing back behind him. '

The gun in Mr Nine Mil's hand coming up and firing. The first round whacking into the wall. Mace taking the second in the arm. The third and fourth smashing into the heads of mounted buck. The fifth smacking into his chest. Mace staggered, turning from the gunman. The sixth, a ricochet, caught him in the back. Mace went down.

Sunday

48

Pylon, in the kitchen upending poached eggs onto croissants, said to his step-daughter, 'Pumla, tell your mother, breakfast's on the way' – giving her a tray with bowls of marmalade, jam and grated cheddar to take upstairs.

Pumla saying, 'I didn't hear you fetch the croissants?'

Pylon plopped out a perfect egg, not breaking the yoke, came back, ''Cos you were asleep. I got them from the deli half an hour ago.'

'Kalk Bay?'

'A new place, nearer.' Licked his fingers.

'Mom'll know,' said Pumla. 'She only likes the Kalk Bay ones.'

'She won't guess.' As he took out the last egg his cellphone rang. Captain Gonsalves. The phone vibrating across the work surface. 'Take the tray,' he said to Pumla, 'tell Treasure I'm almost there.'

Pumla giving him that look he was on dangerous ground.

'Captain,' said Pylon, 'this's Sunday.'

'For some people it doesn't matter,' said Gonsalves. 'One of them's you. You know the Smits? Young couple. Lots of money.'

Pylon tucked the phone in between shoulder and ear, made a mess of getting out the last egg. 'Sure.'

'I'm standing in their apartment. Nice place. Very expensive. I'm looking at this view of the ocean all the way to the horizon. You ever wondered how far that is?

Pylon could hear the cop chewing. Imagined yellow tobacco juice leaking at the corners of his mouth.

'What's happening, captain?' he said.

Mash, mash. 'I think,' said Captain Gonsalves, 'the best thing is you come here and talk to me about some things. We can look at the view.'

'The Smits...?'

'Dead. Four people in one week the name of Pylon Buso's in there somewhere. Sort of coincidence makes a policeman wonder.'

'I'm there,' said Pylon.

He took a bite into his croissant and egg, through the mouthful shouted up to Treasure. 'Emergency. I got to go out.'

Heard her yell for him.

'Later,' he called back. 'This's bad news.'

She got him on his cellphone. 'What's going on?'

He explained.

'I don't know, Pylon,' she said. 'This isn't the way I see family life.'

'Me neither,' he said. 'Be more fun mowing the lawn.'

'Pah!' He could picture the smile on her face. 'You think you're Mr Clever giving me breakfast in bed?'

'Must score some points.' Pylon took another mouthful of croissant.

'If the croissants were Kalk Bay.'

Before he could respond she'd disconnected. The sarky way pregnant women got it was a wonder men wanted children. Maybe explained why so many men ran away.

Gonsalves was out on the balcony of the Smits' apartment with a cup of tea. 'Next door,' he said, 'the people there told me that broad in Basic Instinct came here to a party the Smits gave. Last Christmas. Movers and shakers, hey.'

Pylon said, 'How'd they die?'

'There's tea in the kitchen,' said Gonsalves. 'I made a pot.'

'Come on, captain.'

The cop looked at him over the top of his cup. 'What I could ask first is what you saw them about last Thursday.'

Pylon sat down, pulled his chair round to face Gonsalves. 'It was business, okay. Business. I wanted them in on a development up the west coast'

'You into property now?'

'Investing.'

'And how'd the Smits fit in?'

'They owned some of the land.'

Pylon left it there, Gonsalves signalling with his hand come on, spill it.

'They wanted to go with the other bidder. I told them it wasn't a good idea.'

'Like that? Calm?'

'Ah, save me Jesus, I wasn't threatening them.'

'No? What then?'

'Warning them off.'

'Offa who?'

'Someone called Obed Chocho.'

Captain Gonsalves put down his cup and saucer. 'The one…'

'Yeah, the one whose wife copped it.'

'Serious.'

'Serious.' Pylon tapped his fingers on the table. 'So now you're going to tell me what happened.'

Gonsalves took off his glasses, scratched his eyebrows. Wild flying eyebrows. 'Thursday night they didn't pitch for a dinner with friends. The friends got worried. Couldn't get them on their cells. Couldn't get them here, left messages on the answering machine. Even came round. No answer. They phone some hospitals. Nada. They go to the police, the officer says what's the big deal? Could be a simple reason. They forgot. They're on a flight to New York. The friends say no something's wrong. The officer says come back tomorrow if they've not rocked up.'

Gonsalves took out a cigarette, tore at the tip and unravelled the tube, shreds of tobacco falling into the cup of his hand.

'The next morning the friends are back on the job. Good friends, hey? Phone hospitals, cop shops, even the mortuary. Try again in the afternoon. Naathing. Yesterday, guy at the

248

mortuary listens to the descriptions believes he has a match to two bodies. Wallah.'

Gonsalves rolled the tobacco round his palm with the index finger of his right hand until the fibres had balled, popped the pellet into his mouth.

'That bring meaning to your world?'

'You haven't said what happened?'

'Probably a hijacking.' He glanced at Pylon, raised his wiry eyebrows.

Pylon stayed shtum.

'Upstairs on the parking deck they've got two cars, the Smits. More'n enough for most people. A Saab coupe. BM five-series. What's missing is a white BM. Sort of courtesy car they kept for visiting friends. Thoughtful, hey.'

'Very. They were shot?'

Gonsalves grinned, stopped chewing, the moisture from the tobacco glistening on his lips. 'Leading question.'

'So?'

'So, ja.' The policeman's jaws going at the tobacco again. 'Only not where the bodies were dumped.'

'And that was?'

'Flamingo Vlei. Big wetlands, lotsa reeds. Hadn't been for what they call twitchers counting birds they coulda spent a while there. Ever wondered why you'd wanna count birds? Why you wouldn't wanna count mosquitoes instead? Or locusts?'

'No,' said Pylon. Then: '.22 long by any chance?'

Gonsalves picked tobacco fibres from his lips. 'More like .38s from what I saw. Why?'

'Curious.'

'Spit it.'

'Dlamini and Chocho's wife were head shots. .22s.'

'Nah,' said Gonsalves. 'Not the same at all.'

The two men stared at the horizon: a container ship crossing their line of sight heading for the harbour.

'Obed Chocho, huh,' said Gonsalves. 'Got a shut down on any stuff about his wife, pronto, pronto. No telling when that case'll see the light. You think he's involved here?'

Pylon shook his head. 'Why if they were going in with him would he do that? Knock them off.'

Which wasn't what Pylon thought. Pylon thought Obed Chocho was right at the bottom of this. He and his hitmen. The question was more how to place him there?

'Maybe,' said the captain, 'he'd already got what he wanted. They'd signed a deal?'

'Could be.' Had to be, Pylon was thinking.

'Maybe,' said the captain, 'I should talk to him. Given the business connection. Find out their association.'

'Why not?' Pylon watched the container ship slide from view. 'I'd be interested to know that.'

'Offering some sort of incentive?'

'Depends.' Pylon's phone rang. On the screen an unknown number. 'We can talk about it when you've got it. Whatever it is.' He connected.

49

The pain brought him back. Every breath burned. Vicious, a skewer through his lungs. He lay still keeping his breathing shallow, listened to the night. He heard nothing. When he tried to move, a sear of agony took him out again.

Later, he said, 'Water', felt the cold dampness on his lips. He imagined lying beneath a waterfall with the spray splashing his face. He could open his mouth, swallow clear, cool torrents.

'Papa,' he heard. And his daughter sobbing.

He drifted away to a place with two wounded men. The dead all about, Boers and MK guerrillas. Techipa, Angola. The last months of the war. The one MK clutching at his own entrails, moaning with pain each time he gasped for air. The other MK shot in the thigh, the flesh stripped away, the bone exposed. The left cheek of this man missing, his teeth showing. No other wounds. He saw himself shoot this man first. A heart shot into a cammo T-shirt soaked with blood mess. Took out the one gut-wounded next. Also a heart shot.

He groaned. Felt pressure on his hand and smiled, whispering his daughter's name.

It was light when the pain brought Mace into consciousness and kept him there. He said, 'Christa, Christa' forcing out her name through the stab and rack of breathing.

His daughter's face appeared blurred, hanging above him, disembodied. His vision slowly cleared. Her cheeks streaked with tears, a smear of blood on her forehead.

He managed: 'Are you alright?'

She nodded.

'You've got to help me,' he said. 'Help me sit.'

She tried to prop him up but he was too heavy, the movement causing him to moan with agony. She cried at her father's hurt. A viscid spread of blood oozed from him.

Mace waited with his eyes closed until the pain settled.

'The farmer...' he said. 'Dead? His wife?'

Heard her whisper, 'Yes,'

Mace opened his eyes to see the body of Mr Nine Mil on the floor.

'The man shot him,' said Christa.

'Did he touch you?'

Christa shook her head.

Mace let the moment hang, the throb in his arm and chest sucking away the room. A perfect white pain held him.

Slowly colour came back. He saw his daughter. Heard noise: the racket of guinea fowl. Just bullet wounds, he told himself, you can get up. From the blood soaked in his shirt, slicked on the floor he'd leaked badly. But that'd stopped, mostly. Hardened into a crust. Yet the pain wouldn't let go. Kept him from moving. Kept him from realising he couldn't move.

'Time?' he said.

Christa told him ten.

'Okay,' said Mace, his voice rasping, tasting blood in his mouth. 'Find a phone. In the bedroom. In the kitchen.'

Probably they'd have cut the wires but maybe they wouldn't have bothered.

'I've done that,' she said.

'Pylon?'

Saw her nod. Wanted to say, my girl, but couldn't.

50

Spitz had stopped every five kilometres once through the farm gate. Got out of the car, walked to the fence, threw a gun into the veld. Left hand side, right hand side. First Manga's two nines, then the Ruger without the can, next the silencer, the rifle Manga'd been lugging around, finally he dropped the Mossberg into a river. They'd be found eventually, most of them. One or two might end up with the cops, even that was unlikely.

On the highway he plugged the iPod into the sound system, let the voices of his killer country wrap around his soul.

The right way for a job to finish with all the problems sorted out. He fired a menthol, exhaled a long stream at the windscreen, the blueness tingeing the dark terrain he drove through.

Six hours later Spitz turned into an old mine estate on the outskirts of Johannesburg. Private property notices dangling from the fences and gates, the gates hanging off their hinges. He drove past the old headgear, the abandoned buildings clustered around the shaft, into a bluegum plantation and left the car there. It too would be found, eventually. Before that would probably be stripped.

Spitz walked off with his bag and Manga's. Went through the plantation down into reeds where a stream ran, a rainbow slick of oil along its surface. Plastic, cans, broken bottles strewn about. Old fireplaces ringed by stones.

He dumped Manga's clothes on the bank, threw the bag into the reeds. Went on following a dirt track that took him out of the mine estate onto a tar road. Here Spitz waited for a taxi. Smoked menthols, listened to his tunes, wondered if he could polish the scratches from his brogues.

THE ISSUES

THE ISSUES

51

The surgeon said, 'You're lucky to be alive. You're lucky you can walk out of here. Thank your daughter, Mr Bishop.' Mace walking out of the hospital between Oumou and Christa ten days after the Red Cross had airlifted him in.

The doctor's words coming back at him: 'Your daughter hadn't been there, I'd have given you, what, twenty, thirty hours at the most and you'd have shuffled off our mortal coil. Not a great way to do it, Mr Bishop. Lying there in all that pain, bleeding out.' He'd unscrewed the lid of a specimen container, dropped a lump of lead into Mace's palm. 'That was against your spine. The reason you couldn't move.'

When he was strong enough Mace took the cable car up Table Mountain. Felt he needed the sense of space. Time out of the city. Of being above it. Somewhere he could vent his frustration without being heard.

Alone on the plateau of the mountain he brooded about being caught like a sucker. First by the vagrants, then by the hitman and his sidekick. Brooded about his own uselessness. Gazed down at the beaches, and along the spine of the mountain to the end of the peninsula, forced a bitter laugh at the irony of being a security man.

Brooded until a woman called out to him for help, a Spanish tourist, trembling with fright.

'Please, please, they have stolen my camera. A man with a knife.'

He'd given chase but the man was gone.

Later he'd said to Pylon, 'What they need up there are some vigilantes. That'll stop the mugger.'

Pylon'd raised his eyebrows, said, 'Don't even think about it.'

Except he did.

Mace brooded about whacking the mugger.

Took the cable car up with the tourists and walked away south along a path until he could hear nothing but birdsong. Sat on a rock nursing his wounded arm, nothing in view but wildness and sky, willing the mugger to seek him out. Bastard knocked over tourists daily, why didn't he have a go at him?

Mace thought, do something useful, take out the rubbish. Leave his body for the crows. Who was to know who'd done it?

Get a silenced Ruger like Mr Short Dreads, plop, plop, nobody'd even hear it. Drag the body off the trail into the bushes, it'd be three days, a week before anyone found the corpse.

Mace fantasising about the surprise on the mugger's face, the prick standing there with a rusty kitchen knife looking fearsome. Give me your cellphone. Give me your money. Give me your boots. Suddenly the Ruger up the thug's nostrils. A bit of shock and awe dawning in his eyes.

Cap the bastard.

What a pleasure! Nothing there that would come back to haunt him. Like the justice said, getting rid of the scum.

The desire stirred Mace so much he jumped up to walk it off. Found his way to the path, hoping someone would take him on.

Give him back his self-respect.

That it wasn't for nothing he'd taken lead. The first in a lifetime with guns and ammo. Three bullets that'd almost done it for him. A flesh hole in the bicep, a chest shot that'd skated round a rib and torn out a hole in his armpit, and the ricochet. At a time when he should've been protecting people. Let alone his daughter.

Mace walked back slowly to the cable station, wondering why he had no plan? Sat on a bench looking down at the city and the bay. The murmur of city noise rising loud in his ears. Like the beast was growling. Nothing clear in his head about what to do, he phoned his daughter.

'Papa,' she said, 'I can't talk now.'

Mace brooded:

With Oumou on the Sea Point promenade, the two of them walking there one afternoon. Time out with sun and ice creams.

Mace saying, 'I'm not functioning, Oumou. I'm half a-bloody-sleep. I got to get back to normal.'

A story she'd heard repeatedly over the past month. But he hadn't quit them.

'I could've got us killed.'

A line he trotted out once a day.

'You could not do anything otherwise.'

A line she countered with.

'I could've. I've thought about it. The pistol was in my belt, for heaven's sake. I had the time. I could've done them both. Probably before short dreads got the woman.'

'Mace, cherie.' She stopped, reached out a hand to his good arm. 'We have been over this many times, no?'

He swung his eyes from her face over the lawns to the blocks of flats, an urban cliff along the sea front. Where fatcats lolled in deckchairs, sunning their stomachs. Fatcats needing protection. And he brooded about the short dreads hitman who'd walked out like he didn't care that there were two witnesses. That he could dispense death. Allow life. Untouchable.

'Sure,' Mace said.

'If you stop with blaming yourself, you will feel better.'

'Maybe,' he said.

They leant against the wall. Below some men stretched out on towels soaking in sun and cancer rays, on the rocks a gran with two boys. Mace looked across the sea to Robben Island, the island low in the haze.

'Fat chance I've got of swimming there now.'

Oumou rubbed a hand over his back.

'If Christa can walk again, then you can swim one day.'

'I don't know.'

The self-pity bubbling up in Mace. The way he felt so often: a spare part.

'I've got to do something.' He turned to Oumou, pulled her to him. He could smell clay in her hair.

Mace brooded:

With Pylon, in the office, thumbing through a mining magazine, the face of the gunman smirking at him.

Pylon saying, 'This isn't the end. No ways.'

Mace flipped the magazine onto the coffee table.

'Give it up. Obed Chocho's legal. He's got the contracts. He's got the tender. What're you going to do?'

'He took out Rudi Klett.'

'Oh right. He's confessed?'

'Those guys stayed at Chocho's house.'

'Big deal. The cops would love it.'

'The cops. Who's talking cops.' Pylon jumping up to pace the room. 'Why're you so negative. This isn't Mace Bishop talking. The hellboy.' He stopped next to his partner. 'We should roll over on this? That's what you want?'

Mace let out a long sigh. 'I don't know what I want.'

A silence in the room. Someone revving a bike on the square, someone calling a name. Pylon dropped onto the couch. 'Wake up, brother. Get on the programme.'

'I'm thinking of it.' Mace raised heavy eyes at him. Saw the hard brown stare of the man he'd known for more of his life than anyone else. The pursed lips, the quiver in the nostrils that Pylon got when he was worked up. Felt a deep lethargy dragging him down. Times were he thought to go down with it.

Pylon reached over and slapped his knee. 'Come on. Snap back, save me Jesus.'

Mace straightened in his chair. 'Okay, okay.'

'You with this?' Pylon leaning forward, started tapping off

points on his fingers. 'Here's what we know. We know they connected with Obed Chocho. We know they took out the farmer. We know one of them's still alive. You with me?'

Mace nodded.

'Sharp.' Pylon held up another bunch of fingers. 'Here's what we assume. For the hell of it. We assume this gent, Mr Hitman, did the number on Popo Dlamini. Taking the .22 headshot as a clue. Reason: Popo was screwing Obed's wife and Obed didn't like it. Same reason the lovely Lindiwe got done.'

'Chocho takes a contract on his own wife? Give me a break.'

'Ah, Mr Bishop returns.'

'That shit happens only in movies.'

'Whoa. Whokai. Hey, we're talking assumption. We're talking stories. Let's play it out.' Pylon waiting for Mace to agree. Mace opening his hands with a shrug. Pylon smiled. 'Good. So we assume Mr Hitman took out Rudi Klett. Same sort of headshot. Also a .22. Reason: Rudi Klett could jeopardise Obed Chocho's development plan. All of the details known to Obed thanks to double-dealing Popo Dlamini. How'm I doing?'

'It's a story.'

'Course it is. Now here're the blinds. Who got to the Smits and why? Could be Obed because everything's signed and sealed, but why'd he bother? Also the shooters had a white BM. Could've been the Smits car.'

'Possible.'

'And who got Mr Hitman onto the farmer? No leverage for Obed Chocho there. Except Judge Telman Visser sentenced Obed Chocho to six years. The man could be pissed off. But if we're talking some sort of revenge, why not take out the judge himself?'

'Why not?'

No answer.

Tami came in with the post, handed a bundle to Pylon, another to Mace.

Pylon said, 'How about some sandwiches?' Tami, on her way out the door, paused. 'Make mine gruyere on half rye. With gherkins.'

'Very funny.'

'I'll have the same,' said Mace, waving another copy of Mining Weekly. 'What's this?'

Tami said, 'Search me. Probably a freebie, fishing for a subscription.'

Mace tossed the magazine onto the table.

Pylon said, 'Please, Tami, do us a favour, sisi.'

'Jeez,' said Tami. 'Buti' – giving him a run of Xhosa that brought an embarrassed laugh out of Pylon.

'Hey,' said Pylon, 'remember who's the makulu boss.'

Tami sashayed off in the way that Mace appreciated, her arse tight against the black slacks.

Pylon said, 'Can I have your attention, sir?'

'What for?' said Mace. 'We're getting nowhere.'

Mace brooded:

About the hitman's motive in not killing him, Christa. Finishing the job. Was it scorn? Pity? Ridicule? Was it because he could never be found. Could drive into the vastness leaving no traces of who he was. Mr Invisible. Mr Almighty.

He could hear the man's laughter. See his mouth wide open. His teeth glistening.

Mace phoned Christa, the girl at school on break. Every morning he phoned her, keeping it light. Nonchalant. Like he just happened to do it on the spur of the moment.

'I'm okay, Papa. You don't have to worry.'

Mace saying, 'Just checking.'

One morning Christa responded differently. 'Papa, in life skills we heard about PTSD.'

'Which is?'

'You know, stress.'

'So?'

'So you're stressing.'

'You think?'

'I think,' Christa talking quietly. 'Like hectic.'

Mace calling while on one of his mountain-top walks, hoping to flush out a mugger. 'It bothers you? My phoning?'

'Papa.' A pause with the shrieks of playground noise in the background letting Mace know that the connection wasn't down. Then: 'It's not that.'

'What then? You think I need a shrink? Your Dr Hofmeyer?'

'She's a therapist.'

'You think I'm crazy?'

'I was shot, too, Papa.'

'Been there, huh. Done that?' Regretting the words immediately.

He heard a bell ring for the end of break. 'I've got to go Papa.'

'I'm sorry, C,' he said. 'I didn't mean that.' Realised she'd disconnected.

Mace sat on a rock staring at the back of Devil's Peak. Beyond a plane sank out of the sky. He tapped the phone against his knee, insistently, rapidly. Stressing. He was stressing. His daughter telling him this. That he needed to see someone. The strong silent untouchable Mace cracking up.

The pebble scrape of footsteps snapped Mace back to the here and now. A man coming along the path, eyes focused on him. A black brother, lanky type, cornrow hairstyle, shades, something metallic in his hand. Mace slipped off the rocks, out of the man's sight, planning to circle up behind him.

Except he came round the boulders, the man was right there in his face. Mace going straight for him, spinning the brother, a lock across his throat, slamming him against the rockface. Shades snapping. Whatever the man held clattering as it fell.

'Want to mug me?' Mace said, bouncing the man's head off

the sandstone. 'Think I'm some German pisswilly? Think again, china.' Bringing a knee up hard in a groin mash. The man gasped, Mace let him fall on the sand. Brought out the P8.

'Mountain ranger,' Mace heard him wheeze.

'What?' Mace grinding the barrel against the man's temple.

'Ranger.'

'Oh yeah.'

'Please.'

Mace heard two-way radio static from the handset fallen between the rocks. A voice saying, 'Dumisa, Dumisa? Come in, Dumisa.'

'You're Dumisa?' said Mace.

The man nodded. Mace put away the pistol. 'You should wear a uniform,' he said, walking off.

Mace brooded:

Alone. After being woken by Oumou in the small hours from a dream.

Came awake with her voice soothing him.

'What?' he said, 'what?' – sitting up.

'You are shouting,' said Oumou. 'And jerking about your body.'

Mace collapsed back on the pillow. 'I'm soaking.' Running a hand over his damp chest. 'Ah, that was horrible.' He got up. In the bathroom towelled himself dry, the images from the dream still vivid.

'You are having a nightmare?'

'It's okay,' he said, 'I'm okay.' Standing at the bed. 'I'm going to make some tea. Rooibos.'

Oumou, half upright, resting on her elbows, watched him pull on a tracksuit. 'Mace, cheri, why do you not want pills? With them you can sleep.'

'I've had them,' he said. 'You know what they do to me. It's like being half-asleep all the time. They're not the answer.' He zipped closed the tracksuit jacket, looked down at her. 'There's something I need to do. To get rid of. You know, purge it from inside me. I reckon that's what's my problem. When I get rid of this thing I'll be alright.'

'And this thing is?'

'I don't know. A fear. Something weird.'

'You must see Dr Hofmeyer.'

'No ways. Forget it. You and your daughter both want me on a shrink's couch. Uh uh. I'm not mad.'

'Of course. Macho is the same thing, yes.'

'Not at all.'

'Christa has seen Dr Hofmeyer and she has no problems. No nightmares. But you think you can be shot and be a tough man. Non, mon cheri, it is impossible.'

'Soldiers do it all the time. So do cops.'

'Ah oui, soldiers. Policemen.' Oumou levered herself upright. 'How many policemen kill their families? Shoot at their wives and their children? Every week I hear it on the radio.'

'All right. Okay,' said Mace. 'Just let me work this thing out. Then I'll do it.'

'You are making a promise?'

'Sure.'

'For the sleeping pills and for Dr Hofmeyer.'

'Both.'

She looked at him. The sceptical tilt to her head Mace had seen plenty of times when she wasn't sure if he was playing straight.

'Genuine,' he said.

Oumou pulled her knees up under the duvet. 'Oui, I am going to believe you. But what is your English saying that we will wait and see.'

'You will,' said Mace, at that moment convinced he meant it. He opened their bedroom door. 'Want some tea?'

Oumou shook her head, settled herself again. 'Do not stay up for too long.'

Mace looked in on Christa, a tight ball beneath the duvet. She didn't stir at the click of her door opening. The cat did, made a strange strangled meeou, leapt off the bed, rubbed against Mace's legs. Mace stared at his daughter, the spray of her hair across the pillow. Thought, even when you were with them, you couldn't protect them.

In the kitchen he dunked a rooibos bag in a mug of boiling water. Stood at the counter in the dark with the blinds open so that he could see the city: the bright lights pooled in the bowl. The yellow strings around the bay.

Cat2 sprang on the counter, pushed against him for attention. He rubbed the skin between her eyes, thinking about the short dreads hitman. About why he hadn't killed them? There was no reason. Two more deaths on such a hit list couldn't be a bother. No. He'd let them live because he could. He didn't care. It was a favour. A backhanded donation. The way you'd flip a coin into a beggar's tin. Without thinking. Walking past in your own life, untroubled.

Mace got riled at the thought. At the arrogance. To be dished out charity by a self-styled Mr Death. And then to rub it in.

He spooled through the nightmare again, image for image. Being chased across a stony terrain: the ground rock-strewn, huge piles of boulders scattered about like silent mausoleums. His legs heavy, the muscles too fatigued to move him one step after another. Like he was staggering through soft sand. Panting with the effort. Pylon ahead, looking back to urge him on. The sound of gunfire. Of men shouting. And the face of the short dreads hitman suddenly at his shoulder. The man laughing, showing his teeth he laughed so hard. Bringing up a pistol with a silencer. Pow. Pow. Not gunshots, but the hitman's joke imitation.

Mace felt the sweat break out across his chest and back again.

52

She had visited him in hospital. Looked in on him while he slept, a vulnerable man taped to tubes and drips. His cheeks rough with beard, his face almost peaceful with his eyes closed. Those eyes that were like glass. Cold blue ice. Nordic, like her own. Which appealed to her. Gave them something else in common.

She thought to leave a rosebud. A single stem in an elegant glass vase on the table beside his bed. It would anger him. Maybe even put a chill in his blood. Although she believed Mace Bishop hid whatever troubled him in violence.

She smiled to think of his reaction. Imagined he would backhand it off the pedestal. Summon nurses, security, demand explanations.

Describe her. How? Tall. Striking. High cheekbones. Perfect lips, deep plum lipstick. Her brilliant eyes. Her dark hair, glossy and bobbed. The stylish suit. The black glove on her left hand.

Try to have her banned from the ward. For leaving a rosebud! His insistence that he be taken seriously. The puzzled expressions of the nurses and doctors, nodding, patronising, infuriating him.

For that alone it would've been worth it but she had other plans. Instead she stood at the foot of the bed, photographed him.

She brought up the photographs on her laptop. A series: a long-distance of a stretcher being lifted from an air ambulance; another, closer, of the wounded man on the stretcher being placed in an ambulance, a woman and her daughter standing anxious, looking on; the ambulance under the portals of a hospital, its doors open, the stretcher being rushed into casualty. Two photographs of Mace Bishop in his hospital bed. The next of him leaving hospital on crutches. The photograph tightly framed, sharp enough to catch a wince of pain on his face. Then: Mace walking the promenade, his arm in a sling; Mace at a café, his arm free; Mace at the upper cable station, a photograph taken from behind with the bay in the background. Another of Mace approaching the photographer: a figure in the landscape on a path leading between rocks over low scrub. The top of the mountain, behind the figure the cliffs of Chapman's Peak dropping to the sea.

In recent weeks she had a number of photographs of Mace on the mountain. At first she'd wondered at his sudden taking to the heights. Then noticed they tracked what the papers called the mountain maniac's attacks. How sweet, she thought. He's playing vigilante. Unless he was the mountain maniac himself. The notion brought a smile to her lips.

Leaving the pictures she poured herself a cold white wine, sauvignon blanc, went to stand on the balcony. Above the horizon a sinking sun held little heat. From below rose the voices of tourists on a sunset cruise, heading for the Waterfront. A few waved at the sight of her. She ignored their gesture. Then turned to face into her apartment: the crimson of a westing sun flushing its whiteness. She liked this time, this autumn season, with its hint of winter.

She went in. Plugged the iPod Spitz had sent into her sound system and scrolled through the playlist to a section he'd called Songs of Murder. At first she'd found them too sentimental, too emotional. But on a second listening she'd heard something else: a simplicity that appealed to her. These were songs about people who lived by their own laws. They were ruled by their hearts.

She liked that.

Sheemina February turned the music louder, Love Me Someday, flopped down on a couch. She heard the song through, Jesse Sykes putting out an invitation. And the next. Soft Hand. A driving beat, got her foot tapping. Then the voice, full-on sex. Singing about a soft hand to ease him in. She could imagine doing that. Skin against skin. Reversing the roles. Sitting on him. Her thighs splayed over his. His slow thrusting into her. His hands on her breasts. Her hands around his throat. How gently he could be squeezed into death. She could see him on her laptop, the face of Mace Bishop staring across at her, puzzled.

The song ended and Sheemina February took a swallow of wine. Agitated, went back onto the balcony. The sea was empty now, a breeze scratching its surface. She could hear the music faintly still: another murder, another broken heart. Spitz's anthems. I'll Follow You Down. He Will Call You Baby.

She'd been irritated when he'd sent the iPod. Phoned him. Asked him what he thought he was doing?

'It is nothing,' he'd said in his weirdly formal English. 'A gift precisely.'

'Alright. But this is it, understand.'

Waiting for him to say, 'I understand.'

'I'll be in touch,' she'd said. 'Presently.'

Sooner than she'd thought, as it turned out.

She selected his number on her cellphone. The phone rang once only.

'Everything is fine,' Spitz answered. 'There is no need for any concern.'

'I wouldn't have thought otherwise,' she said, disconnecting.

53

Judge Telman Visser reached across the table and spooned lemon sorbet into the young man's mouth. Smiling, his eyes fastened on the eyes of the young man, his coach, Ricardo, such emerald eyes, such a name. The young man sucked the ice off the teaspoon. With his own spoon scooped a helping from the ball of sorbet in the dish between them and held this towards the judge, the judge opening his mouth in anticipation, his teeth gleaming with saliva.

'A palate cleanser,' said Judge Visser sitting back in his wheelchair, following the tang of the sorbet with a sip of riesling. A 2001 vintage, crisp and clean. His second glass on a starter of grilled haloumi fingers. One of his most successful hors d'oeuvres, a word he used twice as Ricardo carried the plates to the dinner table, pronouncing it the French way. He touched his upper lip with the tip of his finger. 'Sorbet,' he said.

'Ag.' The young man coloured, wiped at his moustache with a serviette.

'And how was that?'

'Righteous, judge. I've never had that before. Legend food.'

'Isn't it,' said the judge. He pointed at the bottles of red wine on the sideboard. 'Will you do the honours?'

The young man pushed his chair back. 'Any one?'

'I think the pinotage, something peppery to go with the duck.' Watching the gym trainer's movements, so lithe, so fluid. The white shirt with the pink stripes, riding up with each step to flash a neat bum in black trousers. Telman Visser imagined running his hand over the curve of that bum.

'Let me invite you to supper,' he'd said to Ricardo at the end of a session the previous week. They'd been out for dinner a clutch of times, met for coffee twice, the judge felt it was time to move things on. Normally he'd have gone in faster but he enjoyed the seduction of the young Ricardo. There was a frisson to be had from the slow unfolding. Also he wasn't sure which way Ricardo swung. Probably back and front, he decided.

'Where'd you learn to cook so well?' said Ricardo, drawing the cork.

The cork coming out with a soft plop like sex, to the judge's way of thinking.

'I took classes. But I've always liked cooking. Since I was a boy. My father hated the idea.' And Telman blew out an amused 'mmm' through his nostrils.

Ricardo brought the bottle of wine to the table, poured a little into the judge's glass as he'd been taught.

The judge swirled it. 'Actually he hated me. Does your father hate you, Ricardo?'

'Never,' said Ricardo. 'He loves me. He tells me that.'

'You're lucky. It's not pleasant when your father hates you. He even tried to kill me in a car accident. Certainly put me into a wheelchair for life.' He tasted the wine, sucking in air over the liquid pooled in his mouth. Swallowed. 'Excellent. Try it, Ricardo.'

Ricardo filled his glass and took a sip, not a mouthful as the judge had once told him.

Judge Visser said, 'I get deep richness. And there cocoa coming through, now the prickliness of the pepper. Lovely. Full.'

'I don't know,' said Ricardo, 'I can't taste that.'

'Take another sip. Hold the wine on your tongue… That's the way, let it rest. And breathe in gently through your mouth. Now swallow and you'll taste the chocolate.'

'Hey, wow, I can,' said Ricardo. Grinning looking down at the judge gazing up at him. 'Amazing.'

The first bullet put a hole in the big pane in the lounge window, buried itself in the opposite wall high up, plaster chips showering the table.

Ricardo dropped his glass and the bottle, wine splashes spotting like blood across the judge's shirt. Vivid on the pale blue. The judge ducked, turning his wheelchair to face the windows.

The second shot came lower down, shattering the pane, embedding at head height in the wall between two of the judge's prize Kentridges: both visions of horror and desolation. Both worth six figures. Glass shards tinkled after the bang.

Ricardo screamed, dropping to the floor.

The judge shouting, 'Bastards, bastards,' propelling his wheelchair at the window.

The third bullet was high again, smacking into the wall above the picture rail.

Then silence.

Then a motorbike revving off at speed.

Then a neighbour's dog barking.

'It's over,' said the judge, breathing hard. 'They've gone. He's gone.' Turning his wheelchair to see Ricardo's head appear above the table, the boy's eyes large with fear. 'Are you alright? Not wounded?'

Ricardo shook his head. His mouth worked but no words come out.

The judge said, 'I think I'd better call someone.' He dug in his pocket for his cellphone, called Mace Bishop.

54

Mace took the call on an intercity bus, a solid mama sitting next to him in the window seat who should have booked a double. Mace jammed between her thigh and the aisle armrest. Five hours he'd endured with another three to go. Not a spare seat in the bus he could escape to.

He saw the judge's name on the phone, said, 'This's a bit late, judge.'

Heard the judge say, 'I've been shot at, can you get here quickly.'

Mace said, 'Where?'

'In my house, dammit.'

'I meant where're you hit?'

'I'm not.'

Mace paused, he could hear someone whimpering in the background. Wasn't the judge. The judge's voice was hard and angry. Said, 'Get the cops, judge. I can't help you. I'm out of town, fetching my car.'

He heard the judge say, 'Christ' before the connection was cut.

Mace thumbed off his phone thinking, what was the judge's case anyway, ringing him? He had security. He had the cops. Strange coincidence though six weeks after his father's killed someone takes potshots at the remaining Visser. Except, even in the middle of the night in the middle of the Karoo, Mace couldn't see a link. Felt he was missing out on something. Or more likely the incidents weren't related. More likely something to do with the arms deal commission the judge headed. For sure if the same person that had arranged the shooting of Justice Marius Visser was involved, then Judge Telman Visser wouldn't be making phone calls.

Mace shifted about in his seat trying to win a little space from the mama, but the woman's thigh didn't budge, the heat of it burning through his jeans. You could see why none but the desperate took the intercity buses. It would've been worth flying. Charging the expense to the judge. Sometimes saving costs wasn't worth the pain.

Almost four hours later, two o'clock in the morning, Mace stepped into a bedroom in the Grand Hotel. Flung himself down on the bed, slept in his clothes till reception woke him at eight. A Meneer Johan Pretorius was waiting for him.

Mace said to reception, 'Hell, man, I agreed eight-thirty.'

Reception said, 'Sorry, sir, he asked to tell you.'

Meneer Johan Pretorius was sitting in the breakfast room, drinking orange juice when Mace got down, still in his travel clothes.

The lawyer stood up, extended a hand. 'Ag, ja, I hope I'm not rushing you,' he said. 'I have a tight schedule.'

Mace wondered why a lawyer in a small town would have any schedule at all, let alone a tight one.

'They do a good breakfast here,' said Johan Pretorius, turning to the buffet. 'You can eat as much as you like.'

Johan Pretorius heaped scrambled egg, sausages, bacon and two fried tomatoes onto his plate. Ordered a rack of white toast. Mace did the same, passing on the toast and the sausage.

'I've got your car outside,' said Johan Pretorius, cutting carefully into the sausage to release a squirt of fat.

Mace watched him, realising the trouble with boerewors was that the sausage looked like a turd, ruptured at both ends.

'Nice car. Goes like a bomb.' He winked at Mace. Grinned. 'No, I didn't drive it around, Mr Bishop, it's okay, though there were a few poppies who begged for a ride.' He winked again. 'But I haven't taken advantage. Your car's all spick and span and valeted at the garage yesterday.'

He reached across and patted Mace's shoulder. 'I'm pleased I can give it back to you. Sometimes the Lord's not so obliging in who he spares. Like Justice Visser. Magtig, a helluva problem these farm killings.' He lifted a forkful of sausage and egg to his mouth. 'Val weg.'

Mace hacked at the bacon. Just the way he didn't like it: too thick, not crispy.

Johan Pretorius said, 'Tragic business, the Vissers.' The lawyer bit into a slice of toast, leaving a smear of butter at the corner of his mouth. 'You know the story about them?'

He swallowed not waiting for Mace's answer. 'Let me tell you. That farm belonged to his first wife. She was a Malherbe. And I can tell you it was a Malherbe farm for about a hundred and fifty years before she got it. Maybe longer. Generations buried there. She was born in the old house, Suzanna, his first wife, an only child. On her death, the farm goes to Justice Visser. That's another story.'

'I know,' said Mace.

Johan Pretorius paused with a forkful of food.

'Justice Visser told me.'

'Magtig, is that so?'

'The bare bones.'

'He never spoke about it usually.'

'He didn't say much.'

'Probably he wouldn't tell you that he remarried six months later.' Johan Pretorius winked at Mace, a small smile on his lips.

Mace tasted the scrambled eggs and wondered how it was possible to make it so rubbery, give it the texture of stiff porridge.

Johan Pretorius was saying, 'The first thing he does is he wills the farm to his new wife because of bad blood between him and his son. If there were Malherbes left they would have shot him.' He sniggered. 'Ja, well, I didn't mean it like that.' And chewed at a mouthful of sausage and bacon. Then lowered his voice, leaning towards Mace. 'Let me tell you, a week before the attack, his lawyer's, old Niemand's office burned down. Old Niemand died too in the fire. Very tragic. But also all the man's legal documentation was destroyed. Of all his clients. So when Justice Visser was killed he was intestate.'

The lawyer leaned back. The smear of butter on his lips had melted. He stared at Mace. 'Do you know what that means?'

'Tell me.'

'It means his son inherits the lot.' Johan Pretorius wiped his mouth with his serviette. 'There is a saying, not so, what goes around comes around? Here is an example.'

The lawyer went through three mouthfuls of food before he said, 'But the story doesn't stop there. The farm is now for sale.'

'Any buyers?' Mace sipped at his coffee, thin and bitter, grimaced.

'No one's been to look.' The lawyer spooned three sugars into his coffee. Brought the level up with milk. He drank off the cup, his Adams apple bobbing. He winked. 'Farm murders, you know. Land claims. These days you buy land, you buy trouble. What can I tell you.'

Mace took a drive to the farm. The gate wasn't locked. Before entering he wracked a shell into the chamber of the P8, put the pistol on the passenger seat. He had an odd feeling about being there. Felt he was watched. Yet he had to go back. He'd always had to go back, revisit places that had gone bad. Places where he'd been and people had died. A mission in Sudan piled with killings. Villages in Congo littered with corpses. Boats in a Somali harbour where the seabirds ate at the dead refugees. Places where sometimes days, sometimes hours before a massacre, he'd traded arms. Places where he'd left ghosts.

He drove slowly, scanning the veld and the koppie ahead for movement. On the stony approach to the house, flushed a flock of guinea fowl, sending them clattering into the eucalyptus trees. He stopped the car, slipped off the gun's safety catch. Waited, watched. Put the gun between his legs, drove on into the shade. At first he kept the engine idling, scanned the shadows, alert for any movement. Then cut the ignition. The silence held until gradually the tick of insects and the movement of birds started again. Mace got out of the car, went up the steps onto the stoep.

The door to the farmhouse was locked but he could see through the windows the black stains on the floor where Visser and his wife and the gunman had died. And the spread of his own blood across the floorboards. He shaded his eyes against the pane: without Christa he might have died there. Thank your daughter, the surgeon had said. His daughter. The child he was supposed to protect. The thought weighed on him. And he spun away from the window, walked fast off the stoep towards the shed where Visser had brewed his moonshine.

The shed door was padlocked. Mace piled some logs under a high window, stood on these. He peered through the dusty glass, made out the still but the bottle racks were empty. Probably the cops hadn't seen any sense in letting good liquor go to waste. While he stood there, balancing, the automatic in his hand, he caught a movement reflected in the glass.

Mace dropped, crouching, the P8 clasped in both hands, sweeping slowly left to right, and back. Nothing. Except the silence, the birds quiet again.

He stood, waited for the bird chirp and the insects.

'Trying to spook yourself,' he said aloud, walking towards where he'd seen the movement, his footsteps a soft sibilance over the dead leaves and fallen twigs. A shadow was how he imagined it, shifting

276

between the trees. Gooseflesh prickled along his arms, crept at the base of his neck between his shoulder blades. A warning. It had kept him alive before.

Twice he spun suddenly but no one lurked behind him. At the tree line, where a swathe of open ground separated the plantation from the cliff edge, he paused. Looked back through the trees at the house almost hidden in the shadow, then started along the path he and Christa had taken to the river. From the krantz top he had a wide view: nothing moved below.

He sat on the rocks, gazed into the trees. Christa had felt they were being watched. He remembered that. Had imagined a man with the head of a buck, as the Bushman had drawn him. Mace shook his head, forced a soft laugh. And then he saw it, well back in the trees, unmoving. Tall, thin, horned. The light dappled about the body. A figure staring at him. Mace brought up the pistol, shouted, 'Hey?' – his finger putting pressure on the trigger. The shape not moving. Then Mace heard voices, far off to his right.

And glanced quickly: saw two men on the top of the ridge walking towards him. And back: but the spectre was gone.

Sometimes the light played tricks. You stared at shadows they changed shape. You looked from the sunlight into the shade, you saw things that weren't there. Mace stuck the P8 into his belt, covered the bulge of the gun with his jacket.

The men had seen him and stopped talking. He waved. One waved back. Young guys, probably in their late twenties, shorts, boots, rucksacks, floppy khaki hats. The one with a map in his hand.

Turned out to be geologists, specialists compiling a scoping report on the lie of the land. Part of a government survey. Were headed to tell the Vissers of their presence.

Mace thought, they don't know. Thought, the justice would've had them with his Mossberg even before the Dobers and the Rotty got them.

He recounted the situation. Flashed them his security card by way of explanation.

The one who'd spoken, who had a quick smile, took his hat off to reveal a dreadlock hairstyle only not as neat as Mr Short Dreads's, went solemn and said, 'That's not a good scene.'

His colleague with the map kept a stern mouth. 'I can understand it,' he said. 'The shit we get from farmers.'

'You'd have had it from this one too,' said Mace.

The geologists went on. Mace watched them out of sight before returning to the Spider. He didn't see the horned man again or even sense him. He drove slowly off the Visser land thinking that the geologist put him in mind of Mr Short Dreads. So did whatever he'd seen among the trees. Made him believe that what he had to do was find the hitman.

55

Obed Chocho stood in the sitting room of the Smits' getaway cottage, the stoep doors open onto the path leading down to the beach. Low tide, beds of kelp lazy on the sea's rise and fall.

Perched on a barstool behind him, Sheemina February looked at his head, shaven and glistening, and the roll of neck fat resting on his jacket collar. The tycoon surveying his domain. Yet all the drive out he'd been bitching about his dead wife. After these many weeks still going on about it. Get a life. Pull another chick, she wanted to tell him. Wasn't as if they weren't clamouring over him. Drawn by the smell of money.

'Mighty fine,' he said, 'mighty fine' – turning towards her.

'Mighty fine what, Obed?' She clicked her fingernails on a piece of driftwood the Smits had used as a countertop. Faint traces of blue paint embedded in the patina. Not so much driftwood as a length of ship's planking, a nice touch that gave the room a beachy feel.

'It is taking too long,' he said, 'the paperwork.'

'That's bureaucracy.' Sheemina February, brushed flecks of pollen off her dress. 'There's a process.'

'I am ready. I have sub-contractors waiting. People with bulldozers and trucks. Every day they're not working I am paying.'

'I warned you to wait.' She watched the bluster build in his face. Couldn't resist irritating him.

'You told me it would be fast. With your contacts.' His face puffed up with anger. 'You told me no problem. Ten days, two weeks we would be on site.'

'It's not ten days. It's been five working days by my count.'

'Five. Ten. Mighty fine. This doesn't matter. I am wasting money. Tens of thousands.'

'Obed,' Sheemina February came off the stool. 'What was my advice?' She raised her eyebrows at him. 'My advice was put the contractors on notice. On notice, not on contract. Wait until the tender's signed, I advised you. Not so?' She walked out the stoep door onto the path of crushed shells. Smelt the air thick with salt. Turned back to him. Obed Chocho standing above her on the steps. 'But what do you do? You get as excited as a boy with a toy.'

Obed Chocho beat his fist against the step railing. 'Mighty fine. To hell with you. Mighty fine. I will get another lawyer.'

'If you want to. If that will make you feel better. Be my guest. But remember the paperwork, Obed. It's a nightmare. The entanglements.'

'Your nightmare. Because of you.'

She ran her tongue over her lips, moistened the plum lipstick. Smiled. 'What were your words, Obed? Lawyer us up, I think was the rather hip phrase you used. Your brief, remember. I acted on your brief.'

Obed Chocho hissed out his breath.

'Think about it.' She climbed the steps until she stood opposite him, put a gloved hand on his arm. 'In another five days, in a week, the bulldozers will be here.' She withdrew her hand. 'In the meantime tell the contractors if they want the job, they must wait. At their cost. Believe me they're hungry, they're not likely to run. Also they'll want to stick close to you. Get in on the action.'

She waited until Obed Chocho said, 'Mighty fine' – watching the pulse working behind his ear. Such a small neat ear.

'Now,' she said, 'when's the architect getting here?' – even as she spoke, hearing the whine of a car in low gear. A big black Mercedes Benz. They watched it approaching.

'Not the architect,' said Sheemina February.

'Buso,' said Obed Chocho. 'Get him off my property.'

'Yes, sir.' Sheemina February snapping a salute. She waited for the visitor at the kitchen door. Pylon taking his time, getting out of his car, admiring the view, walking towards her.

'Mr Buso,' she said, 'this is unexpected. Come to have a last look at your distant dream.'

'I heard you were out here,' he said.

'Oh?'

'Chocho's secretary.'

'How discreet of her.'

'So I thought I'd bring you the news.'

'That's kind.' She stood squarely in the doorway. 'What news?'

Pylon bent to pick up a porcupine quill. 'Actually, not so much news, probably it'll be old news to Comrade Obed but a supposition.'

'Sounds intriguing.' She moved aside to let him enter. 'Go through.'

'You're trespassing,' said Obed Chocho as Pylon came into the sitting room. 'I can have you for that.'

'Visiting,' said Pylon. 'Briefly.'

'For what?'

'To tell you this: we know it's you.'

'Know what, Mr Buso?' Sheemina February standing beside

her client, rubbed a gloved thumb over the smooth elegance of her right hand. 'What mystery is this?'

'Not much mystery,' said Pylon. He pointed the quill at Obed Chocho. 'Just no hard facts.'

'Facts?'

'Facts to put Comrade Obed behind the shooting at Judge Visser's last Friday. Probably also the Visser farm killing. The Smits hijack. Popo Dlamini. Your wife, comrade. My German business partner. Eight deaths.'

'Pah,' Obed Chocho, threw up his hands. 'Bullshit.'

'Careful, Mr Buso, you're on the edge of libel.'

Pylon offered the quill to Obed Chocho. 'Here. This is yours. I found it outside. On your property.'

'Leave,' said Obed Chocho, taking the quill and snapping it. 'Get out. Go.'

'I'm going,' said Pylon. 'But know this: we'll get you.'

Obed Chocho laughed. 'Oh, mighty fine. Mighty fine. Piss off, arsehole.'

'I think you should go,' said Sheemina February, stepping between the two men, ushering Pylon to the kitchen door. When he was halfway to his car she called out, 'Remember me to Mr Bishop. Tell him I still think of him. Often.'

She watched Pylon reverse the big Merc and drive off. Heard Obed Chocho come up behind her. Without turning to face him, said, 'What happened to Judge Visser?'

'How should I know?' said Obed Chocho.

'Frightening the judge, that wouldn't be smart, Obed. You heard the man. He's put it together. He just can't join the dots.'

'Hey,' the word coming out shrill. 'I'm in the dark, okay. The first I've heard of it.'

'Oh yes.' Sheemina February searched his eyes: saw puzzlement lurking there.

56

'Tell me again,' said Mace to Judge Telman Visser. The two of them in the dining room at the judge's house. Mace making him run through the seating positions when the first bullet was fired.

The judge powered his wheelchair to the table, pointed at the sideboard. 'My guest was standing there, opening the wine.'

'Your guest?'

'A friend of mine.'

'Someone important? Another judge? A politician? A mover and shaker?'

'It's not relevant.'

'It could be.'

'A friend, Mr Bishop. Simply that, a friend.'

Mace shrugged. 'The curtains were closed?'

'No.'

'You ever close them?'

'No. What for? I'm a long way from the street. Nor am I paranoid, Mr Bishop. I don't imagine thieves lurking in my shrubs at night.'

Mace, at the window, looked over the garden. A trimmed lawn surrounded by rose beds, most of the roses sad and blown. Not the sort of shrubbery you'd want to go wandering through in the dark.

'They found casings,' said the judge. 'The police. On the lawn. .38s I think they said.'

'Amazing,' said Mace. 'Amazing that that's the best the shooter could do.' He crossed to the wall where the bullet had embedded itself, gazed at the hole above the picture rail. 'Guy wasn't even trying.'

'The second shot was closer.'

Mace studied the damage between the Kentridges. 'Not really. And the third's wider than the first. Some hitman. He's standing out there. He can see you plainly. He puts three bullets way right.'

'I can't be so casual about it, Mr Bishop.'

'Suppose not.'

'I need protection. Private protection. People I can trust.'

Mace nodded, moved to stand in front of the Goldblatt photograph of farm murders. 'So you brought it home.'

'After what happened it seemed even more appropriate. It's a reminder of the state of our country.'

'Despite the bad blood. Between you and your father.'

'Despite it. In recent times he'd been trying to reconcile. In his own way. I wasn't convinced but I hadn't resisted.'

'I heard,' said Mace, flopping onto a couch, 'that you got the farm.'

Judge Telman Visser shut his eyes, brought his hands together, rested his chin on his fingertips. He stayed like that for what Mace thought must've been a full minute. Then opened his eyes, blinked, dropped his hands into his lap.

'It seems you've heard the story.'

'I did. From the lawyer…'

'… Pretorius.'

'Pretorius.'

'A busybody.'

'Told me you had the farm on the market.'

'I have.'

Mace waited but the judge said nothing more.

'I went out there,' said Mace. 'For no reason. Curiosity I suppose…'

'Morbid. But I can understand it.'

'… Bumped into two geologists on a government survey. You've heard about that?' Mace watching the judge slump like he was overcome by weariness.

'No. Nor do I want to, Mr Bishop. I want to get rid of the land. It means nothing to me. Pretorius would've told you it'd been in my mother's family for generations but I am finished with that. Those are ties I no longer want.'

'Fair enough.' Mace stretched out his legs, linked his fingers behind his head. 'What's going on here, judge? Who's shooting at you? Wouldn't be a man called Obed Chocho by any chance?'

'Chocho?' The judge frowned. 'The man…'

'You put away for fraud.' Mace unhooked his fingers and kneaded the tension from his neck.

'He's out, I know. Six weeks ago on parole.' Judge Telman Visser paused. 'You believe… No. What on earth for?'

'It could be,' said Mace, 'that he arranged the hit on your father. Or we could be talking something completely different. We could be talking the arms commission you head. Important people unhappy at your inquiries. People getting people to tell you to back off.'

'Nonsense.'

'Does the name Rudi Klett mean anything?'

'The arms trader?'

'The same.'

'We have subpoenaed him.'

'How very proper. And?'

'The Germans are considering it. But Mr Klett is a hard man to find.'

Mace stood. 'Because he's dead.'

'You know this for certain?'

'Pretty much. He was killed here. In this city. Hadn't been here an hour before they got him. Question is: who are they?'

'I don't know any of this. It hasn't been reported.'

'Under the radar, judge. Lots happens in the static. Most of the time, who really knows what's potting.'

The judge eyed Mace. 'How do you know?'

'A birdie.' Mace winked in imitation of a small-town lawyer, and stood. 'For the moment let's leave it at that.'

The judge propelled his wheelchair towards the door. 'What about my security?'

'I'll arrange it,' said Mace. 'Trust me.'

57

The radio news reported two tourists mugged on the mountain. Not far from the cable station. The two from an early batch of sightseers making the best of a perfect day. The mugger must have gone up at dawn, said the reporter, also making the best of a perfect day.

The couple he attacked was Swedish. Threatened them with a long-bladed knife. Took their cameras, their cellphones, watches, jewellery, their cash, their passports.

'This happened so fast,' said the man in a soundbite. 'After we had given him some things, he snatched at my wife's bag with all our documents.'

'I am grateful we were not killed or hurt,' said the woman.

Mace thought, an hour max he could be on top of the mountain, up Nursery Ravine, head towards Maclear's Beacon. Meet the bastard on his way down.

He drove away from the judge's house along a street quiet, shaded, the mansions of the wealthy either side. Over-arching plane trees canopied the road, their leaves yellowing. Through gaps in the trees the mountain's high buttresses stood visible, a grey edge against the blue. A good day to be up there. He had the P8. Why not? The next client pick-up was in the afternoon. Plenty of time. Mace turned in at Kirstenbosch Gardens.

His cellphone rang. Pylon said, 'We're going to find that hitman. Now. Today. Go pack a bag.'

'You've forgotten something.'

'What?'

'Our clients. The ones flying in to make babies.'

'Tami can sort it.'

'Tami looks like muscle to you?'

'Tami breaks bricks. She showed me. We send someone with her, the clients won't know the difference.'

Mace looked up at the mountain. Thought of the mugger making his way down. 'What's the rush?'

Pylon said, 'I've got forty-eight hours. Treasure and Pumla are away. She won't even know I've gone.'

Mace hesitated.

'Look,' Pylon cutting in, 'you're the one all fired up to find Mr Short Dreads. Now's the moment.'

'What's stung you?' said Mace.

'Obed Chocho. And an old friend, Sheemina February. Told you she was in this.'

'She's lawyering him?'

'By all accounts. Probably shafting him too.'

Mace stopped in the shade of a tree. Killed the engine. The mention of Sheemina February didn't thrill him. The woman shadowing his life, marking anniversaries with a single plum rosebud. The anniversaries of Christa's kidnapping. The anniversaries he killed Mikey Rheeder. A single plum rosebud stuck in the Spider's windscreen wiper. Sometimes when the car was parked outside the gym. Once outside the office. Twice in random places: a city street bay, in a shopping mall parking garage. These two meant she'd been following him. That was the spooky bit, that she was watching. He'd told no one, not even Pylon.

The second time gone to her office. Braced her in reception in front of the receptionist. Held out the flower.

'You're sick. Perverted. No more, okay.'

She'd taken it with her gloved hand. 'How sweet. Thank you, Mr Bishop.'

Mace had stepped towards her, wanting to smash her face. 'You're sick. A bloody psycho. Don't do it again.'

'Or what, Mr Bishop? You'll pulverise my other hand.'

Mace had got out fast before he hit her. What she wanted, to get him on assault.

When the rosebuds persisted he decided, ignore them. Give

her no satisfaction. But they riled him nonetheless. He anticipated them. Got worked up and edgy around the dates. The day was coming, he knew. The day of reckoning.

He swung his legs out of the car, sat sideways in the seat. Priorities. The short dreads man was priority numero uno. Mountain muggers would have to wait.

'All right. How're we going to find him in two days?'

'Start with the dead,' said Pylon. 'The sidekick. Manga whatever.'

'Khumalo.'

'Him. I've got a family address.'

Pylon drove the hire car out of Johannesburg airport saying, 'Oh shit' at the signboards and the highways stacked above him, the windscreen wipers no help against the rain.

Mace said, 'Go straight' – the map book open on his lap.

'Once,' said Pylon, 'I knew this place like home.'

'Once,' said Mace, 'it was home' – tracing the blue line of the highway towards and round the city, shooting off towards Soweto.

'Now it's totally alien. Even the people.' Pylon slammed the gear down to third, shifting right into the fast lane, the car's engine screaming. 'A Toyota's not a Merc,' he said, behind them a Beemer flashed its lights, coming up fast. 'Will you check this brother behind waving us out of the way. Driving like a maniac in the wet.'

Pylon drifted left into the middle lane and the Beemer came past in a waft of spray. Two brothers up front smoking cigars gave Pylon and Mace the hard stare.

'Gangsters,' said Pylon. 'That's what they look like even when they're businessmen. Suits, shades, shaven heads. Who's to know the difference?'

'Keep straight,' said Mace, the city centre mushrooming between the hills, the tall buildings ghosting in the rain. The sight of them always something that thrilled Mace. Pity it'd gone to shit.

'Pity it's gone to shit,' he said.

'Refugees,' said Pylon. 'You let refugees in everything gets buggered up.'

'S'not only refugees,' said Mace.

'Mostly,' said Pylon. 'Zimbos. Yorubas. Congos. Angolas. Any place you can think of that's shot to hell. They're in there, slumming it.'

'Fair number of others, too.'

'Zulus,' said Pylon. 'Mostly.'

At Gillooly's interchange Pylon said, 'Okay now I'm remembering' – taking the hill and over, sorting out the spaghetti tangle to take them past the city centre that wasn't the city centre anymore. A stack of empty buildings you could see right through. Others draped in washing. Barrow sellers under tarpaulins, women with smoking braziers cooking mielie cobs on the streets.

Mace's cellphone rang. He fished it from a pocket, saw the name of the small-town lawyer on the screen and connected. Said to Pylon, 'Go off at Bara hospital.'

'Mr Bishop,' said Johan Pretorius, flannelling straight into a how's the weather, hope you had a nice trip home routine, Mace waiting for him to come out of it. The lawyer not pausing for an answer, saying, 'I have news' – and shutting up.

Mace said, 'That right?'

'You won't believe it. Most people here don't.'

'Try me.'

'A finished deal and nobody even got a whiff of it. Magtig, man. I have my ear to the ground in this town. This whole district not much happens that I don't hear about pretty damn smart. Sometimes even before it's happened. But this. This was tjoepstil. Not a whisper anywhere. And just a few days ago we were talking about it.'

'What?' said Mace.

'Judge Telman Visser,' said Pretorius. 'Today I heard his farm has been sold.'

'That right?'

'Not an hour ago, I heard it. But they tell me it was done yesterday. Signed and sealed.'

'Really.' Mace thinking, why'd Visser not told him. Actually lied to him. Said, 'Who's the buyer?'

'Miners. Zimisela Explorations. Not the first time it's happened in the district. Won't be the last.'

'Interesting,' said Mace – gesturing at Pylon to take the off-ramp, the road signage barely visible in the wiper swish. 'Thanks.'

'Makes the judge a rich man. I thought you might like to know.'

'Why was that?' said Mace. 'Why'd you think that?'

The lawyer gave a burst of laughter. Mace had to hold the phone away from his ear. 'No reason especially. Just spreading the good news. So what d'you think, Mr Bishop?'

'Got nothing to do with me,' said Mace.

'I would've thought…' The lawyer left it hanging. Said, 'Ja, well,' into the silence, wished Mace a happy day further.

Mace clipped the phone closed said, 'How about this: the judge sold out to a mining company. Yesterday. Tells me this morning he's in the market.' Mace musing, tapping his phone against the map book. 'Remember we got those mining magazines?'

'The freebies.'

'Them exactly. Strange, d'you think? Coincidence?'

'Probably.'

Mace opened his phone again, trying for Tami at the office.

The call went to the answering machine. Mace checked the time. Not half past four yet. 'Tami's bunked off.'

'Fetching clients,' said Pylon. 'The fertility couple' – giving a long toot at an iron and scrap merchant swinging his cart into the traffic. 'Save me Jesus, doesn't he understand about cars skidding in the wet.' The horse coming to a stop at the hooting. Pylon slapped down the gears to get round the animal. 'Why d'you want her?'

'Check out the magazines.'

'In case what?'

'In case anything?'

Pylon pointed at a building surrounded by security fences, a car pound visible behind it, said, 'There's the cop shop, can't be far we have to make a left into Sibasa.'

Second robot after a school they turned left, found their way to a house fronting a park. Neat place: face brick, metal windows, corrugated iron roof. Face-brick street wall and a metal gate. A white van in the drive. The drizzle persisted.

Pylon said, 'Ever known anywhere greyer in the rain than Soweto? Even worse than Berlin. Enough to make you slit your throat.'

They went up a concrete path to the front door. Someone was a pot gardener: pots of flowers everywhere, drooping.

The woman who opened the door said yes she was Manga's mother. Said she'd said everything she had to say to the police. Didn't invite them in out of the rain.

Pylon said, 'We're not cops.'

Mrs Khumalo said, 'You look like them.'

'What we want to know,' said Mace, 'was who Manga was with when he died.'

'I told the police,' said Mrs Khumalo. 'I don't know. I told the police Manga brought shame on us. For years he has broken our hearts.'

Mace could see behind her a framed picture of the Virgin Mary, candles burning either side of it.

Pylon said, 'What about girlfriends?'

'At the funeral there were lots of girls. All crying for Manga. All strangers to me.'

'Can we come in?' said Mace, water beginning to drip off his hair. 'Just for a moment.'

'Speak to his sister,' said Mrs Khumalo, giving them a telephone number. Slowly closing the door.

'Great start,' said Mace in the car. 'Such a friendly mother for a Catholic.'

'Wouldn't you be,' said Pylon, 'your son made a living heisting security vans?'

'I'd excommunicate him.'

'She probably did.'

Pylon dialled the number. 'Miss Khumalo,' he said, 'Your mother gave me your number, it's to do with your brother.'

She told him she'd told the cops everything. When he told her he wasn't the cops she said what was his problem? Pylon said, insurance. Manga had his life insured for six figures. She was his beneficiary. Miss Khumalo said her name was Cindy, gave an address in Melville.

Pylon fired the car.

Mace said, 'That pressed her buttons.'

'Money does that,' said Pylon.

'The reality won't please her.'

Pylon grinned. 'For sure.'

He gunned it out of Soweto – 'Not a place to be with the sun going down' – took the ring road to Ontdekkers, shuffled through the robots along the ridge towards the Brixton Tower. They found Cindy Khumalo in a renovated house in one of the avenues: high wall fronting a street of shedding jacarandas, intercom at the street door. She buzzed them into a damp courtyard, the garden plants dripping.

Cindy stood at the door all smiles. An expensive stunner dressed down in pink tracksuit. Her feet bare, her toenails green. Mace thought, someone else had green toenails. What was it with women and green toenails?

She invited them in, sat them down in a sitting room that was all angles. New low-back couches with chrome legs, matching chairs in red. Hi-tech reading lamps bent over the chairs like servants. Chrome and glass coffee table, splatter of magazines on it. And an ashtray: glass inlaid with mother-of-pearl.

She offered them single malt whisky, a choice of three: Dalmore, Arran, Whyte & Mackay – twelve-year-olds. Or beer. They both said beer.

Cindy Khumalo brought Stella Artois in the right glasses for all three of them. Said she was a beer girl at the start of an evening. Fetched a pack of cigarettes, held them towards her guests.

Mace and Pylon shook their heads.

'I have to,' she said, bringing up a flame from a thin roller bar lighter.

'A Sarome?' said Mace.

She gave him the eye. Blew a plume from the corner of her mouth. 'An ex-smoker and a connoisseur.' Handed him the lighter.

'Nice,' said Mace, rubbing his thumb over the rounded corners. Appreciating the featherweight. Handed it back to her.

She didn't look at all like her brother to his way of thinking. Except for something in the smile. A charm. The same sort of smile Manga had used stepping into the Vissers' house waving the thirty-eight around.

Pylon was saying, 'Like I said, you are your brother's beneficiary. Except that when a crime's involved the policy is void.'

'So you wanna cut a deal?' said Cindy. That smile.

Brought out a smile on all those who received it, Pylon and Mace hardly immune. Mace had to admire her cool. Must drive men wild.

Pylon coughed. 'We could do that.'

'Ten per cent.' She took a mouthful of beer, followed it with a draw on the cigarette.

'We'd have to go a bit higher,' said Pylon.

'Because of the police.' She studied the end of her cigarette, letting the smoke trickle from her nostrils. 'Fifteen tops.'

Pylon and Mace looked at one another. Mace giving the shrug.

'We could stick at that,' said Pylon. 'Assuming…'

'I can give you the man with him.'

'Yes. To straighten the paperwork.'

Cindy took another pull at the cigarette, shallow, hardly holding the smoke, crushed out the remainder.

Said, 'You're good, but not good enough. So, guys, what's this about, really?'

Mace looked at Pylon. Pylon held his hands up, nodded.

'It's personal,' said Mace.

She studied him, a gaze Mace was hard-put to hold. Not a blink, a black depth to her eyes, dense as coal. 'Alright,' she said. 'I'll give you what I gave the cops. Seeing as they weren't interested. It's someone called Spitz. Hangs at Melrose Arch. Check out JB's first. That's all I know. All Manga told me.'

'When?'

'About three days before he died. Told me he was in Cape Town with this Spitz.'

'That's all?'

'That's all I'm telling you.' She smiled to take the edge off her words.

'You've looked for him?' said Pylon.

'Not my scene.'

'What is your scene?'

'Insurance. Claims investigations.'

'Very sexy, I thought,' said Mace. He and Pylon at a table in the dining room of the Sunnyside Park hotel, drinking beer. Amstels, not Stellas. 'Little chi-chi boobs and a small bum. Dainty feet, too.'

'You noticed that?'

'I look at feet. Toes especially. Sucking toes can change a woman's attitude.'

'You suck Oumou's toes?'

'The first thing I did.'

'And others? Isa—' Pylon stopped. 'Sorry, my brother.'

Mace finished his glass of beer, shrugged by way of answer.

The waiter brought their steaks, asked if they'd like to see a wine list. They told him they'd stick with beer, ordered thirds.

'Have to give it to her,' said Pylon, slicing into the meat's juiciness – 'that Cindy was one smart chick.' He admired the red stain spreading on his plate. 'This's what I call rare.'

'Got your number,' said Mace, saliva welled in his mouth at the sight of the pink meat.

'Think so?'

'Know so. She was playing you. Right from the get-go.'

The waiter set down fresh lagers. Wished them, 'Enjoy.'

Pylon said, 'I hate that.'

Mace grimaced, what can you do? He slurped a mouthful of beer, then cut into his steak.

Pylon chewed, said, 'This is something.' He swallowed, sliced off another piece of meat. 'That Cindy's too cute for her own good.'

'Probably. Get her into trouble one day.'

'Why?'

'What?'

'Why d'you say she was playing me?'

'Weren't you listening? I asked her. She said she'd used that approach herself once or twice.'

'She said that? When?'

'As we were leaving.'

'Save me Jesus.'

Pylon's cellphone rang. He looked at the screen. 'Oh shit. Treasure.' Connected. 'Babe.'

Mace could hear her saying, 'I phoned home. Where are you?'

'Babysitting,' said Pylon. 'That fertility couple.'

'In a bar?'

Pylon laughed. 'Restaurant. They wanted to eat out.'

'What's their problem?'

'Wanted to see the town, I suppose.'

'His sperm? Her eggs?'

'Oh that.' Pylon spluttered, put down the forkful of meat and chips he had halfway to his mouth. 'Not something we ask.'

Mace heard Treasure cluck disapproval. 'These people are going to adopt as well, I hope. You should make it a condition. Rich people using us to do this nonsense on the cheap. Like there aren't enough people on the planet. I don't like it. People can't conceive they should adopt. Here, say goodnight to Pumla.'

Pylon said, 'Your mom enjoying herself?' Mace couldn't catch the response but Pylon laughed, said, 'Pregnancy does that.' Then said, 'Oh, yeah, I forgot to tell her, I can't fetch you from the airport. I'll get Tami. I'm in Jo'burg all day. Back in the evening.' He said ciao sisi, disconnected. Forked the food straight into his mouth. 'A good kid,' he said through the chew.

Mace said, 'What'd she say? That you said, pregnancy does that?'

Pylon grinned. 'She said Treasure was puking. Again.'

Four beers and a cognac down, Mace came out of the shower into his hotel room whistling. Recognised the tune as one that'd been on Mr Short Dreads's iPod. Matt Ward singing Outta My Head. Thought, huh? Fancy that coming to mind. Maybe it was the possibility of getting into the hitman's face in the morning. Talk to him about lifting an iPod from a shot man lying there bleeding on a farmhouse floor. Among other matters.

Then realised he'd enjoyed the evening chilling with Pylon in the lounge. Especially the nightcap cognac that'd gone down smoothly. A long time since they'd spent an evening together. Talking. Remembering. Laughing easily. After all the evenings they'd spent together in hotels grand and sleazy across the continent and beyond. Sometimes bored. Sometimes anxious. The weapons drop or the pick-up always bringing a special kind of uneasiness. Loose gut, Mace recalled, was what they'd called it.

He had the television on but the sound turned down. The screen filled with Table Mountain, footage of tourists getting off a car at the upper cable station. Mace aimed the remote, brought up the sound. The reporter's voiceover said the mugger who'd attacked two tourists that morning hadn't been caught. The camera came up on the two victims, the woman giving her line about being glad to be alive. Next an official held out the theory that the mugger/rapist might be living on the mountain. A composite mug shot filled the screen: savage, stone-eyed, flat-nosed, thick-lipped face wearing a beanie. A standard mug shot. Mace pressed mute. Said aloud, 'Your time's coming arsehole, faster than you think.'

He phoned Oumou.

'Mace, cheri,' she said, 'this is so late to phone me. I was worried.'

'You could've phoned me,' he said, 'anytime.'

'Ah, oui. You would have liked that in the middle of something.'

'When it's you I'm never in the middle of something.'

She laughed. 'Of course not until I phone one day at the wrong time.' He heard her say 'Merde' off-phone. 'This clay! Nothing will work for me tonight. It is all rubbish.'

'You're still in the studio?'

'Why not? You are not here.' Oumou putting a suggestiveness into her tone.

'Pity I'm not,' said Mace, smiling, catching himself smiling in the mirror. A silly look on his face. 'Tomorrow I'll suck your toes.'

She laughed, lightly, not far off a giggle. 'You say strange things.'

'I've done it before.'

'That was a long time ago.'

'Why I thought it would be a good thing.'

'You have been thinking this during the day? About sucking my toes?'

'It crossed my mind.'

Again the light laughter rising to a giggle. She paused, came back in a softer voice. 'Mace, you are alright, yes?'

'I'm fine. I was even whistling.'

'Be careful,' she said. 'I do not want to have trouble like that again. To be told that you are shot. Please.'

'There won't be a problem,' he said. 'Promise.'

Mace heard her sigh, then she said, 'You must sleep. Go now.'

After they'd disconnected he realised he hadn't asked about Christa. Realised he hadn't thought about his daughter all day. Nor had Oumou mentioned her. He got halfway to phoning back, stopped as he was about to key in the call. Maybe leaving it was better, a sign he wasn't obsessing. He had a photograph of her in his card holder: Christa sitting on a wine barrel in a blue bathing costume. Her face scrunched in a squint. Serious. Frowning. Her hair shoulder length. The summer before she was shot.

58

The next morning the rain had stopped. A blue-sky day. The early sun warming a pungency in the wet vegetation. Mace breathed in deeply, smelt his youth. Smelt freedom. Like after a night he'd run away, slept wild and wet in the hills, never gone back to the home. Freedom and loneliness.

The reason he stayed out of Johannesburg.

On the way to Melrose Arch, they stopped at a mall, bought rolls of duct tape from a hardware store and a tenderising mallet, a wooden one, from a kitchen shop. Asked directions to Melrose Arch.

'Easy,' said the shop assistant, 'you go down Corlett, take a right, it's right there.'

'What is it?' said Pylon.

'Larney,' said the assistant. 'You know, everything mixed up like shops and apartments and cafes and restaurants. Full of black diamonds. People with money to blow.'

They took the assistant's directions down Corlett Drive until they hit the area. Suddenly out of a suburb into a quarter that could've been any city in the world that wasn't at war, even some that were: people at tables on the pavement.

'The thing about Jozi,' said Mace, 'they don't stop building. Give them a bit of open land, a park, somebody says what a waste, this could be making money.'

'Gold diggers,' said Pylon.

'Once and always.'

Mace parked a distance away in the nearest space he could find. They walked into the quarter, Pylon taking JB's because if Spitz was there the appearance of Mace would disturb him.

'Need to keep the brother cool,' said Pylon. 'Don't want him getting uneasy.'

Mace went farther into the piazza, found a little place where he could order a long latte. While he waited got hold of Tami, asked her to find the mining magazines on Pylon's coffee table.

'That could take an age,' she sniffed, 'going through the piles.'

'I'm not planning to hold on,' said Mace.

'And I'm looking for?'

'Any mention of a company called Zimisela.'

His latte was down to a tepid milky wash when Pylon phoned that the man himself had just walked in, looking very dapper. Lacoste polo shirt, white trousers, moccasins.

Mace said, 'Whisper something persuasive to him. I'm there in five.'

He paid for his latte, his phone rang again: Tami. She told him the one magazine was five years old, the other from two years ago. In the more recent one a mention of a Zimisela Explorations. A news piece about a BEE deal behind the company's formation.

'What I need to know is who's on the board?' said Mace. 'Try the internet. And go through the older mag see what's in it.'

'Like what?'

'Like what what?'

'Like what'm I looking for?'

'Don't know,' said Mace, 'until you find it.' He caught her sigh before he disconnected.

Mace paid for his coffee, ambled across to JB's, clutching the plastic packet with the duct tape and the mallet. Pylon and Spitz waiting for him outside. Spitz looking none too happy. Pylon standing close to the hitman.

'You have a place round here, somewhere we could talk?' said Mace.

'It is possible to talk here.' Spitz not moving, rigid, his hands at his sides. Mace seeing himself reflected in the guy's shades.

'I don't think so,' said Mace. 'Somewhere private would be better.'

Spitz said, 'I have an apartment.'

'Excellent,' said Pylon. 'Let's go there my brother.'

Spitz had an apartment four floors up with a view north over the suburbs to the new city at Sandton, the distant mountains beyond. On this clear day, a big-sky view.

'Nice,' said Mace, scanning the décor: modern minimalism not unlike Cindy Khumalo's. Only difference a mega TV screen, more racks of movies than Mace had seen in some DVD stores. Stacked next to a leather recliner, a number of cases with Thelma and Louise on top.

'Haven't seen this one,' said Mace, tapping the box.

'They die,' said Spitz. 'By flying their car into a canyon.'

'That right?' Mace deciding maybe the best way to handle the discussion would be on a stool at the kitchen counter, piloting Spitz in that direction.

'Hey!' said Pylon, picking up a blue iPod, scrolling through the play list. 'Here's the killer country music. You've got taste, my friend.'

He docked the player in a speaker system, brought up Tindersticks.

Mace said to Pylon, 'Probably the stool's going to be the best option. Nowhere else with a flat surface.'

'Sharp,' said Pylon, taking a roll of duct tape from the packet. 'What we're going to do,' he explained to Spitz, 'is tape you to the stool. At your ankles. So that you don't kick out and fall over.'

Mace searched through drawers until he found a wooden cutting board. Waved it at Spitz. 'And your left hand and wrist we tape to this.'

'This business is not necessary,' said Spitz. 'If you ask me some questions I will tell you the answers.'

'Sure,' said Pylon. 'But you might lie to us.'

'I do not lie.'

'That's what you say. Most people in this sort of situation have told us that. But this way we know you're not.'

Mace's cellphone rang. Tami said, 'I can't find anything in that magazine.'

'Tami,' said Mace, 'now is not a good time, we're busy.'

'You don't want to know the directors?'

'Quickly then.'

She rattled off five names. Only the name Obed Chocho meant anything to Mace.

'Have another look through the magazine,' said Mace. 'Might have something to do with mining.'

'That's what it is,' said Tami. 'A mining magazine.'

'You know what I mean,' said Mace.

'Like I can read your mind.' She disconnected.

'That girl,' said Mace, 'has got a tongue on her.'

'Tell me about it.' Pylon, crouching, advising Spitz it was best he sat still.

Spitz did while his ankles were taped to the stool.

'You're a wise man, my brother,' said Pylon, getting up,

next strapping the hitman's wrist and hand to the breadboard. 'Not everyone has been so cooperative with us. I appreciate it.'

Finally Pylon wound a reel of duct tape round the man's torso, binding his arms tightly against his chest. Spitz's forearms flat on the countertop.

Mace placed a pen between the fingers of Spitz's right hand and a pad of Sunnyside Park notepaper beneath it. Asked him to write his name. Spitz did so.

'Good,' said Pylon. 'That's how you communicate with us from now on.'

'You can ask me a question,' said Spitz.

Mace sat opposite him. 'Alright. Here's the one been bugging me: why didn't you kill us, my daughter and me?'

'There was no point. I thought you would die anyway. My job was to shoot the farmer and the farmer's wife.'

'You shot your friend.'

'He was not my friend. We did the job together. When he started shooting I believed he had killed you. Then he would rape your daughter because he had the HIV and kill her too. I thought this was unnecessary.'

'Most noble,' said Mace.

'I thought he would shoot me.'

'Ah. And why was that?'

'Some feeling I had about him.'

Pylon snorted. 'A hitman with feelings.'

'It is possible.'

'Okay,' said Mace, 'this is what we're going to do. Pylon will tape your mouth closed because the process is painful and we can't have you screaming out loud. We are going to flip a coin, him and me. Best out of three wins. That's how we've always done it. The one who wins gets to ask the questions. The loser' – he took the mallet from the packet – 'has to smash your fingers and the bones in your left hand to make sure you answer the questions truthfully. Anything you don't understand?'

'I will answer the questions first,' said Spitz. 'I have done a job. Nothing is secret.'

'Well a whole lot of jobs, we reckon,' said Mace. 'Seven people according to our arithmetic. Not including your mate.'

'That is incorrect.'

'How many then?'

'Five.'

'Okay,' Pylon said, 'probably not the Smits. Different calibre. Different style. So we'll give you five. Plus the sidekick. Six.'

'For who?' said Mace.

'He is called Obed Chocho.'

'A good answer,' said Pylon.

Mace looked at Pylon. 'But we need to test its truth.'

Spitz said, 'It is the truth.'

Mace's phone rang: Tami.

'I've found it,' she said.

'Not now, Tami,' said Mace. 'We're in a meeting.'

She ignored him. 'It is mining. Well, not mining exactly. More like exploration.'

'Tami?' said Mace.

'In this article. About uranium deposits discovered on the farm owned by Justice Marius Visser. The article quotes him. He says no one will ever mine his land.'

'Interesting,' said Mace. Thinking, next question: who sent the magazines?

'Excellent, Tami.'

'That's it,' she said. 'Excellent. What about what this's about?'

'Not now. Later.'

'Jeez. You guys.'

He thumbed off the connection, said to Pylon, 'Obed Chocho's on the board of Zimisela Explorations. Five years back uranium was discovered on the Visser farm.'

Pylon said, 'Ummm.'

Mace said, 'You're thinking what I'm thinking.'

'Probably.'

'Might explain why the judge was shot at. Why he's so nervy. Why he signed on the quiet.'

'Might do,' said Pylon. 'Quite likely, if Obed's playing the heavies.'

Mace turned to Spitz. 'Good to go?'

Spitz said, 'If you ask me the same question my answer will be Obed Chocho.'

'Let's see,' said Mace.

Pylon gagged the hitman, took a five buck coin from his pocket. They flipped the best of three, Pylon winning with two heads. Mace wanted a rerun. Mace taking it on the first and third call with heads. Spitz watching the proceedings.

Before he flipped the third round, Pylon said to Spitz, 'You're very cool, my brother. Most people shit themselves watching us do this.'

'Flip,' said Mace, calling heads.

Pylon did, caught the coin, slapped it onto the back of his hand. 'Tails.'

Second flip went to Mace. Pylon called heads. Mace went through the actions, uncovered the coin on the back of his hand. 'Heads.'

Pylon gave Mace the mallet.

Spitz wrote on the pad, Obed Chocho.

'We haven't asked you anything yet,' said Pylon.

Spitz shook his head, pointed the pencil at the two words.

Pylon said, 'Okay, here's the question: who ordered the hit on Popo Dlamini?'

Spitz underlined the name of Obed Chocho.

Pylon looked at Mace. 'Seems to be our answer.'

'Go through all the names,' said Mace.

Pylon did. Lindiwe Chocho. This time Spitz circled the name. Rudi Klett. More underlinings. Marius Visser. Deep scoring beneath the name. Mrs Visser.

'What was her name?' said Pylon.

'Something weird,' said Mace.

Spitz kept on circling the name of Obed Chocho.

'Now for the moment of truth,' said Mace, smashing down the mallet on Spitz's little finger. Felt the flesh soften, the bone snap.

Spitz jerked backwards sending the paper and pad sliding across the countertop. The stool tippled, Pylon and Mace catching him from falling over. The hitman had tears of pain running down his cheeks. They rearranged him, his hand flat on the breadboard on the countertop, the guy's little finger swelling and bloody, the tip at an angle. They tore off the sheet of notepaper he'd scrawled on, slid the notepad under his right hand, slotted the pencil between his fingers.

'I'm going to ask you the questions again,' said Pylon. 'In case you want to give us another name.' He went through the list, after each question Spitz writing Obed Chocho on the pad. Five Obed Chochos.

Pylon said to Mace, 'I think we can accept this.'

Mace, beating the mallet in the palm of his hand, agreed. To Spitz said, 'Where's the nearest emergency clinic? We'll drop you.'

59

'The way I read it,' said Mace, 'the judge was lucky.'

Mace and Pylon on standby for a Cape Town flight. Sitting to one side at Gate D3, looking out on an array of planes. Pylon hoped, 'If we get this flight I can still pick up Treasure and Pumla, keep on the sweet side of the pregnant lady.' The two men waiting behind the ropes for the last passengers to board. Mace thought of it as penning sheep.

'Lucky he didn't want the farm. He'd wanted the farm, our friend Spitz might've been the last person he saw.'

'Strange guy,' said Pylon. 'Spitz. So cooperative. So grateful for the lift.'

'A hitman,' said Mace. 'Who lost you the West Coast.'

'Nah,' said Pylon. 'That's like blaming the gun. Spitz did it as a job.'

'He doesn't have to. He could do something else. Be a DJ. Guns, you pull the trigger they have to shoot.'

'You offered him a lift.'

'To show no hard feelings.'

Pylon smiled. 'This's the mother left you to die.'

Mace thought about this. 'Probably, in the same circumstances I'd have done the same thing. What I like about Spitz is he shot the Manga man and didn't hurt Christa.'

'Still a hitman. Could be paid to shoot Christa, Oumou next. He'd do it. He's not going to say, no, I pass on this one, Mace's alright. Only smashed my pinkie. You know what? Took me to the hospital afterwards.'

'What're you saying?'

'I'm saying what you said, he's a hitman.'

'And hitmen kill.' Mace laughed. 'Though some of them like good music.' He brought out the blue iPod.

'You swiped that.'

'It was mine. He took it from me, okay. While I was dying.'

'Actually I'd lent it to you. It was his. He's the one paid money for it. He's the one who lost it. Dropped it outside Popo's place. After he'd shot them.'

'Also it's evidence.'

'Of what?'

'Places him at a certain killing.'

'You're kidding. Who's going to believe that?'

'Obed Chocho might.'

An attendant called over that they could board now, unhooked the rope barrier. She smiled at them, even placed them in adjacent seats.

'To get back to the judge,' said Mace, when they'd buckled up. 'He was lucky. Helluva coincidence that he's the judge to put Chocho away.'

'Very ironic.'

'No. Coincidental.'

'Look,' said Pylon, 'irony's when you get stuff happening and the stuff's connected but nobody knows it at the time.'

'Like a coincidence. Two things coming together that're related. The judge sending down Chocho, while Chocho's planning to snuffle the judge's farm. The judge's old man's farm.'

'For Chocho that's irony.'

'Maybe. Except for the judge it's coincidence. Happens out of the blue. It's random. That there's a connection's a fluke. Pure and simple.'

'Kind of an ironic fluke.'

The captain came on said they'd been given clearance to take off. Everyone was to sit back and enjoy the flight, folks.

Pylon said, 'I hate flying. I hate being called folks.'

'It's just an accident. A stroke of fate.'

The plane's engines wound up a notch, Pylon gripped the armrests. 'Like getting the mining magazines.'

'I've been thinking about that,' said Mace. 'Their coming out of the blue. Been wondering who sent them.'

The plane backed away from the terminal buildings, juddered off along the runway into a departure queue.

'Has to be someone with a grudge. Someone wants to tell us Chocho's been after the Visser farm from before he went to jail.'

'That's what I mean, it's ironic. The judge putting him away.'

The captain instructed cabin crew to take their seats. Said the tower had given them clearance for takeoff, folks.

Mace glanced at Pylon. Pylon rigid, staring down the aisle at the cockpit door. The muscles in his jaw clenched.

The engines went to a pitch, the plane started forward. Mace a sucker for this bit: the acceleration, the Gs pushing him into the seat. The plane bulleting on and on down the runway, faster.

Pylon going, 'Lift the nose, lift the nose.'

When the nose came up Pylon saying, 'Oh shit.' Closing his eyes.

Mace waited until the climb gentled out, the plane tilting south over a mosaic of swimming pools, before he said, 'There's a whole lot of stuff here I can't put together. Too many coincidences. Too many things falling in Chocho's lap.'

Pylon said, 'Helps when you contract a hitman.' Gritted his teeth as the plane bounced through an air pocket.

Brought the captain on to say, folks, it was best to stay buckled up, for comfort's sake.

60

Sheemina February and Obed Chocho sat at an outside table at the café in the Gardens, drinking iced coffees. Mid-morning, two other tables occupied by lawyers and early tourists drifting in. A berg-wind day, warm and pleasant. Later the wind would scour your sinuses, scorch your eyes. Tomorrow it would rain. April in the city. Sheemina February looked up at the blue sky, thought of money. Lots of it.

'Why here?' said Obed Chocho.

With her gloved hand Sheemina February took a file from her briefcase, placed it on the table. 'Because it's a sunny day. Because this is the sort of thing we need to do in a public place. Because the last time I confronted these two it was here.'

'Oh mighty fine,' said Obed Chocho.

'Hey. Hold it.' She looked at him, no smiles. 'Humour me. I'm your lawyer.'

Obed Chocho snorted.

She turned the file until the documents faced him. 'This is the deed of sale. Zimisela Explorations now owns the property. Soon it will run a uranium mine. You are a rich man. You will be even richer.'

She closed the file.

'Also in there is a letter permitting your West Coast development. What more does it take to make Obed Chocho happy?' She sat back, caught sight of Mace Bishop and Pylon Buso heading towards them.

'Having you handle the arseholes.'

'Deal with it, Obed. It's you they want to see. I'm here to hold your hand.'

Mace and Pylon stood over their table.

'The gangster and the gangster's moll,' said Pylon. 'Aren't we honoured.' He pulled out a chair, sat down.

'Such a way with words, Mr Buso,' said Sheemina February. She smiled up at Mace. Giving him the icy Nordic eyes. 'Please, Mr Bishop, sit. Tell us what's on your mind.'

'We don't need you here,' said Mace. He pulled out the remaining chair. Sheemina February on his right, Chocho on his left, Pylon opposite.

'But I'm his moll, as Mr Buso so quaintly puts it. His legal moll.' She rested her gloved hand on the table between them. 'When the heavies get heavy, a lawyer is always useful. Keep a sense of perspective. Now.' Looking from Mace to Pylon, back at Mace. 'What's this about?'

'Spitz,' said Pylon. 'Sharp dude, wears good shoes. Into movies and country rock. Says you've… your client's… contracted with him from time to time.'

While Pylon spoke Sheemina February kept her eyes on Mace. Her lips holding a smile faintly. Flicking to Obed Chocho, she said, 'Obed, you know of anyone called Spitz?'

Obed Chocho shook his head.

'You might like to rethink that, my brother,' said Pylon.

'My client's answered you,' said Sheemina February.

Pylon sighed. 'What I didn't tell you last time is I have photographs. Piccies of Spitz leaving Mr Chocho's house. Him and a brother called Manga Khumalo. The same Manga Khumalo turned up dead at the Visser farm shooting.'

'Where I saw Spitz shoot the Vissers,' said Mace. 'And Manga.'

'I'm sorry,' said Sheemina February, 'what's the point of this?'

'Don't play thick,' said Mace.

'Proves,' said Pylon, 'that your client's lying about not knowing Spitz.'

'An oversight,' said the lawyer. 'That this Spitz shot the Vissers has nothing to do with my client. That information you should take to the police.'

'Just an ironic coincidence then,' said Mace, 'that your client's company's bought the farm.'

'Indeed.' Sheemina February drew the folder towards her, slipped it into her briefcase. 'Mr Chocho is on the board of Zimisela Explorations. That's common knowledge. The farm has uranium deposits. That's common knowledge. The farm came on the market, obviously Zimisela would put in an offer to purchase.'

'How convenient,' said Mace.

'No, Mr Bishop. Ordinary, above-the-line market forces. Willing buyer. Willing seller. Nothing dark and devious.' She made to rise. 'If you and Mr Buso have nothing more than this speculation, then there is no longer a point to our meeting.'

'Keep sitting,' said Mace. He glanced at Pylon.

'We can also place Spitz at the shooting of Popo Dlamini and Obed's wife,' said Pylon. 'Thanks to this little thing he left behind.' He placed on the table a blue iPod in a Ziploc bag.

Obed Chocho wiped his hand over his face.

Sheemina February held up the bag. 'Likewise this is

information for the police. Obviously, Mr Chocho would like to see his wife's killer brought to justice.'

'Obviously,' said Pylon, taking back the bag.

'Now. We have to go.' She stood.

'One other thing,' said Mace. 'Yesterday we spoke to Spitz. Maybe a hitman but he's got good points. Like honesty.'

'So?'

'He has agreed to help us.'

Sheemina February sat down. 'Help you?'

Pylon came in, 'As a state witness. Nail Obed here as the contractor behind the killings. We believe the case is looking good.'

Mace and Pylon stood. Mace said, 'Think about it. Suicide's always an option. Sign of the grieving husband, heartbroken. That sort of thing.'

'Two days,' said Pylon. 'Before we go to our friends in blue.'

When they'd left Sheemina February said, 'This's a problem, Obed. Something extra-legal required. Know what I mean?'

Obed Chocho said, 'Mighty fine. Mighty fine. When the going gets tough Obed'll fix it.'

'Very macho, I'm sure.' She pushed back her chair. 'They've given you two days, Obed. Maybe they want an offer. Other hand, maybe Spitz is the answer, hmm? The honest hitman.'

She walked away, Obed Chocho admiring her legs.

Obed Chocho ordered another iced coffee, made a phone call. Spitz.

'Listen, buti,' he said. 'You've fucked me up. You want to get out of this you come down here 'n sort out your mess. Specifically the arseholes Bishop and Buso. Like chop chop. Now now. Any time from five tomorrow I want to hear they are late. For your account. You fuck me up again, you're dead.'

He disconnected, realised Spitz hadn't said a word. Then again, words weren't the issue here. Action was.

He finished his second iced coffee, phoned Pylon. Said, 'I've been considering maybe we could come to an arrangement.' Paused but Pylon didn't respond. 'At the West Coast site ten tomorrow?' Again the non response. 'Okay. Be there. Alone. We can talk.' He disconnected.

Arseholes. Mighty fine. The arseholes thought they'd nailed him. The arseholes would find out about Obed Chocho. Mighty fine they'd find out. If they were still alive.

61

Spitz, watching a high-speed boat-chase through the canals of Venice, popped a painkiller wondering how one small finger could hurt this badly. Wondering what kind of sadist had to go all the way when you'd told him what he wanted? And then take you to hospital. Say, sorry, pal, no hard feelings. And steal an iPod. What sort of person was this?

The speedboat doing the chasing entered a bad situation ramping over a small boat to land on a flat-bed barge loaded with vegetables. The thieves in the getaway boat grinned at one another, powering up towards open water.

Would the brother have done it? Spitz thought probably yes. Maybe wouldn't have broken the bones. Not hit with such force. As if he enjoyed causing the pain. Spitz aimed the remote at the TV screen, getting back to the main menu.

In tens of jobs, never a comeback. Always clean contracts. In out. Money in his account. Never any of this mess Never people tracking him down. Never physical violence. Even threatening to kill him.

He clicked on-scene selection: there's Charlize cracking the safe the moment before the cop steps up and you realise it's not for real. He had to smile at the concentration on the girl's pretty face.

This job was bad from the start. The changes. The add-ons.

Now mighty-fine Chocho telling him, ordering him, to make a hit on his own account. Or he'd put a hit on Spitz-the-Trigger.

On screen, the cop came into the frame and the tension went out of the scene.

Spitz phoned Sheemina February. Told her the story.

She said, 'Join the club.'

Spitz said, 'I am not sure which club this means.'

'The reason, Spitz,' she said, 'that I wear a glove in case you've ever wondered is because they smashed my hand. Like that, with a mallet.'

'How could this happen?'

'Years ago. In the guerrilla camps. Different world, same modus operandi. Mr Bishop and Mr Buso are not nice men, Spitz.'

'I must kill them?'

'If that's what Obed wants.'

'You have changed your mind?'

'About?'

'About the white man. You want him to die now.'

'I think so. Yes. This time.' A silence. Then: 'Tell me, Spitz, why'd you keep my name out?'

'I do not understand.'

'I think you do. I'm asking why you didn't tell the thugs that I work with Obed Chocho? That I was the one made the arrangements with you.'

Spitz scene-hopped to the lovely Charlize in overalls conducting the recce in the fool's mansion.

'There are some reasons.'

'Such as?'

'You are like me. You work for Mr Chocho. You are doing his business.'

'That's one reason.'

'Another one is that they did not ask me about your name.'

He could hear Sheemina February clicking her nails on the desk.

'Fair enough.' Click, click. 'Let me tell you what another reason might be, Spitz. How about you thought that out of gratitude I'd put down a bonus. Not so? How much were you thinking, Spitz? Twenty? Thirty? Fifty even?'

Spitz didn't answer. Sheemina February gave a soft laugh.

'Doesn't matter, Mr Triggerman. I don't hold it against you. Same circumstances I'd have had similar thoughts. Only now you've got to kill them the leverage falls away.'

Spitz flicked back to the main menu, selected Charlize getting some driving lessons in a Mini Cooper. He could imagine Sheemina February in such a car.

Sheemina February saying, 'No hard feelings, Spitz. Go ahead, make your arrangements. Call me when you've booked into a hotel and we'll take it from there. I have some information you'll find useful.'

'I will need a weapon.'

'There was a time when your targets were a source of weapons. Poetic justice, isn't it, that the gun-runners should take a bullet? A nice idea.'

'A point twenty-two with a silencer.'

'I know, Spitz. Relax.'

'Then we can have a drink on the town. You will show me some of your places.'

Sheemina February laughed. 'You're cheeky. Give it up, Spitz, I'm not available. Understand what I'm saying.'

'One drink.'

'Maybe afterwards.'

Spitz said, 'Is that a promise you are making' – realised she'd disconnected. He aimed the remote at the screen, flicked back to watch Charlize waking up to her daddy's phone call. Paused the movie to give full appreciation to Charlize's body. Sheemina February he believed would have a body like that.

62

'That,' said Pylon, 'was the great Obed Chocho.'

Mace and Pylon on a stroll up Government Avenue through the Gardens heading back the long way to their offices. Kids running on the lawns, people on the benches enjoying the sun.

'Wanting?'

Pylon dug out peanuts from a jacket pocket, threw them to a squirrel. 'To offer a deal.'

'Oh yeah!'

'So he says.'

'When 'n where?'

The squirrel stuffed its pouches, sat up waiting for more.

'Tomorrow morning. At the west coast site, the Smits' old cottage.'

'Should be interesting.'

Pylon bent down, some peanuts rolling in the palm of his hand. 'For me.'

The squirrel approached, paused with a paw in the air, sniffing. Pylon kept his hand still.

'What d'you mean?'

'I'm going alone.'

'Forget it.'

'I am.'

The squirrel snatched two nuts, scampered off and up the base of a tree, hung there looking back at the two men. Pylon dropped the remaining nuts on the ground, straightened.

'No way. This's Obed Chocho we're talking about. A guy puts out hits easy as we buy lattes. He's not wanting to deal, he's wanting to whack you.'

'I don't think so. He knows I'll tell you, probably that you'll be waiting not far off. He's not going to pull a number. This's to sort something. Buy us off.'

'Sounds bloody dicey to me.'

'Nah. Not a big deal.'

'I'm going to ride backup.'

'No need.'

'Every need, china. Just don't even argue the toss.'

The squirrel leapt off the tree trunk, snatched at the nuts, retreating into the undergrowth.

'You like this action? Prefer the edge.'

'Makes the day more clear cut. Brighter. Sure. But between this and getting out, I'd still take getting out. Okay there's fun here. Except I'd rather have other kinds of fun. Where it's not deadly.' Mace gave a chuckle. 'Never thought I'd say that.'

'Never thought I'd hear it.' Pylon laughed too.

Vagrants laying out their clothing over benches cackled with the two men, calling after them, 'Hey, my larneys, two rands for a drink, ek sê. Lekker, lekker. On this lovely day.'

Mace waved a hand. He and Pylon swinging behind the school across Hatfield and down Dunkley to the square. The cafés on the square doing good business. Buzzing talk and laughter.

'You'd swear this city was on holiday,' said Pylon.

'Rain's coming,' said Mace. 'People getting in some sun.'

Pylon stopped, gazed across at the scene. A quick Stella?'

'Why not? Think we should get Tami over?'

Pylon shook his head. 'Nah. Gives too much lip.'

They found an empty table, ordered two draughts. Mace stretched out. Looked up at the mountain stark and solid above the city, a cut-out against the azure sky. Days like this you wanted to go on forever.

63

Cape Town wet and miserable. Grey murk across the city bowl. Lights on in houses, the sort of damp cold that made Spitz think of Germany. The old GDR. Training in gloomy dawns. Loneliness and grim barracks.

Spitz stayed well back from the red Alfa Spider. He'd picked it up on the steep downhill street, Molteno, as per the note. Correct to a minute on the outside. Someone had done their homework. Whoever it was Sheemina February used.

'He will drop his daughter at school and proceed to the office on Dunkley Square,' read the note. The note that had been delivered to his hotel. With the gun.

This morning was no exception. Spitz followed the car through the wet streets to a school, where the girl got out, joined other girls bolting through the drizzle into the building.

At Dunkley Square he parked in a bay with his back to the offices of Complete Security, angled the rearview mirror so he could see without being seen. He was ahead of Mace Bishop. He watched the Spider slot into a kerbside space outside the building. The driver get out, unhurried, unfazed by the drizzle, head for the front door.

'Fifteen to twenty minutes later Pylon Buso will arrive in a Mercedes Benz. He will park in the street in a reserved bay behind the Alfa Romeo. It is usual for them to have coffee in a guest lounge downstairs until 09h00. The only other occupant of the building is their administrative assistant, Tami Mogale. She arrives at 08h25 on foot. The security officers employed by Complete Security very seldom report to this office. In the five days to date these three people were alone in the building between 07h50 and 10h00. On Mondays, Wednesdays and Fridays a cleaning organisation, Dust Busters, services the offices at 15h00 for forty-five minutes.'

With the note was a diagram of the building. Front door leading into a long hallway that ran through to a kitchen at the back. Two paces in, a door on the right into the lounge. Three paces beyond that another door on the right where the assistant had an office. Opposite that door a staircase to the upstairs offices of Bishop and Buso. A boardroom on the left before the kitchen. A toilet opposite the boardroom. A door in the kitchen to an outside courtyard.

Spitz's idea was: knock, and the young woman would open. Brush past her, swing right into the lounge doorway: whop, whop, and out. How the woman reacted determined whether she stayed alive. Back to the hotel, check out, catch a midday flight to Jozi. Spitz's idea.

Twenty minutes later Pylon Buso had not arrived. Shortly before half past eight a minibus taxi pulled into the square, let out half a dozen people. Among them a young woman who ran to the row of offices. Tami Mogale, Spitz believed. Another ten minutes no Pylon Buso. Mace Bishop came out, took off fast in the Spider.

Spitz sighed. Reached down, pulled out the Browning Buck Mark from underneath his seat. Unscrewed the can. Ejected the clip. Distributed the parts in the various pockets of his jacket. Phoned Sheemina February.

'And?' she said. A slight huskiness to her voice.

'Mister Buso didn't arrive here,' said Spitz. 'Now Mister Bishop has left.'

'What a pity,' said Sheemina February, the strength coming back into her voice. 'Never mind, Spitz, there will be other occasions today, if not tomorrow morning. Use the opportunity to familiarise yourself with our fair city.'

'I know the city.'

'Not well enough and not the parts they frequent. These are not easy men to kill, I must remind you.'

'That is not necessary, a reminder.'

'I know, but it's worth saying.' She paused. Spitz could hear the clink of a teaspoon stirring a cup of tea. He did not think Sheemina February drank coffee, only herbal tea. 'Another thing, could we meet tonight. At your hotel, about eight.'

'For a drink on the town?'

'Not exactly. I have other business, Spitz. For which there'll be a disbursement. So your trip is not without its compensation.' She disconnected.

Spitz clicked on the rear window wiper: saw the offices of Complete Security showed a light downstairs and one upstairs on this grey and dismal morning. He fired the white Citi Golf. Went in search of breakfast.

64

The judge held the young man's hand lightly in his own. They sat side by side on the bed, the young man, his trainer, Ricardo, his hair wet from the shower, a bath sheet wrapped round his waist. The judge naked. Their shoulders touching, flesh against flesh.

The judge lifted Ricardo's fingers, brought them to his lips. He could smell herbal hair shampoo, cleanliness. He kissed Ricardo's fingertips, lowered his hand until it came to rest on the young man's thigh.

'You are very beautiful,' he said, his eyes not leaving Ricardo's face.

'Ag, judge,' said Ricardo.

'Telman.'

'Telman,' said Ricardo, withdrawing his hand, standing. 'It doesn't sound right.'

Telman Visser laughed. 'I can't make love to a man who calls me judge.' He looked up at Ricardo, beckoned him to step closer. 'Now drop the towel.'

'It's late,' said Ricardo. 'We can't do this now.'

'We're not going to do anything, I just want to look at you.'

'In half an hour I have to be at the gym. For my shift.'

The judge tugged at the towel, loosened it. 'The Constantia ladies can wait. They only want to lech at you, Ricardo. Dream of biting your bum.' He admired the dark crotch, leaned back on his

318

elbows. 'In a Cavafy poem a young man throws off his unworthy clothes "And stood stark naked, impeccably handsome, a miracle". Like you.' He smiled. 'Turn around, my sensual boy.'

Ricardo did. Judge Telman Visser leaned forward, nipped at the young man's rump.

Ricardo yelped, skipped away.

'Aaa hah,' said the judge. 'By the look of things you don't want to leave just yet.'

'No, I've got to,' said Ricardo, searching among a pile of clothes for his boxers. 'The gym'll fire me.'

'I don't think so. If I had a word.'

Somewhere in the house a phone rang three times, an answering machine took the call. The judge sighed. 'Next it'll be my cellphone.' When it rang he gestured at Ricardo. 'Bring it to me. Please. There on the bedside table.'

'See,' said Ricardo, handing him the phone, 'it's very late.'

Judge Visser glanced at the screen, connected. 'Sheemina February. What is the problem?'

He heard her say, 'Are you alone?' – covering the mic with his thumb asked Ricardo to leave the bedroom.

'Without my clothes?'

'Dress in the bathroom. Close the door.'

He watched Ricardo scurry into the bathroom, a last glimpse of the firm backside.

'Ms February.'

'Am I interrupting something?'

'My work on the commission.'

'I'll be brief.'

He imagined the woman with the black glove and the ice eyes somewhere in a public place by the sound of it, wondered if Sheemina February was ever anything other than brief.

'The issue is this, judge,' said Sheemina February, 'there is more paperwork to be ratified. Relating to the sale.'

'What paperwork?'

'A question of capital gains tax. Nothing out of the ordinary. Revenue needs their pound of flesh.'

'Don't they always.' He caught himself about to sigh again but stifled it. 'Send the documents over to my chambers.'

'I can bring them right now, if you like.'

'I'm not there,' said Visser. 'I won't be there today.'

'Then how about this evening? At your house? You could invite me for a drink.'

Judge Telman Visser considered this, a drink with Sheemina February being a low priority. In fact not a priority at all on his agenda.

Before he could answer Sheemina February said, laughter in her voice, 'That didn't set you alight.'

The judge coughed. 'I have other engagements to juggle.' Mostly the other engagements concerned Ricardo. Wining him. Dining him. Screwing him.

'It will take fifteen minutes, judge. You won't have to juggle anything.'

Judge Telman Visser arranged for her to call at eight. He disconnected, called out, 'Thank you, Ricardo. Please come through.'

The bathroom door opened, Ricardo standing there in chinos and his gym T-shirt, his hair combed. Still bare feet though.

'What a pity,' said the judge. 'There are few people I would rather see naked than dressed. You are one of them.' He patted the bed. 'Sit next to me while you tie your trainers.'

Ricardo did.

'Tonight,' said the judge, 'I wonder if you could make it a bit later than usual. I have an attorney calling at eight, she'll be gone by eight thirty at the latest. Perhaps we should make it nine. What do you say?'

'That's okay, judge, anytime.'

'I will arrange prawns. A quick easy supper. But a messy one. Hands on. Tactile.'

'Prawns are good.'

'Queens, I think.'

65

Pylon turned the big Merc off the coast road onto the dirt track that led towards the sea. A grey sea, wild with wind and scudding foam. Clouds rolling off it, dashing rain against the windscreen. He drove slowly, rank thorn scratching the low hang of the car, a Merc the last ride you wanted on dirt. He checked his cellphone: no signal.

What was it with Chocho, they couldn't do this in an office? He knew the answer. Obed Chocho wanted drama. Couldn't resist being out on the contested land. Rubbing in the prospects.

The track turned down towards the cottage, Chocho's black SUV hunched in the clearing at the back door. The SUV his dead wife Lindiwe had driven. No sign of Chocho. He'd be listening for a car's engine, Pylon suspected. Sitting in the lounge, waiting. Waiting with a sawn-off shotgun in his hands? Unlike Mace, Pylon doubted it. Wasn't Obed Chocho's style. This was about buying time.

He stopped beside the other car. Sat for a moment alert to any movement around the house. Nothing moved, nothing human. The northwester shook the scrub, whipped sand across the clearing. Pylon killed the engine, withdrew the keys from the ignition. Got out, shrugging into a fleece. The back door was open. He knocked, calling out as he entered, getting no response.

Obed Chocho sat at a bar stool, diagrams, plans, paperwork spread across the wooden countertop. A bottle of whisky and two glasses weighting down a file.

'My brother,' he said as Pylon paused in the doorway. 'Come

in. Please.' He pulled free a stool – 'Sit' – and slid the diagrams in front of Pylon. 'My development.'

'Big deal,' said Pylon.

'Ah, my brother, don't be so hostile. I am holding out an olive branch.'

'To get you out of shit.' Pylon angled the stool away from Obed Chocho, hoisted himself onto it. 'No reason to play lovey-dovey.'

The two men did the hard glare. Obed Chocho looked away first, pulled back the plans. 'Okay. Mighty fine. If that is how it is to be.'

'It is.'

They sat in silence. Obed Chocho moved the whisky bottle, took a letter from the file. 'I am going to offer a deal.'

'What else?' said Pylon. 'I don't go to the cops. You cut me in on the development.'

Obed Chocho held up the letter. 'This is the planning permission.'

'Congratulations.'

The sarcasm brought a smile to Chocho's lips. 'In our business we must be tough.'

'Killers.'

'Your good German friend Rudi Klett was a killer. Like you. An arms dealer. Selling guns to children.'

'I am not an arms dealer.'

'You were.'

'For the struggle.'

'But sometimes you sold guns to children.' Obed Chocho grinned. 'I know about you, Pylon Buso. More than you think.'

Pylon shifted on the hard stool. 'Cut the crap.'

'Mighty fine.' Obed Chocho gazed at the sea. 'I offer you shares in my consortium. Five per cent. For that you get five per cent of the profits.'

'I must invest in your scheme and shut up?'

'You and Mr Bishop.'

Pylon kept focused on Obed Chocho. Watched the bald head turn towards him, the brown eyes find his own. A stonewall stare. 'Why would I do that?'

'For the money.'

Pylon laughed. 'You're a criminal out on parole. I could have you investigated. Charged. Arrested. Your development would collapse. I could tender again and this time be awarded the contract.'

Obed Chocho set his head nodding. 'You could do all that. Except I have Sheemina February on my side. While that is so you will get no developments in this city. Not even in this province.'

'Perhaps you are forgetting the other story,' said Pylon.

'The other story? What other story is this?'

'The farm story.'

Obed Chocho laughed. Not a forced laugh, a laughter that was deep but ended suddenly. 'The mighty fine farm story. Of course. That is a very interesting story. Like all stories of African farms.' He reached for the bottle of whisky. 'A drink?'

Pylon shook his head.

'Why not? Soon we will be partners.' He unscrewed the cap, poured a measure into a glass – 'To the ancestors' – drank off the liquor, slapped Pylon on the knee. 'I know Judge Telman Visser,' he said. 'For many years.'

'That's why he knocked you down for six.'

'You see. You will not believe me.'

'No.'

'It was a mighty fine trick.'

Pylon waited. Obed Chocho grinning at him.

'Have a glass with me?' Obed Chocho hovering the bottle over the two glasses. 'Yes? No? Yes?' Poured only into his own glass. Before he drank he took a sheet of letterhead from the file and handed it to Pylon. 'My other company, Zimisela Explorations. We talked about it.' This time he sipped at the whisky. Smacked his lips. 'Ummm, a mighty fine malt.' Swirled the whisky, smelt it. 'Perhaps?'

Again Pylon shook his head.

'Perhaps you are not a whisky drinker. For many of our brothers whisky is a learning curve.' He pointed at the bottom of the letterhead. 'There is one name missing.'

Pylon scanned along the list, all the usual big name businessmen.

'Judge,' said Obed Chocho, 'is what I call him, the missing director. To him I'm Obed.' A mighty fine smirk on Obed Chocho's face. 'Judge Telman Marius Visser. He has been in Zimisela for two years.'

'Save me Jesus,' said Pylon. Nobody knew?

'A prayer in need,' said Obed Chocho, finished his second tot. 'Now you have an idea of the players.' He paused. 'Tell me, my brother, in these circumstances, what is it you want?'

Pylon didn't answer, thinking, if Chocho was in with Visser he needed more on that. Details. The full story. He pointed at the whisky bottle. 'A drink.'

Obed Chocho gave his throaty laugh. 'The man sees a little sense. Mighty fine, mighty fine.' He poured measures into each glass, pushed one towards Pylon. 'Going forward,' he said, raising his glass. Pylon drank to it.

Obed Chocho turned on his stool to face the incoming storm. He leant back against the countertop, propped on his elbows. A gust battered the windows, he mock-shivered. 'On a wild day the Cape is dangerous. Even when this is a golf course, there will be days like this. For me, not a place to live.'

Pylon sipped the scotch. Obed Chocho didn't spare himself on his whisky. Stuck to the wall was a photograph of the Smits. Something overlooked when the place was cleared. A small print, the colours faded to pink. The couple arm in arm laughing at the camera. Given the positioning probably a self-timer, Pylon reckoned. He flashed to the photographs Captain Gonsalves had shown him of the couple dead. Individual photographs.

Thought: take the in. Said, 'I haven't got cash for five per cent.'

Obed Chocho shot him a side glance, eyebrows raised, no light in his eyes, a glint on his teeth. He took a swallow of scotch.

'You have made bad choices,' he said. 'In your business. You forgot your comrades. So they have forgotten you. You are small-time, my brother. You cannot do developments like this. In the planning department they see a scheme from Pylon Buso and they laugh. Where are the lunches? The holidays? The little gifts? The generous gestures? The patronage? No, that Pylon, he has turned away from us. This is what they say.'

Obed Chocho popped off his stool, went to stand at the window, his back to Pylon.

'Mighty fine. I have not forgotten you. I remember Comrade Pylon. I remember what he did in the struggle. In the dark days. So' – he turned – 'I know that you have money on the Cayman Islands. I know that you can use this money for the five per cent.'

Pylon kept his eyes locked on the gloating man.

'What I am saying is, mighty fine, let us put the other matters to the side. Let us go forward.' He made to pour another tot into Pylon's glass. Pylon held his hand over the top. 'Do we have a deal on this?'

'I need time,' said Pylon.

'Why not? In the Cayman Islands they are only waking up. Talk to your bankers when they have rubbed the sleep out of their eyes. In a few hours this can all be settled. Inter-account transfer. Cayman to Isle of Man. We live in the days of globalisation, my brother. So much is possible.' He pulled his lips into the rictus of a smile. 'Be in touch. This afternoon.'

66

'How?'

'Doesn't matter, Mace. He knows. We go in we're caught. We

stay out, he'll have Revenue on us. We tell the cops, it'll hit file thirteen. Probably he's already bought off Spitz, if he doesn't whack him. We're stuffed. Up shit creek. No paddles, no canoe, crocs in the water.'

'What about Visser?'

'He's saying Visser's in it. He's saying they're buddies.'

'Visser doesn't know him. Sends him down for six years. That's not buddy stuff.'

'He's saying a con trick. Didn't matter how long the sentence. Visser, both of them, knew Chocho'd only sit for a few months. Face it. He's saying Visser's been on Zimisela for two years. That's from the start.'

'Implying Visser allowed the hit. On his own father. Because of bad blood. Pah. Tell me a story.'

'This happens.'

'In books.'

'In real life, Mace.'

'So we hit Visser.'

'Tie him down, break his fingers.'

'One way of doing it.'

'Another?'

'Put the story together for him, say we're taking it to the newspapers. Play him off against Chocho.'

'Dangerous.'

'Or we don't do any of it.'

'What then?'

'Shoot him. Shoot Obed Chocho. Point two-two, the same gun. Give the cops something to think about. While they're doing that the problem goes away. West-coast tender comes up again, you scoop the deal. Pylon Buso Developments.'

'And Sheemina February?'

'What's she going to do?'

'Maybe she's the leak on Cayman?'

'The bugger.'

'Maybe.'

'So afterwards she'll make a play. Or she won't. If she does. Well…'

'Most of this I don't want to think about.'

'It's an option, Pylon. Or such shit with Revenue it's jail. The money gone. The future truly down the toilet. For the sake of two wankers. The one kills his own wife. The other his own father. Worse, buys someone to do it. And all the rest. Probably also for the sake of that prime bitch Sheemina February.'

'Save me Jesus.'

'Times two. What it comes down to is how far we go. How far we're prepared to take this.'

Mace and Pylon coming in from the courtyard, shaking rain off a golf umbrella.

'And what's that about, standing out there to talk?,' said Tami. 'I'm not trustworthy or something?'

'Not you,' said Pylon. 'Others are listening. And for the moment that's okay.'

'You mean…' – Mace holding a finger to her lips.

'Yeah. Exciting isn't it?'

Tami broke open a stick of nicotine chewing gum. 'Spooky, actually.'

67

The woman from the agency was waiting. By herself in a Jap crap car outside his front door. Obvious as if she was standing on the pavement in fishnet stockings and a bareback teddy. Wasn't for the rain she might have been. Couldn't be a neighbour didn't know she was there.

Obed Chocho pulled into his driveway, not even casting her a sideways glance. Went straight to his front door, hearing her slam out of her car, calling to him, 'Sir, are you Mr Chocho, tata?'

The door open, he turned. She was hurrying towards him. A woman in a long furry coat buttoned to her knees, white with a hood. Holding up what looked like a business card.

'Discreet Service,' she said. 'For Mr Chocho.'

He nodded. 'Mighty fine, mighty fine. Keep down the adverts.' Wondering if her red boots were thigh highs. Flashy plastic boots.

He led the way to the sitting room, went to the sideboard for a whisky. 'Want one?'

'We can't drink on the job,' she said. Standing close enough that he could smell her perfume. A scent he recognised. Something Lindiwe had worn.

'What's the perfume?'

'Glow.'

A whore with expensive tastes.

'You like it?'

'For sure.' Obed Chocho drained off a short tot. Waited until the warmth bounced back from his stomach. 'Have a drink,' he said. 'It's part of this job.'

She shrugged, kept her gaze full on him in the Western way. In that moment he recognised Lindiwe. She'd done that. Spurned the eyes down in respect business. He'd liked that. Showed her fire.

'Vodka lemonade.'

He smiled at the woman. Her hair braided like Lindiwe's. About the same length. 'Playing safe, my sister?'

She brought out a condom from the pocket of her coat, held it towards him.

'I don't do those.'

She leaned forward, dropped it down the neck of his shirt.

'I do, my brother.'

The warmth of her breath on his cheek. Cigarettes and peppermint. Her height about the same as Lindiwe. Same stature. Like it was Lindiwe standing there.

He reached out, caught the woman by the coat, pulled her into him. His mouth coming down hard on hers. Her hand unzipping him. Burrowing into his rods.

Obed Chocho groaned at her touch.

Lindiwe.

When Buso's money was banked, when Spitz had done his job, Spitz was dead.

He pushed the woman away. 'Undress,' he said.

She laughed at him. 'I don't wear clothes.' Unbuttoned the coat, not taking it off. Gave him a full frontal, turned slowly, sweeping the coat back over her thigh, the swell of her buttocks. The boots were thigh-length.

She had Lindiwe's breasts. Small, perfect, dark-nippled. He knew how they would shape when she rode him. Like cones as she arched over his chest.

She moved towards him. Loosened his shirt, picked out the condom. 'Rough rider, baby.'

'Wait,' he said. 'I must make a phone call.'

Obed Chocho opened his cell. With a remote brought up on the plasma screen a DVD of a family at supper. Eating pasta. The dad going on about the boy's homework. The mom heaping more food onto the kid's plate.

'You like them?'

'Who?' she said. Poured her own vodka lemonade.

68

Spitz, parked in the square, watched the two cars arrive. The big Merc first, the red Spider coming in not a minute later. Flicked the wiper to clear the rain blur. Saw Mace and Pylon hurry to the front door. He finished his menthol.

Now, he believed, was as good a time as any. Only three of them in there. Problem: they'd be scattered throughout the house.

The receptionist probably downstairs, the other two wherever their offices were. Upstairs he reckoned.

Which was not ideal, wandering through a house blotting those you stumbled across. Not the quick in pop out scene he preferred. Without collateral.

Although sometimes you had to shrug and shoot. Take out the audience. Sometimes the best plans got screwed up.

Once he'd put away a string of bystanders to reach the main macher: a bodyguard, a servant, a woman in pyjamas wafting mace about like he was a mosquito. On the way out another security with a cannon in his fist. Proved it wasn't size that mattered.

Only people not part of the plan were the servant and the mace sprayer. Spoilt his principle of one payment one hit but Spitz figured security signed up to take a bullet. Knew one day they'd be staring at a gun barrel. Part of the job description. Bystanders were a pity though. No matter how much you minimised the possibilities there was always the unexpected.

The reason Spitz favoured an eight-round clip.

The way he really wanted to operate was like the scene in Panic. A class act. The sort of scene he enjoyed re-running where Macy in a suit walks up to a guy on the street, pulls a gun from inside his jacket, shoots the guy up close, walks on looking sad, drops the gun in a wastebin. Spitz's aspiration. Clean and neat.

He went now, the receptionist would open the door, he'd have to pop her to get in. Standing there visible to the street. Not a busy street in the rain but you couldn't tell at the crucial moment. Just took one person to drive past as the deed was done.

Even on a best-case scenario: he's in the office, the receptionist's dead in the hall, he's dealing with two ex-gun-runners might have heard the whop of the silencer, recognised it for what it was. Be standing there at the top of the stairs fully loaded.

He shook his head. Not worth thinking about. The only option: get in there face the situation unfolding.

Spitz took the Browning out of the glove compartment, fished the silencer from the pocket of his leather jacket. Screwed it to the barrel. Checked the clip. Eight rounds ready to go. He pulled on his gloves.

Was about to crack open the car door, head across the drizzly square when his cell vibrated. Obed Chocho.

'Where're you, Spitz?' said Obed Chocho. Straight in, no cheery hello. 'On the job?'

'I am about to be doing that,' said Spitz.

'Mighty fine,' came back the answer.

'I will be in touch afterwards.'

Obed Chocho coughed. 'No, Spitz. Back off. Leave it for the moment. Just stay close to them. Hear me?'

'I do not understand. Now is a good time.'

'Listen to me. Not now. Later. Getit. Later. When I tell you.'

'This is not the way I work.'

Obed Chocho yelled. Not a word that Spitz recognised. Just a hard bellow. Then quietly. 'If you worked properly, my brother, I would not be talking to you. You would not be here in the rain. You would be at home. I would be happy. Everything would be mighty fine. But nothing is mighty fine. It is a mess.' His voice higher than a soprano choirboy. 'So, my brother, you stick with them. Wherever they go, you go. Invisibly. And when I say, now. Then you kill them. Do you understand me, mighty fine?'

Spitz said he did. Recognised Tony Soprano calling the odds.

'Mighty fine,' said Obed Chocho.

69

On the phone the judge was short.

'I'm reviewing evidence for the arms commission,' he said. 'I shouldn't be disturbed.'

Mace made a yadda yadda mouth with his free hand. 'This is

important.' He and Pylon in the big Merc already on De Waal, Mace looking into the bowl at the city curtained with rain. 'It can't wait.'

The judge sighed. 'Two minutes. What is it?'

'Give me ten,' said Mace. 'I'll tell you personally.'

Pylon coming up behind a truck slow on the climb, thumped the steering wheel waiting for the fast lane to clear. 'What gets me,' he said, 'is someone knowing all our business.'

'Tapes and tapes of it,' said Mace. 'Or is it digital now? CDs?'

'CDs probably.' Pylon growling at the slowness, eyes in the rearview for a gap. 'When we talked about the Cayman it was in my office,' – lurched the Merc into the fast lane, flooring the pedal. 'I've been thinking about it. Most of the other stuff's been out and about.'

'Pays to sit in cafés.' Mace gripping the armrest.

'Except for Rudi Klett. Those details were in-house.'

'You're saying it wasn't Popo Dlamini ran his mouth?'

Pylon easing on the juice at the feeder curve, Mace wondering as always, what caused the smoke from the hospital chimney. Tissue discard. Cancered organs. Foetuses. Medical waste. Sheets soiled with death. 'Huh, you're saying that?'

'I'm saying it was him, mostly. But also someone listening in.'

Pylon took the downhill at a clip, pulled a right across the yellow lines of the split, cars hooting.

Mace saying, 'Christ, I didn't think you were going to do that.'

'This's the way, why shouldn't I?'

'Seemed you were heading for the N1. The airport.'

'N2,' said Pylon. 'Airport's on the N2. How long we been living here?' Pylon, laying down more power along the sweep to Mostert's Mill, his eyes flicking up to the rearview mirror. 'There's a reason for it. The reason's a white Golf.'

Mace angled the side mirror. 'Got it.'

'Been behind us from the city. Dude hangs well back. Didn't

have any problem with the lane switch at the split.'

They kept an eye on the Golf past the university, through Newlands forest, Pylon taking a right into Rhodes Avenue, the Golf following two cars behind.

'Black or white?' said Mace.

'This makes a difference?'

'Might do. General surveillance would be from the same place as the bug. Specific spying would be one of Obed's sidekicks, for instance.'

'General surveillance is going to be white?'

'Dead-end job. You see a brother taking a dead-end job. In the days of black empowerment?'

'No.'

'Stands to reason, then. So: black or white?'

'Can't tell in this rain.'

Pylon took it slowly along the avenue towards Kirstenbosch Gardens, Mace looking up at the mountain cloud, saying, 'Three days ago we had summer. I was planning to shoot the mountain maniac.'

'In your dreams,' said Pylon. 'All that vigilante stuff.'

'Thought you were into that a while ago.'

'Maybe.'

'Chickening out?'

'I didn't say that.' At the T-junction Pylon turned left, checked his rearview mirror, no sign of a white Golf. 'Big brother's changed his mind. Or it was coincidence to start with?'

'Sans irony.' Mace smiling at his use of the French.

Pylon didn't comment, the two silent for the jag through the suburb to the judge's house.

The judge waited for them in the study. The front door opened by their security man, giving them a nod that his lordship was in a foul mood. His lordship straight-backed in his wheelchair not inclined to any preliminaries.

Going to the crux: 'What is so urgent?'

Might be working from home but he was suited: tie neat in a broad Windsor, black shoes mirror polished. Very professional.

Mace and Pylon stopped two metres from him, stood feet apart, hands clasped loosely in front, almost military in their stance. Mace, an envelope in his hand, took his cue from the judge. Said, 'Judge you owe us an explanation here.'

'Of what?'

'Of your connections with Obed Chocho.'

The judge frowned. 'I have none.'

'You found him guilty of fraud.'

'I have found many men guilty of fraud.'

'You handed down a stiff sentence.'

'As one should.'

'Our belief is that this was to deflect attention from your relationship with Mr Chocho.'

'Really?' The judge smiled, brought his hands together, rested his chin on his fingertips. 'Perhaps you didn't hear me. I have no relationship with Mr Chocho.'

Mace took the mining magazine out of the envelope, opened it to the announcement regarding Zimisela Mining.

'What's this?'

'Read it. Please.'

The judge stretching to take it from Mace. 'You are trying my patience.' He read through the article, handed back the magazine. 'So?'

'Today,' said Pylon, 'Obed Chocho showed me a Zimisela letterhead that has your name among the directors.'

The judge shifted his gaze to Pylon. 'Obed Chocho is a racketeer. A man I sentenced to six years for the crime of fraud. That letterhead is another example of his duplicity. A fake.'

'He says you met about five years ago,' said Mace. He replaced the magazine in the envelope, brought out another. Found the article about uranium deposits. 'We believe that he approached you, or you approached him shortly after this report appeared.' He handed it to the judge.

Judge Telman Visser read the report, Mace watching for any tell in his face. Saw nothing but a judge's unconcern. He took back the magazine. 'My patience is exhausted. If this is the purpose of your visit, I suggest you leave now.'

'One moment,' said Mace. 'Hear us out.'

'I have no wish to.'

'All the same.'

'Our business is concluded, Mr Bishop. I no longer have need of your services. I will pay your invoice to date.' He powered his wheelchair behind his desk.

'Judge,' said Mace. 'Hear us out.' Mace not waiting for the judge's response. 'Here's the thing: to our way of thinking you conspired with Obed Chocho to acquire your father's farm. Getting there we believe involved the death of your father's lawyer. Not an accident, a deliberate arson. With Chocho's help we reckon a hitman was hired to murder your father and his wife.'

'Don't be absurd.'

'Contracting our services was another instance of your cunning. A smokescreen. A hoax, playing on the random violence of farm killings. Had I died it would have strengthened your game. Nice one, judge. Very cutthroat.'

The judge shook his head. 'You are sad men, you and your partner, Mr Bishop. Conspiracists. Paranoids. Pathetic.' He glanced from one to the other. 'Your little story is slanderous. Outrageous. To even make these suggestions is beyond comprehension.'

'The press wouldn't think so.'

'Don't tempt me, Mr Bishop. Don't tempt me. If the press gets onto this I will slap interdicts and writs on you that you wouldn't have thought possible. Now, leave my house. And take your goon with you.'

'It's not over, judge,' said Mace. 'You're in with the snakes. Big time.'

'Out. Out.' The judge pointing at the door. Could have been dismissing servants, Mace and Pylon and the Complete Security guard traipsing out.

In the car, staring down the street at the dripping trees, Pylon said, 'Not a bad actor.'

'He's had the training,' said Mace.

The security officer in the back leaned forward, tapped Mace on the shoulder. 'What's his case?'

'A guilty heart,' he was told.

Pylon fired the car. 'So now?'

'Coffee,' said Mace. 'At the office.' Thinking, maybe the potshot attack had been a staging. What it had been was amateurish or deliberately so. Surely hadn't damaged the paintings. As the Yanks put it, smoke blown up their arses.

Pylon took a different route out of the suburb. 'What I think,' he said, 'is we need to stake them out. Him and Obed. Sometime they're going to have to meet.'

'What for? You need more evidence? You think he's innocent? Shit, Pylon, that was an act. You know it? It was bullshit. They're not going to meet. They'd be crazy. They've got other ways of running this. And what difference does it make to us. We're not going to sink them. We've been through this. We took a decision.'

Pylon didn't answer, said, 'How about that we've got company.' His eyes on the rearview mirror. 'Yeah, has to be.'

'You're kidding. The white Golf?'

Pylon said, 'Don't look back. I'm thinking we keep it calm, head for the office. Pick up your car. Make a plan to nail him.'

'A little bit of fun to brighten a dark day.' Mace racked a round into the P8. Stuck the pistol in his jacket pocket.

They came onto De Waal Drive, the Golf way behind.

'Change of plan,' said Mace. 'At the houses, pull over, he's got to go past.'

70

Obed Chocho was loud, running his mouth.

'You've been drinking, Obed,' Sheemina February said.

He laughed explosively. She held the phone away from her ear.

'Because I have the skelm Buso by the balls. In my fist.'

'How nice for you.'

'The bastard thinks I want to be friends. Cousin to cousin. Brother to brother. Black men together. To hell with him. '

'What are you talking about?' said Sheemina February.

'I have made a deal with him. Given him a chance to buy in. With his money from the Cayman Islands. Then I will kill him. When I have his money.'

'Obed,' said Sheemina February, 'you should consult me before you make such deals. I am your lawyer.'

'Pah! So, mighty fine. What would my lawyer say?'

'That you were unwise. Pylon Buso could use your conversation against you.'

'Never. The man is greedy.'

Sheemina February tapped the long fingernails of her good hand on the glass tabletop. A semaphore of red. 'Where are you, Obed?'

'My home.'

'Good,' she said. 'Sober up.'

Sheemina February docked the phone. The trouble with Obed Chocho she'd long realised was his macho attitude. His world of men that allowed for no finesse.

She sighed, went to stand at the French windows of her apartment. Washes of rain came off the horizon; below a heavy sea beat onto the rocks in spume and spray.

She put her damaged hand against the window pane, could feel a shudder at the break of the waves. Imagined the lives of sailors, filled with the fear of shipwreck. The sea thundering against a metal hull. It made no sense surrendering your will. Putting your life at the whim of the elements.

What point if you had no control? No legal niceties. No contracts. Even with them the world was open to the unexpected.

Open to an Obed Chocho doing stupid deals.

The situation, she decided, was too fluid. It was time to intervene.

Her phone rang.

For a moment Sheemina February considered letting it go to voicemail. Then turned into the white room, in two paces could see the name on the display screen: Judge Telman Visser.

Beside the phone, her glove. And next to that a photograph. A photograph of Judge Telman Visser and Obed Chocho.

The photograph was a black-and-white print. Both men in tuxedos. She remembered Chocho wore a red bow tie. A signal of his difference, she supposed. At the time she had yet to meet him. At the time she didn't even realise there were links worth following. That came later, much later, long after she'd learnt about Zimisela Mining and started sweetening Obed Chocho. Yet it was not until she saw Obed Chocho sent down for six years by Judge Telman Visser that she remembered the photographs. Put the links together. You clever bastards, she'd thought at the time. And got herself closer to Obed Chocho. Made herself indispensable.

It'd been a banquet, she recalled. A banquet in celebration of mining contracts. Black empowerment deals. A banquet thrown by the department of minerals and energy. With an in-house photographer making everyone feel important. Except Sheemina February was absent from the photographs taken that evening four years back. As Sheemina February was absent from all photographs taken at the social events she attended.

She picked up the phone. 'Judge,' she said.

'I can't have this,' said Telman Visser. 'I can't have wild talk from Chocho.'

'I'm sorry. Enlighten me.'

'I have just had a visit from Messrs Bishop and Buso. They have threatened me. With the help of Chocho's bluster.'

'How very clever of them.'

The judge paused. 'Sarcasm is inappropriate. These are not stupid men.'

'Then why did you employ them? If you thought Mace Bishop was no fool, why set him up as a blind?'

'Speak English.'

'Con language, Judge Visser. A blind: a distraction, a decoy, something that keeps out the light. All very sophisticated but very dangerous. As you have discovered. As I could have told you. If you'd asked my advice. What did they have to say?'

Judge Telman Visser told her. Sheemina February listened. Stood looking at the photograph of Obed Chocho and Judge Telman Visser shaking hands, beaming at one another while the voice in her ear told a tale of woe.

When the judge stopped, she said, 'Speculation.'

'Accurate speculation, for the most part.'

The judge perfectly calm, despite the revelations. His voice unwavering. An interesting attitude, thought Sheemina February. The man apparently unfazed.

'Accurate it may be but so what? Even if they take it to the press they have no facts. Without facts, where are they? Besides, you are a judge. Above reproof.'

'Among us are the avaricious and adulterers.'

'This is unfortunate, admittedly. Still, nothing is out of hand.'

'I am glad you think not. From where I sit it looks problematic.'

'Judge,' said Sheemina February, 'I will talk to my client. You have fired Bishop, that is good. Other measures are in place that I can't speak of. What I can say is you have nothing to worry about. Believe me.'

'Hmmm. I shall see you tonight.'

That was not a frightened Judge Visser, she thought. Concerned, yes. Maybe slightly anxious but not frightened. How well things were working out.

She replaced the phone in its stand, picked up her glove, worked her fingers into the leather. Across her view a frigate ploughed eastwards, spray breaking over its bows. One of the navy's new toys. She wondered if Obed Chocho had been in the line-up for handouts in the deal that bought the ships. She wouldn't have been surprised. An operator like that would have his fingers everywhere. She shrugged into her long black coat, cast a look around the apartment. Realised that when she got back in the evening, the world would be completely different.

71

Pylon stopped sharply on the side of the road in front of a service truck. The white Golf out of sight still approaching the bend. He watched in the rearview, said, 'Here he comes.' Then: 'Save me Jesus.'

'Spitz,' said Mace as the Golf whooshed past in a fine spray, the driver not noticing them on the side. 'What's his case?'

Pylon shrugged. 'Nothing a little chat won't sort out.'

They watched the Golf slow down before the bridge, Spitz trying to decide which option to take. Up onto Jutland Avenue? Down into Roeland Street? Deciding on Roeland Street.

Pylon pulled into the road, oncoming traffic flashing lights, hooting.

'Don't follow,' said Mace. 'He'll check us.'

'We're going to let him go?'

'Take a bet he's heading for Dunkley. We go the other way, park in the back streets. Surprise him.'

'Who's Spitz?' said the security man from the back seat.

'Country 'n western hitman,' said Mace, catching a glimpse of the Golf stopped at robots opposite the fire station. They'd have followed, they'd have spooked him.

Pylon, took the tight ramp fast onto Jutland, said, 'Probably got a contract on us.'

'You're thinking Obed Chocho?' said Mace.

'Aren't you?'

'Someone wants to kill you?' said the security man.

Mace said, 'We lead exciting lives.'

Pylon gunned the Merc down Jutland into Mill running orange traffic lights as he pulled the car squealing into Hope Street. Cruised to Glynville Street, stopped in the narrow street.

'This's the plan,' said Mace, turning to the security man. 'You hop out, take a walk down Wandel at the end there, my bet is you'll find him somewhere with a line of sight on our offices. Walk past, give us a buzz.'

'It's raining,' said the security man.

'Umbrella's in the boot,' said Pylon.

'Walk past, hey. No funny stuff.'

They watched him out of sight, tall man under a pink umbrella.

'It's depressing,' said Pylon. 'Having someone want to kill you. On a day like this all grey and dripping.'

'Mightn't be the case. We're only guessing. Maybe he's upset with us, 'n it's a personal thing. He does personal, look what he did to his mate.'

'This's true.'

They sat in silence. Couple of minutes later Mace got the call.

'You're bloody right,' said the security man. Gave them the position.

'Stay tight. Out of the rain.' Mace clipped closed the phone, opened the door. 'There's another umbrella in the boot?'

Pylon shook his head.

'This's what I think's depressing.' Mace got out, zipping closed his jacket. 'Getting wet.'

Pylon leaned along the seat towards the open door. 'We could call Tami have her nip one over.'

Mace got back in while Pylon put through the call, told Tami what they wanted and where to bring it. 'Like I'm not supposed to know why?' she said.

'So Mace doesn't get wet,' said Pylon.

She brought three umbrellas – green, blue, black – slid into the back of the car. 'My last job,' she said, 'my boss was a therapist. I can give you his name.'

'Very funny,' said Mace. 'Walk with me, Tami. Up close under the umbrella like we're lovers.'

'This's not sexual harassment?'

'I'm not going to lay a charge,' said Mace, choosing the black umbrella.

They walked down Wandel, Mace's arm around Tami's shoulder, her arm around his waist. The umbrella hiding his face. He could feel her body firm against his. Had to be the kickboxing she did.

'See the white Golf?' said Mace. 'I'm going to stop at the driver's window, tap on it. When he unlocks I'll get in behind him. You can go back to the office.'

'That's it?'

'Sure. If he pulls a gun I'll probably shoot him first.'

Tami said, 'Such fun working for you guys.'

Mace angled them off the pavement into the street. 'Has its moments.'

When they got to the Golf, Mace tapped on the driver's window with the butt of the P8, said, 'Open up Spitz, it's wet out here.' He noticed Spitz jump, but the hitman did as he was told. Mace got in behind him.

'Spitz,' he said, 'what a surprise. How's the hand?' Spitz's left hand out of sight. 'Bring it up, let me have a look. And hold the gun you've got down there by the barrel because what's in my hand will put your face all over the windscreen. If I have to pull the trigger.'

Spitz held up his hand, the bandaged pinky sticking out straight, his other fingers gripped the .22 by the barrel. Mace reached out and took it.

'Nice gun, the Buck Mark Standard. Accurate. You fancy these things in your line of work, don't you?'

'They are good for the job,' said Spitz.

'And I'm assuming,' said Mace, 'we were your next job?'

Spitz made no comment.

'No hard feelings,' said Mace. 'We're not talking about anything personal. The way my mate Pylon sees it you're the same as the gun, a piece of equipment. My position's a little different. Brings in a moral element. But that's getting all philosophical and we don't want to go there. So. Tell you what, we're not keen on this idea of being your next job. We realise this puts you in a predicament with your client, so we've got a proposition. Want to hear it?'

'I am sure you will tell me.'

Mace laughed. 'That's what I liked about you from the start Spitz. A practical man. No bullshit.' He ejected the eight clip from the Browning, left in a single round, jacked it back into the butt. 'We'll talk while you're driving,' said Mace.

'Where is this place I am driving towards?' said Spitz.

'Not a concern. You go up this street, at the top Pylon will pull in front in the Merc. You follow him, like you've been doing all morning.'

72

'How can you tell that he will be at home?' said Spitz.

He and Mace sat in the Golf down the street from Obed

Chocho's house. Pylon in the big Merc parked in the man's driveway.

'Because Pylon has a meeting with him. To discuss high finance.'

Mace's cellphone rang. He keyed it to loudspeaker.

'Good to go,' said Pylon. 'The man's waiting.'

'Fine,' said Mace. 'We're all ears.'

They heard Pylon open the car door, the door slam. Spitz flicked the windscreen wipers: there was Pylon hurrying down the path to the front door. The buzz of the intercom. Obed Chocho saying, 'Mighty fine, my brother, you have seen the light.'

The door opened, Pylon went inside.

Obed Chocho said, 'Time for another whisky. I took a little bet with myself this morning. A little bet that I'd be seeing you again today.' The voices faded, then came on clear again.

Pylon said, 'What was that? The bet?'

'That I wouldn't drink anymore of this bottle unless we had a deal.'

In the car Mace and Spitz heard whisky being splashed into glasses.

'You have spoken to Cayman?'

'Sure.'

'And the money?'

'By now the transfer would have been made.'

'Mighty fine. Mighty fine.'

'Phone your bank,' said Pylon.

'There is no need for that. As soon as it is done I will be notified. Until then we relax with Glenlivet. On a wet afternoon is there a better option?'

'Ah,' said Pylon, 'a Blackberry.'

A fainter Obed Chocho: 'A mighty fine toy. Come, sit, sit. Let me send a message to ask for confirmation.'

'That thing sends emails?'

'From the palm of my hand.'

Spitz's cellphone vibrated where it lay on the passenger seat. Mace placed his thumb over the mic on his cellphone.

'A message,' said Spitz.

'Open it.'

'From Mr Chocho. One word that says, "now".'

'Which means?'

'Now it is okay for me to kill you.'

'Bloody wonderful.'

On his cellphone Mace heard Obed Chocho say, 'Tell me, my brother, why are you doing this? A few days ago I was the bad man. Now we are business associates. It is so sudden. Must I believe you love your money over your idea of justice.'

'There are realities.'

'Realities, exactly. Pragmatism not idealism. The opportunities of a new country.'

'Something like that.'

'Perhaps we should toast to these realities? Our position as developers.'

'Why not?' Mace heard the clink of glasses, then Pylon say, 'Where are the contracts?'

And Obed Chocho come back, 'On the table.'

Mace said, 'Alright, we're on.' He closed his phone. 'We get out together. Any nonsense, you're dead.'

'There will not be any nonsense,' said Spitz.

The two men walked quickly through the rain to Obed Chocho's house. Mace slightly behind Spitz, his hand on the P8 in his jacket pocket. He buzzed the intercom. When Obed Chocho answered, said, 'Courier, package for Mr Obed Chocho.' Was told, 'One moment.'

Mace thought, the nice thing about people, even crooks, was their trust.

Obed Chocho opened the door. Mace slammed Spitz against the big man, the three of them stumbling into the hallway.

Pylon stood alert at the lounge door watching, his automatic clutched in both hands, pointed at Chocho and Spitz. Said to Obed Chocho, 'Off your knees bad man. We've got a new reality here.'

They sat Obed Chocho in an easy chair, kept him under Pylon's gun, Mace with the P8 on Spitz.

'What we didn't appreciate,' said Pylon, 'was your having Spitz fly down to zap us. Not friendly. You could also say that if we didn't know which way to dive before, this kind of convinced us. Okay? Mighty fine!'

'Fuck you,' said Obed Chocho.

'Brave,' said Pylon. 'The bellow of the bull brought to the slaughter. Yakhal'inkomo.'

They gagged him with what remained of the duct tape they'd bought for Spitz. Also strapped his ankles. Took a photograph of Lindiwe framed in silver from among a herd of photographs on the booze cabinet, told Obed Chocho to hold it against his chest. Whichever way he preferred: her image in or out. He clutched her to his heart.

'Touching,' said Pylon.

Mace took out the Browning from his belt, the can from his pocket, screwed it on. He placed the gun where Lindiwe's photograph had stood.

To Spitz said, 'Put on your gloves.' Waiting while Spitz waggled his fingers into the black leather. 'We'll wait in the hall. When we're out of the room the scene's all yours. One load in the clip. Our deal's this: you come through we'll call it quits, no comebacks.'

Spitz said, 'If that is what you want, I can agree.'

'Mighty fine,' said Mace, nodded at Obed Chocho. He and Pylon backed out the room, closed the door. Heard the muted whop of the shot, stepped back into the room. Obed Chocho slumped in the chair, his head fallen forward, blood dripping in his crotch. The angle of his head you couldn't see the bullet hole.

Mace took the gun from Spitz, waited while the hitman pulled off his gloves. Pylon emptying his whisky into a flower pot, wiped clean the glass and put it back on a shelf of similar glasses.

'Forensics'll find it,' said Mace.

Pylon shrugged. 'Maybe. But what's it going to tell them? Someone else was here. Bit of luck they'd have put that together anyhow.'

Outside Mace said, 'So long, Spitz' – giving the hitman the keys to the white Golf. 'I like your work.' He and Pylon watching the man drive off.

'Think that's the last we'll see of Spitz?' said Pylon.

Mace brought up Eugene Edwards on the sound system doing a cover of Sinnerman. 'Probably not.'

73

Captain Gonsalves caught Mace at home.

Mace and Oumou in the kitchen eating breakfast, shouting to Christa that she'd be late for school.

Mace in high spirits, telling a story.

'I'm watching this young guy, neatly dressed in a beige raincoat, ask for change for a hundred bucks. He's stopped a businessman, nice suit, snappy tie, black umbrella popped open over his head. The businessman takes out a wallet gives the guy two fifties. The young guy says, no, what I actually need is a ten. He holds out a fifty to the businessman. The suit's got the umbrella handle clutched under his arm and it's not protecting him from the rain so he's getting wet and he's scratching through his wallet. Comes up with some notes, two twenties and a ten, and takes the fifty in exchange. The young guy's, Thank you, sir, thank you, sir, and sir's smiling putting his wallet in his pocket and hurrying off out of the rain. The youngster heads away in the other direction nice and easy having scored a hundred bucks.'

'He never gave him the hundred rand note?'

'No. Showed it. Then kept it in his fist.'

Oumou looked at Mace over the top of her coffee cup. 'For this Mr Mace Bishop did what?'

'Told him one day he'd get into serious shit.'

'He should have given back the money.'

'The businessman looked like he could afford it. People get conned every day, just got to learn to be wide awake. In a city like this.'

Christa came in reading Le Petit Prince. Sat down to eat without looking up from the book.

'You could say good morning,' said Mace.

Christa glanced at him, smiled. 'Was there really an army of lamplighters before electricity?'

'Oui,' said Oumou, 'how else could people see at night?'

Mace's cellphone rang: Gonsalves.

'You wanna know what I did last night?'

Mace didn't but Gonsalves went straight in. 'Last night I sat in a car inna street watching a house. All dripping night long. My legs frozen. My feet I can't feel. Sat there outside a known gangster's family home. So that when said gangster pitched up I could arrest him. Supposed to be he comes home every night about eleven. So no big deal. He comes home that time, by twelve he's sitting tight with lots of his tattooed chommies in a communal. Doing a getting to know you my brother. By twelve thirty I'm ten minutes away from my shuteye, all's well with the world. Except this gangster doesn't come home. Not by midnight. Not by three a.m. By three a.m. I'm starving for tuna sandwiches. I'm thinking I should of brought a extra supply. Then my inspector says to me, tuna's getting scarce. He's seen this television programme we're gonna have eaten all the tuna in the sea soon. No more tins of tuna. I start thinking. I've been a cop thirty-nine years. Each day I eat tuna sandwiches. On a stakeout I eat double. So I'm thinking in a year

I'm gonna eat maybe three hundred tuna sandwiches. You take off two weeks holiday in the game reserve doesn't really make a lot of difference. On those tuna sandwiches there's probably seventy-five grams of tuna. Means by the end of a year I'm up twenty-two kilos of tuna. Like half a fish. Work it out over thirty-nine years the figures not far short a ton. That's a lotta fish, Mr Bishop. Maybe a whole shoal. Catching criminals cost our seas a shoal of tuna. You add this to what the Jap chaps take down in sushi, you see why the tuna's in trouble. My inspector, he eats burgers. Fast food shit. He's fat. Got a gut like a tyre. He runs he's gonna have a heart attack. Me, on tuna, I got my health. What I'm saying, Mr Bishop, is I'm sitting inna freezing cold thinking of tuna when another call comes through. They tell me forget the gangster get your arse the other end of town. I do, Mr Bishop, now what I gotta say to you is you want the good news or the bad news first?'

'Morning like this,' said Mace, taking in the sky over the city, blue and long, the air washed clean after the rain, 'there can't be any bad.'

Captain Gonsalves cleared his throat. Mace held the phone away from his ear. 'There is. There always is. Believe me, hey.'

'The good.'

'Ten minutes ago I heard Obed Chocho snuffed it. One in the head. That'll please your mate Pylon.'

Mace made no comment. 'And the bad?'

'Where I'm standing,' said Gonsalves, 'the sun's full on the mountain. Very pretty. Fresh and green. No doubt our maniac's heading up there for a day of rich pickings. Wet days like we've had must make a serious dent on his income. I'm standing on the lawn facing the house. Some uniforms here and me. My inspector's gone home. The uniforms were called by the maid, uh, about twenty minutes ago. Ambulance on its way. Behind them the techs. The dead is one Judge Telman Visser. Client of yours I gather from the invoice on his desk.'

'Was,' said Mace.

'Was, exactly.'

'Fired us yesterday.'

'Son of the justice copped it on the farm, am I not right? Where you were shot, I believe. Amazing links, hey.'

'Coincidence.'

'My world doesn't know coincidence. Everything's connected.'

Mace paused a beat, let the captain think he was being profound. 'How? How'd he die?'

'Come'n have a squiz.'

Mace could hear Gonsalves chewing. 'I'll be there now.'

'Join the rush, kiddo.'

'You want a tuna sandwich? From Woolies?'

Too bad the cop had cut the connection.

Mace got to the judge's house the same time as Pylon. The street gate was open, Captain Gonsalves standing on the stoep chewing tobacco. They walked up the garden path between the rose beds.

Pylon said, 'He tell you how?'

'No. Probably wants to surprise us. Get a kick out of the reaction. You know Gonsalves.'

'Angle for a tip-off tip no doubt. A pension contribution.'

'We'll see.'

'No we bloody won't.'

'Such suave gents,' called out Gonsalves. 'You always wear black?'

'Only to collect clients,' said Mace. 'The international set. They appreciate black. It's reassuring.' They mounted the steps to the stoep. 'Where's he?'

'In the study. Room with lots of law books.' He led the way indoors. 'You boykies keep your hands in your pockets, okay.'

Still wearing the smart suit, Judge Telman Visser sat askance in his wheelchair behind his desk. He had fallen forward face down on the desk blotter. A clear plastic bag was over his head, held fast at his neck by a belt.

'Takes a certain type of person, does it this way,' said Gonsalves. 'Usually, in the cases I've seen with plastic bags, they try to tear them off. Sometimes people succeed. Spend the rest of their days in the gaga ward. Drooling. What's a new thing for me is the belt. People use rope, duct tape, elastic bands, that plastic tape you use to seal parcels, that's the best. Strong and tight. A belt's a new one on me. Though you can see the effectiveness. Draw it, notch it. When you're gasping it's too finicky to undo. Alles kaput.'

Gonsalves stripped a cigarette, rolled the tobacco in a ball in his palm.

'Another thing people usually do is drug themselves. Take a packet or three of Panado. But not our judge. He wanted to do this. God knows why.'

'Maybe,' said Pylon.

Captain Gonsalves flat-handed the pellet into his mouth. 'Why'd he fire yous?'

'Said he didn't need us anymore. The state'd stepped up security because of the arms commission.'

'Some security.' The captain chewed. 'Not a spook in sight. Blarry typical. But hey' – he cupped his ear – 'do I hear an ambulance. Twenty minutes later. Just as well the judge's dead.' He ushered Mace and Pylon out of the room. 'Was this worth it?'

'Why would it be?'

'Dunno. You came pretty chop chop.'

Pylon looked at Mace. 'What'd I tell you.'

'Two hundred,' said Mace.

'That's all?'

'Was an ex-client. No stain on our rep.'

Gonsalves spat tobacco juice into a rose bed. 'Such generosity.' Held out his hand. 'Quickly then.'

Pylon palmed him two blue notes.

They grabbed a cappuccino on the café balcony at Kirstenbosch Gardens, the autumn sun warm across their shoulders. Watched the tourist coaches arriving. Mostly Japanese going off to photograph every flower in the gardens. Happy voices rising to them.

Pylon said, 'That was a helluva thing for the judge to do. Conscience or something else, you think?'

'Not his conscience,' said Mace.

'I didn't think so either. Nor did Gonsalves.'

'Thing is,' said Mace, 'when you're in a wheelchair, what're you options? Slitting your wrists. Overdose. Can't drown yourself if you haven't got a swimming pool.'

'If you had you could strap down in the chair, ramp it into the water. Long as the pool was deep enough you'd be okay.'

'True.'

'Hanging's out.'

'Could blow a hole in your head, if you've got a gun which I don't think the judge had.'

'Can't jump off a building.'

'Exactly.'

'Could crash the car except the airbag would pop 'n save you.'

'Could get assistance.'

'Or be assisted.'

The coffee came.

Mace said, 'How about a blueberry muffin?'

'They're still warm from the oven,' said the waitress.

Pylon nodded.

Mace held up two fingers to the waitress. 'With butter.' Said to Pylon, 'Do you believe that?'

'What?'

'Warm from the oven.'

'No.'

'So why's she say it?'

'It's what waiters say. To give you that special feeling.'

Mace shook his head, spooning froth and chocolate dusting from the head of his coffee. 'I never believe them.'

'Very middle class. Treasure loves it. Falls for the bullshit every time, like they're baked just for her.'

The waitress brought the muffins, steaming.

'Probably been nuked,' said Mace, halving his, spreading butter melt over it.

'One problem with blueberry,' said Pylon, 'is that it looks so good. Flavour's so good. Afterwards you wonder what's this metal taste in your mouth. Was it chemicals you ate.'

'You still eat it though.'

'That's the other problem.'

They shut up to eat, getting through half a muffin each before Mace said, 'So what's your take on the judge?'

'Assisted suicide.'

'Meaning someone had a gun to his head.'

'That sort of thing.'

'Why?'

'Could've been arms deal related. Powerful figures involved there. The talk I hear's even fingering the president. One of the sidebars on Obed whacking Rudi Klett was as a favour. For someone near the top of the food chain.'

'Why not just do a Spitz special on the judge, shoot him.'

'Too obvious, maybe.'

Mace took a long pull at his cappuccino, wiped froth from his upper lip. 'This's not about the arms deal.'

'What then?'

'Who then, rather.'

'Who then?'

'Sheemina February.'

'Ah come on.' Pylon stuffed the last of his muffin into his mouth, spoke through the chew. 'She was Obed's sidekick.'

'Maybe she reckoned the judge pulled the hit on Chocho over

the farm killing. Got his bucks and blotted the evidence. Maybe she didn't like that. Having a major money source terminated. I don't know. What do I know? Everything's weird. Except, I know, yesterday, when we saw him, wasn't a flower in his study. Today there's a rose.'

Pylon swallowed. 'He grows roses. All over the garden.'

'Most of them shrivelled and brown. This one was a rosebud. Aren't any rosebuds anywhere in his garden. Plum coloured.'

'Like those she sends you.'

'Precisely.'

'Which proves what?'

'Christ knows. Doesn't even prove it was her. Unless she wanted to tell us something.'

'Like?'

'Like look how powerful I am.'

'Bit macho.'

'We're talking Sheemina February.'

They finished their coffees. Pylon called for the bill.

'Probably we'll never know,' said Mace. 'Doesn't matter anymore. All the baddies are dead.'

Crossing the parking lot to their cars Mace said, 'This sort of day I could go up the mountain and hunt the maniac.'

'Two hours time we've got clients to collect.' Pylon put his hand on Mace's arm. 'Do me a favour, calm down.'

Mace laughed. 'I like it this way. Bit like the old days. I couldn't give a shit.'

'Save me sweet Jesus,' said Pylon ducking into the Merc.

Mace said, 'You're right about the blueberry. Tastes like I've been sucking bullets.'

74

Sheemina February told Spitz to meet her at Rhodes Memorial. At the bottom of the steps. That way she could watch him approach for no reason other than she wanted the drop on him. For the hell of it. Wanted to clip down the steps towards him saying, 'Bang, bang, Spitz boyo, you're dead.'

She got there fifteen minutes early. Banked on being five minutes ahead of him. Knowing he'd case the area first as a matter of habit. She left her car in the upper parking lot near the restaurant, took the path to the memorial, waited in the shadow behind the columns. Gazed across the suburbs and the industrial belt towards the Durbanville hills, beyond that to the Hottentots Holland and the winelands. Thought about money. That of all human inventions money had the measure of each person's heart. Hers was expensive.

She watched Spitz drive up in his white hire, park beneath the stone pines in the main lot. He got out, looked around for her black Beemer. Only seven cars there, none of them a BM. At this hour of the morning no one hanging around either. Too early for tourists. Probably the car owners were walkers, strolling the contour paths, enjoying themselves.

Spitz walked quickly to the lower entrance that led onto the flagstones below the steps. A viewpoint with a wider aspect than the memorial. Almost a bay-to-bay sweep: west coast to Hangklip. He took this in, pivoted to look at the memorial, Devil's Peak rising behind it. Sheemina February wondering what he'd make of a classical folly with columns, steps leading up flanked by walls, eight lions at rest on them. In front, on a plinth, a horse and rider, the rider shading his eyes, squinting at the hinterland. Spitz turned back to the view.

Sheemina February watched him. An elegant man, the crease on his trousers exact. Black polished shoes. The bandage on his little finger encased in a leather sheath. A slender man, and graceful.

She waited until his back was to her before she came out of the shadows and down the steps, her heels clicking on the granite. Spitz spun round almost immediately.

'Do you know, Spitz,' she called out, 'there are forty-nine steps. One for each year of his life.'

'Who is this?' said Spitz.

'Cecil Rhodes. Used to come up here to contemplate, according to the tourist guides. Stare out at the dark continent and think of money.' She came level with the hitman. 'Worked for him.'

'But he did not make even fifty years.'

'Neither did Obed Chocho.'

Spitz looked away. 'I was not able to…'

'Oh, I'm not blaming you Spitz.' Sheemina February touched his sleeve with a gloved hand. 'Things have worked out better than I planned. And for this I have you to thank all along the way. Last night especially. Without you the judge would not have been so… accommodating. Men are much more inclined to listen to other men I find. Particularly to one who's pointing a gun.'

She paused. The dull growl of the city filled her silence, and closer birdsong, insistent sunbirds.

'Up here,' she said, 'you can understand his point. Old Cape-to-Cairo Cecil. The birds make it peaceful.'

'What do you want to tell me?' said Spitz.

She sat down on the low parapet, faced the memorial. Patted the stone alongside her. Spitz sat.

'Obed had a contract with you on Mace Bishop and Pylon Buso, how much was that for?'

'There was no money.'

'You were doing it for free? You?'

'Because I had spoken his name to them.'

She crossed her legs. 'Obed getting his payback. Fair enough. And now, are you going to honour it?'

'There is no point.'

'I suppose not. But there would be a point if I offered you money.'

'Of course.'

'So, I will offer you one hundred and fifty thousand, not to kill them, but to kill the wife of Mace Bishop.'

'That is more than my fee.'

'I know. There is a catch.'

'What is this catch?'

'I don't want you to use a gun.'

'My weapon is a pistol.'

'I know, Spitz. But think about it. You kill her with a .22 or any other calibre and Mace Bishop will not even stop to think who did it. He will think Spitz-the-Trigger. What's more he knows exactly where to find you. Before you got home he'd be waiting inside your apartment.'

Spitz stroked his bandaged finger to ease the throbbing. 'Which is the weapon you want me to use?'

'A knife.'

'I do not use a knife. It is too dangerous.'

'That is why I'm paying you a lot of money.' She smiled at him. 'Let me be generous. How about two hundred thousand? I can afford it.'

She watched Spitz think about this. Not a twitch on his face. No frown. No tightening of the lips. She liked that, the calm contemplation.

'Once,' she said, 'you used a knife.' She drew a finger across her throat. 'Your trademark. No noise. Spitz the silent steps out of the shadows and ssssh the blade slits open the jugular. I know about that Spitz.' She reached out, lightly squeezed his forearm with her gloved hand. 'I might, too, Spitz, have a position for you. In my organisation. A career change. The comfort of a salary. Medical aid. Shares. A pension. The full rooty tooty of the late-bourgeois world.'

Smiled at Spitz staring at her, his lips glistening.

Eventually he said, 'Alright for that much I will use a knife.'

'There is another condition,' said Sheemina February. 'It must be in her pottery studio.'

'It has to be in some place.'

'The pottery studio is underneath their house.'

'I do not like that.'

'Can't be helped. I'm willing to pay a lot of money for this, Spitz. Offering you a future. There have to be some risks.'

She waited. When Spitz made no comment, held out a photograph: Mace, Oumou, Christa eating breakfast beside a swimming pool.

'Happy family. They live on the mountainside. The studio has access onto the lower garden. The only other access is a spiral staircase inside the house. A man with your resources shouldn't have any problems getting in.' She dangled some keys from her gloved hand. 'But these may be a help.' Spitz reached out, she dropped them into his hand. From a coat pocket took out a barber's razor. 'As might this.'

'No,' he said, 'this is not a knife.'

Sheemina let it lie bone-white against the black leather of palm. 'You thought differently once, I am given to understand.' She closed her fist, used the fingers of her good hand to open the blade. 'This is a special razor. It is not something I picked up in a junk store. It has provenance, Spitz. A history. A memento you should leave at the scene.' She held it towards him.

'When I used knives I was a younger person.'

She laid it against his hand, the blade's edge lightly on his skin. 'Take it. This is how I want it.'

'You are a demanding woman.'

'Not demanding, Spitz. Insistent. But generous too. I pay for that over the odds.'

Spitz closed the blade into the handle. Lifted it from her fingers.

Sheemina stroked his arm. 'I'm impressed. Now listen.' She gave him more details: access, the Bishop routine, the best time to do it. 'I must go now, Spitz.' Stood looking down at him. 'I'm sorry we didn't get to have a drink on the town but under the circumstances this would no longer be a good idea.' She held out her hand. 'I must say you have been an easy person to work with. My offer remains open for the future.'

'Please,' said Spitz, keeping a grip on her hand even as she gently pulled away.

'No, Spitz,' she said, using her gloved hand to free herself. 'Some things are not to be.' She headed for the steps. 'When the job is done, you'll get the money in cash at JB's. Special courier. While you're drinking a latte. After that I'll be in touch.' She pointed at Devil's Peak. 'Maybe you'll be able to get up the mountain this time. It's a wonderful view from the top.'

75

Pylon, palms down, felt the heat over the coals, said, 'This's mighty fine.'

'I reckon,' said Mace, giving the nod to the Obed Chocho jibe. Took a plate of sausages and lamb chops from the table, stripped off the foil covering. Gave Pylon a dish of ribs in marinade.

They laid the meat on the grid.

'Has to be Sheemina February, doesn't it?' Pylon licking sauce from his fingers. 'Not bad. This one of Oumou's specials?'

'Deep desert recipe.'

'Nice.' He swigged the last of his beer. With tongs repositioned some of the ribs.

'Your money's on her?' Mace picked up his beer.

'Isn't yours?'

'Probably.'

'Think of it.' Pylon shifted square on to Mace. 'The guys are dead two days, she's head of Zimisela Explorations. Even gets airtime for the announcement. Has to say something.'

'That she manipulated it? Even the judge's death?'

'Has to be.'

Mace finished his beer, put the empties on the table.

'Treasure'll freak at that,' said Pylon. 'You bin empties. Don't leave them littering the place.'

'Our domain,' said Mace. He grinned, fiddled with his tongs at the coals, spreading the heat.

'Myself,' said Pylon, 'I believe she knew their connection, Obed and the judge. Somehow she'd worked it out 'n sidled up to Chocho.'

'It's possible. Knowing her.'

'For sure. Comes over all sharp mover 'n shaker to impress the darkie meanwhile she's putting together the leads. Writing contracts to sew things up. Should something happen to Obed Chocho or the judge, heaven forbid.'

Fat sizzled from a split sausage. Mace moved it to the side.

'Pork sausages, I don't know.'

'Don't know what?'

'If it's best to prick them. You don't prick they burst, you do you lose the juice.'

'I prick,' said Pylon. 'One small hole is enough.'

Mace opened the cooler box, took out two bottles of beer. Uncapped them, handed one to Pylon.

'Something I do reckon, the mining magazines came from her. Part of her grand plan.'

'She did that she did everything else.'

'I'm not arguing.' Mace tipped back two swallows of beer. 'Years ago, in the camp, we should've done ourselves a favour, had her shot.'

They moved a couple of paces away, out of the smoke.

Pylon saying, 'Always she's stirring the shit. You can just see it: once the paperwork was done, stuff had to start happening otherwise what was the point?' He reached down, extracted Cat2's claws from his jeans. 'Maybe didn't happen the way she thought. But she got the result.'

Mace stuck a fork in the split sausage, lifted it off the grid. Clicked his fingers to call the cat, broke off small pieces and cooled them. Cat2 curled about his legs, giving her strangled whisper. He dropped the sausage bits on the patio.

"N there's squat we can do.'

'Unless we figure an angle.'

'Pah!' Mace turned the ribs to even the browning. 'Fat chance.'

Crouched among a cluster of boulders, Spitz looked down on the house. He'd watched the black Merc arrive: Pylon, a pregnant woman, a girl get out. He could see Pylon and Mace now at a Weber cooking meat. The girl and Mace's daughter on loungers beside the pool, reading. No sign of the pregnant woman and the woman Oumou.

He smoked a menthol, considering his options. Go away, come back later. Sit it out, watching them have their fun. His backside getting stiff and sore on the damp ground. This was not an option. Not where it stank of urine. Was littered with broken glass, tins, bottle necks, stompies. He ground out his cigarette among the butts.

On a day such as this. A Saturday. He thought of JB's. The beautiful people coming in for eggs florentine, tall lattes. His people. His city. Not this place under the mountain. The mountain always over everything.

Spitz stood, eased the cramp out of his muscles. Decided waiting was what he did. Sometimes waiting was most of the job. You got on the job you didn't leave it. That was the way he operated. He stretched. Except no point to waiting where bergies and derelicts wasted their lives. Her studio would be more comfortable.

Only he needed the Browning too. A situation like this there could be difficulties. The necessity of self-defence being one.

Pylon said, 'Pumla tells me this joke last night. Something she heard at school and wants to know why's it funny.'

'I know why.' Pumla indignant, not looking up from her book.

Christa saying, 'We're not stupid.'

Mace and Pylon laughed.

Mace said, 'You better tell your mothers the meat's cooked.'

'Burnt, you mean,' said Christa. 'I can smell it.'

'It's juicy,' said Mace. 'Pink and tender.'

'Yuk,' said Pumla.

'Black and crisp, probably,' said Christa.

The girls heading indoors.

'The joke?' said Mace.

'Right.' Pylon stacked sausages onto the plate. 'The traffic cops've mounted a safety check one night on a highway. Pulling over all the cars. A sort of Arrive Alive thing.

'So this traffic cop walks up to a smart Jetta. Black car, tinted windows, new model. He can see two young guys in the front seats. The window comes down, zzzzs. The young guys are both buckled up.

'The cop's impressed. "Hey, guys," he says, "you're the lucky ones tonight." Tells them Arrive Alive's running this surprise reward, they've won five thousand bucks for wearing seatbelts. He's got this envelope bulging with big notes in his hand, gives it to Sipho, the driver.

'"Yo, wow," goes Sipho. "That's so cool, I've never won anything before. This's magic."

'"So what're you gonna spend it on?" says the traffic cop, all friendly, doing good PR for the department.

'"I'm gonna buy a driving licence," says Sipho. "Be legal."

'"No, china, china, china," says Hendrik, in the passenger seat, "what're you saying chommie?" He leans across to speak to the traffic cop. "Don't listen to him, sir officer, he always tries to be funny when he's drunk."

'The traffic cop's getting a squinty look on his face.

'Sipho's saying, "I'm not drunk. Strues, officer, you can test me." Running his words together.

'This wakes Ravi who's been sleeping on the back seat. He pops up, sees the cop and groans, "Oh shit, I told you guys. You gotta keep off the highways in a hot car. There's always roadblocks."

'The traffic cop shines his torch in the back, checks out Ravi, sees bloodstains on the headrest from the hijacking.

'Before he can do anything there's knocking from the boot and a voice calls out, "Please tell me, buti, are we over the border yet?"

'Now the cop's got this frown on his dial. "My brother," he says to Sipho, "seems we've got a little problem here."

'Sipho says, "I can explain."

'"For sure," says the traffic cop. He puts out his hand, palm up. "This is a good explanation."

'Sipho says, "How much?" starts counting the notes into the cop's hand. When he gets to five thou, the cop says, "Is that all?"'

Pylon waited.

Mace said, 'Ja, okay.'

'State of the nation,' said Pylon. 'Geddit?'

'Sure.'

Pylon covered the dish of sausages with foil. 'What's with you and Pumla you can't see the joke?'

Spitz followed a path away from the boulders that looped through a stand of Port Jacksons down to the street where he'd left his car. A well trodden path. Surprising thing was not meeting anyone. This time of day, he supposed, the scavengers were out scavenging.

The street was empty, too. Except he could hear voices from behind the garden walls. People laughing. Settling down to lunch. The shrieks of children playing. The walls high and electrified, tall trees hiding the houses. It was better this way.

He slipped into the Golf, sat looking down on the city: the green block of the park. Wondered why he'd never taken a walk through it. What he'd liked about Europe's cities were the parks. The people in them: sitting on benches, reading, talking. On the grass white girls, so white you could see through their skin to the veins, faces up to the sun like they were worshipping.

All this time in the city he'd never been in the park. Not been up the mountain either. But he had no urge for that. Or to a beach. Not his scene either.

He ate a salami roll bought at a German deli, drank off a bottle of sparkling water. Smoked a menthol.

From under the seat took out the pistol, from the glove compartment, the silencer. Screwed it to the nose. Checked the clip was fully loaded, buried the gun in a deep pocket. The problem with a can it made the barrel so long, awkward to conceal in a windbreaker.

He brought out the razor, opened it, ran his thumb lightly along the blade. Sharp enough to shave with. As men had, maybe a century ago, looking at the pearl inlay. Wondered where Sheemina February had bought it. And why? Why it was important to her for this job. A woman with strange ideas, even offering him an interesting prospect. Something to look into. He folded the blade into the handle, slipped the razor into his pants pocket. Thinking about it Sheemina February was everywhere. The things she knew.

She'd said to him, 'Getting in is easy. The house below has a path up the side. All overgrown. When you're on it nobody can see you. Maybe once it was a public path to the mountain, now not even bergies know it's there. On the street there's a gate, more like a door. It's not locked. Just walk in, climb the steps, push through the hedge plants when you reach the house. There you are.'

'How do you know about this pathway?' he'd asked.

She'd taken off her shades, stared at him with her ice-blue eyes. 'Because I do, Spitz. Because these are the sorts of things I know.'

Spitz fired the engine, drove slowly down to the street with the door onto the mountain. He positioned the Golf for an easy exit. Left the driver's side unlocked.

The garden door had swollen in the rain but gave at his tugging. He stepped through, pulled it closed, paused. The afternoon did not pause with him. No hush to the insects and the birds. No dogs suddenly barking. Spitz started up the steps. The path was cool and shaded, smelt of damp. Of rotting vegetation.

He stopped twice on the climb to keep his breathing easy, his pulse down. Still the autumn heat dampened his armpits. When he came level with the top house he forced a way through the shrubbery into an arbour covered by vines, and waited. A short terrace separated him from the sliding door that Sheemina February said was the entrance to the studio. On the terrace he'd be visible to anyone glancing out of a window above.

Spitz moved quickly across the terrace. Inserted the key, turned once, twice. Gently eased back the door.

They ate in the shade beside the pool. Mace at one end of the table, Pylon the other. Oumou and Treasure side by side opposite Christa and Pumla. On the table dishes of meat, salad, putu pap with a tomato and onion sauce. Chunks torn off Oumou's home-baked French loaves.

TREASURE: They should cut off his balls.

Helped herself to salad.

PUMLA: Ma!

TREASURE: I can use words like that. You can't. What I don't understand is why a bunch of men don't track him down.

PYLON: Exactly what Mace wanted to do.

OUMOU: Non!

MACE: Sometimes the cops can't do it. Not enough manpower. This maniac runs around on the mountain doing what he wants to. How many's he raped? One, that sixteen-year-old. Two that tourist. The young mother. He's going to do it again.

OUMOU: This is breaking the law. To be a vigilante.

MACE: Sure but what good's the law? It's not working. If it doesn't protect.

Cat2 leapt onto the table. Christa gently lifted her off.

CHRISTA: We've got a democracy.

MACE: A sort of democracy.

TREASURE: What's democracy got us, sisi? Unemployment. Still no houses. AIDS. Orphans.

CHRISTA: In history we learnt it's better than we had.

TREASURE: Some people wouldn't know the difference.

Oumou glanced at Mace.

OUMOU: You are not going to do this?

Mace licked his fingers, wiped them on a paper serviette.

MACE: I went up there. If I'd come across the guy I don't know what I'd have done.

CHRISTA: I told you Maman.

MACE: Told you Maman, what?

CHRISTA: You make us worried.

OUMOU: Because sometimes you do strange things…

PYLON: No kidding.

He grinned at Oumou. Ignoring the knife Treasure pointed at him.

OUMOU: Sometimes you think you have the only way.

TREASURE: I wouldn't say anything, Mr Buso.

PUMLA: Ma!

OUMOU: Non. Enough. Enough. No more mountain maniac. We can enjoy this lunchtime.

Pylon finished his beer, patted his stomach.

PYLON: It's hell in Africa.

MACE: I've got to tell you something. Something I didn't know until last night.

He put his hand on Oumou's arm.

OUMOU: What? What's this?'

She looked at him.

OUMOU: Non, ma puce, please.

CHRISTA: Tell them, Papa. Maman, it's the best news.

Mace stood to top up Oumou's and Treasure's wine glasses.

MACE: We need to toast her.

He fetched two beers from the cooler box, flipped off the caps. Handed one to Pylon.

CHRISTA: And us?

Mace looked at Treasure, got the nod from her.

MACE: A small one.

He splashed wine in their glasses.

MACE: Last night, Oumou showed me this email she got. From the Master Potters Association. She's won their platinum award.

Treasure, Pylon, the two girls all over Oumou with congrats.

MACE: I haven't finished. There's a whole story with it. Stuff you wouldn't believe they say about her.

PYLON: So where is it?

MACE: Coming up.

OUMOU: It is a small thing.

Pylon and Treasure protested.

PUMLA: Please, Oumou. We want to read it.

MACE: I'll get the email.

Oumou caught at his clothing to stop him.

OUMOU: No. You do not know where it is.

She stood, moved towards the house.

OUMOU: Wait one moment. I will get it, yes.

Spitz heard footsteps. Reckoned it had to be from the upper storey going down one. Someone possibly barefoot. Light on their feet. Either the child or the mother.

Where he'd been sitting, tucked in a corner behind the spiral staircase, he was out of sight of anyone appearing at the sliding door or descending the stairs. He'd sat there an hour, slightly more, the iPod playing softly in his lap. Killer country songs. Loud enough to soothe him, not so loud he couldn't hear movement in the house.

It occurred to him he could sit there a long time before they finished lunch.

'Late Saturday afternoon she's always in the studio,' Sheemina February had said. 'Alone. It's her private space. That'd be the ideal time, Spitz.'

A nice private space. Along one wall racks of paints, glazes, brushes. Along another racks of pots, cups, bowls, plates. Her wheel in the centre. A bin of damp clay. A bin of broken shards. A desk smothered with magazines and paper, a landline phone perched on a stack of books. Drawings by the girl tacked here and there round the studio. Also desert photographs. One from the air of a small town, looked like it was made of mud. Sudden green patches among the brown of the houses. The floor of the studio, like the desert, brown, studded with lumps of dry clay.

The footsteps softer, crossing the floor. A door opened and closed.

This was too early. Maybe the girl getting something from her bedroom. Spitz checked the time: 2:30, they couldn't have finished lunch yet.

The footsteps were above him. He put aside the iPod. Opened the blade. Stood, moved back into the corner.

He saw her feet on the stairs. Long toes. Soft uncalloused heels. The stretch of the skin and muscles. A woman sure on her feet. A fine silver chain round her left ankle. Her dress swishing below her calves, an embroidered pattern round the hem.

She came down the stairs, stood with her back to him, sifting through papers on the desk. Spitz took two quick paces, grabbed her from behind, yanked her against him. His left arm wrapped around her neck, his right arm slashed the razor across her chest.

He bent her backwards. Cut at her stomach. Once, twice. The blade going in.

The woman struggled, her teeth in his arm. He pushed her away. Blood on his clothing, the razor sticky in his grip. He went at her again where she crawled across the floor. Drew the blade down her neck.

She screamed.

Oumou felt the sear of the cut across her chest. The slices of hot pain in her stomach.

As it had been before. The two men stabbing at her belly, leaving her bleeding on the sand. Going away laughing.

She struck out, the blade slicing her hands. Bit down deeply, and she was free of his grip, on her knees on the floor. The blood leaking from her, her hands stained.

She could hear his panting.

Began crawling round the desk, forcing herself against the pain.

She felt his hand grip her hair, her head jerked back, the blade sliding into her shoulder.

A redness crossed her eyes. Her arms buckled. She gasped as the man tugged at the razor, twisting to pull it free.

She screamed. A howl, long and angry and filled with the sadness of desert nights. A cry of solitude.

Again she was free, crawling away, slowly clawing herself upright against the desk until she stood and faced him. Saw in his eyes the matt gaze she had seen in the eyes of other killers.

He stared at her unmoving.

Her hand slid down the leg of the desk for the sword that hung there in its scabbard. She drew it, the blade coming out smoothly.

She kept her eyes on him. Started forward step by step. Saw the man unzip his jacket, saw the black grip of the gun.

They all heard the scream. Christa stopping in mid-sentence. Pumla frowning. Treasure saying, 'What's that?' Mace and Pylon on their feet.

Hesitating. Glancing at one another. The charge going through Mace like ice in the veins.

'Guns,' said Pylon.

Mace shaking his head. Shouting: 'No time.' Heading indoors, Pylon leaping down the terraced garden.

Mace took the first flight in three bounds. Called out, 'Oumou, Oumou.'

Heard no response above his own noise across the wooden floor to the spiral staircase. Shouting for her again.

He took the stairs carefully, aware of the silence in the studio. Slowing down, ready to act.

He saw the blood first. The smear of it across the floor. Then Oumou's feet and her prone body, the barber's razor in her back, her dress soaked red, the blade slashes across her hands, arms.

The body of Spitz-the-Trigger against the wall, the sword through his stomach, buried almost to the leather handle. The hitman bleeding out, his eyes flickering.

Mace bent over his wife, whispered her name.

76

Mace Bishop on the mountain sat with his back to a rock, gazing south. He could see the blue of False Bay and the blue of the Atlantic. Above a sky without cloud that fell to the cold horizon. In his hand the blue iPod, in his ears the murder music of Tindersticks. His chest was tight. His hands trembled. His daughter stood off a distance.

Mace looked at her. The slim size of her drawn in against the cold. Her hands in her pockets. Her hoodie up. Had they spoken at all? He'd hugged her. Cooked her food. Watched her push the plate away untouched. Come upon her reading in the small hours. Fallen asleep on her bed. Woken in the first light with her gone and called her name and found her in the studio. Sobbing. The two of them dead souls in the house, wandering the rooms. This loss that hurt, more painful than any wound.

These days without her.

The constant replay of those final moments.

'It is in the music,' Spitz had said. His last words.

What? Mace had screamed. What? Kneeling beside the hitman, shaking him.

Spitz had smiled, blood leaking from his lips. Said something that Mace couldn't catch, the words gurgling in the man's throat.

Mace leaned closer. Shouted at him again.

Spitz offered his iPod on a reddened hand. Repeated the words.

Mace said, 'Who hired you? Bloody tell me. Sheemina February? Tell me. For Chrissakes, you're dying. Tell me.'

Spitz said what sounded to Mace like 'It is in the music'.

Mace lost it. 'Who? For fucks sakes who?' Hammered the sword in deeper with his fist.

Spitz jerked. The last move he made.

Sheemina February.

Mace'd stood up, gone to his wife. Drawn her against his chest. Now he called to Christa.

'We've got to go, C.'

Stood up. Watched her turn towards him, the dark shades that were her eyes. They walked back to the cable station, father and daughter.

Groups of tourists huddled against the winter wind at the lookout decks, pointing down at the city, out at the island, admiring the view. People struck by the beauty of the place. Taking photographs beneath the signs. Eleven thousand kilometres to London. Fifteen thousand to Tokyo. Seven to Buenos Aires. Happy people despite the wind chill.

What did they see as they approached, he wondered. A man and a young girl. His hands thrust into his jacket pockets, a man in a beanie and dark glasses. The girl with long silver earrings, her hands not touching the man beside her. Both plugged into their music on a fine winter day after rain.

Mace pulled the plugs from his ears, said, 'Christa.' But left it there. She half turned, reached out her hand for his.

He'd crouched beside Oumou. Stroked her hair. Held her hand. He'd heard Christa screaming. Seen his daughter hurl herself onto her mother. He'd held them both.

Afterwards, long afterwards, he'd swum, lap on lap through the cold dark water until his thoughts disappeared. Swimming until he could no longer. Until his body was as cold as his hurt. When he stopped, the pain came in fast. He'd gripped the edge of the pool, floated there, looking at the lighted rooms of his house. The empty lighted rooms. Christa standing backlit at the sliding doors. Watching him.

Near the cable station Mace and Christa heard singing, children's voices. A school choir. The lilting stabbed a pain across his chest. He turned away from the singers, to stop the cold wind watering his eyes.

Christa said, 'Papa,' – let go his hand. She had a camera, was backing away to take his picture.

There was no choice. He would do what he had to.

'If you like I will photograph you both together,' said a woman. Her voice accented. German.

Mace turned round. A woman in her fifties, blowing on her hands. Her cheeks flushed.

'Thank you,' said Mace. Called Christa back.

'Is she your daughter?' asked the woman.

Mace said, yes.

'So lovely. You will stand together, ja.'

Father and daughter, bereft, in mourning, yet easy now arranging themselves.

'That is wonderful,' said the woman, looking at the image on the screen. 'See.'

She handed the camera to Christa.

'For your memories. Auf Wiedersehen.' The woman, excusing herself, heading off quickly. 'I must get the next cable car downwards.'

The departure siren sounded. They watched the woman board just in time.

'Who's she?' asked Christa.

'Some tourist,' said Mace. 'Let's see it, the picture.'

He looked at the photograph: the two of them locked tight. Christa pulled in against his chest. Both her arms around him. A smile on his lips, and hers. Could anyone tell his wife had been murdered? Could anyone say her mother was dead? The lies photographs told.

'I like it,' said Christa. 'We look okay.'

That was the point, Mace thought, they did. Where was the anger? The pain? The grief? He looked closer at their faces, the glint on Christa's teeth. The smile not in their eyes. Then took in the background: above, a sky of wide and dying crimson. Behind them a terrace and parapet wall. Standing at the wall, a woman in a long coat. A woman with a black glove. Sheemina February.

THE PLAYLIST

Kal Cahoone	If They Cheered
Johnny Cash	The Man Comes Around
Cowboy Junkies	Highway Kind
Tindersticks	Another Night In
Tindersticks	Until Morning Comes
M Ward	Let's Dance
Steve Earle	Goodbye
Woven Hand	Swedish Purse
Jesse Sykes	Reckless Burning
16 Horsepower	Hutterite Mile
16 Horsepower	Outlaw Song
Johnny Cash	I'm On Fire
Tindersticks	Rented Rooms
Johnny Cash	Hurt
Giant Sand	Wayfaring Stranger
Emmylou Harris	I Don't Wanna Talk About it Now
Tindersticks	Sweet, Sweet Man
Calexico	Sunken Waltz
16 Horsepower	Alone and Forsaken
Deana Carter	State Trooper
Jesse Sykes & the Sweet Hereafter	Love Me, Someday
Giant Sand	Sand
The Handsome Family	Far From Any Road
M Ward	Dead Man
Willard Grant Conspiracy	Christmas in Nevada
Billy Bob Thornton	Forever
Jesse Sykes & the Sweet Hereafter	Don't Let Me Go

Alejandro Escovedo	Follow You Down
Jim White	The Wound that Never Heals
Emmylou Harris	Snake Song
Johnny Cash	I Hung My Head
Lilium	Lover
Willard Grant Conspiracy	Soft Hand
The Walkabouts	Loom of the Land
Cowboy Junkies	He Will Call You Baby
M Ward	Outta My Head
Tindersticks	Traveling Light
16 Horsepower	Sinnerman